Palgrave Studies in the Enlightenment, Romanticism and Cultures of Print

General Editors: **Professor Anne K. Mellor** and **Professor Clifford Siskin**

Editorial Board: **Isobel Armstrong**, Birkbeck; **John Bender**, Stanford; **Alan Bewell**, Toronto; **Peter de Bolla**, Cambridge; **Robert Miles**, Stirling; **Claudia L. Johnson**, Princeton; **Saree Makdisi**, UCLA; **Felicity Nussbaum**, UCLA; **Mary Poovey**, NYU; **Janet Todd**, Glasgow

Palgrave Studies in the Enlightenment, Romanticism and the Cultures of Print will feature work that does not fit comfortably within established boundaries – whether between periods or between disciplines. Uniquely, it will combine efforts to engage the power and materiality of print with explorations of gender, race, and class. By attending as well to intersections of literature with the visual arts, medicine, law, and science, the series will enable a large-scale rethinking of the origins of modernity.

Titles include:

E. J. Clery
THE FEMINIZATION DEBATE IN 18TH-CENTURY ENGLAND
Literature, Commerce and Luxury

Mary Waters
BRITISH WOMEN WRITERS AND THE PROFESSION OF LITERARY CRITICISM, 1789–1832

Forthcoming titles in the series:

Adriana Craciun
BRITISH WOMEN WRITERS AND THE FRENCH REVOLUTION

David Simpson, Nigel Leask and Peter de Bolla (*editors*)
LAND, NATION AND CULTURE, 1740–1810

Palgrave Studies in the Enlightenment, Romanticism and Cultures of Print Series
Standing Order ISBN 1–4039–3408–8 (hardback) 1–4039–3409–6 (paperback)
(*outside North America only*)

You can receive future titles in this series as they are published by placing a standing order. Please contact your bookseller or, in case of difficulty, write to us at the address below with your name and address, the title of the series and the ISBN quoted above.

Customer Services Department, Macmillan Distribution Ltd, Houndmills, Basingstoke, Hampshire RG21 6XS, England

British Women Writers and the Profession of Literary Criticism, 1789–1832

Mary A. Waters
Assistant Professor
Wichita State University

© Mary A. Waters 2004

All rights reserved. No reproduction, copy or transmission of this publication may be made without written permission.

No paragraph of this publication may be reproduced, copied or transmitted save with written permission or in accordance with the provisions of the Copyright, Designs and Patents Act 1988, or under the terms of any licence permitting limited copying issued by the Copyright Licensing Agency, 90 Tottenham Court Road, London W1T 4LP.

Any person who does any unauthorized act in relation to this publication may be liable to criminal prosecution and civil claims for damages.

The author has asserted her right to be identified as the author of this work in accordance with the Copyright, Designs and Patents Act 1988.

First published 2004 by
PALGRAVE MACMILLAN
Houndmills, Basingstoke, Hampshire RG21 6XS and
175 Fifth Avenue, New York, N. Y. 10010
Companies and representatives throughout the world

PALGRAVE MACMILLAN is the global academic imprint of the Palgrave Macmillan division of St. Martin's Press, LLC and of Palgrave Macmillan Ltd. Macmillan® is a registered trademark in the United States, United Kingdom and other countries. Palgrave is a registered trademark in the European Union and other countries.

ISBN 1–4039–3626–9 hardback

This book is printed on paper suitable for recycling and made from fully managed and sustained forest sources.

A catalogue record for this book is available from the British Library.

Library of Congress Cataloging-in-Publication Data
Waters, Mary A., 1954–
  British women writers and the profession of literary criticism, 1789–1832 / Mary A. Waters.
       p. cm. – (Palgrave studies in the Enlightenment, romanticism, and the cultures of print)
  Includes bibliographical references and index.
  ISBN 1–4039–3626–9 (cloth)
    1. Criticism–Great Britain–History–19th century. 2. English prose literature–Women authors–History and criticism. 3. Women and literature–Great Britain–History–19th century. 4. Women and literature–Great Britain–History–18th century. 5. English literature–History and criticism–Theory, etc. 6. Book reviewing–Great Britain–History–19th century. 7. Book reviewing–Great Britain–History–18th century. 8 Criticism–Great Britain–History–18th century. 9. Women critics–Great Britain. I. Title. II. Series.
PR75.W36 2004
820.9′9287′09034–dc22   2004044686

10 9 8 7 6 5 4 3 2 1
13 12 11 10 09 08 07 06 05 04

Printed and bound in Great Britain by
Antony Rowe Ltd, Chippenham and Eastbourne

*In Memory of Annie Mary
and Myrtle*

Contents

Acknowledgments	viii
Introduction	1
Part I "Forms scientific and established": The Critical Preface, the Canon, and the Woman Critic	25
1 The British Common Reader: Critical Prefaces by Anna Letitia Barbauld	28
2 Renouncing the Forms: The Case of Elizabeth Inchbald	57
Part II "Fearful ascendency": Women Periodical Literary Reviewers	83
3 "The first of a new genus –": Mary Wollstonecraft, Mary Hays, and *The Analytical Review*	86
4 Periodicals and Middle-Class Dissent: Anna Letitia Barbauld and Elizabeth Moody at the *Monthly Review*	121
5 The Next Generation: Harriet Martineau's Literary Reviews for the *Monthly Repository*	151
Notes	178
Bibliography	206
Index	217

Acknowledgments

Many individuals and organizations have encouraged and supported me in this project, and to them all I owe my deepest appreciation. A few, however, deserve special mention. I would like to thank Kari Lokke, Catherine Robson, and David Simpson for their enthusiastic and challenging readings of early drafts. In particular, Kari Lokke has been a source of encouragement and inspiration since long before the germ of this study took form. Discussions with Alessa Johns during the project's early stages helped me to sort out the shape the project would take. Jan Wellington and Gina Luria Walker read portions of the manuscript as it developed and offered timely and insightful suggestions. Library staff at Shields Library at UC Davis and Bancroft Library at UC Berkeley also receive my thanks, but Nancy Kushigian at Shields deserves special recognition for her valuable research assistance. UC Davis has provided a variety of grants and fellowships, large and small, that have made the research for this project possible. Portions of Chapters 3 and 4 have appeared in *Nineteenth-Century Prose* and *Eighteenth-Century Studies*, and I thank the editors of those journals for permission to include that material here. And finally, my deepest gratitude goes to Noel Phipps, without whose generosity, faith, and encouragement this project would never have arrived at completion.

Introduction

> All men of sense, who know the world, have a great deference for [women's] judgment of such books as lie within the compass of their knowledge, and repose more confidence in the delicacy of their taste, though unguided by rules, than in all the dull labors of pedants and commentators.
>
> – David Hume[1]

In 1977, Susan Sniader Lanser and Evelyn Torton Beck asked a provocative question: "Why are there no great women critics?"[2] Their query was in part rhetorical, for in the very essay to which it gives title, they go on to offer examples of women critics whose work fails to receive its due in standard anthologies and histories of criticism. Names such as Charlotte Lennox, Clara Reeve, and Vernon Lee provide them with instances of groundbreaking women's criticism that since its first appearance has been largely dismissed.[3] Lanser and Beck suggest that women's criticism fails to garner the respect it deserves partly because the difference in perspective between women writers and their male counterparts shapes women's compositions in ways that make them an ill fit with standards and concerns subsequently developed by men from writing by men. Hence, though women's criticism may have been well regarded in its day, it was soon forgotten or, if remembered at all, held up to "some pre-established norms" against which it is "judged to be defective."[4]

One could surely argue that since Lanser and Beck's essay first appeared, women's criticism has begun to come into its own. After all, the work of a woman writer, Virginia Woolf, makes the only complete book-length critical essay in that standard of English literary studies, the *Norton Anthology of English Literature*.[5] Lanser herself has helped edit one of three recent anthologies contributing to the recovery of women's literary criticism before the twentieth century.[6] Moreover, Anne K. Mellor has offered early women's criticism as an object for serious study in an essay arguing that Romantic-era women critics took a position between the "mirror" of mimetic Augustan aesthetics and the "lamp" of Romantic imagination to promote an innovative new aesthetic imaging literature "as a balance or scale that weighs equally the demands of the head and the heart."[7] Yet Woolf's essay aside, many scholars would still be hard put to name a work of women's literary criticism that pre-dates twentieth-century feminist literary studies. The present study takes up Lanser and Beck's question in two ways. For one, it seeks to remind literary scholarship of the existence of women literary critics during the British Romantic era. More importantly, it elucidates those women critics' role in the dramatic literary and cultural changes taking place during that era. In the process, the study engages in some of the most topical debates in British Romantic period studies: about professionalism, the dynamics of print culture, the nascent consciousness of a reading public, nationalism, and the literary canon.

Contributing to the recovery of women's criticism, then, while part of this project's purpose, is far from its most consequential goal. Reading outside the narrow boundaries of today's critical canon reveals new information on the material and social circumstances that made writing, especially certain forms of writing by women, possible during the Romantic era. Not only do women writers depend on the support of a specific culture to enter the field of criticism, but their work reflects the values of that culture and helps shape those values. These women saw themselves as professionals and as authorities on a crucial topic, the nation's literature. They understood that their work had implications beyond the publication at hand. Their criticism shows their engagement with far-reaching public issues – morality, both public and private, the nation's cultural heritage, the essential qualities of Britishness itself. The following pages reveal that many women critics had a sophisticated understanding of the constructed and contested nature of aesthetics and the role of aesthetics in shaping the culture at large. They demonstrate women critics' lively interest in the relationship between author, authorial persona, and reading audience at the time these concepts first began to assume conscious shape. Most importantly, they establish the existence of conscious professionalism among Romantic-era women writers.

This study examines professional literary criticism by Romantic-era British women writers. A project so delineated first becomes possible during the period between the beginning of the French Revolution in 1789, when the first truly professional woman literary critic, Mary Wollstonecraft, appeared and the passage of the First Reform Bill in 1832, when increasing numbers of women began to earn a living from criticism and editing. During these years, many factors combined to cause momentous demographic shifts in the reading and writing public. Such causes include the rapid expansion of literacy, especially among women and the lower middle class, the rise of the periodical press, the phenomenal proliferation of novels and sentimental poetry, the prosperity that increased the amount and altered the employment of leisure time, the declining role of coterie circulation and patronage in publication, and the widespread public debate about the abilities and circumstances of women. One additional change, the rise of the professional woman literary critic, will be shown here to have far more significant implications than the sheer numbers of women critics might suggest.

The professional woman writer had been around at least since Aphra Behn, but paid writing took on new importance for women in the face of economic and social instabilities that marked the late eighteenth and early nineteenth centuries, leaving many women of genteel social standing without the finances to sustain their social position. Edward Copeland points to runaway inflation and burdensome taxation as factors that left middle-class women especially vulnerable.[8] Monetary pressures prompted numerous women to turn to writing as a source of income. Charlotte Smith desperately trying to write her family out of debtors' prison is only one of the more extreme examples that come to mind. Yet though she was one of the most prolific novelists of her time, Smith only briefly enjoyed a precarious respite from the worst of her financial troubles toward the end of her life, after her health was broken from overwork and anxiety. Copeland offers convincing evidence that, contrary to past assumptions about successful women novelists, novel writing alone did not during these years provide enough income for a "genteel competence," the basic income necessary to maintain at a modest level the trappings of genteel life. Copeland points to a few outstanding counterexamples such as Hannah More, who was able to accumulate a substantial fortune largely through the sale of her writing. But More, he reminds us, earned most of her income not from novels or other "creative" works, but rather from less prestigious forms, such as her highly successful *Cheap Repository Tracts* (1795–97). If women were to make much of literary work, they would have to look farther than novel writing in order to do it.

In fact, women had engaged in a wide variety of literary activities before the Romantic era, much of it for money. Not only had they written novels and poetry, but they had been dramatists, moralists, devotional and conduct book writers, translators, editors, composers of children's literature and educational materials. They had written history, philosophy, biography, spiritual narrative, even scientific texts. Alice Adburgham cites numerous instances where women's literary work falls outside the bounds usually thought to circumscribe their activities. Adburgham records that the first Sunday newspaper was published by a Mrs. E. Johnson. Stacy Sowle and Elizabeth Harris were both printers. Sarah Popping, mentioned in Alexander Pope's *Dunciad*, was co-proprietor with Benjamin Harris of a newspaper, *The Protestant Post-Boy*. Elizabeth Powell founded a news weekly directed toward women, the *Charitable Mercury and Female Intelligence*, in 1716. For most of a year beginning in mid-1709, Mary de la Rivière Manley thrice weekly published a political periodical, *The Female Tatler*, a "vehicle for the violently Tory invective of 'Mrs Crackenthorpe, a Lady that knows Everything.'" Manley claimed the papers had been written by her father and another male associate, but her disavowal did not save her from facing a grand jury on charges of being a public nuisance.[9] Paula McDowell offers additional confirmation of the variety of women's work in print culture, especially their role in the production and distribution of political journalism and pamphlets directed toward the lower classes.[10]

By the last decade of the eighteenth century, women had as one facet of this literary activity written and even published literary criticism in a variety of forms. Eliza Haywood contributed theater commentary to *The Tea Table* for a time and later published several periodicals directed to a female audience, the best known of which was the *Female Spectator*, a publication loosely modeled on Addison and Steele's *Spectator* and ostensibly comprised of the contributions of four respectable women, all of whom were probably fictitious personas of Haywood herself. The monitory tales that make the bulk of this publication turn amatory fiction to a cautionary moral purpose, much like Haywood's later novels. But Haywood incorporates literary criticism through reflections on the purposes of reading and the vagaries of taste, and through commentary on Shakespeare and occasionally other writers. Similarly, Frances Brooke also included literary commentary in her magazine *The Old Maid*.[11] Women had also worked sections of critical exposition into novels or their prefaces.[12] A few women had published free standing critical essays as well, an important step in the progress toward the professional woman critic. Margaret Cavendish, Duchess of Newcastle, published the first known critical essay on Shakespeare by a woman in letter CXXIII of her *CCXI Sociable Letters* (1664). Poets such as Anne Finch, Countess of Winchilsea, had privately circulated verse on topics such as inspiration, imagination, and poetic composition. And women had occasionally contributed criticism to literary reviews. The first woman to do so must have been Isabella Griffiths, who probably contributed anonymous articles to her husband Ralph Griffiths' *Monthly Review*, the first modern literary review.[13] Yet the true forebears of Romantic-era British women critics are the Bluestockings of the latter half of the eighteenth century.

All but forgotten for much of the twentieth century except, possibly, as an epithet for an asexual scholarly woman, the Bluestockings have recently become the object of some exciting scholarship inaugurated by Sylvia Harcstark Myers's study of the original Bluestocking group, Elizabeth Carter, Elizabeth Montagu, Catherine Talbot, and Hester Chapone.[14] These women produced a voluminous correspondence as well as several publications, the most interesting to the present study consisting of the Shakespeare criticism by literary patroness Elizabeth Montagu.[15] Montagu's essay proved extremely popular for its vindication of Shakespeare in opposition to the views of Voltaire, who had condemned the British dramatist's work for mixing comedy with tragedy and for violating the Aristotelian unities. Montagu was hailed as a literary patriot for championing the writer who was rapidly coming to be regarded as the national poet. Her essay constitutes a landmark in the development of a British literary canon with Shakespeare at its apex.

Although Myers keeps most of her attention trained on the original Bluestocking circle consisting of the four women named above, her frontispiece features an illustration, Richard Samuel's *Nine Living Muses of Great Britain* (1779), that suggests a different configuration. Samuel depicts writers Elizabeth Carter, Anna Letitia Barbauld, Catherine Macaulay, Elizabeth Montagu, Elizabeth Griffith, Hannah More, and Charlotte Lennox, painter Angelica Kauffman, and musician Elizabeth Linley (later Sheridan). Though Montagu, who appears in both groups, published one of the most important prose essays by a woman to appear before the last decade of the century, Myers's original circle of four accentuates literary amateurism. With the exception of Carter, probably the most learned woman in eighteenth-century England, who depended on Montagu's patronage and the income from her own writing, none of these writers relied on remuneration from their publications as a crucial part of their income.[16] Montagu's *Essay on the Writings and Genius of Shakespeare* (1769) earned wide acclaim, but it meant little financially to this wealthy philanthropist. Chapone experienced pecuniary embarrassments after her husband's death, but she preferred to reduce expenses, declaring that since her publications fulfilled a moral duty, she had no regrets over the modest sums they brought her. Talbot was reluctant even to circulate, much less publish her work.[17] The *Nine Living Muses* group, on the other hand, formed, as Elizabeth Eger observes, an assemblage made up of "women united by their professional status," for all except Montagu made a living from their work.[18]

Eger's essay appears in a collection that enters literary scholarship as it turns its attention to women's role in the formation of aesthetics and their contribution to an "evolving national culture." Its editors view women's participation as "integral to the steady rise of a professional print culture and the renegotiation of the role of the writer in relation to a commercial public."[19] Bluestockings, especially the more inclusive grouping posed by Eger and her associates, effected a number of changes in the British culture of letters that offered to their Romantic-era successors the possibility of a woman's professional life of the mind. Gary Kelly's essay in the same volume credits Bluestocking feminism with "the promotion of an emergent 'national' literature, cultural modernisation, and classical republican politics in opposition to court culture and politics." Through non-professional means such as coterie culture, epistolary networks and emphasis on the civility of mixed company conversations as well as their publications, the Bluestockings helped establish a bond between the gentry and the professional middle class and proffered "an intellectualisation and professionalisation of female subjectivity."[20]

The Bluestocking circle included several women critics who made significant contributions to the emergence of a national literary canon through their "formative contributions to the field of Shakespeare scholarship."[21] Yet although, with the exception of Montagu, the Bluestocking Shakespeare critics can be classed as professional writers, it is not for their literary criticism that they merit that designation. Elizabeth Griffith, who defended the morality of Shakespeare, relied for most of her income on publishing novels and letters, acting, and playwriting.[22] Charlotte Lennox wrote novels and received a small grant from the Royal Literary Fund. Her Shakespeare criticism was scholarly enough for Dr. Johnson to draw on for his own edition of Shakespeare. But because it argued that although Shakespeare offered highly original characterization, his narratives were less original than those of his sources, Lennox's essay was so unpopular that it yielded little profit and damaged her subsequent career as a novelist. Thus, although these women were professional writers who published criticism, unlike their later counterparts, several of whom depended at least for a time on criticism as a significant source of income, they cannot be regarded as professional literary critics. In contrast, the present study trains attention on women writing literary criticism for money under circumstances requiring that they meet the demands and offering them the collegial support of a newly emerging literary profession.

The question of professionalization, especially when refocused away from the rise of the woman novelist, will for some raise the issue of literature versus "hack" writing. The sort of professional writing that constitutes the object of this study has rarely garnered much respect, especially when by women writers.[23] This study contends that a reevaluation of this professional literary work is in order. Scholars of women's writing have long known that hierarchies of literary value ranking one form of writing above another have often served to deny the possibility that truly great writing could come from a woman's pen. Kathy MacDermott relies on Althusser's contention that "at different historical moments strategic words can become the site of a struggle between competing ideologies," to show that the term "hack" itself refers to a historical construct, one of a pair of oppositions, "author/hack," that emerged during the eighteenth century in response to the demise of the patronage system and the rise of an urban popular press.[24] This pairing, with its hierarchy of valuation that throws contempt on one of its terms, depends on and was in part produced by other oppositions that arose concurrently, including "genius/mechanism," "patron/bookseller," high versus low culture, and "art/commerce." Students of the first half of the century's literature will begin to hear echoes in some of these terms of satires like Pope's *Dunciad* and Swift's *Tale of a Tub*, both of which MacDermott identifies as early manifestations of the struggle over the professionalization of the field of letters. Meanwhile, late century and Romantic scholars will identify associations that helped construct the notion of Romantic genius, the very core of what Jerome J. McGann has called "the Romantic Ideology."[25] As MacDermott observes, "the qualitative distinction of high/low directs critical attention away from popular writing."[26] The present study retrains attention onto popular forms that prove crucial to a full understanding of Romantic-era literary practice and argues for their significance as objects of literary study.

Thus the professionalism that defines the work of a few women literary critics beginning in roughly the last decade of the eighteenth century in no way diminishes their achievement. Quite the opposite, in fact. The writers considered here discuss the work of other writers at the behest of a bookseller or editor who directs their work and compensates them in hard cash for it. The women that make up this study spent part of their literary lives as professional critics, elucidating and evaluating the writing of their contemporaries for a rapidly expanding British reading public. At a time when it remained a vexed question whether women had the mental capacities necessary for rational judgment, these women writers applied their judgment in a literary form that was dominated by men, and they did so for the same reasons as did most male critics – they were writers, they needed money, and here was paid work. Though genteel independence for a woman came about almost exclusively through inherited wealth, a few women were able to break through gender and class constraints to find in professional literary criticism a significant source of income. Changes in literary culture opened up opportunities for women to make the effort and the risk attendant on publishing criticism pay – and on occasion pay well.

How could such a departure from past practice prove not only possible but lucrative? The answer must be found by looking beyond the Romantic ideology of the solitary individual genius to the actual practices that govern literary production at that historical and cultural moment. Marilyn Butler suggests, in fact, that "the search for 'Romanticism'" will find its object in the professional intellectual, a figure very much of the culture of the moment, for whom literary journalism provides one important outlet among many.[27] Jack Stillinger goes even further, demonstrating that not only is social and cultural support the ground from which individual literary works spring, but that even the canonical works that have helped construct the Romantic vision of solitary creation turn out to be socially produced. Stillinger exposes the collaboration that interwove the work of multiple identifiable hands into the fabric of 'single author' Romantic literary works.[28]

The implications of such arguments for Romantic-era professional women critics are far-reaching. Like all writing, professional literary criticism by Romantic-era women writers issues from a specific culture, both intellectually and materially. Cultural circumstances and practices make it possible and give it shape. In return, this criticism responds to texts and ideas that construct that culture, making important contributions even on topics of national importance – topics such as the foundation of morality and the role of literature in its development, the nature of national character, the constituents of the nation's literary heritage, and the hotly contested topic of literary taste. What is more, it turns out that a particular subculture of the literary world repeatedly emerges as a powerful support to Romantic era women critics. Dominated by middle-class Unitarians and other Rational Dissenters, revolving for a number of years around radical bookseller Joseph Johnson and the lively, even volatile creative circle associated with Johnson and his shop, and eventually making a part of the vanguard of Victorian secular reform, this culture was, like women themselves, largely disenfranchised through legal and extralegal forms of discrimination. Yet as a culture, it fostered mutual support, collaboration at all levels from the business venture to the creation of a text, a relatively high degree of learning even for women, and social values that awarded to women an important standing as a barometer of the state of the culture. The women critics so intimately associated with this culture reflect these values, whether in their assessment of what makes a good novel, their professional assistance to another woman reviewer, or their definition of what makes an ideal British subject. Far from degrading their achievement, these critics' reliance on this network of affiliations offers a lens through which new insights about this culture come into focus. Women literary critics are not peripheral to British Romanticism. They are instead centrally constructive, making a significant, if at times behind the scenes, formative contribution.

The eighteenth-century culture of religious dissent thus occupies a central place in this study. Whether or not they were themselves Dissenters, the woman writers discussed here enjoyed strong connections to the progressive Dissenting community that included a key part of the London publishing industry. These ties are of interest here less as a matter of faith, though that was important to some of these writers, than as a matter of culture and community, the characteristics of which were defined in part by Dissenter religious views, but which affected much more than their religious practice. It is beyond the scope of this project to offer a full overview of the origins and views of Rational Dissent.[29] Nevertheless, a brief description of a few features and trends can help explain the remarkable coincidence of community among these early professional women literary critics. Dissenter culture was marked by practices of collaborative enterprise that fostered the entrance of women into an untraditional professional field. Further, its theological perspective blended well with the philosophy and aesthetics of sensibility that inform criticism by several of the women studied here.

Although the roots of Dissenting thought can be traced back centuries earlier, the culture of eighteenth-century Dissent was officially created by early Restoration legislation which excluded from the rights and privileges of full citizenship any individuals who failed to conform to the Church of England.[30] Thus established as a separate subculture, Dissenters developed many of their own institutions. Not only did they worship separately, but because they were excluded from official avenues of education, they founded their own network of academies in England, some Dissenters then taking higher degrees at universities in Edinburgh and the Netherlands. Though men so trained often entered such professions as medicine or clergy within their own denomination, Dissenters were barred from traditional avenues of advancement such as government office, the military, and clerical positions within the Established Church. Many turned instead to the rapidly expanding opportunities in commerce and trade, becoming leaders in eighteenth-century economic change.

Meanwhile, partly in response to the excesses of the Interregnum, many religious moderates both within and outside the Established Church felt a renewed commitment to the role of reason in issues of faith. Among Anglicans these ideas were expounded by the Latitudinarians, a group of moderate clergy who insisted on the benevolence of a rationally comprehensible divinity and the importance of good works to salvation and spiritual health.[31] This philosophy proved attractive, and Latitudinarian influence spread. Among Dissenters reason affirmed the possibility of universal salvation and underlay skepticism regarding the doctrine of the trinity. Thus, despite their doctrinal differences, Rational Dissenters came to be more allied in both their thinking and their personal lives to moderate Anglicans than they were to their Dissenting counterparts who ascribed to Puritan and Calvinist doctrines and practices. Or, as R. K. Webb phrases it, "the more moderate conclusions of the latitudinarians survived relatively intact to give a characteristic identity to eighteenth-century Anglicanism, in its upper, more visible sectors, and to provide inspiration and allies for the Rational Dissenters."[32] It is important to avoid overemphasizing the separation between Rational Dissenters and other forms of English religious dissent, for the limited numbers of Dissenters meant that except in London, disparate sects attended the same academies and in isolated areas at times even identified with the same congregation. Still, the moderate influence took hold, and Rational Dissenters, especially Unitarians, came to dominate religious Dissent through the later eighteenth and early nineteenth centuries.

These trends have several implications. R. S. Crane has clarified how emphasis on the naturalness of benevolence and virtue, on the human being as "essentially a gentle and sympathetic creature," with a propensity toward goodwill, promotes the characteristics of sociability, the same characteristics that G. J. Barker-Benfield has identified as a key ingredient of commercial success.[33] Unwilling to worship with their Anglican counterparts, moderate Dissenters nevertheless easily made personal and business contacts among them, thereby enjoying indirect access to some of the economic and social influence that was denied them through more direct channels. Webb hints at a relationship between economic standing and religious thought within Anglicanism in the statement quoted above. Meanwhile, a similar dissociation arose between the various nonconformist sects. Leonora Davidoff and Catherine Hall point out that "Divisions between Anglicans (themselves split between Evangelicals and traditionalists) and nonconformists were compounded by a multitude of nonconformist sects. While ostensibly based on doctrinal issues, these denominational divisions often covered latent social distinctions."[34] While the open air meetings and lay clergy of Methodism, for example, appealed most to the lower classes, Rational Dissent, with its emphasis on individualism, sociability, and religious moderation, attracted prosperous commercial and professional nonconforming Protestants. Rational Dissenters and the Presbyterians to whom they were closely allied "recruited from increasingly wealthy and imposing mercantile and professional levels in society."[35] Thus, though legally and in many points socially and economically a marginalized culture, Rational Dissenters prospered as a group and became a vital part of the English middle class. Especially relevant to this study, by the last decade of the eighteenth century Dissenters owned and operated many of the most influential enterprises in the London publishing industry, including respected bookselling firms, prestigious periodicals, and important presses.

At the same time, emphasis on benevolence and feeling as the basis of religious teachings led Rational Dissenter clergy to emphasize plain language and practicality in preaching, instruction of the young, good works, mutual aid, visitation of the sick, and a personal acquaintance with every parishioner. Influential divines such as Philip Doddridge, a leading mid-century Dissenting minister, theologian, and educator, adopted a style that in making itself accessible even to the lowest parishioners achieved what Webb refers to as "truly the language of the family circle as well as of the reader in his closet."[36] It is easy to see the significance of private and domestic virtues to such a culture. Barker-Benfield, for example, devotes significant attention to the contributions of religious Dissenters to the campaign for the reformation of male manners, one of the cultural and intellectual trends nudging English values toward emphasis on domesticity and sociability. Further, Davidoff and Hall remind us that partly because of their status as a separate culture, one deeply grounded in sociability and domesticity, Dissenters relied on collaboration and familial enterprise in their economic pursuits.

It is not my purpose to overemphasize the importance of particular religious views to the development of eighteenth-century middle-class domesticity and the culture of the "Man of Feeling." Crane himself reminds us that his study locating the genesis of this culture in latitudinarian thinking is not meant to deny the influence of secular thinkers such as Newton, Locke, and Shaftesbury, names that still rank among the most prominent in Barker-Benfield's study so many years later. Instead, Crane offers his genealogy as a corrective to exclusive emphasis on secular thinkers, reminding readers of some intimate connections in the evolution of both religious and secular ideas of sensibility. His latitudinarian divines were well versed in and enthusiastic about the ideas of Locke and Newton, and those ideas animated their developing views. Similarly, intimate connections between Edinburgh intellectual circles and English Dissent meant that Dissenting academies and schools in England promoted the theories of Locke, Hartley, and their Scottish followers. Educated Dissenters were well versed in secular as well as religious intellectual threads that came together in the culture of sensibility.

My point in tying these threads together is to suggest that Rational Dissenters such as Unitarians enjoy a privileged relationship to the culture of sensibility. Both their religious thinking and their social practice emphasized values that have been identified as the core of eighteenth-century sentimental culture. These values lent themselves to business practices that proved highly successful in the newly developing market economy, allowing Rational Dissenters to experience substantial commercial influence and financial success, especially when compared to other non-Anglican sects. Certainly not all Dissenters were prosperous, but in the London publishing industry social and business contacts were so interwoven that Dissenting culture proved surprisingly supportive, not only for Dissenters, but for non-Dissenters of the same social circle. Dissenter emphasis on collaboration and mutual aid offered opportunities to individuals who in more traditional settings might not have enjoyed the same prospects. These possibilities included openings for literary work, including occasions that fell outside the gender constraints enforced by those holding more conservative views. The women writers studied here benefited in finding professional literary work beyond the confines of what previously had been available to women. These same values of sensibility, particularly amenable to women, animated their criticism in complex ways.

Several studies of the eighteenth-century culture of sensibility emphasize the connection between sensibility and private domesticity. Jean Hagstrum, for example, argues that changes in affective relations followed from shaping the discourse of sensibility as the origin of the companionate marriage. Hagstrum ensconces Milton's *Paradise Lost* as the foundational text for both this new discourse and its model of affectionate domesticity. John Mullan identifies mid-century ideals of sociability as grounded in expressions of "the capacity to feel and display sentiments, a capacity that is called 'sensibility.'" Barker-Benfield's work locates the discourse of sensibility as emerging with the birth of a modern consumer society. Arising from late seventeenth- and early-eighteenth century models of sensation and association, theories of sensibility provided a means of articulating accounts of "natural" femininity and masculinity "aiming to discipline women's consumer appetites in tasteful domesticity, but thence reforming male behavior," thereby replacing the model of barbaric aristocratic Restoration male culture with the successful commercial entrepreneur happy to spend his hours of relaxation in his increasingly comfortable middle-class home.[37] All these theories have in common the view that though sensibility is immediately pertinent to the private domesticity, it carries undeniable public implications.

To begin exploring the significance of these public implications to Romantic-era British women literary critics, we need to conceive of the public/private divide as more permeable than most analysis has allowed. Recent discussions of this divide have for the most part depended on Jürgen Habermas's *Structural Transformation of the Public Sphere*. According to Habermas, the public sphere, made up of bourgeois individuals who come together to discuss political issues of consequence to the stability of private property and the free flow of goods and services in the market, fully materializes as a function of shifting discussions from mixed company venues such as the French *salons*, where women were not only admitted but exerted much sway, into masculine settings like the English coffeehouse, where women were present only as workers, not as equal disputants. Habermas's formulation has been much revised, including a recent reassessment by Harriet Guest.[38] Guest resists the polarized opposition between "a masculine public sphere of political power and a sphere of privacy which is much more difficult to characterize, but which almost always includes or overlaps with the domestic."[39] In much recent scholarship on gender in eighteenth-century culture, Guest argues, the analogy of spheres, by obscuring the fluidity or permeability in the relation between the public and private, becomes a hindrance. Anne K. Mellor agrees, for in *Mothers of the Nation* she suggests of the gender defined concept of spheres that "It may be time to discard this binary, overly simplistic concept of separate sexual spheres altogether in favor of a more nuanced and flexible conceptual paradigm that foregrounds the complex intersection of class, religious, racial, and gender differences in this historical period." True, one must not lose sight of the difference between, for example, petitioning parliament and serving in it, however public an activity petitioning might be. Nevertheless, Mellor is correct that at least some women did "participate fully in the discursive or literary public sphere conceptualized by Habermas, self consciously defining themselves as the shapers of public opinion."[40] One of the ways they did so was through published commentary on literature.

Emphasis on fluidity or permeability between the public and private uncovers a recognition on the part of some eighteenth-century writers, several of them women, that private values and many activities regarded as private under most definitions of the public sphere turn out in fact to have broad public implications. In her research on nationalism, for example, Linda Colley argues against the view that women were confined to an exclusively domestic privacy, demonstrating instead that women often participated in activities that were quite public. "At one and the same time," Colley affirms, "separate sexual spheres were being increasingly prescribed in theory, yet increasingly broken through in practice." In her view, women's petitions for compassionate reform or their sentimentalized support for the war effort show the public applicability of privately generated values. On the war effort, for instance, she remarks that "By extending their solicitude to the nation's armed forces, men who were not in the main related to them by blood or marriage, women demonstrated that their domestic virtues possessed a public as well as a private relevance."[41] Thus, in Guest's words, "domesticity gains in value as a result of its continuity with the social or the public, and not only as a result of its asocial exclusion."[42]

By the 1770s and 1780s, Guest argues, domesticity and its associated values come into play as the key ingredient defining a publicly estimable, patriotically beneficial form of sensibility. Excess of sensibility was often interpreted by this time as the sign of corruption, degeneracy, social disintegration. Novels satirized such excess, critics condemned it, and writers on issues such as morality and femininity issued dire warnings. Yet in other circumstances, "Sensibility [...] is central to the issue of women's ability to imagine themselves as patriotic or public citizens" in part "because of its role in the sentimental notion of the continuity of affect linking the family and the nation." "The basis in the affective family," she explains "is necessary to guarantee this value, and to distinguish it from those forms of sensibility that might seem to be merely about polish and superficial affect."[43] Sensibility itself, then, was seen as split between a healthy, 'natural' variety that characterized, even produced, ideal Britishness, both male and female, and a corrosive, "artificial," enervating excess that served as the hallmark of domestic corruption and foreign degradation. The private sphere of middle-class domesticity comes to serve a critical public function in the discourse of nationalism and the construction of British national identity.

As subsequent chapters will show, women literary critics drew on Dissenting culture and its attendant middle-class values of sensibility in ways that indicate that they understood the public implications of their work. The circumstances that make their criticism possible consistently show reliance on and intimate collaboration with supportive family and close friends, virtually all of whom prove either to be Dissenters themselves, or to enjoy their own close business and personal contacts among Dissenters. Probably because it was so important to their own work, women critics attended to issues of collaborative writing practice. Their criticism frequently registers aesthetics grounded in sensibility, such as interest in the promotion of morality based in benevolent feeling, or approval of the entertainment to be derived from depictions of natural affections. These critics shaped the taste of British audiences in the direction of the values that gave them support, all the more because they often discussed popular literary forms that appealed to a wide audience. Furthermore, in their rejection of "foreign" literary inferiorities, including expressions of sensibility's degenerate excess, in their elevation of certain literary values over others, and in their selection and defense of the texts that would make up the definitive canon of national literature, they helped to define the character of the ideal British subject as one in whom reason moderates, even produces the middle-class domestic affections that find, as Guest had said, their "basis in familial privacy."

Recent work on Romantic-era construction of the British literary canon has suggested that literary criticism was one arena in which the discourse of nationalism worked itself out. By the late eighteenth century, writing about literature was regularly brought into service to define the nature of Britishness, in part through the delineation of the essential characteristics of the national literature. Quoting Jacques Barzun, Gerald Newman argues that much literary research during the Romantic period acted as a form of "national literary hero-worship in which the great authors of the past – masters of the native tongue, hence specially attuned, it is believed, to the national spirit – are revived, reappraised, and then presented as 'great figures which common opinion regards as embodying the soul or spirit of a given people.'"[44] According to Newman, the national literary heritage and the national identity that it both exemplifies and constructs worked during the divided and fraught period of the late century "to overcome inherited particularistic loyalties (such as religious, political, and regional ones), replacing these with a mythic ideal of character which functions then to promote a real national community."[45] James Chandler has extended this view, arguing that the turn away from Augustan aesthetics toward Romantic poetics valuing ideals such as originality and individual genius must be regarded as a patriotic response to Burke's depiction of the French Revolution and the anxieties that events in France inspired.[46] Chandler situates his analysis in the Romantic-era controversy over the poetry of Pope, whose cosmopolitan literary aesthetics the idea of a native British literary heritage was constructed to refute. Meanwhile, Thomas F. Bonnell demonstrates the importance during the 1770s and 1780s of collected editions such as Samuel Johnson's *Works of the English Poets* (1779–81) in establishing for the first time a canon of indigenous British literature.[47]

Women literary critics made numerous contributions to establishing and revising the newly emerging literary canon, and to creating the literary values that made it possible to identify and celebrate a native British literary heritage at one of the most divisive moments in British history. Though efforts to delineate a national canon of poets had begun long before, during the years covered by the present study, this project extended into other literary forms, especially more popular genres, establishing canons, for example, of British drama and British novels. Like the earlier projects studied by Bonnell, these projects served a unifying function, in this case bringing the lower orders of the

British middle class together with the more learned and the upper classes who had until then dominated public representation of British value. The work of these women critics stands the traditional class hierarchy on its head, so that their literary commentary re-values domesticity and the middle class as the true location of ideal Britishness.[48] This study will show that women literary critics made landmark contributions to extending the British literary canon, often with middle-class and women readers in mind. Anna Letitia Barbauld, for example, argues for the value of novels because of their greater accessibility compared to poetry for those with only modest learning or those distracted by the concerns of commerce.[49] By the same token, Elizabeth Inchbald turns her theater criticism away from a critical format grounded in learned citation to develop a sort of *bricolage* of basic literary history, remarks on production and staging, and celebrations of recent performances, a format that offered strong popular appeal.

But women literary critics engaged in debates over the literary canon in other ways as well. Certain literary values which we have long associated with distinguishing Romantic from Augustan aesthetics work to elevate a native British literary canon over a more cosmopolitan one. Like most of their male counterparts, women critics continue to rely on standards of value derived from Augustan literary criticism, labeling works they regard as good with "elegant," "refined," "witty," or "correct." But they also show a strong tendency to lean in favor of such evaluations as "new," "original," full of "imagination," displaying "genius," expressions that elevate native British literature and the new Romantic literary experiments over more finished, classically inspired work. Thus, in women's periodical reviews, "elegance" can become "artificial," while originality or imagination can excuse a multitude of violations of the correct. Walter James Graham has identified the reviews of Wordsworth's and Coleridge's work as exemplary of what made the *Analytical Review*, a publication considered radical by some, the most forward thinking literary review in its day. *Analytical* contributions were published anonymously with coded initials, so the authors of most articles are unknown, but Ralph M. Wardle has identified those written by Mary Wollstonecraft, and Derek Roper has speculated briefly about a few that he believes were written by Barbauld and her niece, Lucy Aikin. These identifications include virtually all of the *Analytical* articles on Coleridge and Wordsworth, so that if the attributions are correct women writers turn out to be the authors of the very articles that place the *Analytical* in the vanguard of literary reviews for twentieth-century scholarship.[50]

Moreover, since women were regarded as especially susceptible to the sentimental emotions that were thought to produce corruption on one hand, or benevolent virtue on the other, it was in women's best interest to elevate moderate, domestic forms of sensibility while condemning sentimental excess. Women critics drew on the discourse of sensibility for all sorts of purposes. Middle class women all, they give serious consideration to literary forms such as novels, plays, sentimental poetry, conduct books, and periodical essays, all popular among middle class and women readers. In criticizing these works, domestic sensibility, a natural inclination toward sympathy, affection, and benevolence, defines much of what is worthy of praise, whether in an educational or moral work, or a publication that falls under the rubric of belles-lettres. Meanwhile, condemnation of sensibility in its corrupt or excessive manifestations informs much of their censorious commentary, separating bad novels or poetry from good, revealing laxity in moral work, and articulating the essential qualities that exalt British literature above its inferior competition from France. According to women critics, for example, characters are "natural" when they display emotions consistent with their background and the situation in which they find themselves and "artificial" both when they display emotions that are disproportionate and when they fail to show emotion at all. Morality is good when it proceeds naturally from domestic affection and fellow feeling. When it is based on externally imposed precepts or when it proves harsh, exacting, unforgiving, it can be nearly as bad as immorality itself. And for the women who made significant contributions to Romantic-era revisions of the literary canon, entertainment, the lightening of the burdens of middle-class life through the enjoyment of decent pleasures, especially the pleasures of affection and benevolent sympathy, proves the chief purpose for popular literary forms, whether novels, plays, published letters, or familiar essays. These women critics help tie the discourse of sensibility to that of British nationalism, shaping a vision of British identity that is domestic, benevolent, middle-class.

Disenfranchised, blocked from traditional channels of power on the basis of gender, class, and community, the women writers studied here found themselves in a position to speak to large numbers of the British literate middle class on a topic of utmost public importance – the nation's cultural heritage, and through that heritage, its very identity. Jon Klancher offers an illuminating analysis of how, by the Romantic era, literary discourse had become *discourses*, and through their codes and concerns, their tropes and syntax, their anxieties and moments of satisfaction, texts began to carve up readership into readerships, interpellating an audience whose identity came to hinge on recognizing that they were part of a distinct group. Klancher affirms that in reading non-canonical Romantic prose, "what is at issue is precisely the historical forming of taste," and the consequent redistribution of British subjects from social groupings based on rank so as to produce the emergence of social classes in the modern sense. Thus, "reading and writing themselves are agents, not reflexes, of individual, cultural, and social transformation."[51] Women critics played an important part in this process. Though they deployed their critical values from positions outside official lines of authority, they took the values of that marginalized culture into one of the most public of discourses and offered them as the standards for the nation's culture as a whole.

According to Klancher, the growing consciousness of audience specificity is a key element of late eighteenth- and early nineteenth-century publication. He argues that "The English Romantics were the first to become radically uncertain of their readers, and they faced the task Wordsworth called 'creating the taste' by which the writer is to be comprehended."[52] Male poets, for example, often published criticism openly guiding public taste toward standards that their own work embodied. Wordsworth's famous preface to the 1800 edition of *Lyrical Ballads* comes to mind. Similarly, women critics evince their cognizance of reading audience, showing moments of precise discrimination. Mary Wollstonecraft advises Mary Hays on how, through her book's preface, to best present herself as a creditable author, while Harriet Martineau recognizes qualities that make a book inappropriate for the intended reader. But more generally, women critics seem to have a growing consciousness of just how a book might produce a certain reader – how a novel might make a reader moral, for instance, or, more interestingly, how a series of familiar essays can help bring about a social world dominated by a domestically oriented middle class. In all these examples, the work of women critics reflects their consciousness that what they are writing carries implications that extend well beyond the book at hand.

Part One of this study examines critical prefaces by Anna Letitia Barbauld and Elizabeth Inchbald, both of whom penned critical introductions to reissues or collections of work by other writers. This portion of the project concentrates on sources of women critics' expertise and professionalism. Through their engagement with the discourse of sensibility and their theorizing and defense of popular literary forms, Barbauld and Inchbald offered important contributions to the formation of the British literary canon and to developing views about the nature of British national identity. Barbauld, whose work makes the focus of Chapter 1, had a long history as a poet, educator, author of children's literature, devotional writer, and political pamphleteer before she began to write criticism. Her first major critical essays introduced Mark Akenside and William Collins, both of whom in Barbauld's analysis took their inspiration from Augustan literary aesthetics and appealed to a well-educated, privileged audience. Remarkably learned herself, Barbauld shows her own comfort with these attributes through her essays' emphasis on qualities that make for these poets' elite appeal and in her reliance on systematic scholarly form. Barbauld endorses these conventions at first, but as she begins to introduce other more popular literary forms, she shows increasing consciousness of the interplay between literature and the surrounding culture, so that by the time she discusses novels, the most popular of literary forms, her essays reveal acute interest in the reciprocal relationship between literature and national identity. The culture of British middle-class Dissent fostered Barbauld's literary efforts, and her criticism comes to credit popular literature with producing the typical British subject as one inherently domestic and middle class. These later essays constitute landmarks in the development of a British literary canon. Barbauld's work on the periodical essay and the novel establish for the first time a canon in each of these literary forms, while her essay on the novel marks as well the first substantial effort to bring women writers into the British literary canon. Meanwhile, though Barbauld continues to employ a systematic critical framework, that framework becomes more supple and unobtrusive as she comes to de-emphasize Augustan aesthetics and to argue for the importance of literature with broad-based appeal.

Chapter 2 treats Elizabeth Inchbald's critical prefaces to the plays in the 25 volume *British Theatre*. Unlike the far more learned Barbauld, who seems comfortable with the scholarly framework that, though applied with increasing flexibility, shapes all her criticism, Inchbald, an actress and popular novelist, seems weighed down, handicapped, when she draws upon scholarly apparatus. Her criticism comes into its own when she finds her niche as a critic addressing a popular audience on topics more entertaining than scholarly. Inchbald is the first woman drama critic to be placed in the highly visible position of authoring critical introductions to a prestigious edition of recently acted plays, but although she suffered some harsh condemnation, she also cannily exploited the popularity of her series in an unusual example of conscious authorial self marketing. Like Barbauld's work, Inchbald's essays touch on issues of national identity when she compares the characteristics of British theater to that of other countries. Yet although tied by numerous friendships to the same intellectual and artistic circle marked by so many connections to the culture of Rational Dissent, Inchbald was herself a Catholic, and though she avoids direct reference to it, her views on patriotism and national identity are inflected by this religious and cultural difference. She reveals, for example, distaste for many of the anti-French aspects of British nationalism as well as skepticism over some expressions of British national pride. In addition, taken together, Inchbald's critical prefaces form a coherent theory of closet drama based on principles that retained their usefulness into the later decades of the twentieth century.

Part Two concentrates on periodical literary reviews by women writers. Often a dismissed literary form even when authored by canonical male writers, reviews, when discovered to have issued from a woman's pen, have received especially harsh treatment. Yet reviews carried much influence, influence that sometimes called for applause, sometimes for alarm. As the form of criticism that molds public opinion on the most current publications, reviews exert a cumulatively critical influence on literature and public taste. Three chapters examine the reviewing work of Mary Wollstonecraft, Mary Hays, Anna Letitia Barbauld, Elizabeth Moody, and Harriet Martineau. In every case, the literary reviews that employed these women critics all benefited from close ties to the community of English Rational Dissent. Each woman critic discussed here, even if not a Dissenter herself, still enjoyed similar close ties with the Dissenting community. The material circumstances of women's reviewing reveal the collaboration and mutual support characteristic of middle-class Dissenting culture. At the same time, their reviews promote sympathy, benevolent affection, and morality based in natural feeling, values grounded in the discourse of sensibility, which, while generally widespread in Romantic-era British culture, held special significance for the Dissenting community.

Chapter 3 looks at Mary Wollstonecraft's work for the *Analytical Review*, often regarded as the most forward thinking or even radical of important literary reviews. As the first professional woman periodical reviewer, Wollstonecraft represents a landmark in the study of literary criticism by women. Her work for the *Analytical Review*, lasting through most of her literary career, provides an important index to her ideas about literature, and the evolution of her thinking that led to her most radical as well as her most personal publications. Equally important, her reviewing career also presents an opportunity to study the circumstances that make possible such an unusual career, and the extent to which that career offered the financial, personal, and professional support that made her better known work possible. Wollstonecraft's reliance on the discourse of sensibility to legitimize her critical authority reveals the public implications that women writers had come to attach to private feeling. Plus, in the support and guidance that Wollstonecraft extended to Mary Hays, her career as a writer and editor for bookseller Joseph Johnson represents the first known example of a professional mentoring relationship between women writers.

Chapter 4 returns to Barbauld, this time to examine her reviews for the *Monthly Review*. Part of a close, mutually supportive literary family who, during much of the later eighteenth century, enjoyed personal and professional ties to the Unitarian intellectual elite, Barbauld was, by the time she began to write anonymous reviews, highly respected as a literary authority. Her reviewing practice is grounded in the culture of Rational Dissent and in support from and collaboration with members of her immediate family. Consequently, it sheds new light on the culture of the literary review. That this collaborative interdependence was a cultural rather than a merely familial phenomenon receives important confirmation from the periodical work of Elizabeth Moody, the *Monthly Review*'s only other positively identified regular woman reviewer.[53] Like Barbauld's, Moody's work at the *Monthly* depended on the Dissenting community. Only after her marriage to a middle-class Dissenter did Moody leave behind the dilettante amateurism and coterie circulation of the eighteenth-century upper class in favor of collaboration and professional publication. Barbauld's reviews show both her professional attentiveness even to minor publications and her confidence in her role as a literary authority. Her critical standards shift from emphasis on the "elegance" and "correctness" of Augustan aesthetic ideals to valuing "imagination," "genius," and experimentation with the "new," the same shift that James Chandler has identified as fundamental to Romantic period efforts to identify a native British literary heritage. Furthermore, her work provides a clear demonstration that even the "Catalogue" review, the critical genre of all others that has received the most dismissive treatment, merits consideration as a worthwhile object of study.

Chapter 5 moves the discussion forward to the next generation of women's literary criticism. Harriet Martineau, a younger member of the same progressive, predominantly Unitarian community that had supported professional women's criticism from the first, opens her criticism career quite explicitly as a champion for the Unitarian cause. Her journalism arose first out of sympathy with the *Monthly Repository*'s Unitarian agenda, and like the work of her female predecessors, it reveals the structures of collaboration and support that characterized enterprises originating in Dissenting community. As the years that mark the end of the present study approached, this community began to evolve, shifting its philosophy away from a denominational focus toward the secular vision of social reform that inspires one of the dominant threads in early Victorian thought, a change that Martineau's essays helped bring about. Furthermore, Martineau's work demonstrates her ability to distinguish distinct reading audiences and her understanding of the needs and expectations of those audiences. Meanwhile, she capitalizes on her position in the male dominated field of literary criticism to move into even more emphatically masculine discourses such as philosophy, theology, and social reform, so that her early articles stand as a landmark in the history of women's literary journalism leading up to the early Victorian years.

As a whole, my study argues that criticism by these women writers demonstrates their conviction of the public implications of commentary about literature. Supported by a culture that emphasized mutual aid and found little shame in respectably earning one's own income, women literary critics found themselves in a position to speak to a wide audience on the vital issue of the nation's cultural heritage. They extended the literary canon and helped to redefine aesthetic values, often with women and middle-class readers in mind. During the years that mark the period between the fall of the Bastille and the passage of the First Reform Bill, a time when British literary culture was becoming increasingly commercial and middle class, a few women writers found in literary criticism unprecedented opportunities for professionalism and public authority.

Part I
"Forms scientific and established": The Critical Preface, the Canon, and the Woman Critic

Dissatisfied with the quality of Elizabeth Inchbald's critical prefaces to the plays included in *The British Theatre*, Inchbald's first biographer, James Boaden, explains that like Inchbald, "Mrs. Barbauld had [...] been seduced into the engagement of furnishing prefaces to the entertaining collection of British Novels, which bears her name; but the Aikins [Barbauld's family of birth] were all scholars, and better turned, not to the discrimination of criticism, but its forms scientific and established."[1] Boaden's remark brings together two women critics who, for all their differences both personal and critical, share the distinction of having been solicited during the first decade of the nineteenth century by respected booksellers to lend their names to literary collections offering a definitive selection of British authors in a chosen literary form. They come to Boaden's attention, then, as contributors to large projects that serve as landmarks in the history of bringing English literature to the British public. Both part of the loose-knit circle that included such well-known literary, artistic, and intellectual figures as Mary Wollstonecraft, William Godwin, Thomas Holcroft, Joseph Johnson, Joseph Priestley, Amelia Opie, Mary Robinson, Henry Fuseli, William Blake, and many others, these two women critics share similarities in personal circumstances as well. They were both mature women who came to literary criticism after achieving reputations in other forms of authorship, with Inchbald enjoying an acting career as well. Barbauld's poetry was well regarded by her contemporaries and some of her children's literature continued popular well into the nineteenth century, while Inchbald had achieved outstanding success as a playwright and novelist. Their names were well known – even celebrated – and their association with their respective literary collections could be expected to increase marketability. Still, their previous publications had failed to secure permanent financial security for these two middle-class women, and commissions for paid literary work were welcome.

These similarities should not, however, obscure their differences. Both Inchbald and Barbauld were unusually well read for women in their day, yet their education differed greatly. Neither, of course, enjoyed an advanced formal education. As Boaden suggests, however, Barbauld, born Anna Letitia Aikin, came from a family of scholars. Though a middle-class woman Dissenter, she not only received an unusually rigorous home education from her parents, but profited as well from the family's proximity to the Dissenters' academy where her father, John Aikin, a respected classicist and theologian, taught. As a result, her scholastic attainments would have been worthy of respect even among university men. Her writing, which included poetry, devotional and educational literature, and even political pamphlets, reflected this background, and she had worked for many years as an educator herself. Inchbald, on the other hand, showed precocious abilities in reading, and throughout her life set herself study programs to facilitate professional advancement or self-improvement, but she had only the standard formal education for middle-class girls. Both her writing – mostly plays and novels – and her first profession of acting appeal to the expanding middle-class audience that turned to lighter literary entertainment during their hours of relaxation.

Not surprisingly then, Barbauld's criticism at first shows her alignment with the educated elite, and throughout her career she tends to follow a systematic plan and to offer scholarly apparatus such as classifications and definitions in her critical essays. In a similar effort to lend her work scholastic authority, Inchbald begins with cumbrous citation of sources, but quickly abandons this approach for a format that is varied and casual with a style that is light, entertaining, and often ironic. In turning away from the established forms, Inchbald finds ground for critical certainty in her own experience with the stage. Discussing progressively more popular literary forms, Barbauld too turns away from her initial concentration on the voice and concerns of a privileged few to focus her essays on the values and practices of the middle class. Meanwhile, the criticism of both these writers indicates that they saw themselves as professionals. Engaged for projects that offer specimens of the national literature to an audience increasingly encouraged to think of themselves as part of a cohesive British nation, they both offer visions of the national character and the role national literature can claim in shaping it. And they reveal attitudes about literary composition and the nature of creativity that are at odds with the vision of a solitary, transcendent creative imagination that until recently characterized most accepted views of Romantic self-representation.[2]

1
The British Common Reader: Critical Prefaces by Anna Letitia Barbauld

Boaden's offhand remark – that the difference between Barbauld's criticism and that of Inchbald stems from family background – is more telling than it may at first seem. As religious Dissenters, the Aikin men were barred from most avenues of formal higher education in England. Yet Boaden is right; they were indeed scholars. To prepare their own clergy and to provide educational opportunities for their adherents, eighteenth-century English Dissenters established separate schools such as Warrington Academy. Though outside the elite channels of education that might culminate at one of the prestigious Anglican universities, Dissenting academies, particularly Warrington, were among the best schools in England. The Reverend John Aikin, Barbauld's father, a respected Dissenting clergyman committed to theological and classical scholarship, became one of Warrington's first tutors when the Academy opened in 1757.

Barbauld's childhood brought her into contact with the period's most eminent Dissenters, and after moving to Warrington, her circle of acquaintances constituted a virtual who's who of Dissenting intellectual elite. Joseph Priestley, one of the most esteemed Dissenters of his time, helped found the Academy and served there as lecturer. Gilbert Wakefield, whose "seditious" pamphlet later landed bookseller Joseph Johnson in Newgate, and author and theologian William Enfield were also among the roster of tutors. Jean Paul Marat, at the time simply a young author and physician but later a key member in the French National Assembly, lectured in French and occasionally on scientific subjects. Thus, Warrington provided an education that was broader than that available at Oxford and Cambridge, "which were still very much in the doldrums."[1] Students included Thomas Malthus, known for his theories on population, and several MPs. The Warrington Press, operated by William Eyres, with Joseph Johnson as London agent, issued over 200 separate publications, including works by Barbauld (then Anna Letitia Aikin) and her brother John, Priestley, Enfield, naturalist Thomas Pennant, biographer and historian William Roscoe, and prison reformer John Howard.

Nor was Warrington's vibrant intellectual atmosphere restricted only to men. Before the young John Aikin enrolled in the academy, he and his sister were taught at home, and her education was comparable to his. An eager scholar, Anna attained exceptional competency in French and Italian and conquered her father's reluctance to teaching her Latin and Greek. Though, like its Anglican counterparts, Warrington enrolled only men, she was permitted to attend lectures, and the academy's students comprised much of her circle among those her own age. By the time she reached adulthood, her scholastic achievements were exceptional for anyone at the time, man or woman.

In addition, Anna Letitia Aikin had already proven herself an accomplished writer. The lively and creative Warrington set freely circulated their own literary manuscripts, and her poetry ranked among their favorites. It was at the encouragement of this tightly knit intellectual community that she published her *Poems*, printed on the academy press in 1772, with a London edition appearing in 1773. The individual poems ranged from sentimental to comic, and satirical to almost mystical in tone with subjects as varied as quotidian domesticity, sublime nature, and the island Corsica's independent spirit in their ill-fated struggle for liberation from the French. *Poems* was applauded by both the public and the reviews, and Anna and her brother John soon followed it with their co-authored *Miscellaneous Pieces in Prose* (1773), a collection of essays and short tales on literary and familiar topics.[2] Barbauld's early literary reputation as a writer of imagination, sensibility, and spiritual depth placed her among the nation's most venerated women, worthy of celebration as one of the *Nine Living Muses of Great Britain* in Richard Samuel's painting.

It was a disappointment to those who felt her literary gifts were going to waste that for the next decade this distinguished poet turned her attention to young children. In 1774 she married a former Warrington pupil, Rochemont Barbauld, and the couple established their own Dissenting school for boys in Palgrave, with Anna teaching English composition. The childless couple adopted one of her nephews, and she took charge of his education as well. Faced with a dearth of appropriate children's literature and educational materials, Barbauld determined to fill the gap, producing *Lessons for Children*

(1778-79), then *Hymns in Prose for Children* (1781). Both volumes proved popular, and *Hymns*, which influenced Blake's *Songs of Innocence* (1789), continued on its own account to help shape the imagination of many a child through most of the nineteenth century.

Up to this point, Barbauld had pursued subjects and forms of writing typical for women – poetry, entertaining essays, and devotional and children's literature. During the 1790s, however, she turned in a new direction. With Britain agitated by a domestic drive for reform and debates on the revolutionary political transformations abroad, Barbauld took up her pen in the service of political and social change, beginning with *An Address to the Opposers of the Repeal of the Corporation and Test Acts* (1790). The pamphlet argues for full political rights for Dissenters, predicting that failure to extend religious toleration will lead to the demise of the Established Church. She followed up the *Address* with poems and essays supporting abolition of the slave trade, government accountability, dissenting forms of worship, and rigorous examination of personal conscience in public life. Although social and political critique seems a long leap from the topics of her earlier writing, a consistent thread runs through Barbauld's work stressing heartfelt religious devotion and commitment to democratic ideals inspired by empathy and scrupulous yet forgiving self-examination beginning in early youth. With her exceptional education and her achievements as an author, it is no surprise that even from the first, Barbauld's literary criticism shows an understanding of the discipline's "forms scientific and established."

This chapter examines Barbauld's critical essays prefacing collections and reissues of previously published literary work. Written during the two decades that mark the turn of the nineteenth century, the essays appear after Barbauld had gained recognition as a poet, moral writer, and author of children's literature and educational materials. Barbauld included a few essays that can be classed as literary criticism in *Miscellaneous Pieces in Prose*, but the essays considered here constitute her induction into the field of professional criticism. Introducing the work of other writers, Barbauld's essays enhance that work's marketability. The literary forms that Barbauld is called on to address vary, perhaps explaining a significant evolution in her critical attitudes and concerns. Other external factors, such as the change in social and intellectual climate from the time shortly after the French Reign of Terror, when the first essay appeared, to the days just before the Regency began, may also play a part. Literary values too, changed during these years, with the 1800 preface to Wordsworth and Coleridge's *Lyrical*

Ballads providing the most famous articulation of new literary objectives. And while it can be risky trying to attribute large attitudinal changes to any particularly influential authors, her reading probably played a role, with Mme. de Staël's *De la littérature* (1800) as one likely candidate. Or as she gained experience she may have felt more confident as a critic. Whatever the reason for it, the shift was dramatic. Barbauld begins her critical career introducing poets that she represents as appropriate for only the most highly educated reader. Her analysis not only highlights her authors' appeal to elite readers, it praises their work for the very qualities that make for this exclusive appeal. Meanwhile, in presenting her author as an exemplary British poet, she proffers an ideal of Britishness that corresponds to the elite audience that can fully appreciate such poetry. But as she later finds herself discussing more informal, popular types of writing – letters, periodical essays, even novels – she turns away from a privileged audience and poetic values that affirm that privilege to champion a middle-class reading public and the forms of literature such a public would prefer. These forms tend to eschew intellectual rigor in favor of qualities that lend themselves to reading for amusement. So completely does she reverse her views that entertainment, once an aim to be sniffed at, becomes the chief purpose for at least some literary forms, able to mitigate a multitude of other sins. Her criticism and editing constitute landmarks in establishing a canon of popular British literature. Further, her work on the British novel marks the first substantial effort to bring women writers into the British literary canon, and to establish a canon of women writers. At the same time, her interest in national identity and the British personality as it manifests in both literature and its consumers culminates in representing middle-class domesticity as the quintessence of British national character. Only by examining her critical essays together can we understand her views on the public role of Britain's literary heritage and the criticism that presents that heritage to the nation's readers.

Barbauld's first professional criticism consisted of two prefatory essays that appeared during the mid-1790s as critical introductions to volumes reissuing the work of mid-eighteenth-century poets William Collins and Mark Akenside. Both volumes, *The Poetical Works of Mr. William Collins* and *The Pleasures of Imagination* by Akenside, were published by booksellers Thomas Cadell and William Davies, who held numerous eighteenth-century copyrights in partnership with the firm of Thomas Longman, and their reputation as aggressive defenders of their venerable literary properties may in part explain their motives for reissuing these works.[3] Further, the poetic "effusions" and "trifles" of the poetry of sensibility had been for some time quite common, but by the middle of the decade, fears that the French Revolution might spread to England had left many associating free expression of emotion with Jacobinism. Cadell and Davies probably felt that the time was ripe for the reappearance of some poetry that conformed to more formal and controlled aesthetic standards, but without a fresh marketing angle, recycling work whose appeal had waned could be a risky venture. Following the success of collections such as Johnson's *Works of the English Poets* (1779–81), the addition of prefaces or introductions by a known author as part of repackaging an old literary product in a new and freshly marketable form had become a recognized strategy for success, and Cadell and Davies banked on the same formula. One of the nation's most celebrated women poets, whose reputation dated back nearly a quarter of a century and who had recently published several pamphlet length poems, Barbauld made an attractive choice to pen the introductions. Though characterized at times by emotionally responsive or even sentimental moments, her work had always held excessive emotionalism in check, and while progressive in bent and therefore topical and "new," her recent publications tended to yoke expressions of feeling with reason in the service of advocating reform. Moreover, Cadell and Davies had for many years been associated with Joseph Johnson, Barbauld's long-time publisher and friend, who counted her brother, also a respected man of letters, among his staff of critics for his *Analytical Review*. Cadell and Davies probably knew what to expect from one of this family of scholars – criticism that, if marked by relatively few flights of genius, was sound and systematic, based in accepted literary standards.

If so, Barbauld delivered as expected. The first sentence of her introduction to Collins initiates the systematic classification of poetry into two general categories. The first, in which the verse serves as an ornament to "subjects which in their own nature are affecting or interesting," comprises didactic, narrative, and descriptive poetry, moral poetry that realistically depicts society and manners, and poetry that contains "a lively representation of the *passions*." She offers Alexander Pope's work in illustration. "The other class," she continues, "consists of what may be called pure Poetry, or Poetry in the abstract. It is conversant with an imaginary world, peopled with beings of its own creation. It deals in splendid imagery, bold fiction, and allegorical personages." Lyric poetry is the quintessence of this category, and Collins, who "has cultivated the Lyric Muse with peculiar felicity," serves as a prototype. Barbauld's classification is too general to tell us much about Collins's poetry, or poetry in general for that matter. Nor do the stiff, formal similes she offers help much: "An Epic Poem may be compared to a piece of massy plate finely wrought," she explains. "[I]t is intrinsically valuable, though its value is much increased by the work bestowed upon it. An Ode, like a delicate piece of silver filligree, receives in a manner all its value from the art and curiosity of the workmanship."[4] We need to keep in mind that this essay and the one on Akenside are her first forays into a genre that frequently leaned toward the pontifical. With her unusually strong background in rhetoric and the classics, it should not surprise us if in this unfamiliar context her prose shows many of the flaws and few of the strengths of eighteenth-century formal exposition. Still, anyone familiar with Barbauld's poetry or with the easier, livelier style and more original content of either some of her later critical essays or her youthful contributions to *Miscellaneous Pieces in Prose* will be disappointed with such a beginning. In the face of such disappointment it would be easy to miss what in fact becomes a most interesting design on Barbauld's part.

According to Barbauld, "abstract" or lyric poetry demands a special kind of audience. "[H]aving to do chiefly with ideas generated within the mind," it tends to be "obscure," and so "it cannot be comperhended [sic] by any whose intellect has not been exercised in similar contemplations." It is, in other words, poetry for the highly educated with leisure for intellectual and literary pursuits. Its figurative language renders it "remote from comprehension." Especially the Ode, several of which number among Collins's most successful poems, "will only please those who, by being long conversant with the best models of Poetry in a polished age, have acquired a scientific and perhaps, in some degree, a factitious taste." By contrast, the other type of poetry, the more concrete forms that include narrative, didactic, and sentimental poetries, "have been popular among all that read." In particular, poetry representing the "passions" love, terror, or pity has a popular appeal that Barbauld regards with a touch of distaste. It "commands the attention even of those who are but indifferent judges of the vehicle in which it [the representation of a 'passion'] may be conveyed."[5] According to Richard Wendorf, Collins began his career by patterning himself "on classical and neoclassical models," while his later work is characterized by the "hidden, dark, and difficult."[6] In setting the stage for the reception of the new Collins volume, Barbauld presents this poet who had garnered respect but never a remarkable degree of popularity as worthy in part precisely because of his narrow appeal. Barbauld sets his audience apart and defines them as an elite with highly cultivated taste.

Moreover, the critic of lyric poetry rises above the common reader as well, for "to judge of or relish such a composition requires a practised ear, and a taste formed by elegant reading."[7] As one with the "scientific" (perhaps even the "factitious"?) taste not only to appreciate, but to systematically analyze this poet, Barbauld groups herself with the highly literate, predominantly upper class and masculine elite over and against the audience for poetic forms increasingly popular with women and the middle class. If figurative language is central to what defines this privileged category of poetry and what sets it and its audience apart, then the purpose for the ponderous similes that mark the first few pages of her essay becomes clear. Barbauld includes them less as examples to aid our understanding of her classification system than as markers of her own authority as a critic. As a person she may be a woman from the Dissenting middle class, but as a critic she allies herself with the male, upper-class graduates of the prestigious Anglican universities who dominated the upper echelons of the world of letters, including essay criticism.

Nor does this demarcation exhaust the service that she enlists from this simple classification. Again like filigree, which comes to little when melted down, without the foundation of an intrinsically valuable subject matter, "Lyric poetry will very seldom bear translation, which is a kind of melting-down of a Poem and reducing it to the sterling value of the matter contained in it." In *The Rise of English Nationalism*, Gerald Newman traces how throughout the second half of the eighteenth century, literature and the other arts had played a pivotal role in creating among its inhabitants the popular notion of an English nation, and had helped to shape both the concept and the expression of an English national character. Because it will not bear translation, lyric poetry seems in Barbauld's formulation to be the ideal literary form for expressing national character. Indeed, "who, but a native of France, reads, what a native of France reads with rapture, the Odes of JEAN BAPTISTE ROUSSEAU?"[8] The implications of Barbauld's argument are clear: if lyric poetry is the literary touchstone that separated the native from the outsider, then the reader of lyric poetry embodies the true national character. And if lyric poetry displays features that make it accessible only to an elite, formally educated reader, then the true Englishman, the reader of the English lyric, is just that – an English *man* who ranks among the few who have inhaled their Englishness with the fumes of port and fine tobacco at one of the universities. An allusion to Collins's years at Magdalen College then takes on importance as part of Barbauld's case for Collins, this poet of and for the masculine elite, as a distinctively English poet. Such an undertaking seems rather surprising in view not only of Barbauld's own background and affiliations, but of the fact as well that, if Newman is correct, the concept of an English national character originated among English artists and writers against the perceived cosmopolitanism of the British upper-class. But this essay is one of Barbauld's first contributions to a form of discourse – the signed literary critical essay – that most often was the domain of educated men. A reissue of the work of a poet that Barbauld herself calls "minor," the volume in which her essay appears cannot through its intrinsic importance lend her the authority she needs. Indeed, Cadell and Davies surely enlisted her in the hope that her name would lend stature to the volume. Barbauld constructs her authority instead by shaping a textual identity that aligns her with those whose identity alone serves as adequate authorization, then performs this identity in her criticism. As we shall later see, however, within a few years she reverses her strategy.

Meanwhile, reading through the introduction to Collins reveals what the "forms scientific and established" must have consisted in, at least as Barbauld saw them. It seems that a good critical essay would have introduced a classification system, whether original or established, in which the critic could assign the poet a place. The poet should be ranked on a scheme of relative merit, and Barbauld in fact assigns to Collins the rather vague "respectable rank amongst our minor Poets." One surely must list the qualities that characterize the poetry: in Collins's case, "tenderness, tinged with melancholy, beautiful imagery, a fondness for allegory and abstract ideas, purity and chasteness of sentiment, and an exquisite ear for harmony." Objectivity requires that a few flaws receive mention as well, such as a tendency to be "not unfrequently obscure."[9] Of course, this flaw, like Collins's strengths, helps establish him as a poet for the elite, for since Collins is an "abstract" or lyric poet, if we fail to penetrate his obscurity the fault must lie with our inadequately schooled intellect rather than with the poetry itself. It is not my intention to diminish Barbauld's critical achievement, which is substantial. Indeed, Wendorf ranks her as one of the earliest critics to come to grips with Collins's challenging obscurity, expressed as an elusive sublimity.[10] Instead, I suggest that in addition to providing estimable aesthetic commentary, her essay serves to legitimate her unusual position as a woman critic.

Barbauld sprinkles the early part of her essay with several biographical details, an increasingly material aspect of any complete introduction to an author's work during the late eighteenth century, as masterworks of biographical criticism like Johnson's *Works of English Poets* demonstrate. Then before discussing the individual poems in depth, she briefly digresses to discuss the creative process itself. It is here that the fissures become most apparent in her construction of Collins as a poet of the masculine elite in which she, at least in her textual character as Collins's critic, can be included:

> A real Poet must always appear indolent to the man of the world. The alacrity and method of business is not to be expected in his occupation. His mind works in silence, and exhausts itself with the various emotions which it cherishes, while to a common eye it appears fixed in stupid apathy. The poet requires long intervals of ease and leisure; his imagination should be fed with novelty, and his ear soothed by praise.[11]

As Barbauld sees him, Collins produced only a small body of work because, like any "real" poet, he has loitered about, physically indolent while tossed by emotion until long solitudes yielded the kindlings of imagination that are poetic creation. David Simpson has drawn attention to the affinities between this description and the "society lady" as described by Mary Wollstonecraft and depicted by novelists such as Jane Austen, figures feminized, as was literature in general, over and against a rational "theory" or "system" increasingly associated with the masculine. Simpson argues that this feminization of the literary "produced a series of tensions" that undermined any "neatly defined subject positions for writers."[12] Indeed, as Collins's individual works come under consideration, his poems feature scenes replete with feminine sounding "sweetness" and "keener sensations," with "enchanting" or "affecting" scenes of "tender and plaintive" emotion, including the depictions of distress that were the stock of sentimental poetry. Barbauld by no means approves of these excursions into the realm of feminine popular poetry. "When COLLINS is not sustained by richness of Poetry," she grumbles, "his sentiments will be found to be trite."[13] Yet she names his "Ode to the Passions" as his most successful poem. Her inability to hold her two opposing classes of poetry apart in order to firmly establish Collins on the side of masculine privilege suggests that she finds that associating intellectual rigor with poetic masculinity affords shaky ground from which to reject the emotion of popular and feminine sensibility. The same proves true for her own textual performance of elite masculinity. Simpson observes that the tensions produced by the feminization of the literary "were especially urgent for male writers seeking a place in a social subculture that was, both symbolically and actually, more and more the domain of women."[14] Barbauld's essay reveals her struggle with precisely the reverse, with tensions that were especially urgent for the female writer seeking a place in a social subculture, the subculture of literary criticism, that was, both symbolically and actually, primarily the domain of men. Eventually her textual masquerade proves too unstable as a foundation on which to construct her edifice of critical authority. In the meantime, however, another essay published three years earlier reinforces the point. Whether or not trained and disciplined intellect and systematic analysis truly belong to the poet, they do belong to his critic.

Like the essay on Collins, Barbauld's essay on Akenside introduces a Cadell and Davies reissue of the work of a mid-eighteenth-century poet. And even more emphatically than was the case for Collins, Barbauld's "Essay on *The Pleasures of Imagination*" frames Akenside as an author for the educated elite.[15] The essay includes a short biographical summary emphasizing Akenside's education in the classics, his sources in aesthetic philosophers such as the aristocratic Shaftesbury, his neo-Platonism. In actuality, Akenside appealed to a relatively wide audience. After its original publication, *The Pleasures of Imagination* quickly went into several editions and within a few years had been translated into a number of other languages. It was reissued frequently through the remainder of the century. Collins's work, on the other hand, enjoyed less popularity, but found a place in more of the eighteenth-century collections of poetry.[16] Yet although Akenside addresses a subject from Joseph Addison's *Spectator*, a model of down-to-earth clarity and broad-based appeal, Akenside's treatment is, according to Barbauld, appropriate for the educated classes only: "to the generality of readers it must appear dry and abstruse." Barbauld depicts as ridiculous any objection that "people from the fields and the highways" might find Akenside alienating. "He will wish none to read," she sniffs, "that are not capable of understanding him."[17] The acrimony expressed here reveals the urgency of the threat it is calculated to forestall. Despite recent expansion of the English reading audience especially among the middle and lower middle classes, agricultural laborers and the homeless posed little hazard to Akenside's poetic reputation. The real menace resides with the lower middle- and working-class readers who made up a substantial part of the rapidly expanding audience for more popular literary forms. If reading is not confined to the educated, but instead every tradesman, shopkeeper, or artisan can relax on occasion with a novel or a volume of sentimental poems, what is to differentiate a reader like Barbauld, whose absolute distance from the commercial classes is less than her distance from the typical Oxbridge graduate? And if she can be equated with the shopgirl skimming a novel, on what possible authority could her criticism rest? Only her education and her ability to put that rigorous intellectual training into practice can set her apart.

Figuring Akenside as appropriate only for a highly educated audience not only establishes Barbauld's own status, but releases her as well from any obligation to make his work more accessible: "Those who have studied the metaphysics of mind, and who are accustomed to investigate abstract ideas," – those, perhaps, like Barbauld herself? – "will read [Akenside's poem] with a lively pleasure; but those who seek mere amusement in a poem, will find many far inferior ones better suited to their purpose." Specifically, she contrasts Akenside with Edward Young, the far more popular author of *Night Thoughts*, who though superior to Akenside in "originality," lacks Akenside's greater "taste and judgment" – two touchstones of aesthetic discernment that at least as far back as Addison's *Spectator* papers had required "cultivation," that is, literary training at least from select reading if not from a university education. Even Barbauld's own style and diction seem to exclude the less educated from her audience, stopping their muddy boots, as it were, at the gate to Akenside's text. As in her essay on Collins or much like Akenside's poem itself, Barbauld's formal, highly structured prose, ornamented with elaborate figuration and citing rhetorical theorists like Longinus, aligns with literary values drawn from learning denied to middle- and lower-class readers. "It is easy for the reader who is conversant in the writings of SHAFTESBURY and HUTCHINSON to perceive," she declares, "how much their elegant and fascinating system is adapted to ennoble our author's subject, and how much *The Pleasures of Imagination* are raised in value and importance by building the throne of Virtue so near the bower of Beauty."[18] Presumably the reader not so conversant should find some other company. Yet how stiff, artificial, and conventional this exclusionary sentence sounds, and how tired and trite are such metaphors for a critic who is herself a poet. Fortunately, when she turned her attention to Addison ten years later, Barbauld had made an about-face in her critical concerns, while her prose takes on vitality as a result.

To elucidate Barbauld's discussion of Addison's *Spectator* papers, it is helpful to make a brief detour through the essay she published a few years later, "On the Origin and Progress of Novel-Writing," an exposition of the history of fiction that introduced the fifty volume collection, *The British Novelists*.[19] We will look further at this essay later, but for the present, it is of interest as a fuller, more articulated statement of an issue broached in the earlier introduction to the collection of periodical papers. Probably in response to Staël's *De la littérature* (1800), which Barbauld doubtless read even before it was translated into English, Barbauld discusses literature as very much a cultural product, integrally connected to a social milieu that it helps to create.[20]

Barbauld's essay in *The British Novelists* describes fictional works as taking their distinct tone and features from the culture that spawns them. What is typical about German literature, for example, derives from the folk tales and traditions that modern German writers draw on for their stories, while French literature derives its unique tone from the expressiveness of the French language and the refinement of French culture. Conversely, popular literary works will also effect changes in the wider culture. She recounts, for example, that after the publication of M. d'Urfé's *Astrea*, a sentimental novel featuring a pastoral setting, young gallants began to carry shepherd's crooks and lead tame lambs about the streets of Paris. *John Buncle*, a novel featuring dramatic escapades in the wild landscape of the northern counties, "contributed to spread that taste for lake and mountain scenery which has since become so prevalent." Rousseau's linguistic practice worked its way into every day use, thereby influencing "the intercourse of common life." And, more grimly, publication of Schiller's *The Robbers* and Goethe's *Werther* were followed by a series of what we might today call "copycat" incidents. All of these examples make for little, however, when compared to how Laurence Sterne popularized the culture of sensibility. After Sterne and his followers, "for a while, from the pulpit to the playhouse, the reign of sentiment was established."[21] In her essay introducing the *Selections from the Spectator*, Barbauld only begins to broach a theory of reciprocal influence between literature and culture. Yet although still only partially developed, the tendency can be traced in discussions of how books themselves create a "relish" for reading, and declarations such as "Books influence manners; and manners, in return, influence the taste for books."[22] When Barbauld turns her attention to Addison's own contribution to English culture, however, her views come much more clearly into focus.

Introducing a selection from four popular early eighteenth-century periodicals, Barbauld's discussion of Addison's *Spectator* becomes almost a case study of the way a publication can alter the wider culture. She describes English society when the *Spectator* appeared as vicious and brutal, marked by aristocratic libertinism and deeply divided along lines of political alliance, gender, and class:

> Party spirit was high and bitter, the manners of the wits and fashionable young men were still tinctured with the licentiousness of the court of Charles II., mixed with the propensity to disorderly outrages and savage frolics incident to a people who were still amused by the Bear Garden, [she provides a footnote describing the Bear Garden as a crime-ridden place where the lowest and highest classes intermingled promiscuously for the sake of a variety of coarse and immoral entertainments] and who had not yet been taught to bend under the yoke of a strict police. The stage was in its meridian of genius and fashion, but disgraced by rant and grossness, which offended the sober and excluded the strict. Men lived much in clubs, and of course drinking was common. There was more separation than at present between the different classes of society; and each was more strongly marked with the peculiarities of his profession. There were learned and there were elegant women; but manners had not received a general polish, nor had women the advantage of a general cultivation.

No longer the means for delineating an abstract, polished poet's fit audience, elite erudition has become identified with its restriction to the few and a consequent coarseness in society as a whole. Meanwhile, Barbauld associates popular acculturation or "general cultivation," quite specifically with widespread intellectual improvement among women, a change that has proved consequential in refining society away from this vulgar and libertine state. It is worth noting that the court culture, licentiousness, class extremes, and chaotic intermixing of the socially unequal that mark this passage had by Barbauld's time taken on nationalistic, anti-French associations which would not have been lost on her essay's readers.

Barbauld recognizes the extent to which the *Spectator*'s forerunners relied on politics to carve out an audience along narrow partisan lines. Whether by humiliating political opponents or setting their own allies and views in a favorable light, writers and editors of overtly partisan periodicals expected to influence public opinion. The *Spectator*'s immediate predecessor, Richard Steele's *Tatler*, for example, took an adamant Whig stance. Yet, even with Tory readers alienated on political grounds, Addison and Steele, founders of the *Tatler*'s successor, "had experienced how popular this way of writing was capable of becoming." Thus, when the time came to launch the *Spectator*, "they determined to keep it free from personal satire and party politics."[23] Not that the paper was truly neutral: "It is not difficult [...] for a skilful reader to discern in the general turn of sentiment the political complexion of the writers." Yet in contrast to the caustic personal and political satires of contemporary writers like Alexander Pope and Jonathan Swift, Addison's irony "is so sheathed in urbanity, that it scarcely offends those whom it chastises."[24] Barbauld believes it was Addison's rejection of partisan hostility that made his influence so extensive. In her view, the turn away from aggressive politics constituted a conscious step toward broad-based marketing, and she documents this strategy's success in the *Spectator*'s reputed sales figures. But the paper's real success in her mind must be measured by its profound effect on the wider culture.

Barbauld regards the *Spectator* as pivotal in transforming both English society and English aesthetics. "Addison," she explains, "was one of a cluster of men of genius, who, flourishing at a time when the taste of the nation was forming itself, became in their different walks the standards of literary excellence." True, she recognizes in Addison's condescending pleasantries to women "a contempt for a sex [that he] probably considered in a very inferior light." In Barbauld's day it would probably take a woman critic, or at least a critic unusually sensitive to the nuances of complacent superiority that mark patriarchy's hold on institutionalized male privilege, to recognize this undercurrent of patronization in a publication so popular with women readers. Nevertheless, she feels that Addison changed the culture in ways that benefited women. By means of "humour, taste, and richness of imagination," English society was turned away from the vulgar sensuality of Restoration upper-class culture toward "virtue and good manners, [... d]ecency and sobriety of behaviour." In the *Spectator*, "marriage, the constant butt of the wits and jest of the stage, is treated with just respect, and its duties enforced." Moreover, especially through his fictional creation, Sir Andrew Freeport, a London merchant, "Addison has frequently taken occasion to set the trading part of the community, who were nearly all Whigs, in a respectable light, and to show the connection of commerce with science and liberal principles."[25] These values are those of Rational Dissenters, women, and the middle class, the very values that in Barbauld's day provided the foundation for a fair degree of social and political influence by women.[26] In extolling Addison's periodical papers for promoting middle-class values such as domesticity and respectability, Barbauld offers those same values her strong endorsement.

Barbauld's narrative of Addison's *Spectator* constitutes an assertion that through Addison's influence, English culture had fundamentally changed, that in fact the very nature of Englishness had changed. Once, as she describes it, licentious, coarse, and deeply divided into socio-economic extremes, English society had become, partly in consequence of Addison's contribution, genteel and cultivated, unified around common values of middle-class domesticity. Not that Barbauld was a self-deluded utopianist; her poem *Eighteen Hundred and Eleven* (1812), published only a few years later, would alone provide ample evidence that she was not blind to her nation's distresses. In the decade immediately preceding the publication of her essay on *The Spectator*, she had witnessed a devastating war, widespread government repression, and the failure of campaigns for reform that ran the gamut from Dissenter efforts to gain full rights of citizenship to improvements in labor conditions and abolition of the slave trade. Her own brother had fled religious persecution in Yarmouth, where he tried to establish a medical practice.[27] Literary work, Barbauld's own source of livelihood, had resulted in imprisonment on charges of sedition of several of her friends, complete annihilation of the personal and professional reputation of at least one acquaintance among women writers, Mary Wollstonecraft, and Barbauld herself denigrated along with Wollstonecraft and several other women writers in public venues such as Richard Polwhele's *Unsex'd Females* (1798). These are circumstances against which it is not surprising that Barbauld, shy, aging, probably in an uncertain financial position, and with a husband who was showing increasing signs of the mental illness that four years later would kill him, was not inclined to fight – at least not openly. But her description of the culture Addison helped to bring about sets these abuses in a new light. Outside the values that now define English culture, and in fact reminiscent of an earlier, more aristocratic yet more brutal time, such extremes of abuse would now be, quite simply, un-English.

During the late eighteenth century, large anthologies and collections of the sort that Barbauld edited and introduced became an important force in the efforts of booksellers, writers, editors, and other literary professionals to frame cultural institutions, literary heritage in particular, so as to define a British national identity, heritage, and character. Thomas F. Bonnell describes the place of poetry collections in a reciprocal process between the elaboration of "a notion of English literature" and the evolution of "a sense of national literary identity." According to Bonnell, "Publishing enterprises of this kind and magnitude had never before been undertaken in Britain. Now there were several; they put before the public a cultural heritage apparently vital to be known. Defined for the first time in uniform print were *the* poets, *the* works – in effect, canons of English poetry, worthy of honor, study, and preservation." [28] Similarly, both *The British Novelists* and *Selections from* […] *the* Spectator help to establish the canon of the novel and the periodical essay.

Bonnell locates invention of a canon not in the collection's editor, however, but in the bookseller. In the case of one of the earliest of these great collections, *The Works of the English Poets* (1779–81), marketed under the editor's name as 'Johnson's Poets,' that editor, Samuel Johnson, did not select the poets that would be included. Rather, the booksellers made these decisions on the basis of which poets they believed would sell. The same was probably largely true for the collections that Barbauld edited. In her "Advertisement" for an edition of Richardson's correspondence, Barbauld explains that Richard Phillips, the bookseller who had acquired the letters, asked her to make the selection.[29] Likewise, the number of women novelists represented in *The British Novelists*, especially when considered in tandem with the prominence Barbauld gives to women in the collection's introduction, suggests that she probably had some say in which authors would be represented. Yet in light of her emphasis in both the novel collection's introduction and in the preliminary essay to the *Selections from … the* Spectator collection on Laurence Sterne's contribution to eighteenth-century English culture, the absence of Sterne in *The British Novelists* seems to suggest the opposite – that though Barbauld cannot conceive of a discussion of eighteenth-century popular literature as complete without mention of Sterne, the booksellers, with whom the decision lay, decided for whatever reason to leave his work out. Instead, Barbauld seems to strain to find something positive to say despite her all-too-evident disgust at the narrow-minded prejudices, low jokes, and uninteresting hero of *Humphry Clinker*, which does find a place in the collection. The truth was probably that the selection most often rested with the bookseller. On occasions when the specific selections involved much work and were unlikely to affect profits, such as the selection of individual letters from a single author, he may have delegated the responsibility and labor. But the choice of authors would certainly affect the appeal of any multiple author collection, and issues of copyright ownership might limit what was affordable or even possible to include. In such cases, Barbauld may have carried her point at times, but the bulk of the choice remained with the bookseller. Like Johnson's, Barbauld's name lent authority to the bookseller's selection. Where Barbauld exerts independent influence is less in the content selection than in the critical introductions.

If the two volumes of periodical selections constitute a proposed canon of eighteenth-century periodical literature, then Barbauld sets Addison at the apex of this canon through the disproportionate attention she devotes to *The Spectator* compared to the other three periodicals and to Addison as compared his co-proprietor Steele. Barbauld places Addison in such a position of honor partly because of Addison's own contribution to literary canon making. His papers on literature receive Barbauld's greatest attention because of their importance to British culture, and because his most significant achievement in the arena of literary taste was to prepare the nation to accept the poetry of Milton, like Collins a difficult and obscure writer, but one who by Barbauld's time was considered, along with Shakespeare, one of the two quintessentially English poets.

According to Barbauld, it was Addison who brought to Milton's *Paradise Lost* the literary status it held by her time. Before Addison's papers, Milton's own character, particularly his political sentiments, restricted his poem's appeal, but more importantly, qualities of the poem itself, including several that now cause it to rank among the greatest in the language, made it foreign to the English reading public. In Barbauld's account, Addison's Milton commentary constitutes an act of literary patriotism that is as much a democratic as a nationalistic one. Barbauld identifies the "common reader who was not, as now, familiarised, through the medium of good translations, with Homer and Virgil" as the audience whom Milton's epic structure and blank verse would strike as strange.[30] Addison's service, then, was rendered not to that classically educated audience "who have studied the metaphysics of mind, and who are accustomed to investigate abstract ideas," and are therefore ready to receive poems like those of Akenside and Collins "with a lively pleasure." Instead, it was that other group of English readers, "those who seek mere amusement in a poem," on whose behalf Barbauld thanks Addison.[31] Though Addison, educated at Oxford, became a noted classical scholar, Barbauld downplays the contribution of a background denied to Dissenters, women, and the middle class. Qualified for the task as much by "exquisite natural taste" as by education, Addison brings *Paradise Lost* to the common reader by explaining "the laws and construction of epic poetry in general," after which little need be done but "illustrate the beauties of his author." Thus Addison, "by familiarising the reader with the style of Milton, made way for the more general reception of the entire poem." The result? "This admirable poem [...] is now the boast of every Englishman."[32] Addison receives credit for bringing *Paradise Lost* into the English literary canon, so that it has in his hands become the national treasure of every literate Englishman – and presumably, given its now democratic accessibility and the size of Addison's female audience, Englishwoman, too.

What Addison's accomplishment would have meant to not only to Barbauld but to the wider English reading audience should not be underestimated. James Chandler explores the Romantic-era controversy over the literary canon to conclude that at its core it consisted in the rejection of Augustan poetics, which emphasized formal aspects of poetry as exemplified by the poetry and aesthetic standards of Pope, who took classical poetry as his inspiration; indeed, "Homer stands as a synecdoche for this canon."[33] Outlined by Boileau, Augustan aesthetics had come by the end of the eighteenth century to be viewed as French, a liability in the increasingly anti-French atmosphere after the publication of Edmund Burke's *Reflections on the Revolution in France* (1790). Chandler draws on the work of Lawrence Lipking, to explain the repudiation of Augustan poetics as primarily political in purpose, satisfying

> a hunger for ... "a glorious national poetic pantheon" ...; that is, for a specifically national rather than a global canon of classics. Such a canon would in turn serve political purposes that Lipking sees motivating "the poets of mid-century, Thomson and Akenside and Collins and Gray and Mason and Smart," who all "wrote variations on the mythopolitical theme of Milton; sweet Liberty, the nymph who had freed English pens to outstrip the cloistered conservative rule-bound verses of less favored nations."[34]

Chandler sums up the aim of such a canon as "a definition of the superiority of the national character." British Romanticism, then, responding with increasing conservatism and nationalism to the critical developments in France, rejected Pope, who "was identified in this period with modern French rather than ancient classical ideas about poetry" in favor of a purely British poetic heritage, here originating with Milton.[35] One could say, then, that in crediting Addison with introducing Milton to the British public, Barbauld is in a sense proclaiming Addison to be the author of British Romanticism.

This vision of Addison may seem a bit unusual, to be sure, but let us follow for a moment where it leads. Chandler is explicit in assigning the impulse toward nationalism as the stimulus for the turn away from the Augustans. Quoting Lipking, he argues, "Augustan poets won their title by establishing commerce with the poetry of Greece and Rome and France, not by planting native roots, and a literary history that appealed to them could not afford to be parochial."[36] Or, in his own words, "a literary history that insists on discovering native roots for English poetry could not afford to appeal to, or perhaps even to accommodate, Pope and the Augustans."[37] Though Barbauld makes her own contributions to an expressly British literary heritage, she declines explicit rejection of the French in her aesthetics, a fact not surprising considering that many in her immediate circle were actively critical of manifestations of extreme nationalism. In fact, she draws on French editing practice to describe her own task as editor of the Augustan-era periodical papers:

> The French are very fond of extracting what they call *l'esprit d'un auteur*, which may be translated *the essence of a writer*. In this, which may be compared to the essential oils of plants, resides the genuine and distinguishing flavour of an author's wit; but it commonly bears a very small proportion to his bulk. Whole libraries might by this process be distilled down to a few pocket volumes; as a single phial of *attar* of roses contains the precious product of many acres.

What Barbauld rejects about Augustans like Swift, Pope, and even Steele is their caustic satire, their aggressively Tory politics, and their "supercilious harshness" towards women.[38] Addison promotes an aesthetic that became associated with national identity when he stands "true wit," the "metaphors, similitudes, allegories, enigmas," and so on that make up the standard tools of the poet, in opposition to "false wit," all the word games, poetic puzzles, and puns that, by the end of the eighteenth century, came to be identified with French literature.[39] Addison himself, however, associates them more with classical literature and aristocratic culture. *Spectator* 58 traces the various forms of false wit back to Homer and cites examples in English as well as French court culture. When Barbauld notes these papers as another of Addison's contributions, she makes the same associations herself.[40] In introducing Addison as a sort of white knight of British literary heritage, Barbauld turns away from literary elitism that has now become aligned with the misogynistic and libertarian values of the Restoration aristocracy and its Tory followers. Instead, she substitutes good tempered authors producing accessible prose, publishing in popular literary forms appealing to a middle-class audience, and promoting political broad-mindedness and domestic virtues. Such is now the shape that a truly British literature must take.

At about the same time that Barbauld was composing her essay depicting Addison as the transformer of English culture and promoter of one of the nation's great poets, she was also at work constructing another highly esteemed eighteenth-century author as an ideal of middle-class domesticity. The six volumes of the *Correspondence of Samuel Richardson* feature an introductory critical biography that constitutes Barbauld's most extended and theoretical piece of literary criticism. It also presents Richardson as promoting retirement, private virtue, and middle-class heterosexual sociability. Even the "Advertisement" declares that the selection of letters gratifies a not entirely justifiable "curiosity [...] to penetrate into the domestic retirements, and to be introduced to the companionable hours of eminent characters," suggesting it provides an almost improper peek into private middle-class life. The introductory essay offers Richardson as both a model and a champion of domestic virtues and his chosen literary form, the novel, as the ideal vehicle for the dissemination of these values.

Although the theoretical portion of "Life of Samuel Richardson" is comparatively brief, it merits attention. Barbauld begins the biography not with Richardson himself, but with a history of fiction, gradually narrowing her discussion to concentrate on the novel. As with her essay on periodical papers, Barbauld describes fiction as embedded in the wider culture, as taking "a tincture from the learning and politics of the times" and, conversely, lending its color to the culture by serving as the vehicle for education, politics, or social criticism.[41] We see how far she has shifted since her essays on Collins and Akenside when she defends prose fiction against the greater prestige afforded to poetry on grounds of aesthetics, creativity, and, most important, its value as entertainment. Barbauld's theory of fiction inclines toward realism, her account of its evolution describing its progress toward "a closer imitation of nature" or "stories imitating real life." Significantly, this "real life" refers to portrayals of the middle class. Passing through progressive stages where the romance characters, who "were all removed from common life, and taken from ancient history" are replaced by the often lower-class comic characters of Boccaccio to arrive in the works of Mme de Lafayette at the first approach to "a modern novel of the serious kind," Barbauld finds that "a step is still wanting; [...] the heroes and heroines are princes and princesses – they are not people of our acquaintance [...] they are not the men and women we see about us every day."[42] Not until that depiction of the emphatically middle-class *homo œconomicus*, Defoe's *Robinson Crusoe*, did a model appear for the minute, circumstantial realism of Richardson's novels.

Given that Barbauld views Richardson as, like Milton, one of England's great national treasures, her essay offers an interesting comparison to Addison's papers on *Paradise Lost*. Unlike Milton, whom Barbauld sees as alien until Addison rehabilitated him for the English popular reading public, Richardson was already extremely popular when Barbauld set out to represent him. Yet Barbauld does much the same work for Richardson that Addison had for Milton in explicitly theorizing her author's method so as to place his merits in a stronger light. She includes a section analyzing three possible methods for an author to tell a story, thus, according to Catherine E. Moore, inaugurating the modern study of narratology.[43] Barbauld describes – without our modern designations – the advantages and problems associated with third person omniscient narration, first person narration, and the technique that to her mind combines the best of both worlds, Richardson's own epistolary method. Barbauld's history and theory of the novel enables her to elucidate and justify epistolary narration much as Addison's explanation of "the laws and construction of epic poetry in general" paved the way for Milton's reception by a wider audience. It seems likely that Barbauld saw her work on Richardson as a canon making enterprise much like Addison's own.

After the general overview in which Barbauld construes the novel as a middle-class genre, she turns her attention to what makes up by far the largest part of this more than two hundred page essay, the critical biography of Richardson. Here again, though she broaches other concerns, discussing *Clarissa*, for example, in terms of imagery, characterization, and plot structure, she devotes most of her attention to a narrative that constructs Richardson as an emblematically middle-class hero and to a critique of his novels that centers on their success in elucidating middle-class concerns. In her hands, Richardson's is a story of middle-class virtue surmounting obscure circumstances to attain universal respect and contented domestic harmony, and she stresses the centrality of these qualities to English national identity. Barbauld emphasizes Richardson's humble childhood, the self-made aspects of his career, and his distance from aristocratic origins. She devotes over two pages, for example, to his *lack* of a classical education and his *ignorance* of the "learned" languages. Instead, he showed an unusual affinity for reading, "the cheapest of all amusements," and educated himself in moments snatched from his responsibilities as a printer's apprentice. His personal qualities included a "strong sense of religion," "sobriety of [...] conduct," "punctuality," "abstemiousness," "liberality, generosity, and charity." In habits, he was "sober and temperate, regular and assiduous in business, of high integrity, and undoubted honour," an example of "piety, order, decorum, and strict regularity." As a "careful, kind father, and a good husband, [...] he was enabled to make that comfortable provision for a rising family, which patient industry, judiciously directed, will, generally, in this country, enable a man to procure." Like Barbauld herself, Richardson often did commissioned writing for booksellers, and it was just such a project that led to the first of his great novels. His was a family enterprise in that his daughters, especially the oldest, "were all much employed in writing for him, and transcribing his letters." He preferred his country residence to town, and his novels treat issues of "piety" and "female virtue" so as to produce a sentimental effect on the reader. Even his faults, shyness, a preference for female company, and a tendency toward formal emphasis on family hierarchy, locate him firmly in the feminized and private domestic circle.[44] In short, as Barbauld paints him, Richardson deserves our esteem because he provides in both his life and his works a model of middle-class respectability as it was envisioned not so much in his own time as in Barbauld's.

As was the case when she wrote on Addison, Barbauld not only fashions Richardson as exemplifying genuine English virtue; she introduces his work as promoting the conduct and values that comprise authentic English identity as well. Richardson attains a noteworthy moment of literary success, for instance, when in his novel *Pamela* he portrays the heroine's parents as "true English low life, in its most respectable garb; made respectable by strict honesty, humility, patience of labour, and domestic affection; the whole rendered saintly and venerable by a touching air of piety and resignation." By contrast, she expresses her greatest objection to the depiction of Lovelace in *Clarissa*:

> A love of intrigue, rather than a love of pleasure, characterizes Lovelace; he is a cool systematic seducer, and the glory of conquest

is what he principally aims at. Had such a character been placed in France, and his gallantries directed to married women, it would have been more natural, and his epistolary memoirs rendered more probable; but, in England, Lovelace would have been run through the body, long before he had seen the face of Clarissa, or Colonel Morden.

Though she sees Lovelace as implausible only when his character is contemplated in conjunction with national identity, that consideration is all. In light of her views on Richardson's exemplary virtue and his contribution to English culture, it is hardly surprising that Barbauld is led to contend that it is downright unpatriotic to withhold from him the honor and affection that he deserves. On the exclusion of Richardson from upper-class circles, she declares:

> If the doors of the great were never opened to a genius whom every Englishman ought to have been proud of, if they were either tasteless of his merit, or so selfishly appreciated it as to be content to be entertained and instructed by his writing in their closet, and to suffer the man to want that notice and regard which is the proper and deserved reward of distinguished talent, – upon them let the disgrace rest, and not upon Richardson.[45]

True Englishmen like Richardson stand far above the debased aristocracy that would spurn them.

While her essays on Addison and Richardson represent groundbreaking efforts to theorize the nature of British literature and British authors, by far Barbauld's most substantial contribution to the formation of a British literary canon is her work on *The British Novelists*. This collection, the first of its kind, stands as a landmark in the history of the British novel. Although several large scale collections of British poets had by this time been published and Barbauld's own collection of selected periodical essays must count as a parallel sort of undertaking, no collection that professed to offer the complete texts of a definitive set of exclusively British novels had as yet made its way to the public. International anthologies and selections of abridgments had appeared, as had complete works of a number of British authors. Volumes including short excerpts, selected for some particular point of interest, such as their moral, comic, educational, or sentimental value were quite popular. Novels, usually abridged, were also included in some multi-genre miscellanies that claimed to survey the best of world literature. At least two compilations edited by women writers are worthy of mention here. About 30 years before Barbauld's project, Elizabeth Griffith had edited *A Collection of Novels*, a three-volume complete text international assortment of eight novels. Griffith's brief prefatory essay includes a suggestion that she, like Barbauld, sees the novel as relevant to the emergence of an English national character that was taking place in her day. After the radical swing from the "gloomy Puritanism" of Cromwell to the gay licentiousness of the Restoration, "Decency and good sense, the natural characteristics of the English" began to dominate literary taste, and the novel gained in quality, popularity, and stature as a result.[46] Charlotte Lennox offers a very different sort of collection in *Shakespear Illustrated*. This edition includes a variety of sources for Shakespeare's plays, including work from Boccaccio, Chaucer, Ariosto, and Holinshed, but rather than offering full text originals, Lennox condenses and summarizes most of her sources. She limits her critical remarks following each selection to a brief outline of how Shakespeare used the source in his plays. Barbauld's work, then, is unique in both scope and scale, offering for the first time a canon of British novelists as well as treating this most popular of literary forms as seriously meriting extensive and thoughtful criticism.

The introduction to *The British Novelists*, "On the Origin and Progress of Novel-Writing," is Barbauld's most interesting critical essay partly for the prominence Barbauld gives to women writers in the history and development of the genre. According to Moore, although Barbauld was "not notably interested in specifically feminist causes," she recognizes and welcomes "the dominance of women novelists."[47] Women writers figure prominently in Barbauld's history of fiction, and she usually marks important stages in the development of fiction with a balance of examples from male and female writers. Barbauld explicitly applauds the achievements of women novelists in the remarks that give the title to Moore's essay: "we have more good writers in this walk living at the present time, than at any period since that of Richardson and Fielding. A very great proportion of these are ladies: and surely it will not be said that either taste or morals have been losers by their taking the pen in hand."[48] Yet while praising women writers Barbauld accepts the widespread view that men and women write differently, raising a question concerning the influence of individual circumstances that engaged a number of authors in the early nineteenth century. "Why is it that women when they write are apt to give a melancholy tinge to their compositions?" Barbauld asks. "Is it that they suffer more, and have fewer resources against melancholy? Is it that men, mixing at large in society, have a brisker flow of ideas, and, seeing a greater variety of characters, introduce more of the business and pleasures of life into their productions?"[49] Both Byron and Jane Austen raise the same question in, respectively, *Don Juan* and *Persuasion* as the explanation for women's comparative lack of resilience in the face of disappointments in love. Here Barbauld blames the comparative isolation and enforced idleness that women experience in consequence of their role in the culture for a similar inelasticity coloring their writing. Still, the prestige Barbauld gives to women writers in her history of the novel is reinforced by the number of women novelists whose work is featured in the collection. Only a few more male than female novelists are included, leading Moore to regard this essay as "perhaps the first extended criticism of the woman novelist."[50] As such, the essay and the collection it introduces also constitute the first substantial effort both to bring women writers into the canon of British literature and to establish a canon of British women novelists.[51]

Meanwhile, if social circumstances of individuals affect what and how they write, literature in its turn shapes society. Originating in traditional folk culture and evolving continuously in a process of translation, repetition, and transformation into new stories, fiction is collaboratively produced, all the while exerting a powerful influence on society and culture. Barbauld's phrasing at one point echoes that in her introduction to *Selections from [...] the Spectator*. There she asserted, "Books influence manners; and manners, in return, influence the taste for books."[52] Here in her introduction to *The British Novelists*, she affirms that "Fictional adventures, in one form or other, have made a part of the polite literature of every age and nation [...]; they have been interwoven with their mythology; they have been moulded upon the manners of the age, – and, in return, have influenced the manners of the succeeding generation by the sentiments they have infused and the sensibilities they have excited." Though Barbauld makes an emphatic case for entertainment as sufficient justification for fiction, she says a great deal more in defense of its value. She explicitly credits modern works of sensibility, for example, with refining public conduct: "much of the softness of our present manners, much of that tincture of humanity so conspicuous amidst all our vices, is owing to the bias given by our dramatic writings and fictitious stories."[53] Moreover, by means of their novels, British authors, especially British women authors, cultivate the domestic virtues that constitute the essence of Britishness. Those virtues then protect the British reader from the sorts of pernicious effect long argued as a danger of novel reading. Much praise can be showered on the novels of Fanny Burney and Maria Edgeworth, for example, because they promote the "severe and homely virtues of prudence and œconomy" and encourage "order, neatness, industry, sobriety." These two writers' novels and others like them will help to uproot the faults "which undermine family happiness, and destroy the every-day comforts of common life." Similarly, the "English public" is disposed to reject the more voluptuous novels from France in a show of virtue that "does honour to the national character." Despite the power of literature to shape the surrounding culture, these discreditable novels have left the British reading public largely untainted because "Our national taste and habits are still turned towards domestic life and matrimonial happiness."[54] Her views on popular literary forms have come quite a distance since 1794, when she dismissed those forms as low entertainment. Popular literature now creates national character and can inoculate the British public from foreign literature's pernicious effects.

These popular works are not always wholesome in their effect, however, and at times may even be quite insidious. In language that echoes the deep suspicion that in *A Vindication of the Rights of Woman* Mary Wollstonecraft expresses with regard to the "magic pen" that allows Rousseau to subvert the critical capacities of his reader, Barbauld describes the "seductive" effect of his "glowing pencil," through which "a charm is spread over every part of the work, which scarcely leaves the judgement free to condemn what in it is dangerous or reprehensible."[55] The phrase 'dangerous *or* reprehensible' seems to take us further than a simple Johnsonian view that novels can unduly influence the young and foolish. Indeed, all along Barbauld has argued that literature affects the whole culture, not just a uniquely susceptible constituency. Here, however, Barbauld takes her understanding of the relationship of literature to culture a step further than she had in 1804, declaring that works of fiction "take a tincture from the learning and politics of the times, and are made use of successfully to attack or recommend the prevailing systems of the day." Fundamentally social, novels shape not just the private individual tastes and values, but the most public aspects of society as well, even the intellectual discourses of the power elite – art, literature, philosophy, aesthetics, science, law, and, so important in the two decades that had just passed, politics. As Barbauld puts it, "It was said by Fletcher of Saltoun, 'Let me make the ballads of a nation, and I care not who makes the laws.' Might it not be said with as much propriety, Let me make the novels of a country, and let who will make the systems?" Barbauld says of French writers like Marmontel (presumably not one of the voluptuous French novelists mentioned above), "Writings like these cooperated powerfully with the graver labours of the encyclopedists in diffusing sentiments of toleration, a spirit of free inquiry, and a desire for equal laws and good government over Europe. Happy, if the mighty impulse had permitted them to stop within the bounds of justice and moderation!" In view of the French contribution to the encyclopedic movement – Diderot comes immediately to mind – Barbauld here unmistakably credits French literature with the libertarian impulses that spilled over in the French Revolution, including the excesses of violence that had by this time turned even most of its early British sympathizers against it. Is it any wonder, then, that she likens novels, "numerous 'as leaves in Vallombrosa,'" to Milton's rebel angels?[56]

Yet although Barbauld looks upon novels as potentially so sensational and so public in their effects, her interest in entertainment as their ultimate purpose leads her to describe their influence as more usually in the realm of the private, the domestic. Toward the end of "On the Origin and Progress of Novel-Writing" she includes a section that, though relatively short, leads directly to her concluding comments, and so seems of special importance. Barbauld evinces a much tolerance for transgressions on the part of novels. Indeed, in her own words, "the unpardonable sin in a novel is dullness: however grave or wise it may be, if its author possesses no powers of amusing, he has no business to write novels." This capacity of amusing, of entertaining, makes the novel the most democratic of literary genres, both appealing to middle-class domesticity and elevating its status. Entertainment, the "legitimate end and object" of novels, makes reading "a very high pleasure," and "Reading is the cheapest of pleasures: it is a domestic pleasure." As with the *Spectator* papers, novel reading, though it depends on literacy, requires no advanced intellectual preparation, and so is available to those who lacked access to a university education – women, religious Dissenters, and the literate middle class. "Poetry," Barbauld explains,

> requires in the reader a certain elevation of mind and a practiced ear. It is seldom relished unless a taste be formed for it pretty early. But the humble novel is always ready to enliven the gloom of solitude, to soothe the languor of debility and disease, to win the attention from pain or vexatious occurrences, to take man from himself, (at many seasons the worst company he can be in,) and,

while the moving picture of life passes before him, to make him forget the subject of his own complaints.[57]

Her defense of this "humble," fundamentally popular literary genre brings her to express admiration for its democratic nature and compassion for the distresses of the dispossessed, disenfranchised, and debilitated that popular literature can at least momentarily allay. Barbauld's critical values have come far since a decade and a half before, when she disparaged "those who seek mere amusement in a poem" in favor of the educated elite "who have studied the metaphysics of mind, and who are accustomed to investigate abstract ideas" that make the ideal audience for Akenside's *Pleasures of Imagination*.[58]

When Barbauld identifies those who find amusement and solace in novels with those outside the early nineteenth-century British power structures, she brings us back to a representation of British citizenry, indeed of genuine Britishness itself, as domestic and middle class. When novels go beyond pure entertainment to bring about a change in the individual, it is most often to strengthen qualities and virtues that constitute the essence of middle-class Englishness. What transformed the bear-baiting, libertine, misogynist society that comprises Barbauld's vision of Restoration London to seemly domesticity and egalitarianism is British popular literature, the same sort of literature she once dismissed. In reading Barbauld's essay criticism, we have seen her abandon the exclusionary stance of the introductions to Akenside's and Collins's poetry in order to redefine British literary history in inclusive, democratic terms. William McCarthy and Elizabeth Kraft have characterized Barbauld as an "organic intellectual" in the sense articulated by Antonio Gramsci – that is, "an intellectual who articulates the issues of her own social class at a time when that class is asserting its claims to power and respect." They argue that both her poetry and her experience as an educator served as outlets for her ambition "to intervene in the making of her nation's political and ethical culture."[59] Barbauld's critical essays show that she saw them, too, as venues for influencing the direction British national culture would take.

Barbauld probably came to introduce the poetry volumes partly because Cadell and Davies believed her name might help sales, and partly because she qualified, educationally at least, as a member of the ideal audience for Collins and Akenside as she described that audience in her own essay. Though barred from the universities on the grounds of both religion and gender, Barbauld was one of the most learned women of her day. Truly, as poems such as "A Summer Evening's Meditation" amply testify, she was one of the rare women who ranked among "Those who have studied the metaphysics of mind, and who are accustomed to investigate abstract ideas." Her background, including a family that boasted several publishing critics, prepared her in the "forms scientific and established" that defined the literary criticism of the intellectual elite. It was not the barrier of an insufficient education that prompted the alteration in Barbauld's perspective. Gerald Newman has argued that the exclusionary attitudes of the English upper class toward the predominantly middle-class artists and intellectuals of England, coupled with an almost fanatical patronization of anything French, formed the chief stimulus to the rise of an English nationalism that was as anti-aristocratic as it was anti-French. Despite her conviction of the political and moral danger of some French literature, Barbauld's own anti-elite formulation, although it contains nationalistic elements, is not so purely anti-French as the thinking that Newman describes – witness, for example, the praise she extends to French women novelists such as La Fayette, Genlis, and Staël. If anything, her history of the novel, while it trumpets English national character, is overall more cosmopolitan than parochial. Though, as Newman argues, British aristocratic culture was during the years in question often identified with France and its influences, such a straightforward formulation falls short of describing the perspective that Barbauld reveals in her essay criticism. Instead, Barbauld manages her narratives of literary history to present the eighteenth century as a period during which true literary cosmopolitanism came to reject upper-class culture and the exclusion on which it was based in favor of defining authentic Britishness in terms of the inclusive, supportive, convivial, but private and domestic culture of the emerging middle class. The robust integrity of Britishness so defined makes both her compatriots and British literature itself immune to any pernicious influence from foreign literature, assimilating only that which promotes egalitarianism and domestic virtue.

2
Renouncing the Forms: The Case of Elizabeth Inchbald

Much like Barbauld, Elizabeth Inchbald began writing literary criticism only after achieving professional success in other fields. Born 1753 in Stanningfield, near Bury St. Edmunds in Suffolk, to a family of middle-class Catholics, Elizabeth Simpson was an unusually intelligent young girl, showing an early appetite for both reading and the stage. She had tried unsuccessfully to join Richard Griffith's Norwich theater company, and meeting no encouragement there, at age 18 she ran away to London with the goal of becoming an actor. Two months later she married Joseph Inchbald, a much older established actor who had courted her before she had left home. Shortly after the wedding, Joseph Inchbald engaged with a Bristol theater company in the role of King Lear. Elizabeth Inchbald's stage debut in the role of Cordelia took place toward the end of this production following weeks of determined effort to master the delivery of her lines despite a severe stammer that she was never able fully to overcome. First in the provinces and Scotland and then, after her husband's early death, in London, Inchbald achieved some success in her chosen profession, performing with the celebrated John Kemble and Sarah Siddons, among others.

In London, Inchbald became acquainted with the members of the avant-garde artistic and intellectual circle that revolved around the London shop of bookseller Joseph Johnson, forming friendships with women writers such as Mary Robinson, Amelia Alderson Opie, and, more distantly, Mary Wollstonecraft, while her relations with noted radicals William Godwin and Thomas Holcroft teetered between simple friendship and flirtation. Still pursuing acting, Inchbald began to write for the theater, eventually producing some 20 plays, some original and others translations or adaptations, but most either comedies or farces. *Lovers' Vows*, an adaptation of German playwright

August von Kotzebue's *Das Kind der Liebe*, is best remembered today as the play that threw the Bertram family into chaos in Jane Austen's *Mansfield Park* (1814). Inchbald's novels, *A Simple Story* and *Nature and Art* were also well received.[1] Between her acting and her writing achievements, Inchbald had made for herself a name that would spark recognition from both the reading and the play-going public. As an experienced and successful writer with behind-the-scenes insight and firsthand memory of recent great theatrical productions, she was an excellent choice to pen the introductions when bookseller Thomas Longman and his associates decided to issue a series of recently produced popular plays.[2]

Inchbald's essays appeared in the first large collection of drama that incorporated literary criticism by a woman and the first instance of ongoing criticism signed by a woman writer. She was subject to a malicious public attack for stepping outside the bounds of accepted feminine discourse by entering the masculine territory of literary criticism. Nevertheless, her prefaces show that Inchbald regarded herself as a professional writer, with claims to this province as much as any other, though she found that, weighed against writing and adapting farces, it was an unlucrative and disagreeable occupation.[3] Uncomfortable with the burdensome citation of predecessors that signified critical rigor to demanding intellectual circles, she instead drew on her own experience to contrive a formula for popular success. Her perspective on French and British drama as reflections of national character diverge from those of Barbauld, revealing some cracks in the effort to construct a seamless edifice of a British national literary heritage in which a collection entitled *The British Theatre* figured as a part. Her criticism shows acute understanding of the stage, including observations on what makes drama best for reading rather than staging, comments which, taken together, constitute a coherent theory of closet drama. And, although she praises originality and invention as elements that make for a play's success, her account of drama as collaboratively created runs directly against the grain of those contemporary and modern explanations of Romantic-era literary production that emphasize the genius of an isolated individual author.

The British Theatre was first published one play at a time, beginning in 1806, with the complete collection first issued some two years later.[4] Unlike Barbauld's *British Novelists*, the series was not the first of its kind, though it differed from its predecessors in interesting ways. For at least a century, sizable collections of English dramatic works had occasionally appeared.[5] Still, this collection was more substantial than most, consisting on completion of 125 plays divided between 25 volumes. Moreover, each play was prefaced with a short essay by Inchbald, making the project the first large collection of drama in which literary criticism by a woman played a significant part, and, because of the initial periodical publication, the first instance of ongoing, signed literary criticism by a woman writer. In fact, according to Marvin Carlson, Inchbald "was not only the first British woman to present a series of critical prefaces for a wide range of dramatists, current and classic, but she was in fact the first British critic to do so."[6] The booksellers chose the plays from the recent repertory of London theaters, the selection ranging accordingly from Shakespeare up through the newest work by contemporary playwrights. The text, derived from prompt copies, was often a heavily bowdlerized version, especially in the case of Restoration comedies.[7] Moreover, despite the imposing title, an overview of Inchbald's introductions suggests that the plays were chosen more in consequence of the box office success that they had recently enjoyed than on any judgment of enduring merit. Frequently the selection not only fails the test of time; it leaves Inchbald hard put to find redemptive qualities as well. An amusing example occurs regarding the four plays by Colley Cibber, the hero of Pope's *Dunciad*, which find their way into the collection. Inchbald allows that Cibber's plays "must infallibly create animadversion," but offers for Cibber a rather surprising defense. Rather than claim for him a status he fails to live up to, she instead hints that Pope acted in an ungentlemanly manner when assailing Cibber on a vulnerable point – Cibber wrote so much that he must inevitably produce some works that are dull.[8] Meanwhile, the collection offers only two of the lesser works of Sheridan, whose *School for Scandal* Inchbald regards as "the best dramatic composition since Shakspeare [sic] wrote."[9] *School for Scandal* finds no place in the collection at all. Literary merit seems at best, then, only one – and perhaps not the most important one – among the considerations determining which plays would appear.

If marketability drove the selection of plays for the series, it also determined the decision to solicit Inchbald's contribution. Popular as an actress, dramatist, and novelist, Inchbald was as yet untried as a critic. Still, her achievements had made her, as Paula Backscheider notes, "one of the best-known citizens of London in the 1790's."[10] Fame was not enough, however, to protect her from demands that proved onerous and unrewarding, while exposing her to public censure. As early as March 1806 Inchbald regretted her commitment to this time-consuming project that "added but little to her fortune, and nothing whatever to her fame."[11] She wrote to Longman asking to be released, but Longman would not permit it. Though by the end of the project Inchbald had been told that "her edition of Acting Plays had met with prodigious success," she still had doubts over her abilities as a critic and in fact declined an invitation to contribute to *The Quarterly Review* in consequence.[12] Yet a novel review with the *Quarterly* and a two to four page introduction to a successful play are two quite different things, and Inchbald may have felt equipped to do one but not the other. Whether misgivings over the vulnerable position she had placed herself in already played a part in her request for release is not clear; what is certain, however, is that in consequence of her work on the project she eventually found herself the brunt of some pointedly hostile remarks.

Probably the most discussed portion of Inchbald's theater criticism consists of an exchange of open letters between Inchbald and playwright George Colman the younger. The two letters, one from Colman, and a reply from Inchbald, demonstrate what was at stake for the woman literary critic in Britain during the late eighteenth and early nineteenth centuries. Recall that the plays appeared first with their introductory essays in periodical installments, and that some active contemporary writers had several works represented. Eight of Colman's plays are featured in the series, and when they began to come out, Colman responded to the prefaces with an open letter to Inchbald that he requested be affixed to the next of his plays to be issued. His letter appeared in the bound volume set, along with Inchbald's reply. Dissatisfied overall with Longman's periodical publication of plays that he expected to see issued in more prestigious and dignified bound volumes, Colman expresses particular resentment about Inchbald's criticism of them. Relying superficially on the language and conventions of chivalry, his letter drips with sarcasm, the point of which he turns toward Inchbald purely on the basis of sex. He refers to his plays that had been issued up to that point as

> those dramas of mine which have, already, had the ordeal to be somewhat singed, in passing the fiery ordeal of feminine fingers: – fingers, which it grieves me to see destined to a rough task, from which your manly contemporaries in the drama would naturally shrink. Achilles, when he went into petticoats, must have made an awkward figure among the females; – but the delicate Deidamia never wielded a battle-axe, to slay and maim the gentlemen.

Colman accuses Inchbald of being all wrong in her assessments, of failing to point out what should be criticized while objecting to portions that were above complaint. Had Inchbald applied to him, he would have steered her criticism aright: "I should have been as zealous to save you the trouble," he sneers "as a beau to pick up your fan. – I could have, easily, pointed to *twenty* of my blots, in the *right* places, which have escaped you, in the labour of discovering *one*, in the wrong." Though by this time quite well read, Inchbald had only the formal education standard for a middle-class girl and was vulnerable on this count. In a backhanded insult on the quality of women's education, Colman throws in a bit of Latin, then follows with "I make no apology for writing Latin to you, madam; for as a scholiast, you, doubtless, understand it." As if such gender slurs were not enough, he brings her sex to the fore every few sentences throughout the letter. "But, madam, I tire you," he continues, and shortly after, "Fy on these bitters, madam [...] I should have been gratified, madam, [...] Pray, madam, [...] Pray, madam," and again and again, "Pray, madam, [...]."[13] Male critics who have punctured an author's vanity might be accused of puffery, cronyism, or personal animosity, but it appears that a woman critic's worst offense is her sex.

Following Paul M. Zall, most recent Inchbald scholars view Colman's vindictive letter as ending Inchbald's career as a literary critic. Zall explains that Inchbald was deeply hurt, and that it is because her "sensibility never recovered" that she refused to engage in further criticism after *The British Theatre* was complete. Zall points to records preserved in Boaden of Inchbald's own assessments of her emotional states, which, Zall avers, range through various registers of relative contentment, shifting abruptly to "very unhappy" after Colman's letter, and to her refusal, after *The British Theatre* series, to write any further prefaces. This account has had a substantial influence on perceptions of Inchbald, particularly in her role as a literary critic. Catherine B. Burroughs, for example, relies on Zall, accepting his assessment of the letter's damaging effect. Katharine M. Rogers discusses the same exchange, remarking on the "insufferably patronizing" tone of Colman's letter and accurately observing that "[t]he absurd disproportion between Colman's indignation and the mildness of [Inchbald's] criticism shows that he was outraged simply by her presuming to judge her male colleagues." Rogers misses the mark, however, in describing Inchbald's response as opening on a "distressingly defensive note." Anna Lott takes up the issue where Rogers left it, arguing that Inchbald's response should be regarded not as defensive, but rather as "powerfully duplicitous." "By taking a self-consciously deferential stance," Lott continues, "claiming that a woman's words should not be offensive – should not, in fact, even be taken seriously – Inchbald effectively diffuses and deflects Colman's criticism and any further criticism before it can occur." Lott reminds us that Inchbald's "very real critical power" is demonstrated by the collection's popularity and the continuation of Inchbald's contributions after the exchange took place.[14]

Inchbald did indeed sigh to one friend that the "odium" she encountered as a result of her prefaces constituted the "one sorrow that weighs heavy upon me," but the complaint marks the one dark note in a letter full of "the serenity I have been boasting."[15] In fact, as Lott begins to suggest, whatever her feelings might have been when she read Colman's diatribe, Inchbald was not the sort of person to knuckle under so easily. Throughout her biography of Inchbald, Annibel Jenkins emphasizes Inchbald's independence and resilience. Even Boaden who, as Jenkins rightly points out, is never fully able to understand such a woman, describes Inchbald throughout his *Memoirs* as a woman of independent spirit, capable of an unusual degree of resolution. He notes her insistence on remaining single after her husband's early death, her refusal to conform to many social niceties such as those regarding dress and visiting, her attendance at a masquerade dressed as a male theatrical character, her determination to overcome her severe stammer in order to become an actor. Zall himself tells us, "Whenever her mother indulged her with playgoing in nearby Bury, she would write out the parts before hand and mouth them with the actors, marking those words that made her stammer, then practicing them at home." Inchbald had already been accused of sedition in the *True Briton* for her play *Such Things Are* (1787), and that had not made her leave off writing and adapting plays. Moreover, Inchbald displayed an unusual degree of courage during the repressive mid-1790s. She incorporated a satire of George III into *Nature and Art* (1796), despite, in her words, "[h]aving Newgate before my eyes." And though she asked Holcroft to stop visiting her as his notoriety increased, when he was imprisoned in consequence of the treason trials of 1794, she visited him publicly at Newgate.[16] Though Inchbald apparently found Colman's attack quite disturbing, it is hard to believe that a person like her would have been so intimidated by one person's criticism, however vituperative, of her failure to remain within feminine bounds that she would have on that basis alone changed the trajectory of her career.

On the contrary, Inchbald does not submit to Colman's hostile ridicule lying down, and in the war of wit and words, she has by far the superior weapons. Inchbald does reply frankly to several of Colman's accusations, but these portions of her response sound more matter-of-fact than defensive. One such instance is her ingenuous answer to his charge that she has, in criticizing his father's plays, shown ingratitude for the early support that as a theater owner George Colman the elder gave to her acting career. Inchbald declares quite simply that Colman made the allegation only to give her pain, and give her pain he indeed did.[17] In acknowledging her vulnerability, she seems to trust that emotional honesty can help counter Colman's spiteful invocation of gender stereotypes. Varying her own register between these candid moments and others of ironic humor, this long-time actress inhabits the role that Colman so sarcastically foisted upon her and in what must be described as a performance of femininity, she plays it to the hilt. Mirroring Colman's own sarcasm, but with a far gentler touch, Inchbald too places absurd emphasis on her own femininity in a mocking self-deprecation that turns Colman's attack back on himself. She expresses surprise, for example, that anyone could have taken offense at the remarks of a female critic. She had believed, she claims, that "no one dramatist could possibly be offended, by the cursory remarks of a female observer." Colman need not have concerned himself with a woman critic because "any injudicious critique of such a female might involve her own reputation, (as far as a woman's reputation depends on being a critic,) but could not depreciate the worth of the writings upon which she gave her brief intelligence, and random comments." Her sally very neatly plays upon the available connotations of "reputation" to cast in doubt any connection between gender and sexuality on one hand and literary judgment on the other.

As her reply progresses, the irony, though never rancorous, becomes even more pointed. "Humility, and not vanity," she declares, "I know to be the cause of that sensation which my slight animadversions have excited: but this is cherishing a degree of self-contempt, which I may be pardoned for never having supposed, that any one of my 'manly contemporaries in the drama' could have indulged." Yet when not ironic, she refuses to be put on the defensive. She asks for indulgence, not on the basis of her sex, the more usual ground for such pleas in her day, but one that would help to legitimize Colman's gender-based attack. Rather, she demands to be considered a professional writer when she suggests that the forbearance that Colman demands from critics for authors is even more particularly due to her, a periodical critic writing under pressure of constant deadlines. If her excessively underscored feminine modesty could have been misinterpreted up to this point, Inchbald dispels any lingering questions with her final lines which take up Colman's use of Latin: "I willingly subscribe myself an unlettered woman; and as willingly yield to you, all those scholastic honours, which you have so excellently described in the following play." The "following play" is *The Heir at Law*, a comedy featuring the character Pangloss, whom Inchbald describes as "a satire upon pedantry."[18]

Inchbald's facetious acquiescence in Colman's attack on her capacities as a female critic coupled with her equal willingness to show real vulnerability in the more sincere moments of her reply together sound less like a woman of sensibility devastated and ready to retire from the field than a professional, confident of her overall standing even if a particular performance fails to measure up. The fact is, Inchbald apparently declined to write more criticism not because she was devastated by Colman's letter, but simply because she became canny enough to trade on her celebrity standing without so much effort. Though Zall claims that the turn from happy to "very unhappy" took place suddenly, he himself documents Inchbald's more gradual mood shift dating as far back as 1798 in response to increasingly apparent signs of age and ill health. Further, Inchbald never enjoyed working on the *British Theatre* project and had, as long as two years before, sought release from her contract. Her refusal to write further prefaces seems to have had more to do with the recognition on both her part and that of the booksellers that her name did more than her criticism to boost sales. According to Isaac D'Israeli, despite robust sales,

> [Inchbald] did not please herself, nor the World, by the Criticisms prefixed to her collection of Plays – yet such is the magic of her *Name* in the title-page that the Booksellers Wishing to have what they call a Minor Theatre, (of farces &c) again applied to her. She declined, sick of writing more Criticisms. They made her then a specific offer. To get rid of the business, she in return doubled the demand – & strange to say, they instantly agreed to her price, & I believe not to have any Criticism prefixed, only to insert her Name on the title-page.[19]

Subsequent collections did in fact appear without critical introductory essays. In a letter where she has just complained of a few months dearth of opportunities to earn money with her pen, Inchbald describes her own role in the first of the two sequel projects as follows:

> In my profession I am sometimes idle for months or years; but, when I resolve on writing, I earn my money with speed. No resolu-

tion of the kind has however come to me of late; and yet, the week before last, I earned fifty guineas in five minutes, by merely looking over a catalogue of fifty farces, drawing my pen across one or two, and writing the names of others in their place: and now all those in that catalogue are to be printed with 'Selected by Mrs. Inchbald' on the title-page. The prodigious sale my Prefaces have had, has tempted the booksellers to this offer.[20]

Inchbald views herself as a professional writer, even using the word 'profession' to refer to her writing, and, much as her bookseller does, she views her literary work with a commercial eye. Both D'Israeli's and Inchbald's remarks emphasize not the artistic or intellectual contribution, but the earning potential of professional writing. Her amused irony does not conceal her willingness to exploit the commercial value of her name. Though her prefaces "did not please [...] the World," they did enjoy "prodigious sale." "The World" has ultimately proven to consist not of those who perhaps felt her work lacked adequate rigor, but of willing literary consumers, well pleased with the often desultory remarks of the commodified celebrity.

By the time of her exchange with Colman, Inchbald knew it was these consumers who were her audience. She tells Colman and her reading public that her introductions were written "for the perusal, or information, of such persons as have not access to any diffuse compositions, either in biography or criticism, but who are yet very liberal contributors to the treasury of a theatre" – for, in other words, a popular rather than an elite or highly educated audience. Still, though she eventually earned the approval of both her booksellers and the public, she seems at first to have lacked confidence in her ability as a critic: "Even for so humble a task I did not conceive myself competent," she continues, "till I submitted my own opinion to that of the proprietors of the plays in question." It is not easy to decide whether this passage, coming at the end of a paragraph that begins with a sincere tone, indicates a turn toward irony or instead reveals a genuine trepidation over becoming a critic, at least at the start of the project. Coupled with the disadvantageous terms on which she agreed to participate, however, a look at certain of her essays for *The British Theatre* suggests that the latter is quite likely the case.

Many of the essays in *The British Theatre* are devoted to plays by Shakespeare, placing Inchbald, already rather exposed as a woman critic whose name was attached to a selection that she did not make, in the unenviable position of kicking off a project that committed her to years of such unusual public exposure with discussions of the one English dramatist above all others who had received the most and the best of attention from expert literary critics. Inchbald's essays seem to show a very understandable anxiety, especially in the frequency with which she cites her predecessors. Her opening sentence to the preface for Shakespeare's *Comedy of Errors*, for example, remarks not on her own views about the play in question, but on what is "supposed, by some commentators." The next paragraph supports the assertions of these anonymous "commentators" with citation of George Steevens, a respected Shakespeare critic during the second half of the eighteenth century who had co-edited with Samuel Johnson the 1773 edition of Johnson's *The Plays of William Shakespeare*. Inchbald continues in this vein through much of her Shakespeare commentary, offering her own opinion only when it can be buttressed with the views of already established Shakespeare critics such as Steevens and Johnson. Marvin Carlson also comments on Inchbald's initial reliance on established opinion. "Despite the considerable body of eighteenth-century dramatic and theatrical criticism," Carlson explains,

> there was in fact no clear model for Inchbald to follow. On the one hand there were the scattered commentaries on particular actors and productions [... as represented most often by periodical reviews], and on the other hand there was the tradition of critical prefaces to plays, the prefaces of Samuel Johnson to the plays of Shakespeare being the most familiar example.[21]

But citation of previous authorities had become an accepted critical practice by this time, especially when discussing Shakespeare. A variorum tradition had already taken shape during the eighteenth century, of which Johnson's *The Plays of William Shakespeare*, in which Johnson intended to gather "the best of all previous editions," represents a landmark.[22] In relying so heavily on citation, Inchbald was following accepted procedure, trying through this means to find for her criticism the "scientific and established" formula that would garner respect.

Yet Inchbald was able to find her own critical ground, as even this same essay demonstrates. After demurring to Steevens, whose rejection of *Comedy of Errors* as "no work of Shakspeare's" is supported only with "it is an opinion which (as Benedick says) fire cannot melt out of me;" Inchbald precedes her own comments with "As it is thus partly decided that the work is not wholly Shakspeare's, full liberty may be taken to find fault with it." Backed by this authority, she then censures the play on grounds of probability, a topic that will continue to concern her in other essays as well. She questions, for example, the credibility of a plot where

> one brother comes purposely to Ephesus, in search of his twin brother, his own perfect resemblance, and yet, when every accident he encounters tells him directly, that his brother being resident in that very place is the cause of them all, this is an inference he never once draws but rather chuses to believe the people of the town are all mad, than that the person whom he hoped to find there is actually one of its inhabitants.[23]

The amusing phrasing and minimal analysis lend this and similar sections a light, entertaining quality more appealing than learned citations and ponderous scholarship. In the previous chapter, I argued that Barbauld shifted from addressing a British reading public comprised of the learned elite to a more inclusive and middle-class audience who sought entertainment from their reading. Inchbald's comment on *Comedy of Errors* might not impress a highly educated, scholarly reader, the type of reader, for example, whom Johnson addressed with his own edition of Shakespeare, the reader who opened the volume in order to learn something about the play or, more likely, to have his own status as highly educated elite reaffirmed by the form and texture of what he read. But they would appeal to an audience who read for entertainment during their hours of relaxation – an audience like the middle class one to which Inchbald herself belonged, whose appetite for the theater was keen if not strictly discerning. Jon Klancher describes the efforts by Romantic-era British writers, especially periodical writers, to create an audience through their texts. In a process partly resembling Althusserian interpellation, the writer's diction, syntax, metaphors, and concerns all help shape and affirm a taste for his or her texts and so call into being the appropriate reading audience. Klancher affirms that the effect is nothing less than "the historical forming of taste," and argues that these efforts to define a reading audience coincided with and even produced the emergence of social classes in the modern sense.[24] Was Inchbald conscious of a critical strategy that turned away from the market for the kind of "learned" criticism that she felt unqualified to write? Did she understand that a light, entertaining critical voice would call up an audience among a middle class that wanted recreation rather than erudition? Whatever the answer to those questions, the success of the series confirms that Longman had astute judgment in insisting that his only moderately well-educated middle-class critic continue with her work.[25] The audience for printed copies of recent playhouse successes introduced with short, entertaining essays by a leading theatrical personage materialized almost instantly.

Furthermore, the transition through the rather conventional issue of probability led Inchbald directly to the topic that lent her critical voice its greatest originality and authority – the staging and performance of each play. The "representation" of *The Comedy of Errors*, she avers,

> gives an additional improbability; yet it is necessary that the audience should not see with the supposed eyes of the persons of the drama, for, unless the audience could distinguish one brother from another, which their companions on the stage pretend not to do, the audience themselves would be dupes to the similarity of appearance, instead of laughing at the dupes engaged in the scene.[26]

Though still confined to the well-trodden ground of probability, this remark takes a step in a new direction, one in which Inchbald's extensive experience with writing for and performing on the stage gives her an edge over the more purely literary critics whom she had previously cited. In consequence, she opens a more interesting issue than what her predecessors seem to have offered her – the discrepancy between the point of view of the characters within the play and that of the theater audience when both witness the same events. Inchbald does not pursue these remarks down any of the obvious paths. She does not, for example, follow up with the observation that it is in precisely this discrepancy that much of the play's humor lies, or that the erecting of such an edifice of humor on so precarious a foundation might constitute evidence *for* the play's authenticity rather than *against* it as Steevens argued. Still, she has broken the ground that enabled her to leave behind the stiff, academic sounding tone and the formal citation of experts that arose from her insecurity in the role of a woman Shakespeare critic. She substitutes instead a more natural voice and commentary based on her own observations, interests, and experience. The pressures to keep up with the periodical publication schedule may have had something to with this change. Researching and citing secondary sources is a time consuming business even when, as was the case here, only one or two secondary sources are consulted. Inchbald may not have had the energy to keep up with the same level of documentation that she began with. Then too, the playwrights other than Shakespeare were neither so exhaustively treated in prior criticism nor so devoutly revered. Inchbald could feel freer to comment on difficulties and faults as she saw them without recourse to prior authority. Whatever combination of these or other factors should be credited for it, most of Inchbald's tone and content inhabits a more informal and relaxed register, yielding a criticism far more appropriate to the popular audience for whom, as she will later tell Colman, she was writing.

As Inchbald finds her stride as a critic, she begins to develop a standard format for her criticism. Normally she includes a biographical sketch of the play's author, often freely borrowed from the *Biographia Dramatica*, one of the many contributions to the eighteenth-century efforts to encyclopedically collect and catalog aspects of British culture.[27] These brief sketches usually run less than a page in length and often consist in little more than a notation of the author's place and date of birth with two or three facts or anecdotes about the life. Where several of the author's plays are included, the multiple essays attached to them give Inchbald an opportunity to be more expansive, and she might scatter anecdotes over more than one essay or devote an entire essay to biography. Such treatment indicates that although the essays appeared with their plays individually first, Inchbald was always conscious that they would eventually form a whole, all appearing together. If the play treats of a historical topic, she usually comments on the recorded events that make up the plot. She then ordinarily concentrates on the play's stage history and its audience reception, describing strengths, weaknesses, or special problems in production, and marking especially strong or popular individual acting performances. All the while, she elaborates her views on the differences between plays most suitable for reading and those best seen on the stage, a problem that seems of particular interest to her. She occasionally brings in the social and political milieu of the play's first appearance as well, commenting on how these circumstances shape the play's reception. Though she allows no special leniency to women playwrights, Inchbald notes how the particulars of female existence sometimes bear on issues of authorship. Meanwhile, citations of other critics become extremely rare. The result is an unstructured format, a casual, sometimes almost chatty style, and an emphasis on the play in its social and cultural surroundings – written by persons with complex lives, staged in a theater staffed by particular actors, confronted by specific production problems and competing for attention among other current plays or stagings of the same play, and seen or read by a real audience with interests, prejudices, and political views.

In the realm of politics and social reform, Inchbald is alert to the power of drama to affect public opinion and well aware that a similar understanding lies behind both the popular reception of a drama and censorship of the theaters. Such is the case with Thomas Southern's *Oroonoko*, for example, a stage adaptation of a story most familiar to modern readers through Aphra Behn's work of the same name. Inchbald informs us that Southern's play is "never acted in Liverpool, for the very reason why it ought to be acted there oftener than at any other place – the merchants of that great city acquire their riches by the slave trade." Similarly, the criticism of corruption in government incorporated into Charles Macklin's *Man of the World* has affected its staging history. Though popular in Dublin where it first appeared, the play remained unstaged in London until "the elevation of Mr. Pitt to the high office of prime minister" sparked public hope for reform of that office. Still, the play provoked such controversy on its first night in London that "plaudits and counterplaudits lengthened the time of performance nearly to midnight before the ayes and the noes became all of one mind." This consensus was effected by an epilogue that invoked a sentimental reverence of one's forebears, at which point "all parties united, and the venerable author was hailed with shouts of triumph." In both of these discussions, Inchbald sidesteps the issue of who, precisely, is responsible for the blocking or suppression of political plays, the prejudices and interests of the audience, or official pressure. The absence of *Julius Caesar* from the list of currently staged plays, though, provides Inchbald with an occasion for a more general reflection on the inter-relationship between politics and popular culture, while at the same time moving toward a more definite suggestion of official pressure:

> When men's thoughts are deeply engaged on public events, historical occurrences, of a similar kind, are only held proper for the contemplation of such minds as know how to distinguish, and to appreciate, the good and the evil with which they abound. Such discriminating judges do not compose the whole audience of a playhouse; therefore, when the circumstances of certain periods make certain incidents of history most interesting, those are the very seasons to interdict their exhibition.

Till the time of the world's repose, then, the lovers of the drama will, probably, be compelled to accept of real conspiracies, assassinations, and the slaughter of war, in lieu of such spectacles, ably counterfeited.

In discriminating between a mass and an elite audience, Inchbald makes a point that has proven key to understanding Romantic-era government censorship of the press – that popular audiences were considered more volatile than elite ones.[28] The bite of Inchbald's irony turned to political commentary as above gives an indication of why, during a volatile period like the 1790s, Inchbald had, as she intimated to Godwin, to resort to camouflage in order to remain on the windy side of the law.

Because *The British Theatre* was preceded by several similar collections, Longman's series represents only one milestone among many in the solidification of a British dramatic canon. Still, the name alone indicates that Longman saw the series as entering the market for national literature. Yet Inchbald's essays offer a rather ambiguous affirmation of the British dramatic heritage, often undermining any ambition of this sort. She tries to balance her essays between praising the strengths and noting the faults of each work, but her lack of enthusiasm for some plays causes her to sound hard pressed to find redemptive features. Then too, on the issues that commonly defined British nationalism in her day, her opinion seems divided. True, Shakespeare, "the pride of Britain," "England's most illustrious bard," offers a source of complacency over Britain's cultural legacy, but this view was common enough by Inchbald's time and cannot by itself be regarded as proposing a sustained vision of the glory of true British art.[29] It is certainly in the nature of Inchbald's short commentaries that no sustained, coherent views on any topic can be expounded. Yet Inchbald offers more conflicted testimony than seems inherent in the diffuse format. At times she seems to embrace sentiments of British pride and solidarity, along with the anti-French prejudices that help constitute them. *The Surrender of Calais* by George Colman the younger depicts British virtues in a way that "can do honour to the British." Nearly half of the essay that precedes Shakespeare's *Henry V* is devoted to various versions of the tale of hopelessly outnumbered British forces and their heroic victory at Agincourt. And in *Fontainbleau*, John O'Keefe creates a character who "is, perhaps, an exact Frenchman of the time in which he was drawn; and, as such, the most agreeable object for an Englishman's ridicule." Yet at other points, Inchbald expresses skepticism of uncritical national arrogance and self-satisfaction. Biting sarcasm marks the narration of what she regards as opportunistic changes in political and religious loyalties on the part of John Dryden, a poet laureate. Or, in milder though still quite dry irony, she tells us that through the characters in *The School for Reform*, Thomas Morton (25)

> like a true Englishman, [...] praises the virtues of his own country. It would be somewhat more polite, though not, perhaps, equally just, to carry our eulogisms to neighboring nations; but, the vice of vanity is always tolerated, when national prejudice, or national spirit, is its foundation. Good manners, which, in other cases, oblige every one to praise that, in which they have no concern, and to pass by in silence their own merits, is violated perpetually by the dramatic patriot; whilst he is sure to gain unbounded applause for being a puffer of virtues, that should require no such aid to charm an admiring world.
>
> The author tells us truly, that, 'we have in England, palaces for poverty, and princely endowments for calamity' – The English are charitable, but they are too apt to boast of their benevolent endowments: a higher boast would be, to have fewer paupers who require them.

Seeming at first to accept British self-praise because it is "just," by the end of the passage it has become clear that she is critical of nationalistic self-conceit.[30]

Inchbald takes her critique of the British nearly to the point of lampoon in her essay on *The Distressed Mother*, a translation of Racine's *Andromaque*. Philips earns Inchbald's congratulations for having successfully negotiated the difficulties presented by the essential difference between French and British theater-goers. Inchbald observes that

> The gloomy mind of a British auditor demands a bolder and more varied species of theatrical amusement, than the lively spirits of his neighbours in France. The former has no attention, no curiosity, till roused by some powerful fable, intricate occurrences, and all the interest which variety creates – whilst the latter will quietly sit, absorbed in their own glowing fancy, to hear speeches after speeches, of long narration, nor wish to see anything performed, so they are but told, that something has been done.[31]

The passage does, of course, depict the French as a bit too passive, a commonplace about French national character that had for many years served the British as an explanation of why the French were inclined to submit to absolute monarchy. They are, however, sophisticated, and they bring an alert intelligence with them to the playhouse. The British audience, on the other hand, is not merely unsophisticated, but obtuse and phlegmatic, unable, as she observed some while before, to "appreciate the merit of Shakespeare's plays, so as to be greatly moved, where neither love nor murder is the subject of the scene."[32] In his Shakespeare commentary, Johnson had attributed to the English stage a distressing barbarity arising from a similar cause. The British audience had evolved since Shakespeare's time, as the contents of *The British Theatre*, selected from plays currently being produced, indicates. The more extreme productions of the Elizabethan stage are left out – *Titus Andronicus*, *The Duchess of Malfi*, and *The Spanish Tragedy* come immediately to mind. Still, these London playgoers, it seems, require a jig or a tale of bawdry, or they sleep.

Why would two women critics working at nearly the same time on such similar projects express through those projects such different views on the national literature and character? One might suggest that, as an actress, Inchbald was more closely allied to the fashionable "ton," the upper circles of fashionable society, that according to Newman inspired the nationalistic movement because of their rejection of British art and culture in preference for anything French. Barbauld had cultivated primarily middle-class connections, and because she resided mostly outside London, her social circle was comparatively quiet and intimate. But Inchbald early determined that if she were to retain her independence, she would need to live entirely within her income, and so she too held herself back on the periphery of the more fashionable circles, enjoying some of their diversions at times but explicitly rejecting their excessive demands. A more likely explanation might reside in their different religions. Both women belong to religious communities that had long suffered legal discrimination and a deprivation of the full rights of citizenship – Barbauld was a Unitarian, and Inchbald a Catholic. Barbauld's community, however, had suffered less severe forms of oppression than had Inchbald's. Not only did Protestant Dissenters retain more civil rights, but they had recently seen a nearly successful reform effort that would have granted them equal citizenship. Inchbald, on the other hand, had witnessed the limited amelioration of the Catholic Relief Act of 1778 precipitate the 1780 Gordon Riots. Indeed, Linda Colley argues that it is anti-Catholicism, fueled by an overall drive toward the consolidation of a Protestant British national identity, that was the force behind the anti-French sentiments.

While pro-French comments crop up here and there in Inchbald's criticism, explicit reference to religion is relatively rare. Yet her narrative of the founding moment of Anglicanism and her mention of two seventeenth-century Catholic monarchs seem to provide exceptions. The events in *King Henry VIII*, committed by "hardened perpetrators," could hardly reflect a Protestant perspective. King Henry, whose character "underwent almost a total change" from a youth marked by "personal beauty and grace," who, like his cohort Cardinal Wolsey, had been gay and sociable, a devotee of the arts, "casts from his bed and throne his loving and obedient wife, because his conscience dreads the anger of his Maker." Meanwhile, the Cardinal "devotes himself to pomp, amasses unbounded wealth, and exacts from his neighbours every honour short of adoration." It could not be surprising if the misguided followers of a religion arising from such a grotesque past undervalue the nation's greatest dramatist. In the commentary for *Twelfth Night*, Charles I seems quite literally to have lost his head for Shakespeare as much as for any other reason. According to Inchbald, his admiration of the English national bard "was a crime with the Puritans."[33] But James II went one step further, living out the plot of *King Lear*. Countering the "most learned on the subject" who doubt a historical basis for the Lear story, Inchbald avers that

> If it never did before the time of Shakspeare, certainly something very like it has taken place since. Lear is not represented much more affectionate to his daughters by Shakspeare, than James the Second is by Hume. James's daughters were, besides, under more than ordinary obligations to their king and father, for the tenderness he had evinced towards their mother, in raising her from a humble station to the elevation of his own; and thus preserving these two princesses from the probable disgrace of illegitimate birth.
>
> Even to such persons as hold it was right to drive King James from the throne, it must be a subject of lamentation, that his beloved children were the chief instruments of those concerned. When the king was informed that his eldest daughter, Mary, was landed, and proceeding to the metropolis, in order to dethrone him, he called, as the historian relates, for the princess Anne – and called for her by the tender description of his 'dear, his only remaining daughter.' On the information given to his majesty in

return, that 'she had forsook the palace to join her sister,' the king wept and tore his hair.

Lear, exposed on a bleak heath, suffered not more than James, at one of our sea-ports, trying to escape to France. King Lear was only pelted by a storm, King James by his merciless subjects.[34]

Inchbald brings the two English kings who were deposed precisely for their Catholicism into intimate connection with the writer, above all others, who at the time Inchbald wrote was the most insistently invoked as proof of the superiority of British literary genius. Through this maneuver, Inchbald manages to lace her Shakespeare commentary with a strong critique of anti-Catholic discrimination with no need to resort to mentioning it by name.

While Inchbald's critique of British anti-Catholicism are part of her views on national character, those views also prove central to another of her recurrent concerns – the qualities that divide plays suitable for the stage from those more appropriate for reading. Describing the difference between French and English theater audiences, Inchbald avers that a French audience's keen verbal attentiveness results in French drama that typically is verbal and narrative rather than active and based on a variety of incidents, not only lending itself to a representation of greater dignity of character but possessing a more literary quality as well. French plays therefore will often "gain more favour with a reader than a spectator." That is, French drama more often falls into the category of closet drama. Inchbald brings her own stage experience to the fore in distinguishing between dramas that are most effective when staged and closet dramas. Although the fragmented nature of criticism that appears as a series of separate prefaces obscures the coherence of her theory of closet drama, these prefaces can be culled for the principles of that theory.

Inchbald sees little overlap between those works best appreciated in the theater and those more appropriate to the closet. She defines closet drama primarily on the basis of "literariness," the complexity and poetry of its language and the proportion of such 'literary' language to stageable incident – not a revolutionary theory, to be sure, but one that has retained its serviceability nearly to the present day.[35] The delicate poetry in plays like *As You Like It* and *Winter's Tale*, for example, lends itself better to contemplative reading than to energetic vocalization. Even sheer length of characters' speeches could sometimes tax an audience's attention, making the play more suitable for reading, as was true for *The Clandestine Marriage*. On the other hand, conditions in the theaters meant that some more subtle plays were best enjoyed in solitude. In these days before electric lighting made naturalistic method acting possible,

> Authors may think too profoundly, as well as too superficially – and if a dramatic author, with the most accurate knowledge of the heart of man, probe it too far, the smaller, more curious, and new-created passions, which he may find there, will be too delicate for the observation of those who hear and see in a mixed, and, sometimes, riotous, company.[36]

As Catherine M. Burroughs has noted, "at certain points in her prefatory remarks, Inchbald implies that closet space uniquely provides for the viewing of minute details that add to an appreciation of the psychological richness of certain characters."[37] In doing so, Inchbald begins to move beyond a simplistic characterization of closet drama toward a theory that is more nuanced, emphasizing the effect of the work on its audience.

Furthermore, as she describes the closet drama's opposite, the play that is best suited to the stage rather than the closet, her ideas take on additional complexity. Inchbald recognizes the importance of what talented actors can bring to a performance, and where the play depends heavily on the contribution of its actors, it is suited to the stage and will be found wanting when simply read. In general, comedies, so dependent on timing and on visual support, are almost always better staged than read, and rarely is a play well suited to both: "To be both seen and read at the present day," she declares "is a degree of honour which, perhaps, not one comic dramatist can wholly boast, except Shakspeare." Plus, in cases where the script will not stand up to rigorous scrutiny, the stage can mask what would otherwise come in for censure. Disapproving overall of dialect and colloquialisms, for example, she remarks of *John Bull*, "This comedy would read much better, but not act half so well, if it were all written in good English." Similarly, Lee's *Rival Queens* is better staged than read because of its extravagant rhetoric. "Actors," explains Inchbald, "eminent in their art, know how to temper those failings in a tragic author: they give rapidity to their utterance in the mock sublime, and lengthen their cadence upon every poetic beauty." Plays with deeply flawed or morally reprehensible characters can also pass more easily on stage. A case in point is James Shirley's *The Gamester*, where actors can make an audience pity the characters, while a reader will judge them harshly.[38]

Such comprehensive attention to the contributions of actors stretches Inchbald's drama theory beyond the closet/stage dichotomy into the issue of collaborative composition. Inchbald has much to say about collaboration on many levels. She considers recognized authorial teams such as Beaumont and Fletcher, and George Colman the elder and David Garrick. Yet boundaries between formal co-authoring and the casual and ephemeral fruit of any one production are vague and shifting. Actors and stage managers not infrequently make alterations to the script that become a part of it, lasting perhaps not forever, but through at least a few subsequent productions, often cropping up again in printed versions. One such instance is the epilogue that actor and playwright David Garrick appended to Edward Moore's *The Foundling*, included as a part of the text that Inchbald introduced. The numerous bowdlerizations that appear in the collection provide similar examples. But purely spontaneous contributions emerge as well from any individual production. Not only does a stageworthy play permit of augmentation from the actors; it can depend on such additions as much as or more than on the script itself. *The Mourning Bride*'s "being placed upon the list of acting plays at present, is wholly to be ascribed to the magnificent representation of Zara by Mrs. Siddons." Or again, the actors Garrick and Mossop "contributed to the success of [John Brown's *Barbarossa*] by their skill in acting, as much as the Author did himself by his art of writing." Such a claim should not be interpreted as deprecating the talents of the playwright, however. In *The West Indian*, Richard Cumberland demonstrates superior theatrical judgment inasmuch as "Many of the characters require the actor's art, to fill up the bold design, where the author's pen has not failed, but wisely left the perilous touches of a finishing hand to the judicious comedian."

In making no effort to establish an "original" or "authentic" text, but rather featuring texts derived from prompt copies, *The British Theatre* memorialized many of these ephemeral collaborations for the whole of the nineteenth century and beyond. Individual performances then, or at least significant ones, become a part of a play's textual history, and merit critical attention equal to that given the original text itself. And by this means, even the audience can at least occasionally draw notice. During one performance of *Othello*, Inchbald relates, Booth played the lead with "such uncommon fire and force, that players and audience were electrified." When asked what inspired such a performance, the celebrated actor explained "I saw, by accident, an Oxford man in the pit, whose judgement I revere more than that of a whole audience." What is more, not only do actors construct the text through performance, but the text can, in essence, construct the actors. The role of Polly Peachum in John Gay's *Beggar's Opera* "is endowed with such superior charms, [...] that when she was first represented, every actress who performed the part made her fortune by marriage." In fact, Inchbald claims that the actor who played the first Polly was so fascinating in the part that her consequent marriage elevated her to the rank of duchess.[39]

The biographical notes that Inchbald includes in some individual prefaces reinforce the view of dramatic works as collaborative, with performance a part of the compositional process. Most of the prefaces include a short sketch of the author. Where that author has a history as an actor, as was true of Shakespeare and Charles Macklin among others, Inchbald usually remarks on the contribution of that experience to the writing, a topic on which, as an actor/playwright herself, she would have special expertise. On a few occasions, though, she drops the biography of the author completely, substituting the biography of an actor who gave a landmark performance, the author of a source text from which the play was adapted, or even, in the case of some historical plays, a biography of a significant character. The preface to *The Country Girl*, for example, features no details from the life of author and actor David Garrick, but does include short biographies of Wycherley, author of the source work, and Mrs. Jordan, who played in the first production. Such treatment places actors and adapters on a par with original authors, offering a contribution that if not fully equal to that of the author, is significant nonetheless. According to Burroughs, "Inchbald demonstrates her interest in the bifurcated character of dramatic literature – hovering between text and performance – by frequently citing the performance history of a particular play and providing information about the playwright's life relevant to a play's composition." Moreover, Paula Backscheider observes about Inchbald's own works for the stage: "The method of having the play read by the actors, submitting an acting copy to the examiner, and printing an edition several days after the production opened allowed a kind of collaboration between playwright, manager, and players unknown on the modern stage." Inchbald's own plays reveal her receptiveness to such collaboration in their "attention to the skills of various actors and room for interpretation and enhancement in most of the parts."[40] Though both these views are correct, they come short of describing the full compass of Inchbald's comprehensive account of the genesis of dramatic literature. Her criticism reveals an understanding of the potential for collaboration among source author, actor, playwright, and even audience that suggests that she regards theatrical texts as possessing far less integrity than today's scholarship normally attributes to a literary work.

In *Multiple Authorship and the Myth of Solitary Genius*, Jack Stillinger argues that much of twentieth-century Romanticism studies' mistaken emphasis on the single author as the solitary creator of a literary work is based on precisely what his title implies – a myth. According to Stillinger,

> The biographical study of authors that, in England, got seriously under way in the late eighteenth century (Johnson's *Lives of the English Poets* [1779–81] is the most prominent landmark) quickly became the principle method of writing about literature during the Romantic period, when the personalities of the poets and the essayists were thought to be central in their works and there was widespread discussion of such topics as inspiration, originality, creativity, and genius.

As a result, today "The romantic notion of single authorship is so widespread as to be nearly universal." Where evidence for multiple authorship exists, twentieth-century textual critics most often "call it corruption and try to get rid of it." Stillinger argues that an understanding of multiple authorship, where the contributions of friends, spouses, ghost writers, agents, editors, translators, publishers, censors, transcribers, and printers is taken into account can contribute to a richer understanding of literary works by revealing "the social, cultural, and material conditions in which they were produced."[41] Shakespeare criticism, which, during the eighteenth century, had come to emphasize such issues as authenticity and the original genius of this exemplary British author, would supply a paradigm for the type of account that Stillinger rejects. In contrast, Inchbald generally praises originality of invention, yet substitutes actors, theater managers, and audiences for some of the other potential collaborators on Stillinger's list, thus driving a wedge between the quintessential Romantic constructs of "originality" and "individual genius." She replaces them with a concrete and material account of the genesis of drama, an account consistent with that which Stillinger calls for, and one dramatically divergent from that of Shakespeare critics Samuel Johnson and George Steevens, whom Inchbald had so faithfully cited.

Inchbald continues to push the envelope of textual integrity when she takes up the issues of borrowing, adaptation, translation, imitation, and even plagiarism, in most cases with approval or at least acceptance. The word "plagiarism" comes up only once in Inchbald's prefaces. Defending the originality of one of Colley Cibber's characters, she uses it to describe the repetitions of that character by subsequent authors. Originality is, not surprisingly, a virtue, but plagiarism carries for Inchbald the broad definition that corresponds to our ideas of imitation. Conversely, she describes a portion of Sheridan's *Duenna*, taken from Wycherley, as "not purloined, and the mark taken out, to prevent detection; but fairly borrowed, and used almost to the very letter."[42] This phrase requires a second reading to be properly understood today. If "used almost to the very letter" is a practice of Sheridan, whom Inchbald reveres, that can be contrasted with "the mark taken out, to prevent detection," apparently an unacceptable practice, then "the mark" seems to refer not to the author's name or other formal crediting, but to the exact details that make a part of a play clearly recognizable as the idea of another. In other words, incorporating the ideas of another word for word even without explicit acknowledgment seems at least as acceptable as adapting those ideas while adding one's own original twists – perhaps more so. And although "originality" is to be preferred, reshaping the texts of others, if done well, places a writer on a level with the original author. As a case in point, Inchbald commends the work that Colley Cibber did on John Vanbrugh's *Provoked Husband*, declaring that, contrary to previously held opinion, as Cibber found the manuscript after Vanbrugh died, it contained none of the strengths that made the play successful. Cibber's work on it earns him co-author status on the *British Theatre* published edition.

Inchbald's own work on adaptations provides an additional window onto the forms of casual collaboration that typify composition of theatrical texts in her day. Though many of her plays were original compositions, several consisted in adaptations. The preface to *Lovers' Vows* recounts how Thomas Harris, the manager of Covent Garden, presented her with an unstageable translation of Kotzebue's German play and commissioned her to refashion it into something suited to production. For the completed adaptation, Inchbald enlisted help from another unnamed writer who contributed the prologue and the verse lines of one character. Much like other adaptations included in *The British Theatre*, the printed title page for *Lovers' Vows* features Kotzebue, the original author, on the title page, but it is Inchbald who holds the position of author. Still, Inchbald assures us that "the exertions of every performer engaged in the play deservedly claim a share in its success; and I most sincerely thank them for the high importance of their aid."⁴³ Whether Kotzebue gave permission for Inchbald to alter the text in this case is not clear, but for English audiences, the alterations were pivotal to the play's success. Anne Plumptre had produced a more literal translation directly capitalizing on the success of *Lovers' Vows*, but though it sold well, it could not compete with Inchbald's version for success. Apparently Kotzebue had no objections to either the alterations or the attributions. He brought Harris the script of another play that Inchbald adapted as *The Wise Man of the East*.⁴⁴

By their very nature, Inchbald's short prefaces to *The British Theatre* forestall the possibility of sustained articulation of radically new notions of theatrical arts. Yet as the first woman to have occupied such a visible and influential position in drama criticism, Inchbald's achievement is groundbreaking. Inchbald saw herself as a professional writer, and although she found criticism so unrewarding that she declined any further opportunities to practice it, she took her responsibilities as a critic seriously. Initially emulating the "forms scientific and established" of a structured format and citation of prior authorities, she soon comes into her own. Selected for her marketability rather than her skill, forced to continue a contract she regretted, and attacked on the basis of gender, Inchbald relies on a finely tuned irony to defend her place as a critic. What is more, she comes to know her audience, and it is that that makes for her popular success. As she finds her critical voice and develops her own concerns and flexible format, she creates a body of criticism that relies on her extensive stage experience to elucidate two key concerns. Her views on British drama's role in revealing English national character allow more room for non-Protestant perspectives, or at least more respect for the character of the French than is usual for British writers during this period. And she elaborates ideas on the genesis, production, and reception of drama that turn away from the myth of a solitary author to an account that emphasizes collaborative composition and a mutable literary text.

Part II
"Fearful ascendency": Women Periodical Literary Reviewers

Part One explored essays in which women critics presented literary works as part of the nation's cultural heritage. Among other concerns, the two chapters examined these writers' views on the interplay between literature and the wider culture, with special emphasis on the role of the discourse of sensibility in shaping critical standards and conceptions of British national identity. In the process, they revealed these critics' understanding, even endorsement, of the power and influence of popular literary forms such as drama, the familiar essay, and the novel. This section examines British women's criticism of the most contemporary publications, looking at how a specific subculture facilitated women's commentary on literature. Examining anonymous periodical literary reviewing by women writers clarifies how it was possible, for the first time in the history of British letters, that women were able to break into a profession that until then had been the preserve of men. In their positions as reviewers, these women gained a remarkable degree of influence.

Literary reviews appeared as an innovative form during the second half of the eighteenth century, a time when Britain saw a rapid increase in both literacy and the volume of new publications. Periodicals commenting on literature had for some time enjoyed great popularity and influence, but with an expanding reading public eager for guidance on the mushrooming numbers of new books, the time was ripe for publications devoted exclusively to making sense of all the new publications. Educated professionals expected to keep up with advances in all branches of science and the arts, while the rising middle classes wished to attain the sort of general familiarity with literature that was quickly becoming a necessary mark of status. First conceived in the mid-eighteenth century, literary reviews came to dominate the practice of literary criticism by the beginning of the nineteenth century, determining the shape of Romantic-era popular literary taste. They enjoyed wide readerships, and they transformed this new and diverse audience into consumers of the public conversation about literature and culture. The commentary they supplied educated large numbers of readers whose formal training in literary values was often modest at best. Not only private book purchasers, but reading rooms and circulating libraries in England and throughout Europe and the colonies depended on reviews in publications such as the *Monthly Review* and the *Critical Review* to determine what new books to order. In James Basker's assessment, literary journalism

> introduced new, more accessible forums for critical discussion; it multiplied and diversified the opportunities for critical expression; it fostered new critical values, drew attention to new literary genres, systematized the treatment of established ones, and expanded the audience for criticism. [... I]n subtler ways it affected canon formation, reception history, the emergence of affective criticism, the assimilation of foreign influences, the segregation of 'women's literature', and ultimately the politics of culture.[1]

These are vast claims, but it seems that some were not only conscious of their truth but concerned about the consequences. By 1811 a distressed Josiah Conder complained of literary reviewers that "The fearful ascendency they have gained in the literary world, their extensive and powerful effects on individual character and public opinion, and their consequent importance as a moral and political engine, must awaken the jealous attention of the statesman as well as the philosopher."[2] Accessible to many who had little access to formal education, reviews had taken over from schools and academies much of the role of educating not only the nation's literary taste, but its opinions on the full range of public issues.

The new reviews had other profound effects on culture as well. By offering writers plentiful opportunities for paid work and provided a venue where they could hone their critical and creative skills, they helped drive the shift during late eighteenth and early nineteenth centuries from an amateur literary culture grounded in patronage to a professional one in which the relationship between writers and their booksellers and editors emphasized negotiable but clear terms of payment. Marilyn Butler has argued that we might define the essence of Romanticism not so much in its poetry, as has been usual up until now, but rather in the emergence of the "modern journalist," exemplified in the "man of letters" who "made it his object to carry weight, to wield a kind of moral authority." Under such conditions the woman reviewer, whose work has been largely ignored, takes on importance. Like her male counterparts, women reviewers took seriously their role as, in Butler's words, "critic, watchdog and self-appointed spokes[person]," arbiter in the often contentious arena of literary taste.[3] Their work offers opportunities to reassess periodical literary journalism, a form of writing burdened with unexamined overgeneralizations about reviewer aptitude, dedication, and impartiality – about, in other words, reviewer professionalism – that has fared poorly in twentieth-century literary scholarship. Literary periodicals including reviews were at the center of some of the most momentous changes in the history of literary culture, changes in which women played an inadequately recognized part.

Part II examines periodical literary criticism by Mary Wollstonecraft, Mary Hays, Anna Letitia Barbauld, Elizabeth Moody, and Harriet Martineau. Contributing to three Dissenter-operated literary reviews, the *Analytical Review*, the *Monthly Review*, and the *Monthly Repository*, these women all depended on the culture of English middle-class Rational Dissent for support and encouragement, for the foundations of their critical views, and for their business contacts. Their aesthetic judgment shows engagement in the values of sympathy, benevolent affection, and a morality based in sensibility, values that were widespread in Romantic-era British culture, but that held special meaning for the Dissenting community. Moreover, these women's reviews provide an index to the evolution from a Romantic-era notion of morality inspired by sensibility as the essential quality of the British subject to the emphasis on secular reform that dominates the tone of periodical journalism during the early Victorian age.

The careers of these women reviewers extend from the first professional woman reviewer to the period that saw the woman journalist become an increasingly common phenomenon. Such a transformation in periodical literary culture must be one of the most remarkable events of the Romantic era. The following chapters will uncover structures and ideas that made such an unprecedented change possible. At the same time, they will reassess reviewing as an occupation that placed a few women writers at the vanguard of determining British literary taste.

3
"The first of a new genus –": Mary Wollstonecraft, Mary Hays, and *The Analytical Review*

On 7 November 1787 Mary Wollstonecraft, the 28-year-old former proprietor of an only temporarily successful girls' school and author of a treatise on education, who had recently been discharged from her position as governess with the family of an Irish peer, wrote to her sister Everina: "Mr Johnson [...] assures me that if I exert my talents in writing, I may support myself in a comfortable way. I am then going to be the first of a new genus – I tremble at the attempt."[1] When she wrote this, Wollstonecraft was well aware she was not the first woman to try to support herself through writing. Only recently arrived in London, she had not yet made the acquaintance of the numerous women writers who were to be a part of her circle in the coming years. Still, she had read sufficient educational literature, conduct books, novels, and poetry by women to realize that some women were earning income by writing. In publications by women writers prefaces apologizing on the grounds of financial need for the transgressive immodesty of going public had become common enough to seem almost a cliché. In fact, Wollstonecraft had herself recently turned author to ease financial embarrassments that resulted when she tried to set to rights a family headed by her profligate and inept father. What she recognized as unique about her new relationship with bookseller Joseph Johnson was the nature of the business arrangement. Wollstonecraft differed from previous literary women in that her connection with Johnson was not simply that of an author to the bookseller who purchased her finished manuscripts for publication. That had been their connection before her letter, and it was the usual one for the women writers who were rapidly increasing in number. Rather, Wollstonecraft had engaged with Johnson as a staff writer who would accept the work assigned to her and in return could count on a steady supply of literary work coming her way.

During the decade after her letter, Wollstonecraft's work for Johnson came to include not only her well-known political works, *A Vindication of the Rights of Men* (1790) and *A Vindication of the Rights of Woman* (1792), but editing, translation, authoring stories for children, and voluminous contributions to the soon-to-be-launched literary periodical, the *Analytical Review*. Men had long held similar positions, especially with publishers of the literary magazines that were multiplying rapidly in the second half of the eighteenth century. But Wollstonecraft appears to be the first woman who was relied on in this way, and her work for Johnson commands attention for several reasons. This work was central to her intellectual growth; everything she read and wrote contributed to her fund of knowledge and her cognitive training, laying the groundwork for the books for which she is best remembered. But while literary culture was shifting from amateur practices of patronage and coterie circulation to a new professionalism defined by contracts and remuneration, Wollstonecraft offers the most striking example of the new role these changes made possible for literary women. Her connection with Johnson was professional in several senses. She wrote voluminously, often on demand, and that assigned work, much of it literary criticism, provided the income allowing her to devote herself to writing full time. As her prolific reviewing made her one of the most important contributors to his *Analytical Review*, Johnson soon placed Wollstonecraft in charge of some literary departments for the *Analytical* and possibly some editorial functions for his bookselling business as well. These broader responsibilities then situated Wollstonecraft to provide professional mentoring to another woman writer, Mary Hays.

It is well known that Wollstonecraft's writing, especially *A Vindication of the Rights of Woman*, exerted a powerful influence on Hays's thinking.[2] But it is not this form of influence that I wish to emphasize here. A reconsideration of Wollstonecraft's relationship with Hays discloses that along with Wollstonecraft's intellectual influence and their deepening personal friendship, these two writers developed a professional connection that evolved over time as well. In her role as Hays's mentor, Wollstonecraft provided Hays with opportunities for literary work. Moreover, the specific, practical advice that Wollstonecraft offered Hays on her relationship to her reading audience and on public presentation of herself as a woman author shows that at a time when many writers conceived a new urgency to their connection with their readers, Wollstonecraft held precise and sophisticated views on the creation of an effective authorial persona. Wollstonecraft has long been acknowledged a groundbreaker in the development of feminism and a central figure in the radical British intellectual culture of 1790s. But the lens of Wollstonecraft's commissioned work as a staff writer reveals that she also stands as a landmark in the changing occupations available to women writers. What is more, Wollstonecraft's role as a professional mentor offering expert guidance to Hays, marks the first time in the history of British letters that such a relationship between two women writers can so clearly be traced.

Literary scholarship has long disparaged commissioned literary work such as Wollstonecraft performed for Johnson. Branded with the appellation "hack" writing, it seems precisely the short-notice pecuniary nature of this writing that marks it for contempt. The source of this bias lies partly in prejudices of Romantic era literary professionals themselves. The term comes into play when literary culture began shifting away from publication practices emphasizing patronage and coterie circulation, replacing them with financial contracts and large scale publishing ventures directed to a mass audience. Like their publishers, writers more and more took on an entrepreneurial character, concerning themselves with professional standards and the effect of audience appeal on sales. Yet the illusion of elite dilettantism was still one that many authors wished to maintain. Since commissioned writing was done primarily for the remuneration it brought, writers were often reluctant to have it broadcast that they were engaged in this sort of work. As Kathy MacDermott has argued, the term "hack" itself enacts this conflict between increasingly rare amateurism and the emerging realities of writing and publishing in a mass market.[3] The term carries special liabilities when applied to women writers because it comes into play at a time when an expanding literary marketplace was providing women with new opportunities for literary work, much of it of the kind covered by this label.

Several recent studies in late eighteenth- and early nineteenth-century print culture have examined the emerging professionalism of, in Clifford Siskin's words, "the work of writing."[4] In particular, the rapid proliferation of periodicals has drawn scholarly attention for its role in solidifying a literary culture that was dominated by middle-class professionals. Although men made up the bulk of these newly-created literary professionals, commissioned literary work, and especially literary reviewing, provided at least a few Romantic-era women writers, including Wollstonecraft and Hays, with both publishing contacts and an important source of income. Such forms of writing are consequently far more central to late eighteenth- and early nineteenth-century print culture and its relation to gender roles and the Romantic-era literary career than has been allowed. Study of women's commissioned writing, especially their literary journalism, can help us understand more fully the careers of these women writers in terms of both their intellectual development and the material and social conditions that facilitated or blocked their access to the male-dominated profession of letters. At the same time, it offers a window onto the inner workings of literary culture, helping to illuminate such details as how periodical articles were assigned and what responsibilities inhered in certain types of literary work. Wollstonecraft's work for Johnson marks a critical shift in women's literary employment, one that redrew the map of women's participation in print culture during the following decades. Study of her commissioned work pinpoints some of the dynamics that made such dramatic changes possible.

This chapter examines Wollstonecraft's career as a staff writer and her increasing professionalism, including her consciousness of and ability to adapt to the new, broad reading audience that her reviews were expected to reach. It explores Wollstonecraft's critical practice, noting how she weighs in on social and political topics such as reform and the French Revolution. It isolates some of the bases for Wollstonecraft's critical authority, and in doing so, describes her shaping of an aesthetic that rejects Augustan neoclassical standards and promotes sensibility. Finally, it traces how she draws on the authority of her position to further another woman's literary career, that of Mary Hays. Wollstonecraft's mentoring of Hays was little concerned with the radical thinking for which both women have since become known. Instead, while it progresses from stiff, distant formality to casual assignment of work, the relationship focuses on the development of an authorial persona that is intellectually credible while serving the needs of one's readers. Though this mentorship was unable to bring to Hays secure literary employment, it nevertheless provided an important boost to her writing career.

Joseph Johnson, the "Mr Johnson" of Wollstonecraft's letter to her sister, was a long established bookseller who, though careless with business details, had gained wide respect as a forward-thinking publisher.[5] An extraordinarily generous and personable man, he loaned or even gave money, provided temporary lodgings, and facilitated personal and business contacts for many of the writers and artists associated with him. He had published Wollstonecraft's educational treatise, *Thoughts on the Education of Daughters* (1787), which had enjoyed considerable success, and apparently he had impressed Wollstonecraft with his amiability during the negotiations over this book, for she wrote him several very personal letters during her tenure as governess in Ireland. When she arrived in London after leaving the governess post, she brought with her the manuscript of her first novel, *Mary* (1788). Johnson agreed to publish the novel and offered to board Wollstonecraft at his own rooms above his shop while assisting her to locate more permanent lodgings. Soon after, Johnson extended the offer of steady literary employment that prompted Wollstonecraft's words to her sister.

Wollstonecraft began her work with Johnson writing and editing educational and children's literature and translating French. His first commissions for her were predictable given her background. *Original Stories* (1788) collected Wollstonecraft's own didactic fiction for children. Soon after, she edited *The Female Reader* (1789), an assortment of sentimental, religious, and educational pieces for girls, gathered from sources as varied as the Bible, Addison's *Spectator*, and the sonnets of Charlotte Smith. The translation, however, is surprising. Though she had only recently acquired sufficient French for a governess position, Johnson asked her to translate Jacques Necker's *De l'Importance des Opinions Réligeuses*, a work addressed to the French Academy in complex and dense prose that must have been particularly challenging to an inexperienced translator. Nevertheless, Johnson must have been satisfied with her work; he not only offered her other work translating French, but encouraged her to take up the study of German so that she could translate from that language as well. More significantly, however, she soon found her responsibilities extended in a direction that she probably did not anticipate when she wrote to her sister of her new career. Less than a year later she had already become one of the most important contributors to Thomas Christie's newly founded literary review, launched in May 1788 with Johnson as the editor. Wollstonecraft probably began contributing to the *Analytical Review* with the first issue, and her contributions continue, interrupted only during the three and a half years she spent outside England, until shortly before her death.[6] For most of her remaining years Wollstonecraft's literary criticism for the *Analytical Review* made for a considerable part of her income and a significant portion of her total literary output.

The *Analytical Review* is one of several periodicals that mark a turning point in literary marketing and the imagination of a reading audience. According to Jon P. Klancher, during the eighteenth century periodicals normally mapped their audiences by addressing specific ranks or groups. It was not until the early part of the nineteenth century that they began to obscure differences to tie a diverse audience together.[7] With antecedents partly in the late seventeenth-century learned journals that appealed to the educated upper classes, reviews continued throughout most of the eighteenth century to meet the demands of this audience by recording advances in all fields of knowledge, so enabling readers to keep abreast of the entire spectrum of intellectual developments.[8] Thus in his Advertisement introducing the first issue of the *Analytical Review*, proprietor Thomas Christie solicits notification of breakthroughs in all domains of knowledge, "it being one part of our design to establish a repository for genuine information in every department of Literature and Science."[9] Binding and indexing methods as well as internal references between issues show that reviews were intended to be collected just as volumes of an encyclopedia would be, indicating that they were targeted to an educated audience with substantial time for reading and with the resources and desire to purchase and maintain a library. Unlike modern readers, who, according to Marilyn Butler, "generally look out for evaluative judgments" that compare an author's performance with that of other authors in the same field, this elite eighteenth century audience expected a literary review to provide objective treatment in the form of "a lucid and careful account of a book's contents, aimed at a reader with little or no prior knowledge of the field."[10]

Apparently Christie planned at first to target his new review, like its predecessors, to this learned, mostly masculine audience. He meant the *Analytical Review* to correct what he perceived as a recent falling off from the ideal of pure objectivity. In his initial prospectus, he declares that the purpose of the new review, a purpose that the title was chosen to reflect, is "to give such an account of new publications, as may enable the reader to judge of them for himself." The review would accomplish this aim by providing readers with "accounts [i.e., summaries] and extracts. [...] Whether the Writers ought to add to this their own judgment," Christie demurs, "is with us a doubtful point." Surprisingly, since the reputation that the *Analytical* holds for us today is that of the most radical of literary reviews, Christie meant to hold his periodical aloof from personal, political, and professional controversy, intending instead that his staff strive for neutrality: "Facts, which admit of no doubt, can raise no controversy," he declares. "In relating them, the Writers give no opinion of their own; they appear only as they ought to appear, the HISTORIANS of the Republic of Letters." He envisioned the ideal contribution as consisting of an objective summary of the work with perhaps sufficient extract to allow readers to appraise it themselves without evaluative commentary from the reviewer. Yet as Gerald P. Tyson observes, Christie modified this purely "analytical" plan when he realized that the resulting publication, "though esteemed by the learned and thinking few, would not be sufficiently adapted to the taste of the public at large."[11] He opted for a modified plan combining ideal objectivity with evaluative commentary. In other words, Christie recognized the need to cement a broad-based audience for the new production and altered the plans accordingly. Redesigned specifically to appeal to "the public at large," the periodical to which Wollstonecraft contributed so prolifically offers an early example of a broadly marketed literary product, conscious of the needs of a varied audience. Wollstonecraft seems to have been uniquely suited to assisting Christie's periodical along this new path. Her contributions reflect a turn away from a learned and toward a popular audience in the extent of their evaluation and in their avoidance of the linguistic conventions of learned discourse.[12] Moreover, her later advice to Mary Hays shows an astute consciousness of literary audience.

As a staff *Analytical* reviewer, Wollstonecraft thus found herself in the position – unusual at the time, especially for a woman – of directing the taste and influencing the thinking of a wide public. Klancher argues that targeting periodicals to a broad audience that included middle-class readers had the effect of extending the public sphere. He notes that the eighteenth-century public sphere depended on face to face contact, but "By 1790, the public sphere had itself become an image to be consumed by readers who did not frequent it." Periodicals provided "a phantom social world – an alternative society of the text," a sort of "portable coffeehouse."[13] Klancher is most interested in the part this shift played in the creation of the English middle class, but of course vicarious participation in a now primarily textual public sphere would extend not only to middle-class men, but to women as well. Even more importantly, a periodical whose contributors went unidentified offered not only vicarious consumption, but influential partnership to the woman writer who contributed to a prominent literary review.

Wollstonecraft's reviews show that she had a nuanced sense of her public role as a reviewer. Commenting in one review, for example, that she points out flaws in style "in order that they be avoided in a future edition," she shows that she expects the writer as well as the audience to respond to her reviews.[14] Examining her reviews reveals that she has a keen sense of a broad and varied audience, that she saw herself as performing an important public service, and that as she develops as a reviewer, she more frequently capitalizes on the occasion of the review to nudge her audience in the direction of her own opinions on public issues. But one misunderstood aspect of Wollstonecraft's reviews, their concern with morality, represents as much an engagement with public concerns as her comments on the French Revolution. Ralph M. Wardle, her first critical biographer, dismisses the value of Wollstonecraft's criticism on this basis: "Mary" Wardle declares, "was usually content to judge a work on moral grounds alone; only twice in the first four and a half years of her reviewing for the *Analytical* did she attempt aesthetic criticism of novels. Her view of literature was that of the austere schoolma'am who refuses to truckle with any book which is not somehow uplifting."[15] Wardle's assessment is not only inaccurate in its failure to look beyond Wollstonecraft's moral assessments to other aspects of her criticism, but it mistakenly attributes to Wollstonecraft alone a critical concern that was in her day regarded as of greater public consequence than any aesthetic assessment that she could have offered.

Derek Roper has helped to correct Wardle's misapprehension by comparing Wollstonecraft's reviews to those of her male counterparts writing both for the *Analytical Review* and for other periodicals around the same time. Roper concludes that Wollstonecraft is often more exacting than the male reviewers commenting on the same publication, and that her criticism is successful overall. Apropos of Wardle's view that Wollstonecraft tends to moralize excessively, Roper notes that "To put moral considerations foremost was of course a characteristic of many writers in that age, including Johnson, Coleridge, Southey, Godwin, Fanny Burney, and Mary Wollstonecraft – all of whom wrote reviews."[16] Wollstonecraft's interest in the moral potential of a literary work, then, far from marking her criticism as merely the didactic rants of a repressed "school-ma'am," instead places her with some of the most respected critics of the age.

Wollstonecraft's concerns about the moral potential of novels stem from her sense of who reads them – from an understanding, that is, of the characteristics of a specific reading audience. She expresses wariness of the potential detrimental effects of an overly romanticized plot on female readers, especially younger women. Her first known signed review, for example, a discussion of Charlotte Smith's *Emmeline*, is often quoted:

> Few of the numerous productions termed novels, claim any attention; and while we distinguish this one, we cannot help lamenting

> that it has the same tendency as the generality, whose preposterous sentiments our young females imbibe with such avidity. Vanity thus fostered, takes deep root in the forming mind, and affectation banishes natural graces, or at least obscures them. We do not mean to confound affectation and vice, or allude to those pernicious writings that obviously vitiate the heart, while they lead the understanding astray. But we must observe, that the false expectations these wild scenes excite, tend to debauch the mind, and throw an insipid kind of uniformity over the moderate and rational prospects of life, consequently *adventures* are sought for and created, when duties are neglected, and content despised.[17]

As Wollstonecraft implicitly suggests, her concern that novels may encourage vanity, affectation, or neglect of duty stems from her belief that novel readers are disproportionately young women of the leisured classes who, if they received any education at all, were taught a modest repertoire of ornamental accomplishments such as dancing, French, and embroidery, but who were normally steered away from subjects such as mathematics and classical languages, which required intellectual discipline – they received, in other words, the kind of education that in *A Vindication of the Rights of Woman* Wollstonecraft deplores for failing to develop reason. In addition, these young women often led sheltered lives, so they had little experience to contradict what to a less naive individual would seem simply absurd. Yet Wollstonecraft's review makes a subtle distinction – some books truly promote immorality, but *Emmeline* is not one of them. Smith's novel merely encourages overindulgence of romantic fantasies, making its readers excessively susceptible to the superficial pleasures of emotional excitement.

Clearly stated nearly 40 years before by Dr. Johnson, these same concerns had long been accepted in evaluation of literature. In his well-known *Rambler* No. 4, Johnson argues that because novels "are written chiefly to the Young, the Ignorant, and the Idle," whose minds are "unfurnished with Ideas, and therefore easily susceptible of Impression," and who will regulate their behavior according to the examples they read, "Care ought to be taken, that, when the Choice is unrestrained, the best Examples only should be exhibited; and that which is likely to operate so strongly, should not be mischievous or uncertain in its Effects."[18] As any cursory look at reviews by her male counterparts will reveal, by the time Wollstonecraft began reviewing, Johnson's view was solidly established, and it would retain influence for some years to come. Wollstonecraft would have encountered it in almost any of the models she chose to emulate as she began to write reviews. Then too, she may have adopted this perspective directly from Johnson's own writings, which she admired for what she regarded as their heartfelt sentiments and sound notions of virtue. To cite concern with moral effect as evidence of inadequacy in Wollstonecraft's criticism is to evaluate that criticism by standards foreign to Wollstonecraft's day.

Nevertheless, while a survey of her *Analytical* contributions reveals that Wollstonecraft was concerned with the moral effects of novels, to describe her as solely preoccupied with morality is exaggerated at best. Roper suggests that the majority of scholars discussing literary reviews "seem to have glanced into them hastily, if at all, and then fallen back upon legend."[19] An examination of Wollstonecraft's reviews suggests that Roper has come uncomfortably close to the truth. To begin with, Wollstonecraft's concern with moral effect appears almost exclusively in her reviews of novels, conduct books, and works on moral philosophy. And even with these genres, her moral commentary sometimes serves a larger purpose. For example, she censures a volume whose title, *Woman. Sketches of the History, Genius, Disposition, Accomplishments, Employments, Customs, and Importance of the Fair Sex, in all Parts of the World*, sounds like a complete sociological study but whose description is that of a collection taken mostly from conduct books. She sums up her assessment saying: "Upon the whole we think it very far from being a book calculated to improve women, on the contrary, it will tend in common with novels, to render women more weak and affected."[20] Yet where the same volume records significant intellectual achievements on the part of women, she praises it. These comments, consistent with her arguments in *Rights of Woman*, and many others like them permeating her reviews, show that, consciously or not, while the ideas for her most famous work were ripening, Wollstonecraft was preparing an audience to receive them.

Wollstonecraft shows concern with the social effect of novels throughout her reviewing career, but she increasingly focuses on other aspects of the novels she reviews. As she gains experience at evaluating literary texts, Wollstonecraft becomes more interested in the aesthetic aspects of novels, so that by 1791 it is more usual to find novel reviews that contain no remarks on moral issues. Then too, she reviewed work in other genres almost from the first. In August 1788, for example, the second issue in which signed Wollstonecraft reviews appear, she reviews William Costigan's travel account, *Sketches of Society and*

Manners in Portugal. To attend the lying-in of her friend Fanny Blood (then Mrs. Hugh Skeys) some years before, Wollstonecraft had traveled to Portugal, a destination somewhat off the beaten path of late-eighteenth century English tourism. Hence she may well have been the foremost expert on Portugal that Johnson had on staff. Even in this early review, which stretches over seven pages, Wollstonecraft comments on the morals of the Portuguese as she has observed them, but not on the book's potential effect on the reader's conduct. Instead, she provides her audience with a description of and some extracts from Costigan's book, remarks on the accuracy of Costigan's observations, and makes some chauvinistic comparisons of Portuguese culture to English.[21] Similarly, about a year into her career with the *Analytical*, Wollstonecraft reviewed Olaudah Equiano's autobiography. She treats his work as primarily literary, and comments mostly on its aesthetic qualities. In fact, she seems to suggest that the book would have been improved if Equiano had left the conversion narrative aspect of it out. "The long account of his religious sentiments and conversion to methodism," she complains, "is rather tiresome."[22] Rather than sounding the single note of moral effect, Wollstonecraft flexibly adjusts her critical concerns to fit the type of work her review addresses. Wollstonecraft's review topics continue to broaden throughout her career, so much so that at times the novel reviewing was handed over to another writer, leaving Wollstonecraft free to concentrate her energies elsewhere. At the same time, her critical concerns also broaden, so that in her later articles, her proportionate emphasis on morality continues to shrink.

An overview of Wollstonecraft's *Analytical Review* articles shows a trajectory of expanding responsibility as both the breadth of her assigned topics and the prominence of her contributions increased. Wollstonecraft began reviewing in a narrow compass, discussing genres that suggest that Johnson was assigning reviews cautiously. Her early reviews discussed novels and imitations of sentimental authors, work that made few demands outside the range of competency that might be expected from a woman whose sentimental novel Johnson had recently accepted for publication. The next few numbers added in rapid succession travel narratives, sermons, poetry, drama, letters, essays, educational materials, and conduct literature. Soon natural philosophy, social reform, biography, and the performing arts fell within her purview as well. By September 1789 Wollstonecraft was reviewing books on aesthetics. Her contribution on music led the February 1790 issue. And the March 1790 number even included her short review on the topic of boxing. Within a few months of the first issue, Wollstonecraft's contributions had become so voluminous that the reading and writing required to produce them must have demanded much of her time. At the same time, her articles quickly obtained more prominent positions in individual numbers. To all appearances, as Wollstonecraft proved her mettle, Johnson was very willing to extend her responsibilities. A look at one of these articles will help clarify how Wollstonecraft was able to expand her scope so rapidly.

The February 1790 music article, a review of Charles Burney's *A General History of Music*, has provoked some controversy in attribution of Wollstonecraft reviews. Eleanor Flexner has questioned that an article treating a book on music can be credited to Wollstonecraft, even though it is signed "M," one of Wollstonecraft's known review signatures. She argues that, given Wollstonecraft's recognized interests and areas of expertise, other reviewers on the *Analytical* staff are more likely candidates as this article's author. Flexner doesn't pursue this question to its logical conclusion, but if this signed review cannot be allowed as one authored by Wollstonecraft, it would throw in question the attribution of any review, signed or not. However, the review follows the summary and extract format fairly closely. What evaluative commentary it contains discusses issues such as the book's effectiveness as a free-standing and complete work, and Burney's relative neglect of a composer the reviewer favors. The article demonstrates no expertise in music; rather, it could have been written by any literate and intelligent person who had had a little practice with the review format. Moreover, among the few subjective remarks contained in the article, we find: "people of taste and feeling, who are not professed performers, are most touched by strains addressed to the heart. The mere novelty of harmony will not interest them; and the ingenious contrivance alluded to, sometimes disgusts, as much as fine attitudes in an actor, which, so far from being the expression of passion, spring from study, to produce a stage effect."[23] These are the same lines along which Wollstonecraft defined merit in poetry in "On Artificial Taste," where she contrasts poetry of simple and rural societies, which is "the transcript of immediate emotions," with poetry produced in "a more advanced state of civilization," where the poet's books "become a hot-bed, in which artificial fruits are produced, beautiful to the common eye, though they want the true hue and flavour."[24] On these same bases Wollstonecraft condemned the inflammatory and insincere "turgid bombast" of Burke's *Reflections on the Revolution in France* (1790).[25] The remarks are consistent as well with her later reviews on musical topics such as

Italian opera. In fact, it is hard to imagine lines more typical of Wollstonecraft in both content and diction. With its emphasis on summary and extract, the standard review format lends itself to articles on books that push the boundaries of a contributor's knowledge and expertise. The consequence in Wollstonecraft's case is a clear record of the broadening scope of her reading. This wider reading naturally provoked deeper, more reflective thinking on her part, so in turn further expanding the subjects she could address in reviews.

As her importance with the *Analytical Review* increased, Wollstonecraft's criticism took on more depth as well. With her interest in evaluating morality, she had never fully conformed to the ideal of a purely "analytical" reviewer. But her first reviews often combine several pages of summary and extract with a few paragraphs of evaluation. As she continued to review, though, her departures from this format became more frequent and extensive, especially when reviewing publications that came under her provinces of greatest expertise, such as novels or educational material. Meanwhile, and more interestingly, she framed her comments so that while remaining factual in structure, they provided the sort of evaluation through which reviews had begun to shape literary taste. As she became more capable on a topic, this evaluation grew more subtle, more sophisticated. For example, her review of Costigan's *Society and Manners in Portugal* is her first travel review, and the article consists mostly of summary and extract, interspersed with some exaggeratedly nationalistic sentiments expressed in at times rather extravagant language. She claims that "a childish cruel religion, and the system of dissimulation it has introduced, Moorish customs, and an arbitrary government, have all contributed to turn a savage into a monster." In consequence, the contrast between her idea of English and Portuguese character is so great that she believes Costigan to have fabricated one incident, because "no Portuguese Fidalgo ever married an English woman."[26] To write this review, Wollstonecraft relies on knowledge and prejudices derived only from personal experience. Two and a half years later in a review of Meares' *Voyages ... from China to the North-West Coast of America* (1790), she again questions the author's accuracy, but this time based on her own prior reading in geography and anthropology. She suggests, for example, that Meares has been hasty when describing certain natives, "for canoes of that description, we understand, are not to be met with on the coast, to the eastward of Kaye's Island." In addition, she now envisions several potential audiences for the book and has definite ideas about how her review serves these varied audiences. She notes inconsistencies in geographical observations, for example, "because to professional people, who may hereafter pursue the same track, they are of the greatest consequence." Nevertheless, "Though this work does not appear to us, on account of the inconsistencies which we have noticed, to be a valuable book for professional people, yet it contains much information and amusement for *landsmen*, to borrow a sea-phrase, who only wish to obtain a general knowledge of the face of a coast, and the manners of its inhabitants."[27] In other words, she distinguishes between the book's weaknesses as a specialized work and its appeal for an audience seeking entertainment, and recommends it accordingly. The difference between the two travel reviews suggests that in the interim the reading and writing required for her *Analytical* work both broadened Wollstonecraft's knowledge and matured her as a reviewer. It also suggests an increasingly sophisticated understanding of both her position as reviewer and the diversity of her audience.

Another example of Wollstonecraft's growth as a reviewer occurs in the field of aesthetics. Her *Analytical* reviews include several articles discussing work by one of the eighteenth century's most important aestheticians, William Gilpin. The first review of Gilpin's work extracts a few of his aesthetic principles but makes no attempt to evaluate them. Wollstonecraft's subjective commentary outlines how "observations of taste" must appeal to the sensibility of an audience whose emotional make-up renders them susceptible.[28] Further than that, she merely distinguishes which of the standard aesthetic categories – beautiful, sublime, or picturesque – Gilpin's sketches conform to. Reviewing a second of Gilpin's works in the next volume, Wollstonecraft introduces a few remarks directly addressing one or two specific principles of landscape painting, basing these remarks on her personal response to the effect of certain techniques. A few months later she for the first time cites Gilpin in evaluating the work of another author on landscape aesthetics, a practice she continues, on occasion, throughout her reviewing career.[29] By mid-1791, the next time she turns to a Gilpin volume, she keeps to the "analytical" formula, but arranges her extracts, supposedly neutral, to make a specific and provocative point: that "a picturesque taste must be founded on principles, and that reason and fancy are nearer akin than cold dulness is willing to allow." Her statement directly contradicts a point she made in her first article on Gilpin, that taste is idiosyncratic and cannot be communicated, now showing her as more willing to invoke the psychological issues with which aestheticians were concerned. The remark reveals too that she has taken the neutral summary and extract of Christie's original prospectus and shaped it into a tool to convey ideas entirely her own. The preceding year Wollstonecraft had in *Vindication of the Rights of Men* savaged Burke's gendered aesthetics of the sublime and the beautiful as he had expounded them in his *Philosophical Enquiry* (1757) on the subject. Here she reevaluates a discourse that customarily subjugated a feminized "fancy" to the discipline of masculine-identified reason. In Wollstonecraft's model, these categories no longer fall into an essentialized hierarchical opposition. Instead, such opposition becomes merely the contingent construct of a "cold dulness" that fails to see how the categories are equal, similar, "akin." A year later, her knowledge of the field has further advanced so that she feels authorized to comment on the structure and method of aesthetic disquisition. She criticizes the vague way writers on taste, Gilpin included, deploy concepts like "beautiful" and "picturesque." She also notes connections between Gilpin's discussions in this volume and in his previous ones. The reading she has done in the course of her work as a reviewer has made her solidly competent to discuss work in a field usually considered the province of men, and well educated men at that. Yet her concerns are those of the amateur interested in this extremely popular field – the concerns, that is, of a broad, non-specialist audience.

Wollstonecraft's reviews also reveal both consistencies and shifts in her politics. She is favorable to the French revolution, though affected by its extremes. Some months before the September Massacres she writes,

> These letters develop, in an interesting manner, the polished villainy of court intrigue, and that fatal system of *profusion* and *oppression*, which, in the latter part of the reign of Louis XV. Hurried France to the brink of destruction, and at length brought the affairs of that kingdom to the crisis which gave birth to the present revolution. The French patriots have been reviled, even to a degree of execration, by the *admirers* of *despotism*; but this collection of letters might alone serve as an apology for National assembly, were any apology necessary for the *glorious* labours of that *patriotic body*.[30]

Her encomium is extreme but specific, while its phrasing reveals an effort to enlist public sympathy for the Revolution. The repeated emphases suggest that she is persuading, even propagandizing, and certain turns of phrase recall her responses to Burke. Years later, after the terror in France and the treason trials and suspension of Habeas

Corpus in England, the war between the two nations now raging, she still presents the revolution in a positive light, but her praise is more reserved, less specific. Reviewing an account of a British naval officer captured with his crew by the French, she offers:

> The strange mixture of wisdom and folly, of generous actions and atrocities, and of sufferings and success, which a neighboring country has exhibited during the last six years, the wonderful changes it has undergone, and the immense multitude of important events which it has compressed within so narrow a circle, have naturally attracted our attention strongly towards it.

Lest it seem, however, that she retracts her overall approbation, she remarks on French policies that she finds worthy of British emulation and attributes much that is objectionable to "a people who had recently thrown off the yoke of despotism." "When all the orders of society are shaken together by a political convulsion, similar to Cromwell's usurpation, or the revolution in France," she explains, "a number of ridiculous characters never fail to force themselves into notice." The comparison with England is an interesting one, especially given Burke's refusal to see any similarity between the ultimate outcome of that English revolution and the upheaval in progress in France. In Wollstonecraft's account, England, like France, has survived a bloody revolution, but what English patriot in her day would turn back the clock on those events? Wollstonecraft takes imagery that haunted the British, adding to their fears about events in France, fears that Burke had encouraged, and turns that imagery to account in reducing those fears. She does this in part by distinguishing between theory and practice. After a long section recounting the brutality met by the volume's author and his crew at the hands of their French captors, she offers evidence that "their ill treatment was rather attributable to the low agents of government, than to government itself."[31] The distinction is one that she has long made with reference to England, too. Years before, she had remarked on the "theoretical excellencies which exalt, and the flaws in practice that disgrace, our respectable constitution."[32] She sees no contradiction in extolling the British constitution while condemning the present government. By the mid-1790s, Wollstonecraft had come to agree that the excesses of the French revolution were excesses, but she continues to cultivate respect for its merits and to advocate forbearance in condemning its faults.

Wollstonecraft evolves, too, in the degree to which she takes advantage of reviews to advocate for social reform. In the course of her career, she reviewed works that allowed her to comment on such social issues as slavery, prostitution, prison reform, treatment of the poor, and child labor. Her earliest articles tend to minimize her own views on social topics. The 1789 review of Equiano's slave narrative, for example, remarks on aspects of the narrative that Wollstonecraft finds affecting, but at no time tries for a coherent statement against the institution of slavery. After a little more than a year as a reviewer, she capitalizes on a chapter concerning the penal system in Catherine Macaulay Graham's *Letters on Education* to insert her own lengthy and pointed footnote harshly criticizing conditions in the hospitals for the poor.[33] A discussion of prostitution seems to retreat from such unabashed social criticism when she merely observes that the poem in question portrays the "misery" of prostitution in a manner that is "forcible," followed with an extract that illustrates this affecting depiction.[34] Yet when she returns to the issue of criminal justice in 1792, her review consists not in an account of the book under discussion, but in her own denunciation of solitary confinement instead.[35] Though her own views are partially concealed behind the publications she discusses, Wollstonecraft often exploits the opportunity to address a large audience on social concerns. These and other similar departures from Christie's original ideal of pure objectivity indicate that Wollstonecraft understood the potential of her position as reviewer. Rather than allowing the reader to "judge [...] for himself," she nudges her review audience toward her own view not only of the publication at hand, but of the wider political and social issues under discussion as well.

Wollstonecraft began her career as a sentimental novelist and author of children's literature and works on the education of girls, all literary forms addressing female readers. Interestingly, as Janet Todd has observed, Wollstonecraft's prefaces to these publications seem to reject the need for a congenial relationship with her readers, and her letters at the time reinforce the picture of a writer who believes her audience merits little respect.[36] Unlike the above examples from the *Analytical Review*, these prefaces preach to readers, yet give little indication of a belief that those readers will hear. The prefaces of her two *Vindications*, on the other hand, written around the same time as these reviews, avoid antagonizing the reader. Where contempt is expressed at all, it is reserved for the same writers attacked in the body of the *Vindication* texts. Much like her political writings, literary reviewing brought Wollstonecraft explicitly into the public sphere. The earliest known example of long-term regular periodical literary reviewing by a woman, her literary criticism reflects a growing consciousness of the public importance of her position as she addressed a broad and varied audience, and an increasing willingness to engage that audience's thinking in terms of intellectual respect rather than condescending didacticism.

The potential benefit that Wollstonecraft may have derived from the standard summary and extract review format should not distract from the extent to which she in fact deviates from that format. Though Christie altered his plans in response to market pressures, he initially meant to establish his review explicitly to recapture an objectivity that he believed his competitors had lost. Assuming that Johnson shared this vision at least to some degree, what must he have thought of his contributor, Mary Wollstonecraft? As we have seen, Wollstonecraft was assigned work in an ever-broadening range of subject matter, her contributions claiming ever more frequently the most prominent positions in their respective monthly numbers. Meanwhile, she shows an increasing propensity to evaluate the merits of a book herself, rather than setting judgments aside for the sake of objectivity, and to turn the review of a book into an opportunity to express her own views on related topics. These trends in Wollstonecraft's articles have additional significance in that they may offer some of the early signals of what would become the dominant trends of nineteenth-century reviewing practice under the leadership of the *Edinburgh Review*. But for now, Wollstonecraft's progressive reliance on her own assessments and her penchant for including sometimes highly controversial commentary points to greater self-confidence in her capabilities as a reviewer, a shift that her expanding responsibilities almost certainly encouraged. Yet her letters reveal that, despite her inexperience and a formal education that, compared to that of most of her male competitors, could only be called rudimentary, and notwithstanding the extent to which she depended on the income from her work for Johnson, Wollstonecraft showed a surprising independence from editorial prescription even from the first. Writing to Joseph Johnson, her editor, about a review of a work by Samuel Johnson, she declares, "If you do not like the manner in which I reviewed Dr. J[ohnson]'s s[ermon] on his wife, be it known unto you – I *will* not do it any other way – I felt some pleasure in paying a just tribute of respect to the memory of a man – who, in spite of his faults, I have an affection for."[37]

How could a woman who had, in the words of her biographer, "tumbled up with some schooling," a neophyte in a job she desperately needed where, she must have known, most of her colleagues were learned men with extensive experience, how could such a person show such self-assertion to her employer?[38] While the preferred format for *Analytical* contributions can explain her development and confidence when she conformed to it, it cannot tell us how she could have shown such assurance when departing from that format so early in her career. The anonymity of *Analytical* reviewers surely played a role in her confidence before the public; if readers did not know she was a woman, they could not dismiss her work on the basis of gender. In addition, the corporate voice that was standard for reviewing, the "we" that framed the expression of opinion, lent any single reviewer the authority and prestige of the entire periodical and its proprietor. That same "we" meant, though, that the editor or proprietor saw himself as responsible for the opinions each article expressed, and some editors consequently demanded uniformity in opinion between the various individual contributors.[39] Neither anonymity nor corporate voice, then, can explain such self-assertion toward Johnson. Personality must have played some role here. Johnson's personal affability was legendary, and, as her letters show, his willingness to extend material support and lend a sympathetic ear had already encouraged Wollstonecraft to regard him as a valued friend. Then, too, Wollstonecraft's letters suggest that her success in meeting the many personal challenges she had faced had given her a self-confidence that, though it was sometimes tenuous, could inspire her to rely on her own judgment even in circumstances of great risk. But along with the effects of personality, the intersection of the culture of rational Dissent and aesthetics of sensibility played a role as well.

Although not a Dissenter herself, Wollstonecraft nevertheless enjoyed close ties with the community of Rational Dissent. In 1783, Wollstonecraft and her friend Fanny Blood opened a girls' school that they soon moved to Newington Green, one of the eighteenth century's principal centers for religious Dissent. While at Newington Green, Wollstonecraft became acquainted with some of the most prominent Dissenters of the day, including Mr. and Mrs. James Burgh, Joseph Priestley, and the Reverend Richard Price. Though she did not convert to their faith, Wollstonecraft did at times attend Price's Dissenting services, and she formed several close attachments within the community. She particularly admired Price, and he became a close friend as well as an intellectual and spiritual mentor. At Newington Green Wollstonecraft first met Joseph Johnson, who, himself a Dissenter, had long served as the most important publisher of Dissenters' work. Wollstonecraft retained strong ties with many members of the

Dissenting community throughout her life, and several of them deeply influenced her thinking.

Eighteenth-century religious Dissent was grounded in a respect for individual judgment. Against the doctrines of the Established Church, Dissenters believed that worshippers should read the Bible and come to understand religious truth themselves rather than accept the authority of the clergy in matters of faith. Their belief in autonomy extended to secular judgment as well, thereby permeating much of their intellectual tradition. Tracing the influence of seventeenth-century Commonwealth thought on the Dissenting culture surrounding Wollstonecraft, G. J. Barker-Benfield explains that by the late eighteenth century, the followers of Price and Priestley, the period's two most influential Dissenters, considered individual independence of mind as an essential right. In Price's words, "to be obliged from our birth to look up to a creature no better than ourselves as the master of our fortunes and to receive his will as law – what can be more humiliating? What elevated ideas can enter a mind in such a situation?"[40] Though Barker-Benfield is interested in the tie between these ideas and the feminism of *A Vindication of the Rights of Woman*, it is not difficult to see how such a doctrine would also encourage Wollstonecraft to take a stand when she disagreed with her editor. One can recognize as well the role of such a philosophy in the prospectus of the *Analytical Review*, a periodical owned, operated, and for the most part staffed by Dissenters. And at a review founded explicitly on a plan of encouraging readers to exercise independent judgment and operated by members of a community that believed that such judgment was an individual right, how could the editor refuse the same right to one of his contributors?

Moreover, the culture of sensibility provided Wollstonecraft with a footing whence to pronounce literary judgment. At the time Wollstonecraft took her stand on the Johnson review, sensibility had attained the status of a key constituent of human psychology. Permeating most theories of intellectual functioning, sensibility held a place second only, and sometimes even superior, to reason. It was, for example, often regarded as akin to the creative or poetic faculty, and so was particularly fitting as a measure for evaluating literature. Furthermore, while the ideal man was a feeling one, women were regarded as having an especially direct connection to their feelings. Thus, sensibility, in which women were superior, might provide a foundation for judgment that could compete with the supposedly more developed reason of the educated man, a foundation that could, in fact, be more suitable than reason under some circumstances. Wollstonecraft regarded herself as a person of unusually acute sensibility. Indeed, as Mary Poovey has argued, much of Wollstonecraft's suspicion of excessive sensibility arose from her consciousness of the pain her own capacity to feel sometimes caused her.[41] Any sensitive reader of Johnson must recognize a deep strain of pathos running through much of his writing, and this particular work, a sermon penned at a moment of profound grief, makes an especially apt object for a sympathetic approach. In her review of it, Wollstonecraft capitalizes on the opportunity to affirm that it is in sensibility that we express our humanity: "It is natural to sympathize with a fellow creature enduring what we are all liable to endure, some string of our own hearts is touched and vibrates, – and we may mournfully repeat – 'and I also am a man!'"[42] Wollstonecraft's reference to herself as a "man" marks the universality of human emotion; it does not negate her conviction that it is women who possess the deeper emotional responsiveness. While the classical education of many of her male counterparts might allow them to avow superior rational judgment and knowledge of literary correctness, as a woman of acute sensibility, Wollstonecraft clearly believed herself to have the edge here, where feeling counted most.

According to Mitzi Myers, Wollstonecraft's concern with moral potential arises from her engagement with the aesthetics of sensibility. Myers argues that in her novel reviews Wollstonecraft recognizes that, "Literary commentary [...] is never purely aesthetic but always socially implicated. [...] Novels of sensibility matter because they shape behavior and serve as an index to broader cultural ills."[43] By Wollstonecraft's time sensibility was widely accepted as a potential stimulus to moral development and virtuous action through its status as the natural foundation of human sympathy. Literary depictions of distress were presumed capable of transforming public opinion on issues such as poverty, the prison system, and the slave trade. Similarly, by eliciting sympathy for the distresses of others, sentimental novels could deepen sensibility and promote moral development and domestic virtue. Wollstonecraft shares many of these views and her praise of moral works draws on concepts such as sympathy, benevolence, and natural human goodness that were the stock-in-trade of the positive manifestations of sensibility.[44]

As a guide to morality, sensibility was independent of, perhaps even in conflict with, a classical education or the reason that education was supposed to develop. Moreover, it was often associated with the middle classes and with religious Dissent, both groups to which Wollstonecraft had close ties. In a review of a collection of Johnson's sermons,

Wollstonecraft summarizes Johnson's own concern that "morality, wanting a firm *visible* support, becomes a bending principle easily warped by the prevailing impulse; and that reason is oftener employed to excuse than correct the favourite propensity, when a rule of action is not recurred to."[45] For Wollstonecraft, sensibility in its moderated form can guide behavior more reliably than could reason, or at least reason alone without the assistance of the emotions. Yet she also believed that the excesses of sensibility in the overly romanticized plots of sentimental novels could turn the literary deployment of sensibility from a moral force to a sinister one. Without the tempering of reason, sensibility could forestall the cultivation of rational judgment, and become twisted, distorted, "false." In young women so naïve as to mistakenly regard such plots as realistic, these novels could have a insidious effect.

Despite her censure on moral grounds of its excesses in some novels, Wollstonecraft derived much of her critical judgment from an aesthetic based in sensibility. Throughout her career, its vocabulary helped her articulate her assessments of a wide variety of publications. After all, the above-mentioned review of Burney's *History of Music* departs from the standard *Analytical* format to assert that "people of taste and feeling […] are most touched by strains addressed to the heart."[46] In one of her later reviews, she praises Elizabeth Inchbald's *Nature and Art* (1796) for "those artless strokes which go directly to the heart."[47] Even her review of a book on boxing, a province so distant from what might conventionally be apportioned to a woman reviewer that it led one of her biographers to relinquish any hope of reliably identifying even signed reviews, "considered boxing from a humanitarian angle."[48] Indeed, Wollstonecraft not only relied on this aesthetic; she worked to construct it as well.

Wollstonecraft's only stand-alone essay of literary criticism, "On Artificial Taste," explores in depth the superiority of sensibility over taste, judgment, or education as the source of poetry. "Artificial" taste arises when an individual incapable of responding directly to the beauties of nature is stirred by technically-polished descriptions in literature. Much as William Wordsworth would soon contend in his preface to *Lyrical Ballads*, Wollstonecraft argues that good poetry "is the transcript of immediate emotions." Her rejection of Augustan literary standards is even more emphatic than Wordsworth's, however. For her, the revisions made "during the cooler moments of reflection" may have more technical grace, more "elegance and uniformity," but they will always affect us with less force than "ebullitions of animal spirits." Like hot-house grown "artificial fruits," poetry that arises from reading and reflection will "want the true hue and flavour." Her essay invokes the physiological foundations of sensibility in describing how "the finely fashioned nerve vibrates acutely with rapture." The connection of sensibility to virtue emerges in her praise of poetry that can "rouse the passions which amend the heart." Her analysis relies on principles that extend back to Locke: "the first observers of nature," she explains, "exercised their judgment much more than their imitators. But they exercised it to discriminate things, whilst their followers were busy borrowing sentiments and arranging words." Though her "poet" in this essay seems implicitly male, Wollstonecraft condemns the "barrenness" of mind characteristic in "Boys who have received a classical education" who are able to compose "tolerably smooth verses."[49] In doing so, she implies superior, because more natural, abilities on the part of those to whom a classical education was denied: women, Dissenters, and the middle class, the very groups with which Wollstonecraft most strongly identified. "On Artificial Taste" does not endorse sensibility without reserve; the final paragraph points to the danger that, if excessively indulged, sensibility may lead to libertinism. Nevertheless, sensibility gave Wollstonecraft a solid intellectual ground for authoritative independent judgment. In her expression of that judgment, she steered public taste toward sensibility's more sophisticated – indeed, its more rational – expressions, where its cultivation could "enable the reader to judge [...] for him[- or her-]self." [50]

One site to observe the shaping and promotion of an aesthetic of sensibility in Wollstonecraft's reviews is in her comparisons to Shakespeare and Milton, those poets who were to her contemporaries the quintessentially English poets, and Rousseau, the preeminent writer of sensibility. Wollstonecraft never reviews either Shakespeare's or Milton's poetry – though new editions might have offered the opportunity – but she refers to the work of each as an example of poetic ideals that disdain the confinement of strict unity and precise versification in favor of the spontaneity of "bold flights of genius." Shakespeare, "nature's darling child, [...] may disdain to stop to adjust slight ornaments; and, giving a whole, in characters and passions, may neglect the plot, or sportively introduce heterogeneous matter."[51] Despite reservations about Milton expressed in *A Vindication of the Rights of Woman*, Wollstonecraft dismisses Lord Chesterfield's ridicule of *Paradise Lost* as unable to "cloud the reputation of that sublime poet, unless true taste and feeling give place to sinical [sic] refinement, or to that fastidious nibbling criticism, which [...] never catches that glance of the poet's design, which calling forth a sublime glow of admiration, makes us feel that he is true to nature." In the same review, she makes what is probably her most common comparison, especially when discussing matters of style. This time, it is Lord Shaftesbury who suffers. Because of his highly finished style, she is led to doubt his sincerity. His sentiments, she avers, "appear in rather a suspicious garb in his affected inflated periods; and this parade of words, has ever led the writer of this article to suspect, that his heart was unmoved [...], so little does it contain of that subtle fluid, which running along Rousseau's lines, finds the nearest way to the heart."[52] Wollstonecraft guides her readers to reject Augustan critical standards, here represented by British aristocracy, in favor of a more democratic literary ideal that takes sensibility as the essence of everything from poetic genius to persuasiveness to an admirable writing style.

Though sensibility may have offered Wollstonecraft a source of authority that she regarded as privileging her over her male counterparts because of her immediate access to her own feelings, sensibility as a foundation for judgment was by no means restricted to women. Meanwhile, the anonymity of reviews meant that a woman writer could trespass on territory usually reserved for men, and no one other than her employer need be the wiser. It is not far-fetched to suggest that Wollstonecraft's consciousness of her own accomplishments in a man's job influenced her *Rights of Woman* argument in favor of careers for women. As she proved in the course of each day's work, reason and judgment were ungendered. Able to negotiate the potential pitfalls that might have marked her as a woman writer and so subjected her and Johnson's review to public ridicule, Wollstonecraft must have developed a strong sense of the conventions of masculine versus feminine discourse, and a consciousness that these differences arose not from nature but from strategies of language. The Gilpin review above, among others, shows how Wollstonecraft at least occasionally exploited her anonymous position to subtly revise accepted notions of gender without risk of being dismissed because she was a woman.

At the same time, criticism was decisive in Wollstonecraft's career. It served as a stable, reliable source of income that allowed her to leave behind the tenuously profitable, labor-intensive work of educating girls to become one of the late-eighteenth century's most important women of letters. It was the occasion for broad and intensive reading and voluminous writing, all within the restrictions imposed by deadlines. Though on one hand her use of the term "hack" encourages undervaluation, Wollstonecraft's biographer, Eleanor Flexner, concisely and accurately sums up the important contribution of her reviewing work to her career as a writer:

> In general, what was important about Mary's work for the *Analytical* was its professionalism. She had assignments to meet, and her subsistence depended on her doing the work, whether she wanted to or not. She also faced the kind of competition offered by other established and more experienced hacks who would be watching her work for judgment, style, and literacy. She was adding to her general stock of information and writing more easily and fluently. She was demonstrating to herself and to others that she had the necessary intelligence, ambition, and energy to meet the incessant challenge and strain of such work. The *Analytical*, together with the group she met at Johnson's, provided the climate in which Mary Wollstonecraft attained intellectual maturity in an astonishingly short span of time.[53]

Wollstonecraft's professional development at the *Analytical Review* progressed rapidly – extremely rapidly, in fact. Johnson was soliciting contributors to his new project at least as early as July 1787, indicating that he and Christie already contemplated founding an "analytical" review when Wollstonecraft arrived in London to launch her literary career. The rapid increase in both the quantity and prominence of Wollstonecraft's work shows that Johnson needed her. Though periodical literary reviewing was still almost exclusively a male occupation, Johnson was willing to extend Wollstonecraft's responsibilities as quickly as she could prove herself capable of meeting them. Before long, these responsibilities encompassed even more than regular reviewing. At the *Analytical Review*, evidence suggests that the more important reviewers had charge of entire departments and would "exercise discretion in choosing works for review, paying attention only to those that were significant contributions to their discipline."[54] Often the only reviewer of certain genres and regularly the most prolific contributor in several others, Wollstonecraft seems to have had charge of a variety of departments at times, especially those that would fall under the rubrics of belles-lettres, education, and moral and religious topics.[55] In this position, she would have exerted considerable sway not only in the content of individual reviews, but in deciding what books to call public attention to in the first place. What is more, the circumstances surrounding her acquaintance with Mary Hays suggest that by the time her second *Vindication* appeared Wollstonecraft had become Johnson's editorial assistant in an even broader sense. In this capacity Wollstonecraft significantly influenced Hays's literary career.

Wollstonecraft's professional work for Johnson provides an unusual opportunity to study an early woman to woman literary mentoring relationship. That mentoring is significant in that it focuses our attention away from concerns of literary influence, turning it instead toward the nuts and bolts of becoming a professional in the world of letters. Wollstonecraft provided Hays with opportunities for literary work, gave her practical suggestions for improving her literary criticism, and helped her refine her public textual presentation of herself as a woman writer. She pointed out the special pitfalls that Hays would face on account of her sex, and offered her strategies to present herself as intellectually credible, deserving not of sympathy or gallant condescension, but respect. Wollstonecraft's counsel emphasized that one writes to be read and so must keep her audience in mind. In other words, Wollstonecraft mentored Hays in the professional aspects of literary work.

Wollstonecraft became acquainted with Mary Hays after George Dyer, a long-time close friend who had encouraged Hays's literary and intellectual development, gave her a copy of *Vindication of the Rights of Woman* in June 1792. Hays wrote Wollstonecraft an admiring letter, and sometime in the next few months, the two women met at Joseph Johnson's shop.[56] Whether she knew the specifics of Wollstonecraft's critical and editing work or not, Hays must already have had reason to believe that Wollstonecraft had responsibilities to Johnson that went beyond those of an author to her publisher. She wrote to Wollstonecraft to enlist her influence with Johnson on behalf of *Letters and Essays, Moral and Miscellaneous* (1793), an outgrowth of Hays's reading of Wollstonecraft's *Rights of Woman*. The book followed a format common in works addressed to women but took radical positions on religion, social equality, and gender relations. Perhaps surprisingly considering the influence of her own ideas on this text, Wollstonecraft responded with only minimal encouragement, and the book was issued the following year by T. Knott, who had already published Hays's *Cursory Remarks on [...] Public or Social Worship* (1791).[57] Still, Wollstonecraft's response to Hays merits remark on two grounds.

First of all, Wollstonecraft advises Hays not on the content of her main text but rather on how she presents herself to the reading public – how, in other words, to market herself effectively as a new author. Wollstonecraft offers Hays some brusque criticism of the preface to

Letters and Essays, encouraging her to eliminate both pleas for reader indulgence and a recounting of verbal praise that her manuscript had garnered in private circulation. Inclusion of both this type of apology and similar puffery was conventional at the time. Women writers in particular could by such means preserve an appearance of modesty while boldly launching their work into print. For the most part these women writers, like Wollstonecraft in her own first publications, addressed a female audience. In her anonymous reviews, however, Wollstonecraft had learned to present herself as credible in a masculine discourse addressing a broad audience, and her experience shows in her counsel to Hays. She begins this portion of the letter declaring "I am now going to treat you with still greater frankness – I do not approve of your preface – and I will tell you why." Continuing then for two substantial paragraphs, she points out specific flaws and explains her reasons for objecting to them. She declares, for example, that

> Disadvantages of education &c ought, in my opinion, never to be pleaded (with the public) in excuse for defects of any importance, because if the writer has not sufficient strength of mind to overcome the common difficulties which lie in his way, nature seems to command him, with a very audible voice, to leave the task of instructing others to those who can. [...] I should say to an author, who humbly sued for forbearance, 'if you have not a tolerable good opinion of your own production, why intrude it on the public? we have plenty of bad books already, that have just gasped for breath and died.'

Wollstonecraft's use of masculine pronouns highlights the assumption that ordinarily authors, especially authors of expository prose, were male. If Hays was to achieve credibility with controversial book identifying its author as a woman, it would have been especially important to present that work as standing on its own merits. Addressing Hays's inclusion of testimonials, which she labels "vanity," Wollstonecraft points out the special vulnerability that gender expectations create for the woman author. "Your male friends will treat you like a woman," she cautions, and many men "have insensibly been led to utter warm eulogiums in private that they would be sorry openly to avow without some cooling explanatory ifs." Women, in turn, will be especially susceptible to such flattery. Her advice to this new author concludes as it began with attention not to literary or even political issues, but with guidance on self-presentation: "till a work strongly interests the public true modesty should keep the author in the background."[58] Hays took the critique to heart; not only does the published version appear without most of the material that Wollstonecraft objects to but Hays echoes these views some years later in her own advice to young novelists.[59]

The letter's second point of interest appears in the opening remarks. They suggest that by this time Wollstonecraft may have assumed responsibilities with Johnson that were extensive indeed. She tells Hays, "I yesterday mentioned to Mr. Johnson your request and he assented desiring that the title page might be sent to him – I, therefore, can say nothing more, for trifles of this kind I have always left to him to settle."[60] Though only a hint, these lines raise speculation over what Wollstonecraft's editorial offices must have been and whether she was at times making publication decisions independently from Johnson. Such a possibility is not at all unlikely, for Johnson was notoriously disorganized and inefficient in business matters, and by this time his health was often poor. Wollstonecraft had spent much of her life taking over and setting to rights the affairs of various family members and friends, so it would hardly be surprising if she did the same with Johnson.

Wollstonecraft's next extant letter to Hays reveals even more of the mentoring relationship. Referring to Hays's *Cursory Remarks*, Wollstonecraft again centers her comments not on the content of Hays text, but rather on issues of self-presentation. She compliments Hays on avoiding conventional tactics, "the superlatives, exquisite, fascinating, &c," characteristic of the "feminine" writer. Remarking that Hays's work suffers nonetheless from a tendency to obscurity, Wollstonecraft then assures her that "if you continue to write you will imperceptibly correct this fault and learn to think with more clearness, and consequently avoid the errours naturally produced by confusion of thought."[61] With both observations Wollstonecraft has Hays's relationship to her audience in mind. The former reminds Hays that certain uses of language mark her as a "feminine" writer and so might undermine her credibility. It is worth noting that the perspective has now shifted from male and female writers to "feminine" and "masculine" ones, with "feminine" the term of discredit. As a woman writer, Hays might be especially susceptible to being branded "feminine," – though presumably a male writer could employ the same wording and would therefore be "feminine" as well – but she can minimize the hazard through certain strategies of language. The latter of the two remarks reminds Hays that she must write so as to be clearly understood, a point that comes up again as their relationship progresses. In the same letter Wollstonecraft also mentions that she will correct some proofs for Hays, and that she will pass on some communications from Hays to Johnson. Clearly their association had already advanced to include various forms of literary facilitation.

Shortly after she wrote this letter, Wollstonecraft left London, traveling first to Paris, then elsewhere in France and, after a brief return to London, to Scandinavia. Her friendship with Hays shows its next advance in late 1795, soon after Wollstonecraft returned permanently to London and resumed her reviewing and editing work for Johnson. At Johnson's urging, Wollstonecraft invited Hays to a dinner at his shop. In the meantime, Hays had herself taken up literary reviewing. At some point in 1795, Hays began writing for the *Critical Review*, a periodical with a Tory bias for much of its career, but which during the years in question leaned under George Robinson's editorship toward Whig politics and religious Dissent, a perspective that Hays would have found congenial.[62] Hays's friend Dyer was himself a contributor to the *Critical Review*, and it was probably through him that she began writing for that periodical. With Wollstonecraft back at the *Analytical Review*, her friendship with Hays grew closer as Hays began once again to rely on her for literary advice.[63] Finally, sometime around January 1797, Wollstonecraft asked Hays, now initiated as a reviewer and recently established as a successful published novelist, to review a novel, Jane West's *Gossip's Story* (1796), for the *Analytical*.[64] The review appears in the January 1797 issue, signed with the initials "V. V."

Study of periodical contributions by eighteenth- and nineteenth-century writers whether men or women is complicated by difficulty identifying their work. As these cryptic initials show, neither Hays's nor Wollstonecraft's reviews are an exception. Editors and proprietors of periodicals believed that anonymity facilitated objectivity; that is, a reviewer was presumed to be less tempted to amend criticism of a friend or colleague's work when the author reviewed could not identify who wrote the article. Contributor embarrassment over writing for money played a part as well. Moreover, in the case of these particular reviewers, anonymity would also protect both them and the periodical's proprietor from imputations that the publication was compromised because it employed women, who were presumed to lack the analytical abilities necessary to criticism. In the proportionately few cases where periodical contributors were identified, it was usually by pseudonym or by initials that often bore no relation to the writer's real name. This practice prevailed at the *Analytical Review*. At first few reviews were signed at all, but Johnson soon settled on printing at least some articles signed with the initials of a pseudonym. Nevertheless, a fair degree of agreement has been reached over which *Analytical* articles can be attributed to Wollstonecraft.[65] The same principles can be followed to identify contributions by Hays.

The article on *A Gossip's Story*, published so soon after Wollstonecraft asked Hays to review the novel, has by now been accepted as authored by Hays.[66] The heavily subordinated and elaborately balanced sentence structure, quite different from Wollstonecraft's own writing, matches the characteristics of Hays's expository prose. Moreover, in its first sentence the review begins a defense of the social value of novels by affirming that "the most effectual method of giving instruction, is by interesting the imagination and engaging the affections." Some months later Hays published a critical essay defending the novel in the *Monthly Magazine*. There she used nearly the same words, arguing that "The business of familiar narrative should be [...] to interest the imagination, exercise the affections, and awaken the powers of the mind."[67] These ideas are not unique to Hays, but the remarkably similar phrasing along with an appeal to critical values based in sensibility together reinforce the documentary evidence provided by the letter to suggest that Hays is probably the author of this review.

The *Gossip's Story* article marks the first time the "V. V." signature appears in the *Analytical Review*, suggesting that it is probably Hays's first contribution to that periodical. Evidently Wollstonecraft had read some of Hays's reviews in other periodicals, for her letter counsels Hays on avoiding certain habitual reviewer errors that once again reflect Hays's failure, in Wollstonecraft's opinion, to take her audience adequately into account. She tells Hays,

> In reviewing, will you pardon me? you seem to run into an errour which I have laboured to cure in myself: you allude to things in the work which can only be understood by those who have read it, instead of, by a short summary of the contents, or an account of the incident on which the interest turns, enabling a person to have a clear idea of the book, which they have never heard of before.[68]

Wollstonecraft's comment is not only clear and specific, but, unlike her response to the preface to *Letters and Essays*, penned several years earlier when Wollstonecraft barely knew Hays, the remarks here are considerately phrased, especially since Wollstonecraft's own reviews show no such "errours" even from the first. While her first advice to

Hays might well be thought an attempt to discourage Hays, Wollstonecraft here obviously intended to encourage her. No longer dismissive, she assumes responsibility for guiding Hays's professional development. The letter's conclusion implies that this review is the first occasion when Hays's literary work fell under Wollstonecraft's direction, suggesting both that Hays's work at the *Analytical* depended on Wollstonecraft's facilitation and that Hays answered to Wollstonecraft, not Johnson. The *Gossip's Story* review appeared in the *Analytical* immediately following a signed review by Wollstonecraft, as though Wollstonecraft had submitted it packaged with her own contributions for that month.[69] Yet unlike most of Wollstonecraft's own reviews of similar length, it contains no summary or character description, no extracts, no notion of either the plot of the novel or the overall quality of its execution. Instead, it concentrates on the novelist's avowal of her instructional intent. It shows the same characteristics, then, that Wollstonecraft had objected to in Hays's prior reviews. Yet Wollstonecraft apparently felt sufficiently satisfied with Hays work. Another letter, written around the same time, mentions sending her other material to review.[70]

No signed reviews by either woman appear of the following three numbers, but in May, the month featuring her last signed contributions, Wollstonecraft reviewed a travel volume and a few novels. Immediately following Wollstonecraft's own last signed novel review, the section ends with a novel review signed "V.V.," the signature Hays used. Not only is this review marked like its predecessor by the elaborately subordinated style characteristic of Hays, but it includes comments that can be fully understood only by someone who has already read the novel – again, precisely the weakness that Wollstonecraft nudged Hays to address. Hays's "V.V." signature appears next in July following a series of three novel reviews, the two unsigned of the series, though too short to offer conclusive evidence, containing enough stylistic and content similarities to Hays's previous and subsequent signed reviews to suggest that she probably authored all three. After another interval of several months, a pause that the death of Wollstonecraft, her closest friend, easily explains, Hays's signature accompanies a series of three novel reviews in February 1798. The style and content of the first two unsigned reviews suggest that another writer may have authored them, but the last in the series, the signed review, shows traits consistent with Hays's other signed work. After this issue, Hays's "V.V." continues as the only signature in the 'Novels' section through May of that year, and in these subsequent issues all reviews including the unsigned ones show enough similarities to Hays's known work to suggest that for this period Hays probably had the full responsibility for the periodical's commentary on novels. Indeed, the unsigned review leading the "Novels" section for April alludes to Wollstonecraft's posthumously published *Wrongs of Woman*, which had just appeared the previous January. This sort of prompt tribute to her much admired friend is precisely what one might expect from Hays at the time. It appears that for a few months, Hays was probably the *Analytical*'s only novel reviewer. In view of Johnson's practice of assigning departments, it seems likely that Hays assumed editorship of the "Novels" department during these months.

Hays ceased writing for the *Analytical* just before Johnson, who had been indicted the previous January, was tried on 17 July for selling Gilbert Wakefield's "seditious" publication *A Reply to Some Parts of the Bishop of Llandaff's Address to the People of Great Britain* (1798). Though Johnson was not sentenced until the following February nor imprisoned until some months after that, an issue of the *Analytical Review* was introduced as evidence at the sentencing hearing, presumably to show his insurrectionary leanings.[71] Meanwhile, William Gifford's *Anti-Jacobin Review* targeted the *Analytical Review* as perfidious and its reviewers as incompetent. The climate had grown more hostile as well for women writers who, like Hays, had associated themselves with radical causes. Having witnessed several friends imprisoned after the treason trials of 1794, Hays probably saw the writing on the wall and shied away from Johnson's most notorious publications while political animosities ran so dangerously high.

Like Wollstonecraft, Hays grounded her criticism in the ideology of sensibility. In "On Novel Writing," her only known literary theory publication, she argues for realistic character development as the best means of creating this salutary sympathy. As did Wollstonecraft, whose own literary essay had appeared only a few months before, Hays returns to Johnson's *Rambler* No. 4, in her case taking exception to Johnson's dictum that novels should contain only characters displaying ideal virtue.[72] She questions, "In fitting beings for human society, why should we seek to deceive them, by illusive representations of life? – Why should we not rather paint it as it really exists, mingled with imperfection, and discolored by passion?" Rather than requiring novels to meet strict moral criteria, she reasons "It is not necessary that we should be able to deduce from a novel, a formal and didactic moral; it is sufficient if it has a tendency to raise the mind by elevated sentimens [sic], to warm the heart with generous affections, to enlarge our views, or to increase our stock of useful knowledge." Her reviews in the *Analytical* hold consistently to these principles, criticizing improbability and praising plot and characterization that create sympathy and "interest."

Though good frank advice and a few months income from the *Analytical Review* would be much to a struggling woman writer, Hays may have owed even more to Wollstonecraft. Hays and Johnson had been distantly acquainted for some years, but Hays's literary contacts with this publisher had taken place through Wollstonecraft. Her *Analytical* reviews were the first of her work that Johnson published. When Wollstonecraft left for France, Hays had to find other sources of literary work. Hays's connection with bookseller George Robinson illustrates the complexity that could characterize the relationship between a woman writer and her publisher. Robinson was proprietor of the *Critical Review* when Hays began writing for it, and within a year or so after Hays first contributed to his literary journal, Robinson became Hays's publisher, issuing her first novel, *Memoirs of Emma Courtney* (1796). Similarly, after Hays established a professional relationship with Johnson through her *Analytical Review* contributions, she was able to follow it up on her own even after Wollstonecraft's death. Johnson became her publisher for her next two books, and she continued to publish with him intermittently through 1808, the year before Johnson himself died. In fact, she produced *Harry Clinton; or a Tale of Youth* (1804), consisting of excerpts from *The Fool of Quality* (1765–70), Henry Brooke's successful novel of sensibility, at Johnson's request. Moreover, Johnson was the friend, mentor, and close business associate of Richard Phillips. Hays contributed several articles to Phillips's *Monthly Magazine*, a production that Johnson helped produce and sold at his bookshop. Yet a contribution in March 1797 suggests that at that time Hays did not know Phillips, but instead submitted unsolicited letters, a format that made a fair portion of this publication's content.[73] Hays's last contribution to Phillips's periodical, however, suggests a growing relationship with Phillips. The article, an obituary of Wollstonecraft, appeared not as an unsolicited letter, but as part of the editorial content in the September number for the same year.[74] Soon after, Phillips commissioned from Hays another article on Wollstonecraft for his *Annual Necrology for 1797–1798* (1800). As Johnson's deteriorating health and increasingly disorganized business practices were beginning to affect his ventures, Hays's essays on Wollstonecraft led to further work with Phillips. Most significantly, he commissioned *Female Biography: or Memoirs of Illustrious and Celebrated*

Women of All Ages and Countries (1803), Hays's most ambitious work and, with *Memoirs of Emma Courtney*, that for which she was best remembered well into the nineteenth century.[75] The project itself provided Hays with an important source of income, and was later to lead to her last substantial literary effort, *Memoirs of Queens Illustrious and Celebrated* (1821), commissioned to capitalize on the popular furor over the Queen Caroline affair. Johnson, whose reliance on Hays had begun with the work that Wollstonecraft assigned her, almost certainly facilitated Hays's initial contacts with Phillips. In the years after Wollstonecraft and Johnson had both died and her relationship with Phillips had cooled, Hays often found herself in pinched circumstances, unsuccessfully seeking literary work.[76] Both directly and indirectly, then, Wollstonecraft seems to have offered a significant boost to Hays's literary career.

Most Wollstonecraft scholarship to date has neglected her commissioned literary work in favor of concentrating on her two *Vindications*, her letters from Scandinavia, and her unfinished novel *The Wrongs of Woman* (1798). Yet this work, especially her periodical literary reviewing, proves important on several counts. Unlike her better-known publications, each of which can reflect only a part of her literary career, Wollstonecraft's "hack" writing – that is, her work as a staff writer for Joseph Johnson, the late-eighteenth century's most respected bookseller – spans virtually her entire writing career. Her articles for the *Analytical Review* provide a record of her reading, reading that facilitated rapid intellectual growth, the course of which the reviews allow a glimpse. The reviews show as well that Wollstonecraft was conscious of their potential for public influence, and that she sometimes used them to subtly shape reader opinion, including on issues of gender. Further, in contrast to the unpaid apprenticeships facing most women novelists, this often-disparaged contract writing provided Wollstonecraft with a stable income, allowing her to leave the tenuous vocation of teaching girls and devote herself entirely to literary work. With the income from reviewing to rely on, she authored several books, including the *Vindication of the Rights of Woman*, one of the most exciting and controversial publications of the 1790s. It may be that the anonymity of literary reviewing, by liberating her from the constrictions on feminine literary forms and the presumed limitations of a female audience, opened the way for the evolution of her views on the ungendered nature of reason. Certainly the commissioned work resulted in administrative and professional responsibilities that were unusual for a woman in her day. The ensuing years would offer women increasingly varied roles in the literary public sphere, especially in the fields of editing and literary journalism. Wollstonecraft's work at the *Analytical Review* offers a window onto these changes as they first began to take shape. Her new responsibilities then positioned her to provide professional advice and even publication opportunities to another woman writer – our most striking early example of professional mentoring of a woman by a woman in the English literary world. In a literary culture shifting itself to address a broad audience for the first time, the focus of that mentoring shows consciousness of the textual presentation of self, clear views on what sort of self a female author should present, and a realistic assessment of the obstacles that gender conventions imposed on the woman writer.

4
Periodicals and Middle-Class Dissent: Anna Letitia Barbauld and Elizabeth Moody at the *Monthly Review*

The preceding chapter demonstrates the professionalism of both Mary Wollstonecraft and Mary Hays and situates them in a lively and supportive community that encouraged their intellectual development and offered them opportunities to turn writing into a source of much needed financial support. Anna Letitia Barbauld too seems to have felt the pinched circumstances that plagued the English middle classes, especially during the inflationary war years of the late eighteenth and early nineteenth centuries. Although by this time women frequently turned to writing to supplement their incomes, criticism for a well known literary review remained by and large the province of men. Barbauld enjoyed an early ascent to literary fame, but like Wollstonecraft, she worked for a time as an educator before turning to writing for her income. And for Barbauld, too, literary criticism proved crucial. For Wollstonecraft, however, criticism became not merely a reliable source of financial support. Rather, it brought her into the literary marketplace in ways unprecedented for a woman. Similarly, while the earnings criticism offered were surely most welcome, Barbauld too found more than just income in writing criticism.

Chapter 1 establishes that Barbauld, British Romanticism's most important woman literary critic, came by means of her essay criticism to speak from a position of prominence and authority on issues of national importance. The years preceding the British Victorian era present few opportunities to examine the work of a professional woman literary critic, and among those that can be identified Barbauld stands out for the quantity, range, and professionalism of her critical work. This chapter will turn to her work as a literary reviewer. For over seven years Barbauld reviewed books and pamphlets for *The Monthly Review*, Britain's first modern literary review and for half a century its most prestigious. She authored hundreds of articles, all of them published in the *Monthly Review*'s Monthly Catalogue or Foreign Catalogue, both sections devoted exclusively to brief reviews. These Catalogue contributions are precisely the type of brief criticism that most scholars have dismissed out of hand, yet they offer a rare glimpse of a woman writer's role in one of the most professional forms of Romantic-era literary work. Examination of Barbauld's periodical criticism reveals not just a broader, more nuanced picture of her views about literature and writing, though that is much. Barbauld's literary journalism offers insights into the culture of literary production and marketing during the early nineteenth century and the role of a woman writer in that culture. It demonstrates Barbauld's authority and confidence as a highly educated and respected writer, and her conviction that reviewing even minor works provides an important service for a society in which literacy and print production were expanding at an extraordinary rate. Barbauld's reviews demonstrate the changes in aesthetic values that facilitated the evolution of a British national literary canon and they show how these new values were disseminated not only in prestigious landmark publications, but broadly in the briefest and most obscure literary commentary. Her Catalogue articles reveal signs of the shifts taking place in reviewing standards from an ideal of objectivity to an expectation that reviews would evaluate – a shift that contributed to twentieth-century underrating of these articles. Her reviewing practice counters prejudices in favor of literary amateurism, prejudices that Romantic-era writers were actively revising. It reveals instead a journalistic professionalism that disproves many preconceptions that have blocked understanding of the function of these short articles and opens the way to a reassessment of what literary reviews reveal about the changes taking place in literary culture. Barbauld's contributions to the *Monthly Review* document her own professionalism and authority as a critic. That authority emerged from a collaborative notion of literary production that is both intertextual and interpersonal, and that is grounded in the culture of Rational Dissent, a community that played a highly influential role in the late eighteenth- and early nineteenth-century publishing industry.

A few decades ago scholarship began in earnest to question the view that Romantic literature can best be understood through the figure of the solitary poetic genius. Among those arguing for a revised definition, Jack Stillinger documents that the real compositional practices of prominent Romantic writers show literary production to be collaborative, with even those texts most associated with isolated consciousness revealing the presence of multiple hands in the final product. Barbauld's literary work springs from Dissenting middle class culture, a culture which, as Davidoff and Hall have shown, emphasized collaborative enterprise as its key to commercial success. Study of Barbauld's work for the *Monthly Review*, a Dissenter owned periodical, shows that collaboration and mutual support figured in her understanding of the purpose of literary reviews and brought her to a form of literary work still very unusual for a woman. That this support and collaboration was culturally specific is reinforced by the career trajectory of Elizabeth Moody. Daughter of an affluent lawyer, Moody remained a coterie poet until marriage to a Dissenting clergyman brought her out of the fashionable world of the Anglican establishment and into the middle-class culture of Rational Dissent. Like those of Barbauld, Elizabeth Moody's literary reviews show the marks of their cooperative origin, lending us a fresh perspective from which to reassess both the status of reviewing and practices of literary production during the early Romantic period.

The *Monthly Review* was Britain's first modern literary review – that is, the first periodical exclusively devoted to informing the public about a broad range of new publications. Ralph Griffiths, a young, recently established bookseller, founded the *Monthly Review* in May 1749 and retained sole editorial control for more than 50 years. A Dissenter in religion and a Whig in his politics, Griffiths felt that advocating these views in his review was consistent with the high editorial standards he set for it. He assembled a staff of experts who discussed work appropriate to their specialties, and to ensure impartial treatment of all publications, he concealed the identity of reviewers not only from the public, but from each other as well. Moreover, no reviewer could review the work of a known enemy or friend, and unsolicited reviews were declined because they were likely to be prompted by bias.

For a few years, the *Monthly Review* remained the only publication of its kind, until in 1756 the *Critical Review*, a Tory-leaning rival adopting a number of the *Monthly Review*'s editorial practices, emerged under the editorship of Tobias Smollett. Yet even as challengers became more numerous toward the end of the century, no review could equal the *Monthly Review*'s sales or prestige until after Ralph Griffiths' death in 1803, when his son, George Edward Griffiths took over as editor, a position he held until 1825. The son is generally regarded as less competent and more irascible than his father, and is held much to blame for the *Monthly Review*'s displacement during the early nineteenth century by the new style reviews led by the *Edinburgh Review* that moved lively or even bellicose debate and emphasis on the reviewer's opinion to the fore in extended treatments of only a limited number of new works in each issue. The *Monthly Review*'s more complete and objective coverage retained its appeal for many, however; it survived with a few changes in editorship through 1844.[1]

When Griffiths first set the goal of complete and objective coverage, he fused two purposes that had governed early eighteenth-century commentary on literature. The *Monthly Review* found its immediate antecedents in the learned journals that first appeared during the late seventeenth century on one hand and literary magazines and periodical essays such as Addison's *Spectator* on the other. Pitched to an educated, elite audience, the learned journals sought encyclopedic coverage of selective and specialized publications while often explicitly barring discussion of imaginative literature. They insisted on objective treatment of their material through summary and extract, and on an elevated tone. By contrast, the literary periodicals appealed as much to the middle as the upper classes as a polite source of entertainment partly by including the discussion of poetry and fiction that was excluded from the learned journals. These literary periodicals often featured a section at the back announcing new publications, sometimes accompanied by a brief "puff" by the bookseller or his agent, and rival periodicals competed for the most complete coverage in this list.[2] Thus, when Griffiths established his new review, objective coverage of virtually the entire literary market formed part of his goal.[3] He proposed that the new periodical would "register all the new Things in general, without exceptions to any, on account of their lowness of rank, or price."[4] As rivals appeared, they took up the same challenge. The *Critical Review*, for example, opened its first number by declaring its intention "to exhibit a succinct plan of every performance."[5] Meanwhile, the considerable summary and extract that makes up articles in both these early reviews testifies to the conviction that this was the path to truly objective treatment.

The goal of universal coverage was never fully attained, and even from the first Griffiths was forced to revert occasionally to the older practice of relegating a few works to mere publication announcements in the back pages. Soon, however, shorter treatment of some minor or mediocre works made it possible to give full consideration to the more important, innovative, or interesting publications while neglecting little outside the most technical literature in specialized fields. The briefer articles were collected at the back in a "Monthly Catalogue," a section so reminiscent of the old publication lists that mere announcements were sometimes interspersed with reviews of only a paragraph or two in length. But by the early nineteenth century when Barbauld joined the *Monthly Review*'s staff, the climate of periodical reviewing had changed substantially. New periodicals were springing up, and the field had become much more competitive. As the sheer volume of new books and pamphlets increased, the goal of universal coverage became increasingly difficult even to approximate. Innovative new reviews like the *Edinburgh Review* and its most important rival, the *Quarterly Review*, soon responded to the proliferation especially of novels and poetry by dropping the ambition of complete coverage altogether, reverting to the practice of regularly appending a substantial list simply announcing new publications. The older, more established reviews like the *Monthly Review* and the *Critical Review* were eventually forced to conform to a similar format, but they managed to retain the program of encyclopedic coverage for many years partly by relegating most works of imaginative literature, not just the mediocre ones, to the brief articles of the Monthly Catalogues. The main articles sections around this time featured 10 or 12 longer treatments (approximately the same quantity as the total number of articles usual in the *Edinburgh Review* during the same years) ranging from four or five to 20 or so pages, and dominated by learned works in the sciences, philosophy, theology, and the like. While the *Critical Review* still often featured one novel in the main articles, only rarely by this time did a novel review appear among the *Monthly Review*'s main articles, and although most issues did include a main article on poetry, it was usually of a kind appealing to an elite – and emphatically male – audience, such as translations from the learned languages or original works by peers or university men. The Catalogues had meanwhile become quite substantial, containing at times upwards of 30 articles ranging in length from a few sentences to a few pages, organized into categories, and discussing not just "light" or imaginative literature, but works on such varied subjects as history, sermons, biography, natural history, music, the slave trade, education, prostitution, and the question of paper money.

Given their size and their ambitious goals, late eighteenth-century and Romantic-era literary reviews such as the *Monthly Review* have received surprisingly little close scrutiny. In general, reviews tend to be dismissed as "hack" work done by the poorly qualified and wretchedly paid cast-offs from the world of letters, who combine extensive excerpts from the work reviewed with short sections of bookseller "puffery" or with partisan rehearsals of political or personal vendettas to create articles with virtually no value as criticism.[6] And if reviews have fared poorly with literary scholarship, the Catalogues have been especially deprecated, dismissed even by those sympathetic to longer reviews. Roper, for example, normally sympathetic to reviews, declares that "In the Catalogues, dealing for the most part with cheap fiction to which 'canons of imaginative art' could not seriously be applied, reviewers often did little more than separate the harmless from the possibly harmful."[7] Yet the *Monthly Review* was a popular and prestigious publication conforming to the high standards of an exacting editorial program. Catalogues evolved as a way to better meet that program. By the time Barbauld began writing for the *Monthly Review* Catalogues, those sections of brief articles had expanded to address a considerable share of new publications in a competitive market. The effort required a large and well qualified staff of reviewers. The *Monthly Review*'s Catalogues are valuable for the light they can shed on the practice of reviewing and on the transition from a literary culture based in patronage to a professional one. That they offer a rare occasion to see one of the Romantic era's most remarkable woman writers engaged in some of the most professionalized literary work available at the time only adds to the Catalogues' importance.

As Chapter 1 shows, when Barbauld first turned to professional literary criticism she was a mature writer of proven range and depth and tremendous popularity. Her career as a critic began in 1794 when, already a renowned poet herself, she introduced an edition of Akenside's *The Pleasures of Imagination* with an original critical preface. Over the next decade and a half, her work as a critic and editor not only resulted in expanding critical responsibilities, but merits notice today for its usefulness and insights. A few years after the Akenside edition, Barbauld again authored a critical preface, this time to William Collins' *Poetical Works* (1797). This essay places Barbauld as noteworthy among Collins's early critics. Barbauld also accepted editing work, resulting in the 1804 publication of *Selections from the* Spectator, *the* Tatler, *the* Guardian, *and the* Freeholder and *The Correspondence of Samuel Richardson*, both prefaced with her critical essays. The introduction to the periodical papers offered a strong argument for the cultural significance of a literary form that had been regarded simply as entertainment. The Richardson collection remained the standard edition of Richardson's letters through much of the twentieth century, while its critical introduction established Richardson as an exemplary British author and has been credited with inaugurating the study of narratology. Finally in 1810, the 50-volume series *The British Novelists*, a collection of 25 full text novels that stands as a landmark in establishing a canon of British novels, features "On the Origin and Progress of Novel-Writing," Barbauld's introductory essay tracing the history and cultural significance of prose fiction, along with her critical biography of each of the novelists whose work finds a place in the collection. Barbauld's editing and signed essay criticism represent a remarkable body of work, one that shows her turning away from earlier eighteenth-century upper-class models of literary production and merit to concentrate on promotion of middle-class writers and middle-class values. In doing so, she creates a place in the literary canon for that quintessentially middle class, quotidian, often feminine literary genre, the novel. But during these same years, while she was exploring in those essays a variety of concerns, some expressly literary, others more broadly cultural, she also began to contribute anonymous reviews to various literary periodicals. If we couple the outline of her essay criticism with Barbauld's known periodical reviewing, a picture emerges of a literary professional whose career as a critic spans two decades and who saw her criticism as having considerable public impact.

As was the case with Wollstonecraft's work for the *Analytical Review*, Barbauld's periodical criticism presents difficulties to identification, only some of which can be surmounted. Partly to encourage objectivity and partly to protect reviewers from embarrassment, reviews were normally published anonymously, and like the *Analytical*, the *Monthly Review* conformed to this practice. Identification of Barbauld's reviews is further complicated by lack of a modern biography and by the destruction of a store of her papers in the bombing of London during World War II.[8] Nevertheless, though the individual reviews in the *Monthly Magazine* cannot be identified, Barbauld contributed at least some fiction reviews between 1796 and 1806, while her brother, John Aikin was literary editor. During 1798 she contributed reviews to the *Analytical Review*, edited by Joseph Johnson, Barbauld's good friend and often her publisher as well. Barbauld wrote for the Belles-Lettres section in the early volumes of her nephew Arthur Aikin's *Annual Review*, founded 1802, reviewing Scott's *Lay of the Last Minstrel* among other works. She was almost surely one of the "various members of his own family" whom, according to Thomas Rees, John Aikin employed as a contributor when he founded the *Athenæum* in 1807. The published letters between Barbauld and Maria Edgeworth indicate that she placed at least one piece of criticism in the *Gentleman's Magazine* in 1809 or early 1810, and was probably contributing to other periodicals as well.[9] And finally, she contributed short brief reviews on a variety of genres to the Monthly Catalogue section of the *Monthly Review* from July 1809 until at least October 1815, when a change in the editor's method of tracking contributions makes identification of further reviews impossible. As this summary of her known work indicates, at roughly the same time as she began her editing and essay criticism Barbauld also embarked on a career of periodical literary criticism that continued relatively uninterrupted for the next 20 years.

When Barbauld began reviewing for the *Monthly Review* Catalogues, she was already, at age 66, a mature writer with an established literary reputation stretching back more than three decades. Originally joining the staff as a novel reviewer, she soon expanded to reviews of poetry, plays, memoirs, collections of essays and letters, children's literature, conduct books, educational materials teaching a variety of subjects, French and Italian literature, translations, and travel writing. Though she contributed only to the Catalogue, she quickly took on importance in that section, so that within a few months of her first article she had authored the entire collection of poetry, novel, and educational reviews in some Catalogues, sometimes authoring the entire Foreign Catalog as well. It was only the rare monthly number that included none of her Catalogue reviews.

Barbauld's voluminous *Monthly Review* contributions reveal that, contrary to prejudices held ever since the first reviews, even reviewers responsible for the briefest articles were professionals in the best sense of the word. As a reviewer in the *Monthly Review*'s Catalogue sections, Barbauld was surrounded by colleagues who numbered among the most highly educated and respected individuals in the kingdom. Though regular woman reviewers were rare, Barbauld held the same professional status at the *Monthly Review* as her male counterparts: like them she received assigned work on the basis of expertise, and, like them, she took her role as critic seriously. Constituting by far the largest portion of her writing during her later years, these reviews help make visible the contours of literary professionalism, especially as it affected women writers. Meanwhile, Barbauld's work for the *Monthly Review* provides a window onto a rarely studied form of criticism.

Barbauld's credentials in the fields she reviewed not only attest to her own qualifications, but confirm as well the expertise of *Monthly Review* Catalogue reviewers. When Barbauld began reviewing novels for the *Monthly Review*, she was in the midst of work on *The British Novelists*, a landmark project that required a full history of prose fiction and extensive novel criticism. She was an accomplished poet and essayist, and had written criticism on both genres to accompany her collections and editions. She had been an educator for many years and had developed innovative educational materials and written some of the eighteenth century's most enduringly popular children's literature. Though a woman Dissenter, she had benefited from informal access to exceptional educational opportunities and had attained a level of learning unusual for anyone at the time, man or woman. Her background in French and Italian was particularly strong, and her reviews demonstrate that expertise. She not only reviewed work in both French and Italian, but offered detailed critiques of the quality of translations from those languages and evaluated the accuracy of instructional materials designed to teach them as well. And she had already demonstrated her competence as a reviewer with contributions to several other respected literary reviews.[10]

If Barbauld's own qualifications were above question, those of her counterparts were equally strong. As a regular contributor to the *Monthly Review*'s Catalogue, Barbauld was in the company not of a stable of semi-literate drones, but rather of a group of respected literary professionals such as William Enfield, a former Warrington tutor in belles-lettres whose enduringly popular *Speaker* (1774) served as the model for Barbauld's own *Female Speaker* (1811), John Aikin, Barbauld's brother, both a physician and a prolific literary man who edited a number of periodicals and authored several biographical and historical series, Abraham Rees, mathematician, philosopher, Dissenting clergyman, and editor of *The New Cyclopædia* (1802–20), the *Encyclopædia Britannica*'s only serious competitor for many decades, and William Taylor of Norwich. Taylor, a former pupil of Barbauld and her husband at their school at Palgrave and the most esteemed Germanist of his day, was one of the period's most prolific and respected reviewers, authoring just short of 1,800 known reviews during his career. His commentary in the *Monthly Review* introduced German literature to the Romantic-era British reading public and, according to Benjamin Christie Nangle, was consequently "among the most important and influential to appear during this period." William Hazlitt further credited him with introducing the innovative reviewing style that was to later make the *Edinburgh Review* the preeminent literary review for many years.[11] These few examples only begin to suggest the extent to which even for its Catalogue articles the *Monthly Review* drew upon a capable staff of esteemed literary professionals.

For Barbauld as much as for her male colleagues, it was this solid expertise that determined reviewing assignments. The extent of Barbauld's contributions on novels, poetry, and educational materials could raise speculation that she was "ghettoized" in the Catalogue to genres appropriate to women writers but beneath the dignity of men, yet the evidence reveals a far different picture. Every genre that Barbauld reviewed, including novels and poetry by women, was also reviewed in the same Catalogues by respected professional men. Though she often handled all the Education reviews, for example, it is hardly surprising that C. E. Schwabe, German clergyman and later German tutor to the Princess Victoria, and James Manning, Jr., a barrister with proficiency in Spanish and Portuguese, were brought in to review instructional materials for German and Spanish, languages of which Barbauld knew little. Clergyman and Welsh antiquarian William Rees reviewed the same sorts of French instructional works that Barbauld herself reviewed, at times even in the same issues. Similarly, Barbauld sometimes discussed conduct literature and fiction side by side with Dissenting clergyman Christopher Lake Moody, a hardworking writer and editor who not only operated his own periodical but was also among the *Monthly*'s most productive reviewers. Though novels seem to have been one of her particular provinces, Barbauld shared space in Catalogue "Novels" sections with contributors such as barrister Thomas Denman, her former pupil and the man credited with authoring the 1832 Reform Bill, surgeon Thomas Ogle, who for a time served as surgeon to the Prince Regent, Francis Hodgson, a fellow at King's College, Cambridge and a prolific reviewer not only at the *Monthly* but at the *Critical Review* and the *Quarterly Review* as well, and George Edward Griffiths, the *Monthly*'s editor at the time. Hodgson also reviewed poetry alongside Barbauld, as did Griffiths, Rees, and commercial agent Joseph Lowe. Indeed, Moody reviewed every type of literary production that Barbauld also reviewed, often in the same monthly number.

By the same token, many of the works Barbauld discussed, works such as travel literature, the letters of literary men, and conduct literature for boys, would fall outside the stereotypical purview of the woman writer. They would, on the other hand, benefit from the expertise of someone like Barbauld herself, experienced traveler, former operator of a boys' school, and editor of one of the period's most significant collections of literary letters. Then too, the anonymity of review articles even among the periodical's other reviewing staff meant that the editor need fear no discredit to his publication for assigning a woman work outside preconceived limits on female competence. Barbauld was assigned volumes for review on the basis of her talents and experience rather than gender considerations. Like the eminence of many of her male colleagues, Barbauld's expertise in every field she reviewed calls into question statements that reviews, even the brief contributions to the Catalogues, were the work of unqualified hacks who took whatever came their way.

In the face of such powerful evidence that *Monthly Review* Catalogue reviews were for the most part the work of experts, one cannot help asking why they have been so unanimously dismissed. The answer may in part lie with the brevity of these articles. Mark Parker has recently observed that although the single essay literary periodicals of the early eighteenth century have long garnered scholarly interest, late eighteenth- and early nineteenth-century literary periodicals, rather than receiving attention in and of themselves, tend to be treated "largely as an archive from which scholars draw evidence to use in other arguments," especially reception studies of individual authors. Even Parker himself, who argues that "literary magazines should be an object of study in their own right," turns away from purely review periodicals to examine a number of more broadly conceived literary magazines.[12] If review articles have been valued mostly as a mine for evidence about reception, the brief, rarely indexed Catalogue articles yield proportionately little harvest for the work involved in their retrieval. As the questions driving literary research evolve, however, these articles may have more to offer to these new lines of inquiry. For one, Catalogues have a unique role to play in the social and cultural changes ascribed to literary journalism precisely because they tend to be the section where less prestigious literary publications were featured. Since many of the novels, minor poetry, elegant extracts, and popular sermons that made the stock of circulating libraries and reading rooms would have been reviewed in the Catalogues, the survival of many volumes of popular literature may be a result of a Catalogue review. Furthermore, despite some notable exceptions especially among novelists and poets, women writers tended to fall to the margins of the kind of professionalism that now claims the attention of Romantic-era literary studies. If literary journalism carried significant influence, it is surely important to try to discover where women writers practiced it professionally, and to examine that practice in detail. And as Barbauld's work for the *Monthly Review* shows, it is a good bet that the less prominent section of the review is a promising place to look for work by the marginalized professional reviewer.

But twentieth-century disparagement of the Catalogue review may also arise in part from eighteenth- and nineteenth-century complaints about them, at least some of which were clearly conventional posturing the type that often comprised the prefatory remarks in new novels and poetry. A case in point is a review of J. Amphlett's *Ned Bentley*, one Barbauld's first articles in the *Monthly Review*. Barbauld remarks with good-natured irony on the author's prefatory grumbling over the relegation of his work to the "slovenly monthly catalogues." "Judging of others from himself," Barbauld observes,

> he affirms that "a novel writer enters the list of authors with his mind made up to receive every species of ill-usage, like an ill-used ass by the road side, who screws up his hide in expectation of receiving a blow from every person who goes near him." After this humble though sturdy declaration, Mr. Amphlett proceeds to avow that he is "content if his work be allowed to class among the least exceptionable ones of its kind;" and we shall proceed to inquire how far it may claim such a character.

Barbauld's review of this novel is a brief but complete treatment including a balanced and specific assessment of plot, characterization, style, and moral. Her greatest objection is to its contradictions and improbabilities:

> We see a boy, who had been brought up as a servant till his seventeenth birth-day, suddenly emerging from the kitchen, well acquainted with living manners and dead languages: we meet with a barber gifted with similar gentility and acumen; and we are introduced to another footman, who had not even virtue and the classics to recommend him, but who, after having attempted various robberies and murders, marries a gentlewoman who is acquainted with his history.

If this description is accurate, the novel certainly offers much fuel for skepticism. The article ends, however, noting the novel's strengths, including attention to realism in most characterizations, a spirited style, "interesting" description, and "affecting and natural" emotional scenes.[13] Though amusing and brief, the review can hardly be classified as "slovenly," nor can it be considered a dismissal. Considering that in another article on the same page Barbauld observes, "we consider the want of probability as a fault much more deserving of toleration, and more susceptible of amendment, than the want of spirit or interest," her final assessment of *Ned Bentley* seems quite positive.[14] Certainly not all reviewers see their task in the same light, nor would any one reviewer, Barbauld included, give equal treatment to every publication.

Amphlett's anticipation of ill usage is, however, so attractively quotable that Barbauld herself was unable to resist. It would hardly be surprising if similar passages exerted a lasting influence on scholarly perceptions of Catalogue reviews, especially if at times they issued from the pens of widely respected authors.

If recent scholarship has uncritically accepted eighteenth- and nineteenth-century author complaints about the quality of literary reviews, it has also been guilty of too lightly falling into accord with prejudices that emerged from the aristocratic culture of literary amateurism, the same prejudices that, as I argued in my introduction, Romantic-era authors themselves were contesting and revising. Arising from publication practices based on coterie circulation and patronage and from literary values that emphasized classical forerunners, these biases dissociated the possibility of literary merit from remuneration and the contemporary marketplace. Put simply, that which was written for money could never be good. Yet Edward Copeland documents that during the inflationary decades ending the eighteenth and beginning the nineteenth centuries, no woman, not even one such as Fanny Burney, who commanded a truly exceptional price for some works, was able to earn a "genteel competence" from novel writing alone.[15] Presumably male novelists and most poets of both sexes experienced similar economic pressures. While other motivations also played a role, the careers of many respected male literary figures, both poets and novelists – Goldsmith, Scott, Southey, and many others – show that they wrote criticism primarily for the remuneration it could bring them. As Samuel Johnson once said, "No man but a blockhead ever wrote, except for money."[16] Contrary to prejudices both then and now, remuneration and literary quality were not mutually exclusive.

Financial pressures do seem to have induced Barbauld to write criticism. Though little is known of her personal pecuniary circumstances, her brother, John Aikin, the heir presumptive to whatever competency Barbauld's father may have been able to provide, himself turned critic to relieve the monetary pressures that hounded him over the years. Driven repeatedly to Yarmouth in the hope of expanding his medical practice, then back again to London to escape provincial religious discrimination, and finally forced to retire from medicine due to weak health, finances so pressed him at one point that he sighed, "I seriously fear that it will become a country in which a man of moderate resources and with a family to provide for, *cannot live*, and then what will it signify debating about our constitution?"[17] Always a man with serious literary interests, Aikin turned to his pen in order to supplement his narrow income, becoming a prolific writer with numerous volumes of history, biography, and moral essays as well as many reviews and the editorship of several literary periodicals to his credit. Yet, though forced into the literary marketplace by necessity, he found a community in its middle-class, professional character. Unlike his fashionable London medical clientele, the same letter continues, "My *booksellers* will never expect me to visit them in my chariot." Barbauld is, of course, not her brother, but her lifelong engagement in remunerative work, whether teaching or writing, suggests that she was no more financially independent than he was. In fact, she began a demanding schedule of reviewing for the *Monthly Review* when in her mid-sixties, a time when most people who are free to do so consider reducing their labors. Still, reviewing for pay no more implies that the reviewing must necessarily be shoddy than teaching for pay inevitably attests to poor instruction. Barbauld's reviews help bring under scrutiny facile assumptions about the quality of paid literary work.

One of the standards by which recent scholarship has judged periodical criticism – and found it wanting – is the proportion of an essay devoted to summary and extracts as compared to criticism.[18] Normally reviewers were paid according to the quantity of writing they provided, and scholars have often assumed that summaries and extracts served as padding, allowing reviewers to increase their earnings without more work. But it was not until the second quarter of the nineteenth century, partly as a response to some of the innovations introduced by new publications such as the *Edinburgh Review* during the first quarter of the century, that readers and reviewers took it for granted that evaluation should be a part of a review article.[19] Before then reviewers generally saw their task as one of accurately informing the reader of the nature and content of a work, primarily through summary and extract. Yet if evaluation did not become a standard element of literary reviews until some years later, Barbauld's Catalogue reviews offer a window onto the shift in that direction. Looking at the body of Barbauld's work for the *Monthly*, one is struck by the high proportion of evaluative commentary. When discussing prose work, Barbauld may include short quotes by means of illustration, but only rarely does she extract at length. When reviewing poetry, she normally extracts only from the better work, and only at a length sufficient to give the reader an impression of the texture of the verse. What is more, she never relies on summary as a substitute for criticism.

Almost all of Barbauld's articles include explicitly evaluative commentary, and in those cases where she includes only a summary, that summary implicitly contains value judgments. For example, Barbauld opens one of her earlier reviews with "In treating of some works, description answers all the purposes of animadversion." She follows with an outline of the novel's plot, which indeed can only be described as absurd, marred with implausibilities and overworked devices expressed in trite and conventional language. The review describes an improbably innocent hero being drawn by irresistibly lovely singing through the forest to the lonely cottage of the innocent and inexplicably elegant and refined heroine and her mother. "After having passed through the usual routine of dangers and discoveries, the lady and gentleman have the comfort of being happily married, and of seeing their enemies punished: but, at last the heroine turns out to be an Italian countess!" There is no mistaking the nature of Barbauld's objections to this novel – it is the reliance on a conventional formula, unbelievable in itself but all the more objectionable because of its overuse. She ends the review with a comment that implicitly criticizes romantic fiction in general for failures in two areas that consistently claim her attention – probability and originality:

> These tinsel coronets multiply on us so fast, that we have sometimes resolved to read no novel which does not give a circumstantial account of the heroine's birth and parentage in the first chapter; because, where this is wanting, we read in constant dread of her overwhelming us in her last moments with a mass of uninteresting evidence to prove that she is a countess in her own right.[20]

Though the review consists in little more than a brief summary with a few sample quotations, it succeeds nevertheless in conveying unmistakable value judgments, and any fiction writer would have done well to heed the implicit advice it contains.

Even Barbauld's shortest reviews, some of which consist of only one or two sentences, evaluate, though in such cases that evaluation necessarily remains at the most general level. When she has more room to expand, as in reviews of a page or more in length, Barbauld provides a full, comprehensive treatment. Reviews of narrative works include discussion of plot and characterization. Barbauld prefers realism, though she allows flexibility in genres such as Gothic novels, folk tales and ballads, imitations of the Ossian works or of Elizabethan verse romances, and the like. Historical fiction, on the other hand, which she disapproves of generally for its "mixture of truth and fiction," she holds to a particularly strict standard of realism.[21] Poetry reviews include remarks on the imagery, metaphors, diction, and versification, while prose works are evaluated for diction, style, and grammar. Where appropriate, reviews include comments on the moral value of the work, an important consideration to most critics at the time, especially if the work was intended for the young or poorly educated. Almost all include an evaluation of how well the work is likely to serve its intended purpose, whether that purpose be education, moral improvement, persuasion, or sheer amusement. Although the constraints of length force her to offer general remarks on some aspects of almost any work she reviews, in the longer reviews Barbauld includes specific examples of the qualities that prompt at least one or two of her assessments – a few lines, for example, from a poem whose versification she commends or censures, an "inelegant" prose phrase or two, a description of an "affecting" plot incident, a historical inaccuracy.

The thoroughness of Barbauld's Catalogue articles despite space restrictions and the extent of her commitment to evaluation would suggest that she took her task as a reviewer seriously, that as opposed to seeing herself as a mere drudge separating the harmless from the harmful, she saw herself as a professional performing an important service. Nor, apparently, did pecuniary considerations supersede for her the work of real criticism. Barbauld's articles convey their information in a compact form, containing somewhat fewer and shorter extracts than the reviews by many of her counterparts, so that on the whole they tend to be shorter than the work of most of the other reviewers in the same sections – so much so that it is sometimes daunting to grasp how many volumes she would have had to familiarize herself with in order to provide her well over 300 reviews. The demands of the professional reviewing schedule may perhaps explain why not all of her Catalogue articles feature a uniformly professional tone. Barbauld surely must have felt time pressure in turning out the number of commentaries she did, and in later years may have begun to feel rather exhausted in the bargain. Such a possibility seems to animate her groan over yet another preface offering excuses for the publication's flaws: "Perhaps scarcely any work can be found which will not *admit* of an apology, but we sigh for such as require none." Again in a later review, she verbally flings the book down in exasperation: "Really," the review opens, "this novel is almost beneath criticism."[22] Consistency in tone may have demanded more attention to each article than Barbauld was at times able to give, and perhaps it is here, rather than in superficial treatment and heavy padding with excerpts that, at least in Barbauld's case, the demands on prolific

Catalogue reviewers begin to show their effects. Nevertheless, her overall commitment to evaluation indicates that she accepted a definition of review that was progressive for the context within which she worked, one that would take at least another decade or two before it became widely accepted as standard.

If Barbauld saw accurate and thorough assessment of new publications as valuable to the reading public, her reviews prove that she understood her criticism to be serving another constituency as well. Amphlett's "humble though sturdy" *Ned Bentley* preface did not get his novel promoted out of the "slovenly monthly catalogues," but it does point to the attention that authors paid reviews. By the time Barbauld was writing for the *Monthly Review*, even major writers not only read reviews and addressed prefaces and postscripts to reviewers, but they had begun as well to revise their works in response to reviews, and review editors accepted responsibility for steering these revisions by means of their publications.[23] In arguing that current myths of Romantic literature as the production of solitary genius need to be replaced by an account of the collaboration that routinely went into literary composition, Stillinger points to the intervention of agents, editors, transcribers, and printers, among others, all of whom contributed to the final form of published literary texts. Barbauld's *Monthly Review* contributions help illuminate just how deeply this sort of literary collaboration reached, for they show that even Catalogue reviewers had their part to play.

Many of Barbauld's reviews show that she viewed this interchange between writer and reviewer as not incidental, but central to her responsibilities as a reviewer. As an experienced educator, Barbauld would have special expertise in judging the promise of young writers. She comments at times on a writer's potential, even occasionally recommending intellectual preparation to improve future works. She recommends, for example, that Felicia Dorothea Browne, who published a volume of poems written between the ages of eight and thirteen, "content herself for some years with reading instead of writing," after which "we should open any future work from her pen with an expectation of pleasure." Browne later became the early nineteenth century's most successful woman poet under her better known married name, Felicia Hemans. Barbauld questions, on the other hand, whether even with "time and study" John F. M. Dovaston's "compositions would rise above mediocrity." Or, she will mention possible improvements to the work, especially those that might be implemented without substantial revision. A case in point is *History of France*, which, though serviceable as it stands for purposes of instruction, would be improved as a book of reference by the addition of an alphabetical index.[24] She also on occasion mentions when reviewing a second edition that the writer has revised flaws that she or another reviewer had pointed out as being present in the first edition. In 1809, for instance, she reviewed the *Poems* of William Hersee, a sort of rural prodigy whose work showed promise despite a few ridiculous poetic contradictions that Barbauld quotes. When in 1811 she has occasion to look at *Poems, Rural and Domestic* by the same author, she notes that many of the poems appeared in the original volume, but "The lines which then appeared to call for censure are now altered and improved."[25] Concluding one especially thorough review, in which she censures such weaknesses as incidents that excessively violate probability and the disappearance of characters that played a conspicuous part early in the work, Barbauld remarks: "We should not have dwelt so largely on the defects of this tale, if we had not been still more struck with its merit; [...] We have read Faulconstein Forest with pleasure; and we look forward to the future productions of the author as a source of amusement which, we hope, will be refined but not checked by animadversions."[26]

Even pointing out printing or grammar and usage errors, which one might at first glance attribute to tedious overnicety, turns out on closer inspection to offer support for a collaborative view of literary production. Especially in the case of instructional materials, the periodical review serves as an extension of the text's notations of errata. Barbauld offers her corrections because, as she says in the case of one French language style guide, left uncorrected, the errors "may mislead." At other times, her detailed objections show that she has possible revisions in mind. She lists, for example, a number of class marking usage errors in one volume of poetry because these expressions "should be corrected, if an opportunity be afforded by a second edition of the work."[27] Barbauld sometimes regards the occasion of the review as an opportunity to educate the writer, to offer suggestions or guidance geared not toward the work at hand, but toward the improvement of the writer's future productions. At other times, Barbauld's reviews show that she regards even published work as in progress and subject to a process of revision in which she or other reviewers take an active and constructive part. Basker has suggested that authorial responses to these sorts of corrections were a sign that "Review critics [...] were quietly editing the text of eighteenth-century literature."[28] Barbauld regarded this function as so important that in some cases it makes up the greater part of a short Catalogue article.

Barbauld's confidence, her apparent conviction in the value of her commentary, and her forward-thinking definition of a literary review all suggest that she felt a degree of certainty over both her position and her own judgment that might surprise, given what we know about the position of women writers during the late eighteenth and early nineteenth centuries. She surely derived self-assurance from her solid qualifications, but that self-assurance also arose from the very nature of the review periodical itself, and especially from the specific periodicals to which Barbauld contributed, periodicals founded and conducted from within the Dissenting community, a circle of which Barbauld had long been a respected member, and which had in the cases of Hays and Wollstonecraft among others already proved itself to be generally encouraging to the professional woman writer.

Eighteenth- and early nineteenth-century middle-class Dissenters formed a close knit, politically active and intellectually vigorous community wherein social relationships merged into professional ones. Perhaps the best known example of these connections would be the dinners at the home of the radical Dissenting publisher Joseph Johnson, where a formidable list of the day's literary, artistic, and political figures, including Barbauld herself, gathered to participate in lively conversation and stimulating arguments and to make contacts that proved both personally and professionally instrumental. Daniel E. White demonstrates that Barbauld's early literary publications materialize out of a familial collaboration that was characteristic of the Dissenting community surrounding the esteemed Warrington Academy, where Barbauld's father served as tutor, and where Barbauld herself resided from 1758–74, forming life-long friendships with a number of tutors and students.[29] In Chapter 1 I outlined the intellectual and social circle that sprang up around Warrington Academy and extended into London. White is certainly correct so far as he goes, but Davidoff and Hall's research reveals that collaborative production and communal enterprise was characteristic not just of the circumscribed community that existed around Warrington in the 1760s and 1770s, but among Dissenters as a group, and indeed among the English middle class as a whole, for most of the late eighteenth and early nineteenth centuries.[30] While Barbauld's early publications provide White with a lens through which to study the dynamics of familial collaboration in the publication of her early poems and essays, her periodical reviews help reveal these same dynamics on a much larger scale, where they lent support to woman writers engaged in literary work of a kind still dominated by men.

Barbauld's niece, Lucy Aikin, offers a model of Dissenting familial collaboration in her account of what she calls her father's "social and communicative habits of study." It was John Aikin's habit, Lucy Aikin affirms,

> never to commit a single page to the printer without causing it to be previously read aloud by one of his family in his own presence, and in that of any other members of the domestic circle who could be conveniently assembled. During these readings he listened with close attention, often mentioning the alterations which then suggested themselves to his mind, or the new ideas which struck him; and not only permitted, but invited and encouraged, the freest strictures even from the youngest and most unskilful [sic] of those whom he was pleased to call his *household critics*.[31]

Similarly, Barbauld had circulated her poetry among the members of the Warrington circle, and her first poetic publications came in response to encouragement from that community, and especially from her brother John. It was in a joint publication with that same brother that her first criticism, "On Romances," appeared. And it was he who later exhorted her to return to writing when her absorption in teaching and issues of education distracted her from it. White correctly describes the collective nature of Barbauld's early career. But these early partnerships take on additional interest when Barbauld's periodical reviewing is studied because here, too, we see that collaboration is crucial.

In every known instance of Barbauld's periodical literary reviewing, John Aikin and often other members of the family contributed to the periodical. And in all cases, if the periodical itself was not a family project, as, for example, the *Athenæum* or the *Annual Review*, it was operated by another Dissenter and it employed numerous Dissenting contributors from among Barbauld's family and friends. Barbauld began her reviewing career at a journal edited by her brother. From there she moved on, under the wing of that same brother, to her first contributions to a periodical devoted exclusively to reviews, the *Analytical Review*, edited by Johnson, Barbauld's own publisher and friend, and an editor known to have encouraged the careers of women writers like Mary Wollstonecraft and Mary Hays by employing them at the same review. Contributions to other periodicals operated by her brother and her nephew followed. At a time when the woman periodical reviewer was an exception, Barbauld's career in periodical criticism advanced along a trajectory marked out by family alliances and friendship, culminating in her regular contributions to the *Monthly Review*, a Dissenter operated periodical drawing a number of its contributors from among Barbauld's family and friends, including many former members of the Warrington circle.

It would be possible to argue that the values of middle-class Dissenting culture that emphasized collaborative production and familial models of commercial enterprise were coincidental to Barbauld's reviewing career or that they were idiosyncratic, with no explanatory value outside Barbauld's special case, were it not for confirmation of this model revealed in the reviewing career of Elizabeth Moody, the only other woman during this period to regularly contribute to the *Monthly Review*. A close contemporary of Barbauld and one of the earliest known women periodical reviewers, Moody is of interest on those grounds alone. Moody contributed to the *Monthly Review* between 1789 and 1808, her work there ending a little less than a year before Barbauld began to write for the periodical, thus suggesting that perhaps the editor of this prestigious publication had come to value having a woman on staff.[32] But Moody also provides a pivotal example of the contrast between the upper-class literary amateurism that had characterized much of women's literary production, especially their commentary on literature, prior to the last few decades of the eighteenth century and the emerging forms of literary professionalism that marked the Romantic era. As was the case with Barbauld, Moody's engagement on the staff of a prestigious literary review is supported by the middle-class culture of religious Dissent. In Moody's case, it was the move away from fashionable literary circles into the culture of middle-class Dissent that launched her from private circulation of her writing to publication. Further, like Barbauld's, Moody's reviews show the kind of familial collaboration typical of the economic enterprises of the Dissenting middle class which, when the family enterprise was literary, brought some women into varieties of literary work from which they were still usually barred.[33]

Born in 1737 to a family affluent enough to afford a large house in the fashionable suburb of Kingston upon Thames, Elizabeth Greenly was raised in a region that was, as Jan Wellington phrases it, a "hot-bed of wit and art." Little has been discovered of her education beyond what can be deduced on the basis of her sex, her family's status, and the evidence provided in her poems and essays, but she is known to have devoted much time to English, French, and Italian literature, and to have achieved unusual fluency in French and Italian. Her father passed away when she was thirteen, leaving his wife and each of his daughters rather modest legacies for a wealthy lawyer. Still, as long as her mother lived and retained, as was customary, the use of the family home, Elizabeth remained "comfortably, if not extravagantly, provided for."[34] Under the guardianship of her uncle, she enjoyed the diversions of the London season, but she remained unmarried. Meanwhile, she became part of a fashionable circle of literary correspondents that included poet Edward Lovibond and literary dilettante George Hardinge, and in that circle she began the private circulation of her aesthetic observations and verse that served as her only form of literary publication for many years. Finally in 1777, after the death of her mother, Elizabeth Greenly, now aged 40, married the 23 year old Dissenting clergyman, Christopher Lake Moody.

According to Wellington, the Moody marriage appears to have been a truly companionate one, both parties sharing lively wit and a love of literature and criticism, but Christopher Moody's income and social standing were beneath what Elizabeth had been accustomed to, and the couple were often strapped for cash. Dr. Moody did, however, possess "a keen appreciation for the marketplace of letters."[35] He became one of the most prolific contributors to the Dissenter-operated *Monthly Review*, and purchased a share of the profitable *St. James's Chronicle*, a periodical without an explicitly Dissenting focus, but sympathetic nonetheless to contributions championing Dissenter legal rights and the Dissenting point of view. Publisher Ralph Griffiths, himself a Dissenter, had a share in both periodicals, and the connection Moody formed with Griffiths at the *Chronicle* probably brought him over to the *Monthly* staff as well. Rapidly becoming one of the most important contributors to both journals, Dr. Moody apparently encouraged his wife to publish in the *Chronicle*, and her verse and epistolary contributions soon became such an important feature of that journal that it marketed her as one of its selling points, touting the "Muse of Surbiton" (Elizabeth Greenly's home town) as resident poet. Wellington is of the opinion that the couple's personal acquaintance with many of the *Chronicle*'s readers and contributors made this venue a sort of middle ground for Elizabeth Moody between the coterie circulation that she had been accustomed to, and the public exposure that a wider print audience inevitably involved. Moody published in a variety of genres – poetry, open letters on literary and social topics, and literary reviews – and, Wellington believes, her work at *St. James's Chronicle* may have extended into other forms of literary occupation such as editing. In late 1789, presumably in consequence of her husband's already strong connection to the journal, Elizabeth Moody too began contributing reviews of poetry, fiction, and educational literature to the *Monthly Review*.

Like Barbauld's, Elizabeth Moody's *Monthly* reviewing practice shows characteristic marks of the middle-class family enterprise. Though she had circulated her writing for many years, Moody first began to publish when she joined the ranks of the Dissenting middle class. The need to augment the family income had some bearing on her decision to go public. Moreover, her publications appeared in venues owned and operated partly by family and friends, who encouraged and supported her appearance before the public. And like those of Barbauld, Moody's reviews at the *Monthly* reveal signs of collaborative authorship.

Four of Elizabeth Moody's 29 reviews were co-authored, one with Ralph Griffiths, two with Griffiths's son George Griffiths, who took over as editor and proprietor after the elder Griffiths's death, and one with her husband, Christopher Moody.[36] To Moody's discussion of certain objections to *The Denial* by James Thomson, Ralph Griffith's adds two paragraphs, one consisting of numerous examples, with page number citations, of the objectionable practices, and the other an additional objection to the manner in which Thomson refers to characters holding the rank of peers. George Griffiths adds a rather thin one sentence witticism to conclude the review of *Les Souvenirs de Felicie L****. To her review of *Lettres de Mademoiselle De Launai* he appends a biographical table of significant French women of letters copied from the volume under review, as well as the sentence with which the article concludes. And, according to the editor's notations of authorship, the review of Marmontel's *Noveaux Contes Moraux* was fully co-written by Moody and her husband.

A skeptic might argue that such collaboration served as a necessary corrective to the inexpert work of a woman reviewer. A number of Barbauld's reviews, after all, feature similar insertions authored by the younger Griffiths. In reality, however, both Griffithses were in the habit not only of authoring occasional articles on their own, but of adding to articles authored by both their male and female staff as well. In one example, George Griffiths co-authored a review by William Taylor of Norwich, one of the principal reviewers on the *Monthly* staff.[37] Taylor had not long before rejoined the *Monthly* staff after a long absence precipitated by a tiff with Griffiths over editorial autonomy. Griffiths' addition to Taylor's review shows both that even reviews by an expert such as Taylor could sometimes represent a collaborative effort and that Griffiths believed that, despite their strained relationship, Taylor would be unlikely to regard such additions as untoward interference. The fact that Taylor continued reviewing after this date indicates that Griffiths was probably correct.

Because Moody contributed a limited number of reviews, only modest evidence is available of her expertise. Still, like Barbauld, she commented mainly on genres falling within her areas of exceptional competency. Her unusually high attainments in French and Italian meant that besides discussing the quality of translation in English renderings of French and Italian works, a number of her reviews examine untranslated works in those two languages. In fact, her first review evaluated an epic imitation of Milton in Italian. The article appeared among that monthly number's main articles, a status that for whatever reason none of Barbauld's contributions ever attained.[38] Possibly it was Moody's unusual qualifications as an established poet who could also boast exceptional skill in Italian that made Griffiths take the unusual step of employing a woman critic in the first place. On the other hand, Griffiths seems to have extended his notion of Moody's expertise from poetry and fiction in French and Italian into educational materials in those languages as well. Barbauld too was soon to handle many of the educational works treated in the *Monthly Review*, especially those published in or teaching French or Italian. But Barbauld was professionally qualified to review educational material; she had not only raised her nephew, whom she and her husband had adopted, but she drew as well upon an expertise gained through long years of experience in teaching and authoring educational materials and literature for children. Moody, on the other hand, had no childrearing, teaching, or relevant authorship experience. It is sobering to realize that despite his willingness to take the unorthodox step of employing women reviewers, Griffiths may still have fallen prey to stereotypes that prompted him to regard Moody as qualified in educational and children's works simply because she was a woman.

Wellington offers a thorough account of the contents of Moody's individual reviews, eliminating the need for the same ground to be retrodden here. She explores Moody's own relatively ornate prose, her preference for realism, her deft reshaping of the standard summary so as to convey opinion and evaluation. She appreciates Moody's "persistent, fine-tuned irony," and cites a few instances when Moody turns that irony on her own "critical cross-dressing," her position as a woman writing anonymously in a genre almost exclusively dominated by men. As Wellington observes, Moody explicitly identifies herself with "the harder sex, as men, and of a still harder *race as critics*." In a particularly amusing instance of playing with the masculinity to which her position as critic usually would attest, Moody follows a description of a gothic ghost with an avowal that "though familiarized very much, lately, to these apparitions, we did not feel inclined to go to bed, till we had puffed away the recollection of this spectre in a whiff of tobacco, and re-animated our fleeting spirits by a double draught of old October." Clearly Wellington is on the mark when she affirms that Moody "revelled in a persona that allowed her to be what women of her time decidedly weren't."[39]

Moody's irony offers one ground for comparing her reviews with those of Barbauld. Like Moody, Barbauld often takes an ironic tone, indicating that both critics assume a degree of sophistication on the part of their readers. In one early example, she observes that reminding herself of the author's Shakespearean epigraph, "Lend thy *serious* hearing \ To what I shall unfold," served her as her "only defence against the risibility which was excited by various passages that seem intended to be sublime."[40] In Moody's work, however, the irony is often much sharper, more satirical in tone. In one instance, she remarks of a tale translated from French, "The author had probably some meaning; and intended to illustrate some moral, in this poem: but our dulness [sic] is at a loss to discover either." Then in response to the translator's hope, expressed in conventional words of modesty, that his own part in the production might not fall short of the original, Moody says of the translation itself, "It is with pleasure that we assure this *humble* copyist, that we think full *as well* of his translation as we do of the *original*."[41] Though not all of her reviews are dominated by irony, Moody tends to hold more consistently to an urbane, ironic voice throughout her essays, while Barbauld offers only a mild, amusingly ironic remark or two in the course of some articles. Barbauld's far more demanding reviewing schedule may partly explain this difference; she had no time to give each review the attention required to craft consistently amusing essays. The contrast may reflect a difference in the two critics' sense of purpose as well; Moody seems more committed to entertainment than Barbauld, whose essays inform first, and only secondarily amuse. Moreover, Moody's irony serves as the vehicle for her masculine critical persona, the means of performing her masquerade. Barbauld does not indulge in the same kind of performance. She does at times refer to female authors as "the fair" writer or author, but other than the slight distancing effect of this epithet, she generally shuns devices that would mark her reviews as the work of either a male or female writer. With no need to enlist irony in the aid of gender performance, Barbauld can be much more flexible about when to draw upon it.

A further ground for comparing the *Monthly Review*'s two women critics can be found in their attitudes on national character. Both Barbauld and Moody possess language skills that enable them to comment on foreign literature, especially work from France. Wellington registers but devotes only minimal attention to what she describes as Moody's "vehement patriotism."[42] As that phrase would lead us to expect, Moody's remarks on national character are often more extreme than those of Barbauld. In Chapter 1 we found that Barbauld's essay criticism develops a comprehensive understanding of national character, one too extensive to be replicated in the diffuse format of short periodical reviews. Still, a few aspects of Barbauld's attitude toward these issues can here be extrapolated from her reviews.

To begin with, these articles do reaffirm that Barbauld believes in the existence of national character. She censures, for example, one French travel fiction because "No difference of national character is perceptible; the *dramatis personæ* are all French; a Persian fair one acts and writes like a French coquette, [...]." As the comment indicates, she partakes of a comparatively mild version of common British anti-French stereotypes. Cumulatively, her reviews portray French character as shallow and prone to flirtation or gallantry, often irrational and prejudiced, and at times sexually frank to the point of indelicacy. One French novel offends by "the slanders which it conveys against the English nation; as when it accuses us (Vol. i. p. 190) of 'fighting dishonourably,' and (p. 214.) of 'ill treating prisoners of war.'" Another novelist "offers [his] work as a picture of French society, and its English readers may rejoice that it bears little resemblance to the manners of their country." Other national groups fare similarly; Italian poets are characterized by a "melancholy and morbid sensibility," while German writers tend to be obscure.[43]

Yet unlike Moody, Barbauld cautions that national differences can be overplayed. The disparity between the customs of one country and those of another, she explains,

> may, perhaps, be made to account to us for a poor painter's inviting the Rector Schulten to spend the rest of his life with him, on the first day of their acquaintance; as also for the ready acceptance of this invitation, and the fluency with which the Rector talks Greek to ladies and *valets de chambre*: but the impulse of parental affection is the same in Germany as in England; and in neither country

would a father, on first learning that his son nourishes a hopeless passion, amuse himself with "taking his picture in the character of Antiochus, languishing for Stratonice."[44]

Whatever their culture, she implies, human beings possess certain natural impulses in common, and it would be a mistake for either reviewer or reader to take for evidence of national difference what is mere foolishness on the part of the writer. The first few lines here are surely to be read as ironic – though she knows too little of, for instance, German education to be sure, Barbauld certainly no more believes that German women and servants routinely possess fluency in Greek than she believes in a nation of unnatural fathers. She does, however, believe in a certain competency on the part of her *Monthly Review* audience. The unexplained reference to Antiochus and Stratonice implies that she expects her readers to be at least familiar with the classical legends, if not with their original language.

Though we can, on occasion, find remarks on the characters of other nations, Barbauld's reviews offer few direct statements on the nature of Britishness. We must extrapolate her views on British character based on its contrast with the defects of other nations. For example, the narrator of the French tales of Persian travels "displays an excess of complaisance in the disposal of his heart, which is difficult for an English reader to imagine."[45] Throughout Barbauld's reviews British national character seems to consist in whatever contrasts with French gallantry, coquetry, shallowness of feeling, and sexual nonchalance, Italian morbidity, and German intellectual murkiness and emotional excess. What emerges most clearly about Britishness, then, is its moderated but deeply sincere emotional integrity. Such a picture is not surprising considering the views on national character unfolded in Barbauld's longer essays. Sincerity and moderation, especially in the realm of feeling, is entirely consistent with her description of true Britishness as domestic and middle class.

Like those of Barbauld, Moody's ideas on national character are dispersed in scattered remarks throughout her essays. Her references to issues regarding national character consist mostly of allusions to what she variously denominates "the commotions of Paris" or the horror inspiring "revolutionary tragedies." In a few instances, however, her remarks extend beyond recent events to assert more generally the existence of intrinsic differences between national groups. "French and English *Nature* differs," she affirms in one review, "and the author is acquainted only with the former; – whom we consider as a degenerate goddess." This degeneracy consists, we find a few years later, in "refined and romantic sentiments of prudery, truly *French, and extremely artificial and unnatural.*" These "French" sentiments characterize a novel depicting, according to Moody, French divorce law as little more than the legal discarding of mistresses by men whose epicurean sexual tastes prompt them when sated with one woman to supplant her with another. Moody's disgust with this legalized concubinage is unmistakable. "Of all the absurd and capricious institutions," she seethes, "which France, under either her old or her new *Regime*, has dignified by the name of *Law*, the modern divorce claims the pre-eminence for cruelty and injustice." What is more, Moody views not only the morals and laws but even the language and poetics of the French as degenerate compared to English. When a French anthologist offers a cosmopolitan collection of love scenes from Homer, Virgil, Tasso, Ariosto, Camoens, and Milton, Moody praises his efforts until "he sets foot on the hallowed ground of the most sublime of our English bards." Comparing the original English with the "masquerade dress" of the French translation, Moody declares that the translator, "from not understanding the majestic march of our blank verse, is unable to perceive the ludicrous effect produced by the change into paltry diminutive rhiming [sic] couplets."[46]

Both Linda Colley and Gerald Newman have shown that British nationalism and the idea of a British nation grew out of self-definitions of Britishness as opposed to the "other" of foreign cultures, cultures that manifested what, as far as the English were concerned, British character was not.[47] Partly because of almost constant warfare between the two nations and partly in response to French cultural hegemony, especially among the British upper classes, it was France more than any other nation that served as the paradigm for all that was not British. But both Moody and Barbauld were deeply grounded in Dissenting middle-class culture. Though neither enjoyed close ties with its most radical members, they were part of the same circle of literary, scholarly and artistic innovators that encompassed both the Warrington group and Joseph Johnson's circle in London, the same circle that had proven sympathetic to France during the early years following the Revolution. Moreover, these reviews were written for the *Monthly Review*. The *Monthly* was not quite so forward thinking as *The Analytical Review*, for which Barbauld also wrote, but then it was a far more prestigious periodical with a much longer history. Of the reviews that could claim a stature approaching that of the *Monthly*, none were more consistently progressive.[48] It is true that except for Moody's observation about "commotions," the comments by both writers date after the September massacres, when opinions in even the most sympathetic circles began to shift. In fact, most of Moody's and all of Barbauld's commentaries appeared after several long years of Napoleonic imperialism had made the democratic ideals of the Revolution's early days seem far distant. Yet only recently in her longer essays, Barbauld had expressed her ideas of British character over and against not the French, but rather the aristocracy and upper class of England itself. Both writers' remarks on national, and especially French character sound casual, as though they were commonly agreed upon. Indeed, their very brevity and sporadic appearance seems to suggest that neither author deemed them in need of defense or explanation. In her extended criticism, Barbauld framed her notions of British character so that the culture that supported her and made her literary efforts possible became the very pattern of true Britishness. Yet the *Monthly* reviews show that nationalism expressed in anti-French terms had by that time become so ingrained in even progressive literary culture that both writers allow it to slip into their writing almost unaware.

And what of Antiochus and Stratonice? In her longer essay criticism, Barbauld had evolved her ideals of British middle-class domesticity partly through the rejection of an exclusive, learned, upper-class alternative. Yet her reviews show other signs that she imagined a highly literate reader. Along with similar classical references, they contain numerous allusions to and quotations from Italian and French poets, especially Dante, and from Alexander Pope, who was soon to become the touchstone for a cosmopolitan Augustan literary canon that many of the foremost Romantic critics and poets wished to replace with a nationalistic, exclusively British literary history.[49] The *Monthly Review* was one of the few, and by far the most prestigious, of literary periodicals that at the time Barbauld contributed still conceived of themselves "as instalments of a continuous encyclopaedia, recording the advance of knowledge in every field of human enterprise."[50] Such a program presumes a large audience among scholars, professionals, civic and commercial leaders, the whole of educated Britons. Further, although in her essay criticism Barbauld turns away from the clubby world of the Anglican university, her own middle-class culture of Rational Dissent was by no means an unlearned one. Dissenter schools were often better than those of the Anglican establishment, and many Dissenters ranked among the leading intellectuals of their day. Without benefit of formal matriculation at a school, Barbauld had flourished within that culture to attain a level of learning that was nearly comparable to that of an Oxbridge graduate. As in her history of the novel in "On the Origin and Progress of Novel-Writing," Barbauld looks at literature through a cosmopolitan lens. While her reviews show her rejecting certain aspects of French character as expressed in their literature, she sees no need for literary parochialism as a foundation for patriotism. Rather, a cosmopolitan understanding of literary history and theory provides Barbauld in both her critical essays and her reviews with a broader measure with which to gauge British literary achievement.

As Marilyn Butler points out, "Literature, like all art, like language, is a collective activity, powerfully conditioned by social forces."[51] In particular, the periodical literary review began as a collaborative enterprise by nature. Publishing reviews without identifying signatures and using the corporate "we" as the first person pronoun instead of the "I" of individual self-representation, review editors expected contributors to conform to a corporate opinion that would be uniform throughout the review as a whole. Since the editor was therefore by implication responsible for all opinions expressed, it is not surprising that as a rule the better reviews employed writers of talent and expertise. Meanwhile, writing as part of a collective authoritative voice lent the individual reviewer influence and prestige. At a time when women writers were only beginning to enter the field of literary journalism as professionals, Barbauld's contributions to the Catalogues of the *Monthly Review* provided her with opportunities to speak with authority on issues of literary taste, one of the most dynamic and contested subjects of her day. Her reviews show that, like her colleagues, Barbauld was assigned work on the basis of her expertise, and she regarded the work as serving a worthwhile purpose for both the reading public and the authors whose work she reviewed. The specifics of her reviewing practice add evidence to our understanding of the function of reviews, particularly the rarely studied Catalogue reviews. Barbauld's Catalogue contributions help illuminate a composition and publishing practice that was in its essence recursive, intertextual, and public, with the reviewer contributing to a text's final form. Her reviews offer early examples of the shift from eighteenth-century ideals of objective treatment in reviews to the subjective evaluations that came to define reviewing during the nineteenth century and after. Her contributions to the *Monthly Review* Catalogue offer a window on some of the specific contours of Romantic-era journalistic professionalism, especially as it pertains to women writers. Those "slovenly monthly catalogues" have proven worthy of a second look.

5
The Next Generation: Harriet Martineau's Literary Reviews for the *Monthly Repository*

When Mary Wollstonecraft called herself "the first of a new genus," she probably did not yet see the shape the new classification would take. Yet her metaphor fits in more ways than one. Not only did Wollstonecraft represent a departure from past limitations on women's participation in the literary profession, but she exemplified a "first" that was soon followed by a "second" and a "third," new members of the species emerging singly at first, but by the early 1830s, the period that traditionally marks the beginning of the Victorian age, in increasing numbers. In her introduction to a special issue of *Victorian Periodicals Review* devoted to women contributors, D. J. Trela affirms that from the 1830s onward, some time before George Eliot's significant role in the *Westminster Review*, increasing numbers of women worked as editors and critics. Trela argues that while Eliot's contribution has been used "to allege that it is only the exceptional woman who could break into and successfully dominate periodical literature and fiction, the scores of less prominent but nonetheless successful women who were able to earn a living writing and editing are more important in demonstrating a pattern that became more prominent as the Victorian age advanced."[1] The early reviewing of one of these women writers, Harriet Martineau, illuminates features of women's participation in the culture of criticism between the end of Barbauld's known reviewing and the first years of the Victorian era when the period of interest to Trela and her colleagues begins. It shows how periodical journalism, including literary reviewing, could open doors to other professional literary work. It offers illustrations of the radical shift in review content and format during the same period. Moreover, Martineau was the leading contributor to the *Monthly Repository* during the time that it transformed itself from a Unitarian to a secular periodical. Martineau thus played a prominent role in the shift among Unitarians from a religious based to a secular vision of social reform. Study of her early reviewing sheds light on the world of women's periodical work and the place of that work in wider British culture.

This chapter examines Martineau's development during the third decade of the nineteenth century from an amateur to a professional writer. During these years, the shifts that took place in periodical journalism were substantial. Not only did women journalists become more numerous, making possible both Trela's claims and the other studies featured in her issue devoted to women, but the content and format of literary reviews changed substantially as well. The first literary review editors saw their purpose as that of providing an accurate impression of a book and so strove for objectivity and inclusive coverage. Reviewers may have departed from this standard, but as Thomas Christie's announcement for his new *Analytical Review* indicates, such departures were to be regretted, not cultivated. By the time Martineau began reviewing, however, reviews more commonly served as a starting point for a full length article on the topic that the book reviewed. As the book became less frequently the sole focus of reviews, the line between reviews and other types of expository articles began to blur. Meanwhile, flamboyant controversy, no longer something to be avoided, became instead a tool to spark reader interest and increase sales. We will mark some of these changes in Martineau's own review articles. These changes also opened new prospects for Martineau, possibilities that had been unavailable to the previous women critics. Martineau, like most women contributors to miscellanies like the *Monthly Repository*, continued to publish poetry, fiction, and occasionally reviews. But while her reviews began to more closely resemble philosophical and social commentary, she wrote independent articles on those topics as well, without the pretext of a book to be discussed. Thus, although this chapter will concentrate on her reviews when discussing content, it is not possible in her case to consider the development of her reviewing career or the cultural context that made her early reviewing possible while still regarding her reviews as completely separate from her other journalism.

Martineau's professional literary work emerges from the same Dissenting middle-class culture that had supported the work of so many other writers studied here. As was the case for her predecessors, the collaborative, supportive practices of that culture proved crucial to Martineau's early career, both facilitating her intellectual growth and assisting her in turning writing into her profession. Martineau shares with her earlier counterparts an interest in a writer's relationship to her audience, and she develops this issue a few steps further than had the women reviewers who preceded her. Further, Martineau's first literary articles draw on the conviction that private sensibility as the true foundation for public virtue must constitute the core of British national character. Yet during the first decade of her literary work, the decade in which she matured from a prize-winning amateur to literary professional, Martineau's literary reviews show some new features as well. Martineau began with a reviewing format that had already begun to shift away from summary and extract, the format that had derived from the mission to provide, in Butler's words, "a lucid and careful account of a book's contents."[2] Before her first decade of reviewing was over, Martineau had adopted the form of literary article that had made the *Edinburgh Review* such a formidable rival to the long-established monthlies. At the same time, her specifically Protestant views of public virtue and national character gave way to a commitment to secular reform grounded in Utilitarianism, the same shift that characterized so much public policy discourse during the early years of the Victorian age.

One characteristic of the careers of the women critics we have examined so far is the personal and professional support that enabled their work. These writers broke through strong prejudices about both what sorts of writing were appropriate for women and what sorts of writers could make creditable critics. It in no way detracts from their achievement – rather, it helps illuminate the extent and importance of that achievement – to recognize that it depended on a circle of friends, acquaintances, and sometimes family who, themselves literary professionals, could encourage the woman critic's intellectual growth, assist her with contacts in the profession, and provide outlets for her critical work. What is perhaps surprising, however, is that for all of the women we have studied here, it is the same circle that furnishes this support. Some of these women critics – Barbauld, for instance – were themselves Dissenters. Others, like Inchbald, were Catholic, or, like Wollstonecraft, Hays, and, at least during her younger years, Elizabeth Moody, Anglicans. A few hailed from the most marginal ranks of the lower middle classes, as did Wollstonecraft, while others, like Moody, grew up in families that ranked among the fashionable. Their political views differed as well, the radical politics of Wollstonecraft contrasting sharply with the anti-French patriotism of Moody, while Inchbald held a more skeptical view of nationalism and national character. Yet despite their differences, all found themselves part of the same progressive, even at its most extreme Jacobin, circle. This circle, consisting largely but not exclusively of middle-class Unitarians, tied the Norwich Dissenting community to probably the most important part of the London publishing industry in a vibrant, encouraging, and often collaborative society of artistic and intellectual creativity. The literary reviews to which these women contributed were owned and operated by Dissenters or by men sympathetic to the Dissenting point of view. These reviews were regarded as forward thinking, and they played an important role in introducing new ideas – new scientific thinking, diverse points of view in religious and political debates, experiments by British writers in new forms and aesthetics, foreign literature – to the English public. The volumes that featured essays by these women critics issued from publishers who, affiliated with the same congers, shared business interests and often personal friendships as well. Among these women's social and business contacts, the same names recur. In fact, each of the writers featured so far knew personally at least one of the others. And in most cases, we can trace how the community facilitated the entry of the woman writer into the profession of literary criticism – an opportunity acceptable to each of these women because of financial pressures that made the remuneration that professional criticism could offer most welcome.

By the end of the Napoleonic wars, the approximate time that we lose track of Barbauld's contributions to the *Monthly Review*, the two decades or so when this vibrant and progressive circle had enjoyed its full bloom were over. Many of its members had died, and most of those who remained were aging, their years of greatest productivity and influence now past. Further, the threat represented by the French Revolution and subsequent wars had left the British economy in shambles and helped to fuse public opinion into conservatism, one effect of which was the publication of anti-feminist attacks against several of the women we have examined so far. Contrary to most currently accepted views, however, these women continued their professional writing after the attacks, even in some instances under their own names.[3] Still, pressure on genteel women to avoid the unfeminine intellectualism of serious, much less professional, writing was intense. Yet a new generation of women critics began to arise, eventually to become numerous enough to warrant Trela's claims. Martineau was among the first of this new generation, and examination of her early periodical contributions helps illuminate how the same middle-class Dissenting circle fostered her entry into the literary profession, to become, by the end of her career, one of nineteenth-century Britain's most noted names among professional women writers.

A Dissenter herself, Martineau began her career at a Dissenting publication, and her early work was facilitated by familial encouragement and intense intellectual collaboration. The events that mark her early career confirm well-known views of early nineteenth-century gender limitations on writing and intellectual activity, but they show too that such constraints were as much about class as gender. Initially forced to conceal most of her study and writing, Martineau was freed from such restraint by financial crisis. Her effort to make her way in the most genteel remunerative work commonly available to women, teaching, failed completely. Faced with a choice between needlework and writing, Martineau found in literary reviewing the means of turning writing into a lucrative career. Even counter to some of Martineau's own professed beliefs about the value of professional support, her early career demonstrates that the collaborative, supportive practices of middle-class Dissenters in the London publishing world made all the difference for the professional woman writer.

Harriet Martineau was born into a family of prosperous Norwich Dissenters. Her father, Thomas Martineau, a successful wine and textile merchant, had been a pupil of Barbauld and her husband at their school at Palgrave, and the two families, the Aikins and Barbaulds and the Martineaus, were acquainted and enjoyed many family connections.[4] The Norwich Dissenting community was intellectually vigorous and politically progressive, and the Martineaus shared these traits. In her autobiography Martineau describes her own unconventional education. As she observes, she grew up at a time when serious study for girls was frowned on as tending to encourage "bluestockingism." Nevertheless, although her family was emotionally undemonstrative, they were forward thinking on this issue, substituting care of their children's intellect for open displays of affection. Their encouragement combined with circumstance to provide Harriet with an unusually rigorous education for a girl of her day. Showing an early affinity for literature, composition, languages, and religious study under the uneven tutoring of her older siblings, Harriet found extra time for reading and writing in the early morning and late evening. Then from 1813–15 she, along with one of her sisters and a few other local girls, attended a nearby grammar school, where seating was segregated, but the curriculum and teaching methods for boys and girls was the same. After the school folded, the family engaged masters, and her education continued, supplemented with her own voracious reading in, among other topics, logic, rhetoric, and history.

Harriet had suffered from poor health almost from birth, and by the time she reached the age of fifteen, her parents' concern prompted them to try her in a change of scene. She was sent to Bristol to stay with an aunt, Mrs. Robert Rankin, who ran a school. There Harriet came under the intellectual and religious influence of Unitarian minister and educator Lant Carpenter, who introduced her to the philosophy of Locke and Hartley and their Scottish followers and who inspired her to an intensive course of Bible reading. When she returned to Norwich, Harriet's praise for Carpenter led her parents to send her younger brother, James, to Carpenter's school for boys, and from school James, with whom Harriet had long been extremely close, guided her by letter in a course of continued philosophical reading. Harriet saw her early and unusually rigorous education as central to her later success as a writer. Looking back over her literary career, she writes: "I have no reason to believe that the natural aptitude was particularly strong in myself. I believe that such facility as I have enjoyed has been mainly owing to my unconscious preparatory discipline."[5] With this solid groundwork for serious devotion to intellectual work, some time around the age of 20 she took the first steps that led her to a literary career.

During the early 1820s, partly to divert her from the loneliness she felt when he returned to school after one of his breaks, James Martineau encouraged Harriet to try her hand at writing. In response, she composed an essay entitled "Female Writers on Practical Divinity," which she anonymously submitted to the *Monthly Repository*, a small, struggling Unitarian periodical with a strong theological focus.[6] Martineau cites this essay as the moment when she embarked on a literary career. Because the *Monthly Repository* lacked funds to pay contributors, it always needed material, and at the time not all articles that appeared in its pages were notable for their quality. Martineau's essay stood out as superior to recent contributions. Not only did the editor call in the "Notice to Correspondents" for more contributions from its anonymous author, but this first effort gained her some family support for her literary and intellectual avocations. In her version of the story, when the article came out, Martineau found herself at a small family gathering where her older brother Thomas, unaware that it was hers, read the article aloud, stopping often to exclaim over how refreshingly good it was. When Harriet failed to express equal enthusiasm, he pressed her until she admitted in confusion that she was the author.

"He made no reply;" Harriet continues, "read on in silence, and spoke no more till I was on my feet to come away. He then laid his hand on my shoulder, and said gravely (calling me 'dear' for the first time) 'Now, dear, leave it to other women to make shirts and darn stockings; and do you devote yourself to this.'" From a member of her usually reserved family, such a gesture of affection and respect left a striking impression. No wonder she declares, "That evening made me an authoress."[7] Between the alternatives of needlework and writing, Martineau's choice seemed no choice at all.

Over the next few years Martineau sent poems, stories, and religious or moral essays to the *Monthly Repository* until in August 1828 its editorship was taken over by William James Fox, another Norwich Unitarian, but one from a very different circle than that of the Martineaus. Son of an unsuccessful Calvinist farmer, Fox was early sent to work as a weaver's boy, an errand boy, and finally a clerk in a bank, a position that allowed him time for reading and study.[8] The literary skill he attained enabled him to write occasionally for the newspapers until he entered the Independent College at Homerton. He took orders as a Calvinist minister but soon converted to Unitarianism, rising rapidly in this new, more liberal religious community. Meanwhile, his interests shifted toward politics, journalism, and literary criticism. Yet though Fox occasionally raised eyebrows among Unitarians for his theological radicalism, he was soon recognized as a leader within the Unitarian establishment and as a minister whose formidable writing and oratorical talents made his sermons an extraordinary success. Beginning when the British and Foreign Unitarian Association, an organization which Fox helped to found, purchased the *Monthly Repository* from Robert Aspland in 1826, Fox became increasingly important to that periodical, operated then as an organ of Unitarinism. In September 1828, just after he assumed editorship, Fox published a call for contributions. Still in fragile health but chafing under the remaining months of a year-long medical prohibition against writing, Martineau soon responded, sending Fox a packet of essays and suggesting that he employ her to write literary reviews as well. "Works on Metaphysics & the Belles Lettres," she told him, "suit me best."[9]

Martineau was well aware that the *Monthly Repository* had no funds to pay contributors. This circumstance would have made little difference to her for she was interested in "the cause" of Unitarianism, except that her family, comfortably prosperous for most of her life, suffered serious business losses with the market crash in 1825–26. Already constrained, their financial picture worsened on the death of Thomas

Martineau soon after. Nevertheless, though she was obliged to supplement the family income through needlework, "[Fox's] reply to my first letter was so cordial," she tells us,

> that I was animated to offer him extensive assistance; if he had then no money to send me, he paid me in something more valuable – in a course of frank and generous criticism which was of the utmost benefit to me. His editorial correspondence with me was unquestionably the occasion, and in great measure the cause, of the greatest intellectual progress I ever made before the age of thirty.[10]

Finally in 1829, the failure of their remaining investments left the Martineau women destitute. Rather than viewing this disaster as a setback, however, Martineau describes it as a final liberation from the gender constraints imposed by genteel social standards, the same constraints that had forced her all along to snatch time for writing between domestic obligations, and to conceal serious study completely. In her words,

> The effect of this new 'calamity,' as people called it, was like that of a blister upon a dull, weary pain, or series of pains. I rather enjoyed it, even at the time; for there was scope for action; whereas, in the long, dreary series of preceding trials, there was nothing possible but endurance. In a very short time, my two sisters at home and I began to feel the blessing of a wholly new freedom. I, who had been obliged to write before breakfast, or in some private way, had henceforth liberty to do my own work in my own way; for we had lost our gentility.

The Martineau women looked for a solution to their financial woes in the usual vocations for women – teaching, governessing, and needlework. In Harriet's case, however, a growing deafness made the first two options impractical, and when a plan to conduct courses of study by correspondence failed to yield any pupils, she was left with only the last of the three. Expecting that it would end her career with his periodical, she wrote Fox that her changed circumstances meant she could no longer provide unpaid contributions. Fox replied, according to Martineau,

> by apologetically placing at my disposal the only sum at his command at that time, – fifteen pounds a year, for which I was to

do as much reviewing as I thought proper. With this letter arrived a parcel of nine books for review or notice. Overwhelming as this was, few letters that I had ever received had given me more pleasure than this. Here was, in the first place, work; in the next, continued literary discipline under Mr. Fox.

Working her needle by day and writing at night, "It was truly *life*," she exclaims, "that I lived during those days of strong intellectual and moral effort."[11]

The exact nature of the "literary discipline" during these early years of Martineau's relationship with Fox is elusive. Later in life, Martineau determined to control the image she left behind through her autobiography and the associated memoirs by Maria Weston Chapman, with whom she had left materials for that purpose. Any other correspondence that remained in her hands she destroyed, and requested that her correspondents or, in some cases, their survivors do the same. Though negligence or in some cases refusal to honor her request left a respectable number of letters still extant, only a very few of Martineau's early letters to Fox, and even fewer of his to her survive. Still, even from these few we can glean something more of their intellectual exchange than the "course of frank and generous criticism" that Martineau describes above. Surviving letters show, for example, that Martineau was accustomed to ask Fox for research source suggestions. She consults him about problems that she encounters in her writing, whether in regard to structure or content, sounding out possibilities for solutions and asking for recommendations. Further, although we lack such evidence as multiple drafts or marked copies of Martineau's published work, her letters to Fox suggest that collaborative composition was as much the practice at the *Monthly Repository* as it had been in some of the other settings discussed in previous chapters. Martineau responds to Fox's proposed changes, sometimes of several paragraphs in length, in finished work already submitted to him, and in some cases her reply indicates that he has already made the change and published the altered version before the notifying her. Further, at least one article was fully co-written by Martineau and Fox.[12] Then too, it appears that Fox was always on the alert for literary work for Martineau. She asked for his assistance in publicizing her proposed teaching-by-correspondence venture, and thanks him for his efforts on behalf of some early stories illustrating issues of Political Economy. Martineau's work at the *Monthly Repository* under Fox reflects the same intellectual collaboration and mutual professional dependence that has characterized the careers of other professional women critics working in the middle-class Dissenting culture of the most important and influential part of the London publishing industry.

Martineau soon left for London, where she spent the winter living with relatives while under Fox's tutelage. She worked daily in his study, receiving intensive guidance on her literary work. Fox and his wards, Eliza and Sarah Flower, the former an accomplished musician and the latter a poet, began introducing Martineau to their London connections. Martineau recounts with gratitude the generous acceptance that she, an "absurd and disagreeable" person, met with from Fox's circle.[13] Fox kept his eye out for literary work, but the only present offer was a poorly paid proofreading position. Martineau intended to accept this humble offer, preferring it to leaving London and her hope of a literary career to ply her needle in the provinces. According to Martineau's friend and memoirist, American abolitionist Maria Weston Chapman, the plan was undermined when Harriet's aunt secretly convinced Harriet's mother that "her daughter's hopes of a literary career should be crushed," whereupon Mrs. Martineau issued a peremptory summons home.[14] Though outwardly obedient, Harriet's response only thinly conceals the resentment she must have felt. She writes of Fox's advice that she remain where she was and reminds her mother that while she had no literary connections elsewhere, she had concrete opportunities in London. "There is no periodical work ever sent into the country, and my choice lies between the little stories for Houlston and Darton, and original works, which I have neither capital nor courage to undertake."[15] She conditioned for a return should her opportunities for literary work dwindle at such a distance, and at length worked out an arrangement to spend three months a year in London. Meanwhile, she continued to send Fox the bulk of her literary work. In this way, contributing poems, essays, and tales as well as reviews, Martineau became the *Monthly Repository*'s leading writer from 1829–32, the period that inaugurated her literary career.[16]

Though Martineau credits her brothers with encouraging her first literary efforts and gratefully acknowledges Fox's contribution to her intellectual and professional development, her view of the role community and professional connections played in her early career seems oddly contradictory. In the *Autobiography* she affirms,

> I do not believe that 'patronage,' 'introductions' and the like are of any avail, in a general way. I know this; – that I have always been anxious to extend to young or struggling authors the sort of aid

which would have been precious to me in that winter of 1829–1830, and that, in above twenty years, I have never succeeded but once. [...] every other attempt, of the scores I have made, to get a hearing for young or new aspirants has failed.

Yet this observation follows on the heels of her admission that, without literary connections other than Fox, "I could not get anything that I wrote even looked at; so that every thing went into the 'Repository' at last."[17] It seems probable that Martineau considered her relationship with Fox professional, and therefore not one of patronage, though her mention of "introductions" and obtaining a "hearing" seem to indicate assistance similar to what Fox had offered her. In fact, her account of her first commercial literary success, the publication of her series of tales, *Illustrations of Political Economy*, shows just how heavily she relied on Fox.

Martineau's Political Economy series sprang out of the connection with Fox. She had high literary aspirations and was then thinking of trying her hand at a novel. Whether because it would distract her from his periodical or because he thought her still too green, Fox discouraged her from undertaking a longer work, urging her to continue writing tales instead. Meanwhile, he began steering the *Monthly Repository* away from a religious agenda, concentrating instead on the reform issues that now claimed his interest, a transition that culminated in his purchase of the periodical from the Unitarian Association in 1831, after which he abandoned the religious focus altogether. Martineau's contributions during these years show that she too was turning away from religious concerns toward issues of reform. She first thought of a series of tales illustrating the principles of political economy in 1827, when she read Jane Marcet's *Conversations on Political Economy* (1816). During an 1831 visit to her brother in Dublin she received his encouragement and wrote to some Dublin publishers, but was rebuffed. On her return to London, she and Fox unsuccessfully tried to elicit interest from other firms. Finally, Fox brought her an almost insultingly disadvantageous proposal from his brother, Charles Fox, a small bookseller. Besides offering her an inordinately small share in the profits, Charles Fox demanded that Martineau solicit a list of subscribers, a process that she found mortifying. Even at that, his apprehensions just before the series was to begin led him to stipulate for success in its first two weeks' sales. His fears proved ungrounded, however. The series was begun in February 1832 with a printing of 1500 copies, and by the 10th of that month Charles Fox wrote to Martineau requesting corrections for a second printing of

2000. Three postscripts were added, so that by the time the letter was sent, the number proposed for the second printing had reached 5000. "From that hour," Martineau writes, "I have never had any other anxiety about employment than what to choose, nor any real care about money."[18]

Demands for reform were escalating, so the time was ripe for Martineau's series, and she may very well have soon found more advantageous terms with a larger firm. Still, no one would look at the series until Fox drew on his own family connections for a publisher. Though their close intellectual and professional ties were soon to suffer a nearly conclusive break when Fox left his wife to set up household with his former ward, Eliza Flower, Martineau looks back on the time when she worked under Fox as her professional apprenticeship, and she avers that those years were the period of her greatest intellectual progress. Her brother's encouragement led to her first tentative literary efforts, and that encouragement continued on occasion to play a part in her early career. Yet despite her denials, Martineau's account suggests that without the guidance and professional connections that she found with the reform-minded editor of one small Unitarian periodical, the twentieth century would never have known one of the most familiar of British Victorian women writers.

Notwithstanding the remarkable success of her Political Economy series, Martineau found herself the brunt of the same sort of gender-based attack that had been leveled at Inchbald some two decades before. We will see a new twist, however, in the use gender is put to by hostile reviewers. A sharply sarcastic *Quarterly Review* article ridiculed story after story, denouncing Martineau's series as "unfeminine." Besides foregrounding Martineau's gender through heavy-handed use of such markers as "Miss Martineau" and "authoress," the author trivializes the principles that the stories were designed to illustrate in ribald hints that the issue of population control makes political economy an inappropriate topic for a woman. In one instance, for example, he suggests:

> A little ignorance on these ticklish topics is perhaps not unbecoming a young unmarried lady. But before such a person undertook to write books in favour of "the preventative check," she should have informed herself somewhat more accurately upon the laws of human propagation. Poor innocent! She has been puzzling over Mr. Malthus's arithmetical and geometrical ratios, for knowledge which she should have obtained by a simple question or two of her mamma.

In the penultimate paragraph, a most indirect allusion on Martineau's part to a married couple's ability to limit family size provides the occasion for defamation of both Martineau's own sexual virtue and that of Unitarians in general: "Has the young lady picked up this piece of information in her conferences with the Lord Chancellor?" the reviewer inquires, "or has she been entering into high and lofty communion on such subjects with certain gentlemen of her sect, famous for dropping their gratuitous advice on these matters into areas, for the benefit of the London kitchen-maids?" In an escalating list of absurdities, the reviewer exclaims in horror at "a *female Malthusian*. A *woman* who thinks childbearing a *crime against society!* An *unmarried woman* who declaims against *marriage!!* A *young woman* who deprecates charity and a provision for the *poor!!!*"[19] For this reviewer, the author's age, gender, and marital status suffice to explode the theory and condemn its illustration.

Martineau records the incident in depth. The review was written, Martineau recounts, by a Mr. Poulett Scrope, who soon after asked a friend to inform her that while he did indeed acknowledge the criticisms of Political Economy, "he hoped he was too much of a gentleman to have stooped to ribaldry." That portion had been added by John Wilson Croker and John Gibson Lockhart, who made no secret of their part in the published article, Croker even acknowledging that he had intended to "destroy Miss Martineau" for the sales revenue such controversy would bring. Lockhart had second thoughts about the article, however, and removed some of its most offensive passages before it went to press, leaving the bulk of responsibility for the attack squarely on the shoulders of Croker, whom even the *Dictionary of National Biography* recognizes for his sarcastic, biased reviews. Croker is often blamed as well for cutting short Barbauld's public career with his harsh, gender-based criticism of her poetic critique of the Regency, *Eighteen Hundred and Eleven*.[20] The implications here are substantial. If Croker, a journalist already known for acrimonious calumny in his own articles, turns out to have been brought in to increase the vitriol of other reviewers' work, it seems possible that much of the partisanship and bias that recent scholars so despise in some reviews may be the work of far fewer individuals than has been recognized. On the other hand, his having been brought in precisely for this purpose may also indicate that some editors aggressively exploited controversy, flamboyant rhetoric, and sexual innuendo couched as policing morality in order to boost sales. At any rate, Martineau observes that although this article failed in its immediate effect, "In the long run, there is no doubt that the Quarterly injured me seriously. For ten years there was seldom a number which had not some indecent jest about me."[21] She encountered numerous potential readers over the years, she explains, who refused to open her work in anticipation that they would find it indecent. Indeed, *Fraser's* soon followed suit. The brief review by William Maginn, the periodical's founder, returns to phrases like "the preventative check" and compares Martineau's series with the "shameless books" of "Mother Woolstonecroft."[22]

Two other reviews of Martineau's series suggest, however, that while Croker and Maginn relied on gender bias as their vehicle, Martineau's politics may have been their real target. The *Tait's Edinburgh Magazine* review roundly congratulated Martineau on her work. Like the *Quarterly* and *Fraser's* critiques, this article begins with the author's sex, remarking that "The ladies seem determined to make the science of Political Economy peculiarly their own." Far from regarding this determination as a pernicious tendency that must be squelched, though, the reviewer argues that Political Economy is a woman's special province by virtue of the parallel between the economy of the nation and that of the family. Martineau's contributions to the topic "have all the value of truth and all the grace of fiction."[23] Although the review becomes patronizing toward women as it develops its argument from the perspective of separate spheres, it contains no negative comments on either the appropriateness or competence of Martineau's participation in such a discourse. Similarly, the *Edinburgh Review*, though more skeptical of the parallel between domestic economy and the economy of the state, still argues that the superior emotional responsiveness of women makes at least one aspect of Political Economy, "the protection and comfort of the poor," the privileged province of women. Authored by William Empson, who was eventually to become the periodical's editor, the article continues with a largely positive exposition of both Martineau's series and the work by Marcet that had inspired it.[24] The difference between the two extremes lies in the periodicals' political slant. Both the *Quarterly* and *Fraser's* were Tory-leaning publications. The *Quarterly* had been founded in opposition to the Whig-leaning *Edinburgh Review*, while the initial prospectus of *Fraser's* declares its purpose to be "to support [...] the established institutions of the country." "Our leanings," it continues, "have been conservative throughout."[25] *Tait's*, on the other hand, was founded in the more progressive community in Edinburgh by men with strong ties to reform-minded journalists such as John Bowring, Jeremy Bentham, and John Stuart Mill, all affiliated with both the *Monthly Repository* and its better known but like-minded counterpart, the *Westminster Review*. Meanwhile, although the *Edinburgh* is sometimes regarded as narrow-minded for its dismissal of the Lake poets, it had from the first number run articles promoting Political Economy, including some by Malthus himself. In this case, Martineau's gender apparently served as cover for a controversy that was more political than sexual. Employing gender role conservatism to add an undertone of sexual titillation to what was actually a political attack, the *Quarterly*'s and *Fraser*'s articles exemplify how eighteenth century goals of critical objectivity had given way to reliance on inflammatory controversy as a means of increasing sales.

And what of Martineau's own literary journalism? Her work at the *Monthly Repository* includes only a few reviews discussing literary works on aesthetic grounds, most of them printed in the "Critical Notices," a section of short articles similar to the Catalogue sections of periodicals such as the *Monthly Review*. That Martineau was offered little of this type of work is not surprising. Her aesthetic judgments in these articles are general, and her language unilluminating. Her treatment describes Byron's Letters, for example, as characterized by "vigour, originality, and beauty," while in Thomas Moore's biography of the poet: "The style is simple, the narrative conducted with grace, and animated throughout with an interest." Similarly, Eleanor Snowden's poetry features "elegance" and "liveliness of fancy." Clearly, discussions that are primarily aesthetic in nature are not Martineau's strong suit. Her talents as a literary journalist lay in another direction. The Snowden review improves as soon as Martineau leaves aesthetics behind to comment on the writer's self-presentation. Martineau recognizes the conventions that so often trivialize the work of women writers hoping to circumvent an accusation of immodesty in bringing their books before the public. "Considering that the writer is a lady," Martineau says of Snowden, "and as we understand, a very young lady, the absence of all deprecation of criticism, all apology for publication, is an augury of a very creditable independence of spirit, and a clear understanding of the relation between authors and the public."[26] We can hear in this assessment echoes of Wollstonecraft's counsel to Hays many years before: if your work is worthy, let it stand on its own merits without apology; if it is not, do not plague the public with it.

Her remarks on Snowden's self-presentation turn our attention toward other instances when Martineau shows a strong understanding of the relationship between a work and its audience. By the time of this review, Martineau had already distinguished herself as especially capable in differentiating a specific audience. Not long before the time of the Snowden review, the Central Unitarian Association held a triple award contest for the best essays justifying Unitarianism to Catholics, Jews, and Mohammedans. Martineau had anonymously submitted essays for all three contests, and by May 1830 she had been awarded all three prizes. Her success of course indicates not so much that she had a clear understanding of, for example, an audience made up of actual Moslems; rather, it shows that she was able to respond to the demand to discriminate between audiences in a manner that would be credible to the real audience of all three essays – the Unitarians themselves.

Similarly, Martineau shows in her criticism an understanding that a publication's particular audience makes certain demands on the work. She criticizes, for example, a publication offering religious instruction to a popular audience as characterized by excessively figurative language, which she finds to be "an unsuitable style of expression: and in a book addressed to the people, style is an important consideration." "The enlightened reader" she explains, "can easily strip the argumentative matter from its incumbrance of heterogeneous illustration; but, it is to be feared, the multitude of readers will so occupy themselves with the types as to overlook the thing typified." Similarly, excessive attention to technical detail can make a work unsuitable for its intended audience. A collection of sketches describing great figures in the legal profession, for instance, "forms a part of a series of popular works; and therefore we know that it is designed for general readers. From its contents we should have inferred that it was intended for the profession." Meanwhile, because another legal work "contains nothing more than may be found in the law books in use in the profession, we conclude it was designed solely for popular reference; and it is therefore to be wished that the style had been more popular, and that the points had been put in a more familiar and prominent way."[27] As previous chapters show, our critics were becoming increasingly aware of the relationship between an author and his or her audience. Martineau's criticism seems to take that awareness a step further in the clarity of her comments on this emerging concern.

If Martineau received few of the belles-lettres assignments that she had told Fox might suit her, she accepted many that might fall under the rubric of "metaphysics." Theology and the defense of Unitarianism dominate much of Martineau's early work for the *Monthly Repository*. Indeed, her first contribution, "Female Writers on Practical Divinity," straddles the line between literary criticism and theology to discuss religious writings of Hannah More and Anna Letitia Barbauld.[28] Part of a three-article series, these two articles work as feminist tracts as well. Martineau identifies Barbauld's and More's devotional writing, and, more broadly, women's writing in general with an aesthetic based in sensibility. Indeed, Barbauld, whom Martineau designates "our first living female poet," may show in her devotional writing a bit too much imagination, but Martineau is willing to overlook "what borders on extravagance" because of "the justice with which she paints our passions and emotions, and touches every chord of feeling in our bosoms." Women writers possess a unique ability to impart religion and virtue because "the peculiar susceptibility of the female mind, and its consequent warmth of feeling," allow them to "find a more ready way to the heart than those of the other sex."[29] Because of their superior capacity to move the emotions, women are especially able to affect public values.

The relationship between female emotionality and women's influence on public virtue is one that had by Martineau's time often grounded discourse on the role of women outside the private world of the domestic circle. John Mullan has argued that since mid-century, "a sociability which is dependent upon the communication of passions and sentiments" was increasingly sought as the controlling characteristic of a non-familial but still private, domestic, predominantly middle-class social realm where free, spontaneous, and virtuous communication inspired and guided by feminine sensibility effaces the commercial and political divisions increasingly regarded as intrinsic to the public world dominated by men. As Linda Colley has shown, by Martineau's time, this freedom from the corrupting taint of the most obvious venues of public activity – commerce, the professions, politics – and a consequent emotional integrity had seemingly paradoxically become the basis for some to argue for a unique public role for women. Harriet Guest points out, for example, that Elizabeth Hamilton and Lucy Aikin argued that "middle-class women's exclusion from paid labor allowed them to cultivate a statesmanlike knowledge of the world that was no longer available to professional or landed men." Such women, according to Guest "did not see their exclusion from participation in the public life of the nation as natural." Guest ties such developing arguments for the public role of women to the discourse of British nationalism, explaining that sensibility "is central to the issue of women's ability to imagine themselves as patriotic or public citizens [...] because of its role in the sentimental notion of the continuity of affect linking the family and the nation." Among other examples, she offers in illustration the ways in which "Biographies of women of the past as well as celebrations of living 'extraordinary English women' acquire a new significance to emerging – and changing – notions of the national identity."[30] Though it dates from roughly a decade later than Guest's examples of Aikin and Hamilton, Martineau's essay, certainly in part a celebration of at least two extraordinary English women, similarly explores the significance of her two authors in terms of national character, here in explicitly religious terms. Colley has argued that the connection between religion and the development of British nationalism, including both its anti-French permutations and its claims about the importance of female virtue, was fundamentally grounded in an equation of true Britishness with Protestantism. Martineau's essay on Barbauld and More offers an opportunity to elucidate this argument, for she compares her two writers with their French counterparts, concluding that it is British Protestantism that inspirits the work of her countrywomen.

Martineau sounds the connection between female virtue grounded in sensibility and ideal British patriotism from her first sentence, which emphasizes that the "most useful *English* works on Practical Divinity" are by female authors (emphasis mine). By her second paragraph, the associations take on the recognizable tone of anti-Catholicism. English writers like Barbauld and More outshine their counterparts elsewhere, for example, because "our religion" has been "purified from the degrading superstitions of the Romish Church." Given the discrimination still experienced by Dissenters in England, it is a measure of the strength of invoking the opposition between foreign Catholicism and British Protestantism that Martineau, herself a Unitarian writing for an explicitly Unitarian publication and discussing More, an Anglican, and Barbauld, a Unitarian, feels confident that a reference in such a context to "our religion" requires no clarification. She later explains that although "I differ nearly as much from the author [More], with respect to religious belief as one Protestant can from another," she finds it "highly unreasonable and absurd" to reject her moral instruction on doctrinal grounds.[31] As long as one is Protestant, then, it seems to matter little what kind.

Of course, superior emotional sensibility can prove very miry ground for female superiority, as Martineau was well aware. She recognized the danger that female emotionalism could be deployed as evidence of female irrationality and so correlated with intellectual incapacity, an especially problematic connection for a young woman writing the sorts of philosophical criticism that dominated Martineau's work at the *Monthly Repository* over the next decade. In fact, the third article of this series on women, "On Female Education," is in part an attack on this very formula. Much like Mary Wollstonecraft, whose work Martineau had been taught since childhood to admire, Martineau argues that women must be educated first before it is possible to determine whether they have the same capacity for reason as men.[32] As the description of Catholicism as a religion based in "superstition" might suggest, "feeling" may be a necessary, but it is not a sufficient condition for true religion. Gary Kelly argues that as far back as Elizabeth Carter, women writers, including both Barbauld and Wollstonecraft, mounted an attack on the masculine hegemony of "hard-line" Anglicanism through their insistence that "both reason and 'the heart' are necessary to true faith."[33] Like her predecessors, Martineau subverts the opposition of reason and emotion, declaring that her countrywomen, "whose works are conspicuous for their force of argument, for their simplicity, and for that earnestness which can be expressed only because it is felt," offer their readers moral truths which are "as evident to the understanding as they are interesting to the heart."[34] In English women writers, reason and feeling coexist in reciprocal harmony.

For Martineau it is not the sheer absence of either emotion or reason that differentiates French women authors from their English counterparts, however. Rather, it is the moderation in both that characterizes English women. The work of Madame Genlis, for example, reveals "affected feeling," and "long drawn-out sentiments." Similarly, Madame de Staël displays both "brilliant imagination" and "warm feelings," so that Martineau places Staël above Barbauld "For genius, [...] but our countrywoman has been taught to fix her standard higher, and has consequently made the greatest advances." Martineau locates the superiority of English women writers quite explicitly in "the influence of a pure religion." The work of French women authors, by contrast, may please at first, but will soon be found to be marred by "some defective morality, some hidden licentiousness, or at least some artificial sentiment, which proves that they have drawn their ideas from that source which is tainted by the foul admixtures of superstition, instead of from that well-spring of life [...] under the influence of a pure religion."[35] David Simpson has argued that English ideas of the French, previously evaluating the French character as excessively and coldly intellectual, were colored after 1792 with the legacy of Rousseau's celebration of "spontaneous emotionalism." In the eyes of the British, the French were "unable to negotiate a place of rest between the two extremes of mathematical abstraction and chaotic emotionalism."[36] For Martineau, that place of rest is to be found in Protestantism.

Martineau's early contributions to the *Monthly Repository*, then, tie sensibility, nationalism, and Protestantism together in such a way that she presents emotional depth animated by Protestant piety as the key to what makes British women devotional writers a source of national pride. While Martineau conjoins these three elements in a manner that is her own, her emphasis on the interrelations between them carries echoes from the work of several of the other woman literary critics who have made a part of this study. Furthermore, these early reviews exemplify the shift in format that characterized reviews at the time her contributions began, a transformation that becomes all the clearer in her later work.

Previous chapters have argued that the assumption that literary criticism is the province of men not only dogged the careers of women critics during the period here under discussion, but has also continued to govern many assessments of the quality and even frequency of Romantic-era criticism by women up through much of the twentieth century. In countering some of these assessments, I have discussed the relationship between the format that women periodical critics followed and contemporary expectations regarding the contents of literary reviews. Specifically, twentieth-century dismissals of reviews in general, and those by women writers such as Mary Wollstonecraft in particular, often rely on anachronistic expectations about an article's relative proportion of summary and extract versus evaluation. Such assessments have been brought into question by Derek Roper and Marilyn Butler, both of whom argue that these expectations originate in standards that did not become common until the second quarter of the nineteenth century. Martineau's contributions to the *Monthly Repository* offer an illustration of the new review format while confirming the assertion that it was custom and not gender that determined the overall shape of reviews.

The leader of the new review format, the *Edinburgh Review*, began publishing in 1802, but only over time did it settle on the formula for which it became known. It took even longer for its influence to be so strongly felt that fledgling periodicals routinely conformed to the new design and it became necessary for older, established journals to follow suit or perish. The difference that the *Edinburgh Review* initiated was to abandon any ambition for comprehensive coverage and treat only a limited number of books in any one issue. At the same time, articles designed to provide extensive knowledge of the book itself gave way to those that used the book as a starting point for the journalist's exploration of the book's topic. Reviews many pages in length often feature only a few paragraphs about the book that gave rise to the article. The *Monthly Repository* followed this new format fairly closely while Martineau was contributing reviews, more so during the period when she contributed regularly than during her first years there. A case in point is her article on Sir Walter Scott's *Letters on Demonology and Witchcraft*.

Martineau's review of Scott's volume begins with a paragraph devoting a few sentences to describing the book, the rest sarcastically questioning where Scott obtained his information. Recall that the women critics featured in previous chapters have employed irony sparingly. By contrast, except in their salacious insinuations, Croker's two *Quarterly* reviews vilifying Barbauld and later Martineau offer excellent examples of the tone that dominated that periodical and the *Edinburgh*, the journal that the *Quarterly* was established to compete with and on which it was modeled. Unfavorable articles often employed harsh sarcasm to attack both the book and its author, while even positive articles are marked by consistent irony. Thus, though serious topics always merit from Martineau a serious tone, that portion of her Scott review devoted to the work itself more closely resembles the tone that had become common amongst the writers of her time than it does the work of her female predecessors. Here, the sarcasm is liberal, obtrusive, often far fetched. "Can anybody tell where Sir W. Scott had been since he last met the public?" she opens.

> Will Mr. Lockhart avouch that he has not found his way after Dante to Tartarus? Will Mr. Murray declare that he has not been up to the moon to gather matter for the Family Library? It may be that he has only a legacy of some of Faust's folios; but something has happened to open his eyes upon the living population of a world which we had wrongly imagined to have tumbled back into chaos long ago. Considering the marvels he has to relate, we can but admire his condescension in choosing so humble a vehicle as No. XVI of the Family Library.

Even the extracts she offers, while professedly intended to "do our author the justice to offer his data in his own words," are selected and edited to present Scott's work as absurd, grounded in long abandoned superstitions and unworthy of the serious reader's time.[37] Still, though generous at times with her sarcasm, Martineau does not indulge in the same sort of personal calumny that Croker was soon to use against her. Much like the average article in the *Edinburgh*, this introductory paragraph on Scott is followed by two paragraphs of extract, another of very general description and evaluation, and 14 pages of exposition of

Martineau's own ideas on the topic of demonology and the supernatural. Of course, twenty-first century readers recognize in Martineau's criticism a failure to take Scott's work on its own terms as a contribution to Romantic-era revisions of the literary canon through recuperation of antiquarian and native British literary works. But to dismiss her article on that basis repeats the same failure with regard to periodical criticism. While Martineau's much shorter Critical Notices still address the books in question, the Scott article is representative of her work featured in the *Monthly Repository*'s main article sections and similar to articles by other contributors, including both Fox and some of his most respected male colleagues. It exemplifies the extent that periodical review culture changed since Wollstonecraft first began writing for the *Analytical Review*, and adds weight to the argument that women reviewers failed to meet today's standards for quality periodical criticism not because they lacked the ability, but because those standards were not the ones either they or their male colleagues followed at the time.

Besides illustrating the evolution in review format and standards, Martineau's reviews show her movement along with the *Monthly Repository* in the direction of secular reform. When Martineau penned her articles on Barbauld and More, the periodical, like Martineau herself, was staunchly Unitarian. But when Fox took over its editorship, he began to direct it away from its former religious bent, fully achieving his intention of turning it into a non-sectarian organ for reform when he purchased it outright. Meanwhile, Martineau was turning away from her explicit emphasis on Unitarianism. Though she continued for some time to review works of Unitarian interest, Martineau had begun in articles on less explicitly religious subjects to moderate her view that Protestantism was the tie through which feeling produced virtue. By the time of her political economy series, she had left affect behind as well, replacing all notion of personal virtue with strict utilitarianism. The transformation can be traced in her philosophical essays, some of which explicitly take up issues of religion and human feeling. In her reviews, the relationship between virtue and sentiment as mediated by Protestant faith gave way to cause and effect analysis. Two articles, one on slavery, the other on William Godwin, illustrate Martineau's distancing from religion while retaining a confidence in sensibility as the foundation of virtue; two slightly later ones on social issues show her turn away from emotion toward strict utilitarianism instead.

Martineau opens her article "On Negro Slavery" linking religion and virtue, but here instead of one promoting the other, the connection fails. She hypothesizes an extraterrestrial visitor to Earth, remarking that such a visitor would find much to condemn. Though such should only be the case where Christianity is unknown, slavery is to their shame permitted in Christian nations as well. Martineau has dropped the denominational discrimination that played such an important role in her early pieces on women and that allowed her to rank Britain above France in moral sincerity. Not only do Protestantism and Catholicism come together as a common faith that should inspire virtue, but they both fail to do so. She returns to a religious foundation for virtue, but before doing so she first turns to feeling, explicitly divorcing it from the religion that had given it its power in her earlier work: "There is not a heart actuated by the common feelings of humanity," she declares, "we will not say in a Christian country, but in any country, which would not be moved by a recital of the wrongs of the slaves in our colonies, and therefore a bare statement of the facts which have been perseveringly adduced by their advocates form a strong and universal appeal." Indeed, virtue, she argues, is the purpose of feeling, but in making this argument, she circles back to religion, though of a most general kind: "For this cause is it that human sympathies are imparted; for this cause is it that they become tenderer and warmer as the mind is more fully informed by the wisdom which is from above." By the time her article really gets under way, she has returned to a strong reliance on religion, declaring slavery's abhorrence "to those who know any thing of the life and beauty of religion, to those especially who have been made free in the liberty of the gospel." "Thus feels every Christian," she continues. "If he feels not thus, he usurps the name."[38] The religion remains, however, that umbrella of Christianity that includes not only Protestantism but the Catholicism that had been so abhorrent to her years before.

By contrast, Martineau's review of Godwin's *Thoughts on Man* drops the religious aspect of virtue altogether. Martineau likes Godwin's work in general, but she is disappointed in *Thoughts on Man* because "This work contains sketches of man in his individuality as striking, perhaps, as any ever drawn by the same hand; but they are not, as formerly, fixed in their right place as illustrations of some principles. We have faithful interpretations of some mysteries of human emotion; but they are not, as formerly, brought home as lessons of social virtue." Virtue and feeling remain connected, but Martineau now attributes the connection to what would have at the time been labeled "Natural Philosophy." "The great impediment to a true understanding of the purposes of human life," of which the exercise of virtue is the most important, "is prevalent ignorance or error respecting the primary laws of sensation and thought."[39] Virtue has become innate to human beings, while at the same time, the feeling that gives rise to it has been reduced to its physiological processes.

The period between the articles on slavery and Godwin's work is not long. Partly because of Fox's influence, and also, as her biographers show, in response to her reading, Martineau's thinking was changing rapidly.[40] She had been writing her own stories on Political Economy for some time when, six months after the Godwin review, she reviewed Thomas Cooper's published lectures on the topic. Martineau begins with a long defense of Political Economy and, except for an introductory sentence or two, does not discuss the work at hand until nine pages into the ten page review. She sees Political Economy as a science where general principles, not human emotions, guide reform. "If the abuses of the pauper system were abolished," she declares, "and the wisest of all possible measures substituted, its operation would be impaired if the public persisted in giving alms and maintaining soup charities, and clothing charities, and other well-meant institutions which do nothing but harm." Rejecting charity, public or private, she replaces both religious feeling and sympathy with reason. Ironically, her only objection to the publication at hand is to its structure, its lack of a rational "principle of arrangement."[41]

Utilitarianism comes to guide almost all of Martineau's literary assessments. Even in travel literature, the pleasure of "narratives of adventure" should give way, she argues, to the practical information the work can offer a potential colonist. Her article on an account of Van Diemen's Land comments briefly on the book's structure, but quickly dispenses with literary concerns to consider the merits of resolving Britain's economic problems by "transport[ing] our surplus population." "We would fain show [England's poor]," she explains, "that, on this side the grave, there is a better land, and send them to seek it."[42] The compassionate virtue of a decade before is gone, replaced by a secular sanctimony that grates harshly on the ears of those who listen from a distance. The hint of compulsion only adds to the disagreeableness. Nevertheless, Martineau is applying a theory that had many highly respected adherents, that was often elucidated in persuasive language, and that made a significant contribution to the drive for reform that would have been approved even by those who grew indignant when Dickens's Ebenezer Scrooge echoed the sentiments a decade later.

The issue of involuntary emigration eventually brings Martineau around to penal transportation, to which she is as strongly opposed as she was in favor of transportation of the poor. In the Van Diemen's Land article, she objects that conditions in that nation were formerly so harsh that the threat of exile there served as an effective deterrent. Recently, however, circumstances have become so easy that they "must act as a premium on crime: and so it has proved." Now,

> Those who are under sentence of transportation, know that their friends are making exertions to procure good situations for them, and indulge in visions of wealth and happiness such as the honest poor man knows he has no chance of attaining in his native land. [...] What wonder that people induce their relatives to commit crime in order to get them well established, as stated by Mr. Busby? Or that a magistrate has been asked what extent of crime would ensure transportation.[43]

The merits of this argument need no commentary, but what is interesting is Martineau's shift in perspective a few months later. Martineau contributes a two-part series on penal measures, the first of which includes one of her increasingly rare reversions to an explicitly religious view.[44] "Our treatment of the sinning part of our population," she exclaims, "is as largely compounded of folly and cruelty as if our Christianity were no more than a name, and our civilization a false and conceited assumption." She expresses the same vehemence throughout. She recognizes government obligation "to protect its subjects from the aggressions of crime, and, in consequence, to seclude or otherwise render powerless its criminal members," yet "We cannot discern whence is given the power to inflict arbitrary suffering in the case of guilt more than in any other case." Any punishment that does not proceed from "the natural consequences of guilt," she argues, should be left to "the Almighty."[45] When the sentence is incarceration, it is perhaps illegal and certainly un-Christian to multiply the penalty with prison conditions that are excessively cruel. Her energetic denunciation of excessively cruel punishment puts in perspective the next month's contribution on the same topic. There Martineau echoes her Van Diemen's Land article in declaring the opposition to transportation as a criminal penalty, but she does so for reasons that sound as though she finds transportation to be intrinsically cruel. "Instead of convict-importation being a boon to Australia, it is the most fearful curse which any country has ever dared to inflict on any other country" she proclaims. "Can there be a stronger proof of our iniquity in selecting a portion of God's earth to be the nursery of crime, the spot where guilt and misery may be so fostered as that they may speedily travel abroad, and make a hell of every place which has relations with their special abode? Was anything so daring ever done as establishing a depot of vice?"[46] If Tasmania is a bit too cushy to qualify as punishment at all, Australia is so bad that it constitutes a "secondary" or additional punishment beyond the original penalty of transportation. It is disconcerting to recall that Martineau had only a few months before argued in favor of measures for the poor that she now finds too cruel for criminals.

In general, though the terms may distress today's reader, Martineau's later review articles advocate strongly for reform. She promotes amelioration of prison conditions, a national system of education, reorganization of the Established Church, even reform of administrative practices in colonial India. These reviews hold prominent positions, many ranking as lead articles. They play a decisive part in the *Monthly Repository*'s turn away from the Unitarian focus in favor of utilitarianism and reform. Further, their content adds dimension to the relationship between Martineau and the *Westminster Review*, the Benthamite periodical where George Eliot soon became so prominent, and which shared several contributors with the *Monthly Repository*, including Fox, John Stuart Mill, and, a few years after her work for the *Monthly Repository* ended, Martineau herself. As with the *Monthly Repository*, the *Westminster Review* emphasized a reform-minded political program over the literary even in most of its literary reviews. Martineau's *Monthly Repository* contributions well prepared her for her association with the more prestigious and longer lived *Westminster Review*. Along with similar articles by her colleagues at the various progressive periodicals that sprang up in the 1820s and 30s, they also exerted strong pressure on popular opinion, turning it toward sweeping social and political reform.

Martineau's work for the *Monthly Repository* provided the key to her entry into professional writing; hence, that work and the circumstances that made it possible reveal structures that enabled a women writer to make writing a lucrative career while working outside the usual restrictions on writing by women. Criticism provided an opportunity to pronounce on public issues that were usually considered the province of men. Martineau's work depended on support from and collaboration with an established literary professional whose own connections, like those of Martineau herself, relied on the community of Norwich Dissenters and their close associates, the same community that had already enabled several other women writers to become professional literary critics. As Davidoff and Hall have demonstrated, middle-class Dissenters routinely formed communities that emphasized cooperation, professional interdependence, and intellectual exchange while promoting political and social views that leaned toward the progressive, or at times even radical. Martineau's criticism reveals her own shift in a progressive direction. Initially she elaborates established views that women, especially British women, contribute to public virtue through their refined sensibility, a quality that had come to be regarded as the special province of women partly because of their distance from the sorts of public activity engaged in by men. By the time she attained professional success, however, Martineau addressed a wide variety of economic, social, and political issues. In the process, she became the *Monthly Repository*'s lead writer, thus playing a critical role in turning that periodical away from its explicitly religious focus toward the "ideas in politics and literature" that, as Garnett and Garnett observe, were "characteristic" of the early Victorian era, the views agreed on by the period's "most thoughtful and progressive intellects."[47] At least one of those thoughtful and progressive intellects was a woman professional periodical literary critic.

Notes

Introduction

1. Hume, *Essays Moral, Political and Literary* (London: Oxford UP, 1963) 278, qtd. in Gary Kelly, "Bluestocking Feminism," *Women, Writing and the Public Sphere, 1700–1830*, ed. Elizabeth Eger, Charlotte Grant, Clíona Ó Gallchoir, and Penny Warburton (Cambridge: Cambridge UP, 2001) 166.
2. Susan Sniader Lanser and Evelyn Torton Beck, "[Why] Are There No Great Women Critics? And What Difference Does It Make?" *The Prism of Sex: Essays in the Sociology of Knowledge*, ed. Julia A. Sherman and Evelyn Torton Beck (Madison: U of Wisconsin P, 1979) 79–91.
3. Charlotte Lennox, *Shakespear Illustrated: or the Novels and Histories, on Which the Plays of Shakespear Are Founded* (London: A. Millar, 1753–54); Clara Reeve *Progress of Romance* (London: G. G. J. and J. Robinson, 1785); Vernon Lee, "On Literary Construction," *The Handling of Words and Other Studies in Literary Psychology* (London: John Lane, 1923).
4. Lanser and Beck 87.
5. Virginia Woolf, *A Room of One's Own, Norton Anthology of English Literature*, ed. M. H. Abrams, et al., 7th ed., 2 vols. (New York: W. W. Norton and Co., 2000) 2c:2153–214.
6. *Women Critics 1600–1820: An Anthology*, ed. Folger Collective on Early Women Critics (Bloomington: U of Indiana P, 1995). The other two volumes are *Women Reading Shakespeare, 1660–1900: An Anthology of Criticism*, ed. Ann Thompson and Sasha Roberts (Manchester: Manchester UP, 1997) and *A Serious Occupation: Literary Criticism by Victorian Women Writers*, ed. Solveig C. Robinson (Peterborough, ON: Broadview, 2003).
7. Anne K. Mellor, "A Criticism of Their Own: Romantic Women Literary Critics," *Questioning Romanticism*, ed. John Beer (Baltimore: Johns Hopkins UP, 1995).
8. Edward Copeland, *Women Writing about Money: Women's Fiction in England, 1790–1820*, Cambridge Studies in Romanticism 9, ed. Marilyn Butler and James Chandler (Cambridge: Cambridge UP, 1995).
9. Alison Adburgham, *Women in Print: Writing Women and Women's Magazines from the Restoration to the Accession of Victoria* (London: George Allen and Unwin, 1972) 183, 57, and passim.
10. Paula McDowell, *The Women of Grub Street: Press, Politics, and Gender in the London Literary Marketplace, 1678–1730* (Oxford: Clarendon P, 1998); Other sources on the range of women's print activity include Patricia Crawford, "Women's Published Writings 1600–1700," *Women in English Society, 1500–1800*, ed. Mary Prior (London: Methuen, 1985) 211–74; Lenore Davidoff and Catherine Hall, *Family Fortunes: Men and Women of the English Middle Class, 1780–1850* (London: Hutchinson, 1987); Catherine Ingrassia, *Authorship, Commerce, and Gender in Early Eighteenth-Century England: A Culture of Paper Credit* (Cambridge, Cambridge UP, 1998); Judith Phillips

Stanton "Statistical Profile of Women Writing in English from 1660 to 1800," *Eighteenth-Century Women and the Arts*, ed. Frederick M. Keener and Susan E. Lorsch, Contributions in Women's Studies 98 (New York: Greenwood, 1988) 247–254; and Cheryl Turner, *Living by the Pen: Women Writers in the Eighteenth Century* (London: Routledge, 1992).

11. On eighteenth-century women's literary criticism, see Terry Castle, "Women and Literary Criticism," *The Cambridge History of Literary Criticism*, 8 vols., *The Eighteenth Century*, ed. H. B. Nisbet and Claude Rawson (Cambridge: Cambridge UP, 1997) 2:434–55.

12. See, for example, Charlotte Lennox, *The Female Quixote* (1752); Sarah Fielding, *The Cry* (1754) and *The Countess of Dellwyn* (1759); Frances Sheridan, *Sidney Biddulph* (1761); Fanny Burney, *Evelina* (1778); and *Camilla* (1796); and Clara Reeve, *The Old English Baron* (1778). Mellor's "A Criticism of Their Own" offers numerous examples of the variety of forms taken by Romantic-era women's criticism, from poetry to essays and prefaces to letters and even conversation. In doing so, it implicitly links Romantic-era women's criticism with that of their Bluestocking predecessors discussed below.

13. Betty Rizzo, "Isabella Griffiths," *A Dictionary of British and American Women Writers, 1660–1800*, ed. Janet Todd (Totowa, NJ: Roan and Allanheld, 1985) 143. See p. 182 n. 53.

14. Sylvia Harcstark Myers, *The Bluestocking Circle: Women, Friendship, and the Life of the Mind in Eighteenth-Century England* (Oxford: Clarendon P, 1990).

15. Elizabeth Montagu, *An Essay on the Writings and Genius of Shakespeare, compared with the Greek and French Dramatic Poets. With Some Remarks Upon the Misrepresentations of Mons. De Voltaire* (London: J. and H. Hughs, 1769).

16. Carter's translation of Epictetus (*All the Works of Epictetus, which are now Extant: Consisting of His Discourses, preserved by Arrian, in Four Books, Then Enchiridion, and Fragments.* [London: Printed by S. Richardson, 1758]) earned her the very substantial sum of £1000, enough to purchase a house for herself and her father.

17. Harriet Guest, *Small Change: Women, Learning, and Patriotism, 1750–1810* (Chicago: U of Chicago P, 2000) 127.

18. Elizabeth Eger, "Representing Culture: 'The Nine Living Muses of Great Britain' (1779)," *Women, Writing and the Public Sphere, 1700–1830*, ed. Elizabeth Eger, Charlotte Grant, Clíona Ó Gallchoir, and Penny Warburton (Cambridge: Cambridge UP, 2001) 107.

19. Elizabeth Eger, Charlotte Grant, Clíona Ó Gallchoir, and Penny Warburton, "Introduction: Women, Writing, and Representation," *Women, Writing and the Public Sphere, 1700–1830* (Cambridge: Cambridge UP, 2001) 11, 13.

20. Gary Kelly, "Bluestocking Feminism" 172, 176.

21. Eger, *The Nine Living Muses of Great Britain (1779: Women, Reason, and Literary Community in Eighteenth-Century Britain* (Ph.D. dissertation, King's College, Cambridge, 1999)) 130. Eger's work is significant as one of the few studies to date that examines women's role in the emergence of a British literary canon.

22. Elizabeth Griffith, *The Morality of Shakespeare's Drama Illustrated* (London: T. Cadell, 1775).

23. A few exceptions to the disparagement of pre-Victorian male writers' periodical reviewing include Walter James Graham, *English Literary Periodicals* (New York: T. Nelson, 1930); John O. Hayden, *The Romantic Reviewers, 1802–1824* (Chicago: U of Chicago P, 1968); and Derek Roper, *Reviewing before the* Edinburgh, *1788–1802* (Newark: U of Delaware P, 1978).
24. Kathy MacDermott, "Literature and the Grub Street Myth," *Literature and History* 8 (1982): 159–69. The *OED* cites the first instance of the word "hack" used to mean "a literary drudge, who hires himself out to do any and every kind of literary work" as Oliver Goldsmith's 1774 epitaph on "poor Ned Purdon/ Who long was a bookseller's hack" (*Oxford English Dictionary*, CD-ROM [Oxford: Oxford UP, 1992]). Goldsmith was himself a notorious "bookseller's hack," reviewing for several periodicals, including the *Monthly Review*.
25. Jerome J. McGann, *The Romantic Ideology: A Critical Investigation* (Chicago: U of Chicago P, 1983).
26. MacDermott 168.
27. Marilyn Butler, *Romantics, Rebels, and Reactionaries: English Literature and Its Background 1760–1830* (Oxford: Oxford UP, 1981) 9, 70.
28. Jack Stillinger, *Multiple Authorship and the Myth of Solitary Genius* (New York: Oxford UP, 1991).
29. Sources on British religious Dissent include James E. Bradley, *Religion, Revolution, and English Radicalism: Nonconformity in Eighteenth-Century Politics and Society* (Cambridge, Cambridge UP, 1990); *Enlightenment and Religion: Rational Dissent in Eighteenth-Century Britain*, ed. Knud Haakonssen, Ideas in Context (Cambridge: Cambridge UP, 1996); Davidoff and Hall, *Family Fortunes: Men and Women of the English Middle Class, 1780–1850* (Chicago: U of Chicago P, 1987); and Robert M. Ryan, *The Romantic Reformation: Religious Politics in English Literature, 1789–1824*, Cambridge Studies in Romanticism 24, ed. Marilyn Butler and James Chandler (Cambridge, Cambridge UP, 1997).
30. The Act of Uniformity of 1662 required Anglican communion. The Conventicle Act of 1664 limited the numbers who could gather for religious purposes. The Five Mile Act of 1665 forbade ministers ejected from the Established Church from coming within five miles of their parish or of any center of population. After the "Glorious Revolution" of 1688, increased tolerance of dissenting worship became the rule, but legislative modifications and various forms of official and unofficial discrimination continued into the early nineteenth century.
31. See R. S. Crane, "Suggestions Toward a Genealogy of the 'Man of Feeling,'" *ELH: English Literary History* 1 (1934): 205–30.
32. R. K. Webb, "The Emergence of Rational Dissent," *Enlightenment and Religion: Rational Dissent in Eighteenth-Century Britain*, ed. Knud Haakonssen, Ideas in Context (Cambridge: Cambridge UP, 1996) 21.
33. Crane, 222; G. J. Barker-Benfield, *The Culture of Sensibility: Sex and Society in Eighteenth-Century Britain* (Chicago: U of Chicago P, 1992).
34. Davidoff and Hall 23.
35. Webb, "The Emergence of Rational Dissent" 37.
36. Webb, "The Emergence of Rational Dissent" 31.
37. Jean H. Hagstrum, *Sex and Sensibility: Ideal and Erotic Love from Milton to Mozart* (Chicago: U of Chicago P, 1980); John Mullan, *Sentiment and Socia-*

bility: The Language of Feeling in the Eighteenth Century (Oxford: Clarendon P, 1988) 61; G. J. Barker-Benfield, *The Culture of Sensibility* xxvi. Other important studies on the topic include *Sensibility in Transformation: Creative Resistance to Sentiment from the Augustans to the Romantics*, ed. Syndy McMillen Conger (Rutherford: Fairleigh Dickinson UP, 1990); Claudia L. Johnson, *Equivocal Beings: Politics, Gender, and Sentimentality in the 1790s: Wollstonecraft, Radcliffe, Burney, Austen*, Women in Culture and Society, ed. Catharine R. Stimpson (Chicago: U of Chicago P, 1995); and Janet Todd, *Sensibility: An Introduction* (London: Methuen, 1986).
38. Jürgen Habermas, *The Structural Transformation of the Public Sphere: An Inquiry into a Category of Bourgeois Society*, trans. Thomas Burger with the assistance of Frederick Lawrence (1989; Cambridge MA: MIT P, 1991) For other revisions of Habermas's theory, see Rita Felski, *Beyond Feminist Aesthetics: Feminist Literature and Social Change* (Cambridge, MA: Harvard UP, 1989); *Habermas and the Public Sphere*, ed. Craig Calhoun (Cambridge MA: MIT P, 1992); Dena Goodman, *The Republic of Letters: A Cultural History of the French Enlightenment* (Ithaca: Cornell UP, 1994); Joan Landes, *Women and the Public Sphere in the Age of the French Revolution* (Ithaca: Cornell UP, 1988); Joan Landes, ed., *Feminism, the Public and the Private* (Oxford: Oxford UP, 1998); and Jon P. Klancher, ed., *Romanticism and its Publics: A Forum Organized and Introduced by Jon Klancher*, Spec. issue of *Studies in Romanticism* 33 (1994): 527–88.
39. Guest 11.
40. Anne K. Mellor, *Mothers of the Nation: Women's Political Writing in England, 1780–1830*, Women of Letters, ed. Sandra M. Gilbert and Susan Gubar (Bloomington IN: Indiana UP, 2000) 7, 9.
41. Linda Colley, *Britons: Forging the Nation 1707–1837* (New Haven: Yale UP, 1992) 250, 261.
42. Guest 15.
43. Guest 16, 192.
44. Gerald Newman, *The Rise of English Nationalism: A Cultural History 1740–1830* (1987; New York: St. Martin's P, 1997) 126, quoting Jacques Barzun, "Cultural Nationalism and the Makings of Fame," *Nationalism and Internationalism: Essays Inscribed to Carlton J. H. Hayes*, ed. E. M. Earle (New York: Columbia UP, 1950) 3.
45. Newman 127.
46. James Chandler, "The Pope Controversy: Romantic Poetics and the English Canon," *Critical Inquiry* 10 (1984): 481–509.
47. Thomas F. Bonnell, "Bookselling and Canon-Making: The Trade Rivalry over the English Poets, 1776–1783," *Studies in Eighteenth Century Culture* 19 (1989): 53–69.
48. In *Desire and Domestic Fiction: A Political History of the Novel* (New York: Oxford UP, 1987), Nancy Armstrong explores how domestic fiction and educational and conduct literature for women, two literary forms of particular interest to women critics, similarly worked to reverse traditional class hierarchies, shaping the values that were to define British Victorian middle-class domesticity as the foundation of individual worth.
49. In *Mothers of the Nation*, Mellor credits such remarks with instituting the revolution in literary hierarchies that promoted the novel to the position of

dominant literary genre today (See especially Chapter 5, "Literary Criticism, Cultural Authority, and the Rise of the Novel.")
50. Graham, *English Literary Periodicals*; Wardle, "Mary Wollstonecraft, Analytical Reviewer," *PMLA* 62 (1947): 1000–9; Roper, *Reviewing before the Edinburgh* 92n.
51. Jon P. Klancher, *The Making of English Reading Audiences, 1790–1832* (Madison: U of Wisconsin P, 1987) ix, x.
52. Klancher 3.
53. Moody's reviewing for the *Monthly Review* began in 1789 and ended shortly before Barbauld's contributions began, interrupted by some years during which she contributed no reviews. Besides Barbauld and Moody, Fanny Burney contributed an obituary on William Seward in the July 1799 number. In addition, Betty Rizzo offers a strong argument for attributing a series of reviews published between 1757 and 1763 and signed "N.," a signature never before identified, to editor Ralph Griffiths' wife, Isabella Griffiths, who may have assisted her husband by occasionally contributing reviews during the early years of his editorship of the periodical.

Part I Introduction

1. *Memoirs of Mrs. Inchbald: Including Her Familiar Correspondence with the Most Distinguished Persons of Her Time. To Which Are Added* The Massacre, *and* A Case of Conscience; *Now First Published from Her Autograph Copies*, ed. James Boaden, 2 vols. (London: Richard Bentley, 1833) 1:165. *The British Theatre* carried the full title *The British Theatre; or, A Collection of Plays, Which Are Acted at the Theatres Royal, Drury Lane, Covent Garden, and Haymarket; Printed under the Authority of the Managers from the Prompt Books; with Biographical and Critical Remarks; by Mrs. Inchbald*, 25 vols. (London: Longman, Hurst, Rees, Orme, and Brown, 1808). It was originally issued in periodical installments beginning 1806, with bound volume publication beginning in 1808.
2. As Marilyn Butler phrases it, "recent American Romanticist orthodoxy declares the great Romantic topic to be the alienated individual consciousness," taking as its most canonical text *The Prelude*, "that autobiography of a post-revolutionary recluse" ("Revising the Canon," *TLS* 4 [Dec. 1987] 1360). Milestones in this view would include M. H. Abrams, *The Mirror and the Lamp: Romantic Theory and the Critical Tradition* (London: Oxford UP, 1953); Harold Bloom, *The Anxiety of Influence – A Theory of Poetry* (London: Oxford UP, 1973); and Geoffrey H. Hartman, *Wordsworth's Poetry 1787–1814* (New Haven: Yale UP, 1964).

Chapter 1

1. P. O'Brien, *Warrington Academy, 1757–86: Its Predecessors and Successors* (Wigan, UK: Owl Books, 1989) 30. Further information on Dissenter education and Warrington Academy is provided by Herbert McLachlan, *Warrington Academy: Its History and Influence* (Manchester: the Chetham Society, 1943) and Daniel E. White, "The 'Joineriana': Anna Barbauld, the

Aikin Family Circle, and the Dissenting Public Sphere," *Eighteenth-Century Studies* 32 (1999): 511–33.
2. Aikin, J[ohn] and A[nna] L[etitia], *Miscellaneous Pieces in Prose* (London: Johnson, 1773).
3. On publishing practices of Cadell and Davies and their associates, see Thomas Rees, *Reminiscences of Literary London from 1779 to 1853* (1896; *Reminiscence of Literary London from 1779 to 1853* by Thomas Rees and *The Rise and Progress of the Gentleman's Magazine* by John Nichols, The English Book Trade 1660–1853 [New York: Garland, 1974] 129–32) and Charles Gerring, *Notes on Printers and Booksellers with a Chapter on Chap Books* (London: Simpkin, Marshall, Hamilton, Kent, 1900), especially 59–60.
4. Barbauld, "On the Poetical Works of Mr. William Collins," *The Poetical Works of Mr. William Collins* (1797; London: T. Cadell, Jun. and W. Davies: 1802): iii–l. I discuss Barbauld's essays in reverse order of their publication because the essay on Collins, treating a poet especially noted for his intellectual difficulty, presents the better occasion for developing my ideas. The Akenside essay then offers further confirmation.
5. Barbauld, "On [...] Collins" iv–vi.
6. Richard Wendorf, *William Collins and Eighteenth-Century English Poetry* (Minneapolis: U of Minnesota P, 1981) 87, 103.
7. Barbauld, "On [...] Collins" vi.
8. Barbauld, "On [...] Collins" v.
9. Barbauld, "On [...] Collins" vi–viii.
10. Wendorf 22, 104.
11. Barbauld, "On [...] Collins" vii–viii.
12. Simpson 123.
13. Barbauld, "On [...] Collins" xxiii.
14. Simpson 123.
15. Barbauld, "Essay on *The Pleasures of Imagination*," *The Pleasures of Imagination by Mark Akenside* (London: T. Cadell, and W. Davies, 1794; Philadelphia: B. Johnson, J. Johnson, and R. Johnson, 1804) xiii–xx.
16. Foxon, David F., *English Verse, 1701–1750: A Catalogue of Separately Printed Poems with Notes on Contemporary Collected Editions*, 2 vols. (Cambridge: Cambridge UP, 1975) 1:14, 132–3; *The Cambridge Bibliography of English Literature*, ed. F. W. Bateson, 4 vols. (Cambridge: Cambridge UP, 1940) 2:335–8, 350–1).
17. Barbauld, "Essay on *The Pleasures of Imagination*" xiii.
18. Barbauld, "Essay on *The Pleasures of Imagination*" xiii, xv, xvi.
19. Barbauld, "On the Origin and Progress of Novel-Writing," *The British Novelists*, 50 vols. (1810; London: F. C. and J. Rivington, 1820) 1:1–59.
20. Barbauld read French fluently, reviewed French literature, and gave French fiction a central place in her essay "On the Origin and Progress of Novel-Writing." Moreover, Joseph Johnson was key in introducing foreign, particularly French, publications to English audiences (Leslie F. Chard, "Bookseller to Publisher: Joseph Johnson and the English Book trade, 1760–1810," *The Library: Transactions of the Bibliographical Society* 32 [1977]: 153). Johnson would have called Barbauld's attention to a publication like Staël's work.
21. Barbauld, "On [...] Novel-Writing" 37, 15, 40.

22. Barbauld, "Preliminary Essay" to *Selections from the* Spectator, Tatler, Guardian, *and* Freeholder, 2 vols. (1804; London: Edward Moxon, 1849) v–vi.
23. Barbauld, "Preliminary Essay" to *Selections* xiii, xii.
24. Barbauld, "Preliminary Essay" to *Selections* xii, xv.
25. Barbauld, "Preliminary Essay" to *Selections* xiv, xv, xiv, xxii.
26. In her "Womanpower" chapter of *Britons*, Colley argues that during the latter years of the eighteenth century, the exclusion of women from public life and their restriction to the private or domestic sphere paradoxically enabled them to achieve some authority as arbiters of issues and values that were fostered in domestic life and to advocate for the pertinence of those values to public issues and policies.
27. Lucy Aikin, *Memoir of John Aikin, M. D. with a Selection of His Miscellaneous Pieces, Biographical, Moral and Critical* (1823; Philadelphia: Small, 1824), esp. 89–90.
28. Bonnell 54.
29. *Correspondence of Samuel Richardson, Author of* Pamela, Clarissa, *and* Sir Charles Grandison; *Selected from the Original Manuscripts, Bequeathed by Him to His Family*, 6 vols. (London: Richard Phillips, 1804; New York: AMS P, 1966) 1: vi. The "Advertisement" appears on 1: iii–vi, and Barbauld's critical essay, "Life of Samuel Richardson with Remarks on His Writings" appears on 1: vii–ccxii.
30. Barbauld, "Preliminary Essay" to *Selections* xviii.
31. Barbauld, "Essay on *The Pleasures of Imagination*" xiii.
32. Barbauld, "Preliminary Essay" to *Selections* xvii–xviii.
33. Chandler 503.
34. Chandler 486–7, quoting Lawrence Lipking, *The Ordering of the Arts in Eighteenth-Century England* (Princeton: Princeton UP, 1970) 328–9.
35. Chandler 487, 494.
36. Chandler 487, quoting Lipking 330.
37. Chandler 487.
38. "Preliminary Essay" to *Selections* ix, xiv.
39. Addison, *Spectator 62, Essays in Criticism and Literary Theory*, ed. John Loftis (Northbrook, IL: AHM Publishing, 1975) 71–7.
40. "Preliminary Essay" to *Selections* xvii.
41. "Life of Samuel Richardson" viii.
42. "Life of Samuel Richardson" xiv–xvi. The germ of this view of novelistic realism as accurately depicting the same type of people as make up the bulk of novel readership can be found in *Miscellaneous Pieces in Prose*. There Barbauld also remarks on the limited appeal of heroic epics, observing that by contrast, "everyone can relish the author who represents common life, because every one can refer to the originals from whence his ideas were taken" (Barbauld, *Miscellaneous Pieces in Prose* 42).
43. Moore, "'Ladies ... Taking the Pen in Hand': Mrs. Barbauld's Criticism of Eighteenth-Century Women Novelists," *Fetter'd or Free: British Women Novelists 1670–1815*, ed. Mary Anne Schofield and Cecilia Macheski (Athens, OH: U of Ohio P, 1986) 383–97.
44. "Life of Samuel Richardson" xxxii–li.
45. "Life of Samuel Richardson" lxi, cv, clxxiv.

46. Griffith, *A Collection of Novels, Selected and Revised by Mrs. Griffith*, 3 vols (London: G. Kearsly, 1777) sig. A$_2$.
47. Moore 388.
48. Barbauld, "On [...] Novel-Writing" 56.
49. Barbauld, "On [...] Novel-Writing" 14, 42.
50. Moore 394. *The British Novelists* includes 13 male writers and 8 women, far closer to a 50:50 ratio than any previous collection.
51. Claudia L. Johnson offers a cogent analysis of why Barbauld's canon, asserted so forcefully in such a major canon-making enterprise, failed to retain its position as definitive. See "'Let me make the novels of a country': Barbauld's The British Novelists (1810/1820)," *Novel: A Forum on Fiction*, 34 (2001): 163–79.
52. Barbauld, "Preliminary Essay" to *Selections* v–vi.
53. Barbauld, "On [...] Novel-Writing" 1–2, 46–7.
54. "On [...] Novel-Writing" 47, 48, 29, 55.
55. Mary Wollstonecraft, *A Vindication of the Rights of Woman* (1792), *The Works of Mary Wollstonecraft*, ed. Janet Todd and Marilyn Butler, 7 vols. (London: William Pickering, 1989) 5:Ch. 1; Barbauld, "On [...] Novel-Writing" 19.
56. Barbauld, "On [...] Novel-Writing" 2, 59, 22–3, 36.
57. Barbauld, "On [...] Novel-Writing" 45, 44, 44–5. Reading may have been the cheapest of pleasures, but it was by no means cheap. At 12*l*. 12*s*., Barbauld's *British Novelists* cost more than a fourth of the annual income of most British families (in *Women Writing About Money*, Edward Copeland cites Eric J. Hawsbawm's claim [*The Age of Revolution*] that in 1800, all but 15 percent of British families had income less than £50 [Copeland 221, n. 38]). At around £1 per copy, even a single novel represented a prohibitive expense for most. Circulating libraries were springing up, but in 1800 the annual subscription fee for them ranged around a guinea, a price, as James Raven puts it, "hardly affordable for most" (Peter Garside, James Raven, and Rainer Schöwerling, *The English Novel, 1770–1829: A Bibliographical Survey of Prose Fiction Published in the British Isles*, 2 vols. [Oxford: Oxford UP, 2000] 1:111). The second-hand market opened some possibilities, but these books were neither the newest nor the best, and for many even second-hand prices would have been prohibitive. And although borrowing from acquaintances was an option for some, one had to have acquaintances that could afford to purchase a book in order to borrow from them.
58. Barbauld, "Essay on *The Pleasures of Imagination*" xiii.
59. "Introduction," *Anna Letitia Barbauld: Selected Poetry and Prose*, ed. William McCarthy and Elizabeth Kraft (Petersborough, Ont.: Broadview, 2002) 13, 17.

Chapter 2

1. *A Simple Story*, 4 vols. (London: G. G. and J. Robinson, 1791); *Nature and Art*, 2 vols. (London: G. G. and J. Robinson, 1796); *Lover's Vows* (London: G. G. and J. Robinson, 1798).
2. Unless otherwise noted, biographical information in this chapter is summarized from Boaden's *Memoirs of Mrs. Inchbald* and Annibel Jenkins's *I'll*

Tell You What: The Life of Elizabeth Inchbald (Lexington, KY: UP of Kentucky, 2003). Other biographical studies include S. R. Littlewood, *Elizabeth Inchbald and Her Circle: The Life Story of a Charming Woman (1753–1821)* (London: Daniel O'Connor, 1921); William McKee, *Elizabeth Inchbald, Novelist* (Washington, DC: Catholic U of America, 1935); and Roger Manvell, *Elizabeth Inchbald: England's Principal Woman Dramatist and Independent Woman of Letters in 18th Century London, a Biographical Study* (Lanham, NY: UP of America, 1987).

3. Inchbald's career as a critic was brief. Other than the *British Theatre* project, her only identified criticism was an amusing essay usually referred to as "On Novel Writing," which appeared in the form of a letter to *The Artist* (1 [13 June 1807]: 9–19), Prince Hoare's short-lived periodical devoted to literature and the arts.

4. This initial periodical publication creates some difficulties in discussing the series. Collections bound for the booksellers do not present the plays in the order of publication. In addition, some extant copies were assembled and bound by private collectors. As a result, bound copies vary, not always presenting their contents in the same order, and sometimes lacking some feature such as one or two of Inchbald's essays or some of the illustrative frontispiece engravings. Pagination extends not through entire volumes, but only through single plays, each play beginning its own pagination anew. Furthermore, some readers wishing to consult the essays may prefer *Remarks for the British Theatre (1806–1809) by Elizabeth Inchbald*, the single volume reprinting of Inchbald's essays alone, edited and introduced by Cecilia Macheski (Delmar, NY: Scholars' Facsimiles & Reprints, 1990). For these reasons, I cite Inchbald's remarks by the name of the play to which they are appended rather than by volume or page number. I thank Macheski for pointing out and explaining the discrepancy between copies.

5. Jenkins documents that *The British Theatre* was a continuation of *British Theatre Plays*, a series and later collection compiled by bookseller John Bell that was first issued in 1780 and saw numerous expanded editions over the next quarter century, reaching at least 47 volumes in the 1791–97 edition. Bell sold the rights to his series to long time business associate Thomas Longman, who conceived of the idea of adding critical prefaces when he revived it.

6. Marvin Carlson, "Elizabeth Inchbald: A Woman Critic in Her Theatrical Culture," *Women in British Romantic Theatre*, ed. Catherine Burroughs (Cambridge: Cambridge UP, 2000) 210.

7. Though Longman or his representative selected the versions included, Inchbald seems generally to approve of bowdlerizing. She objects to Nahum Tate's version of *King Lear*, for example, not because it is bowdlerized, but because Tate failed to go far enough when he left in the "savage and improbable" gouging of Gloster's eyes ("Remarks" on *King Lear*, *The British Theatre*).

8. "Remarks" on *She Wou'd and She Wou'd Not* by Colley Cibber.

9. "Remarks" on *The Rivals* by Richard Brinsley Sheridan.

10. "Introduction," *The Plays of Elizabeth Inchbald*, Ed. Paula R. Backscheider, 2 vols. Eighteenth-Century English Drama (New York: Garland, 1980) 1:x.

11. Boaden 2:87.

12. The invitation to contribute to the *Quarterly* appears in Boaden 2:115–18, where Boaden reprints letters from *Quarterly* proprietor John Murray and his agent, a Mr. Hoppner, soliciting from Inchbald reviews of Mme. Cottin's *Amelie Mansfield* and Tobin's *School for Authors*. Patricia Sigl cites evidence from Samuel Smiles, *A Publisher and His Friends* (London: John Murray, 1891) 1:53, showing that Inchbald "had no confidence in her ability to match wits with men of learning in print" and that she declined to contribute to the *Quarterly Review* because of "her fears about the gaps in her reading which disqualified her as a critic" ("Prince Hoare's *Artist* and Anti-Theatrical Polemics in the Early 1800s: Mrs Inchbald's Contribution," *Theatre Notebook* 44 [1990]: 65). The Smiles reference turns out to consist of a letter from Inchbald to Hoppner, not reprinted in Boaden, in which Inchbald explains that, because of gaps in her reading, she feels wholly unqualified to review any literature except novels, and has reservations over reviewing even those. She does, however, agree to review the book promptly, should Hoppner still desire her to. Apparently she changed her mind or Murray did, because no review of either book appears in the *Quarterly*.
13. Quotations from the exchange are taken from Colman's letter and Inchbald's reply published in *The British Theatre* just preceding the "Remarks" on *The Heir at Law*.
14. Zall, "The Cool World of Samuel Taylor Coleridge: Elizabeth Inchbald; or Sex and Sensibility," *The Wordsworth Circle* 12 (1981): 270–3; Burroughs, *Closet Stages: Joanna Baillie and the Theater Theory of British Romantic Women Writers* (Philadelphia: U of Pennsylvania P, 1997); Katherine M. Rogers, "Britain's First Woman Drama Critic: Elizabeth Inchbald," *Curtain Calls: British and American Women and the Theater, 1660–1820*, ed. Mary Anne Schofield and Cecilia Macheski (Athens, OH: U of Ohio P, 1991) 277–90; Anna Lott, "Sexual Politics in Elizabeth Inchbald," *SEL: Studies in English Literature, 1500–1900* 34 (1994): 635–48.
15. John Taylor, *Records of My Life* (New York: J. & J. Harper, 1833) 228.
16. Zall 271–2. Zall repeats the anecdote about *Nature and Art* from C. Kegan Paul, *William Godwin: His Friends and Contemporaries*, 2 vols. (London: Henry S. King, 1876) 1:140–1, and he takes the anecdote about visiting Holcroft from Holcroft, *Life of Thomas Holcroft*, ed. Elbridge Colby, 2 vols. (London, 1833) 2:57, who is himself quoting from Boaden 1:330. Zall slightly exaggerates the Colby anecdote, claiming for Inchbald an "open carriage" when in fact Colby relates that she and her close friend, bookseller George Robinson, went together in a "coach," normally a closed vehicle.
17. The younger Colman accused Inchbald of ingratitude to the man who first produced one of her plays, calling his father the "*very man*, on whose tomb she idly plants this poisonous weed of remark, to choke the laurels which justly grace his memory." As a part of her response, Inchbald affirms that though she was grateful, the actor manager had shown her "no more than those usual attentions which every manager of a theatre is supposed to confer, when he first selects a novice in dramatic writing, as worthy of being introduced, on his stage, to the public." One might argue that Inchbald could be trying to underrate her debt to the elder theater

manager, but Ellen Donkin's study of women playwrights and eighteenth-century theater practice suggests that Inchbald's version of her obligations is closer to the truth than Colman's (Ellen Donkin, *Getting Into the Act: Women Playwrights in London, 1776–1829* [London: Routledge, 1995]. See her Chapter 5, "Advantage, Mrs. Inchbald.").

18. "Remarks" on *The Heir at Law* by George Colman the younger. Jenkins notes that Inchbald's barb was especially sharp here, for Colman had dropped out of the university and could in no sense be described as a scholar.
19. Letter from Isaac D'Israeli to John Murray dated 28 July 1809, quoted in Patricia Sigl, "Prince Hoare's *Artist* and Anti-Theatrical Polemics," 71–2. *The British Theatre* was followed by *A Collection of Farces and other Afterpieces which are acted at the Theatres Royal, Drury-Lane, Covent-Garden, and Hay-Market*, printed under the authority of the Managers from the Prompt Book, selected by Mrs Inchbald, 7 vols. (London: Longman, et al., 1809) and *The Modern Theatre; A Collection of Successful Modern Plays, as Acted at the Theatres Royal, London ..., Selected by Mrs. Inchbald*, 10 vols. (London: Longman, et al., 1811).
20. Boaden 2:132–3.
21. Carlson 209–10.
22. Simon Jarvis, *Scholars and Gentlemen: Shakespeare Textual Criticism and Representations of Scholarly Labour, 1725–1765* (Oxford: Clarendon P, 1995) 166.
23. "Remarks" on *A Comedy of Errors*.
24. Klancher, *The Making of English Reading Audiences* ix.
25. Jenkins takes exception to the charge that Inchbald was uneducated, pointing out that Inchbald pursued a course of reading that included not only many of the most revered British authors, but many classical authors as well. Yet while Inchbald's educational achievement would have set her well above much of her audience, it must be distinguished from the systematic training that was the goal of a university education, training that would ideally have prepared the scholar in the "forms scientific and established."
26. "Remarks" on *A Comedy of Errors*.
27. Isaac Reed, *Biographia Dramatica*, 2 vols. (London: Rivington, 1782).
28. "Remarks" on *Oroonoko*; "Remarks" on *Man of the World*; "Remarks" on *Julius Caesar*. William Godwin evaded prosecution for the potentially seditious message of *Political Justice* (1793) because unlike, for example, Thomas Paine's *Rights of Man* (1791–92), Godwin's book was too expensive to reach and inflame many lower class readers. Censorship of Inchbald's own *Massacre*, a tragedy based on the fate of Louis XVI during the French Revolution, may provide a comparable example. Though the play was printed, it remained undistributed and unstaged, apparently withheld by Inchbald herself. John Taylor, to whom Inchbald applied for advice on whether to publish the play, remarks that he had advised her to suppress it (*Records of My Life* 228).
29. "Remarks" on *Othello* by William Shakespeare and "Remarks" on *The Earl of Essex* by Henry Jones.
30. "Remarks" on *The Surrender of Calais*; "Remarks" on *Henry V*; "Remarks" on *Fontainbleau*; "Remarks" on *All for Love*; "Remarks" on *School for Reform*.
31. "Remarks" on *The Distressed Mother*.

32. "Remarks" on *Henry IV, Part 2*.
33. "Remarks" on *Henry VIII*; "Remarks" on *Twelfth Night*.
34. "Remarks" on *King Lear*.
35. As recently as 1978, Om Prakash Mathur defined closet drama as "drama which, on account of an undue predominance of the 'literary' element, 'reads' much better than it acts (if it is at all intended to be produced), and communicates its full characteristic pleasure in reading and not in a theatrical performance" (*The Closet Drama of the Romantic Revival*, Salzburg Studies in English Literature under the Direction of Professor Erwin A. Stürzl [Salzburg, Austria: Institut für Englische Sprache und Literatur, Universität Salzburg, 1978] 1). Wiebe Hogendoorn similarly lists the characteristics that enable classification of a play as closet drama, with literariness standing preeminent among them ("Reading on a Booke: Closet Drama and the Study of Theatre Arts" *Essays on Drama and Theatre: Liber Amicorum Benjamin Hunningher*, ed. Erica Hunningher [Schilling Amsterdam/Baarn: Moussault's Uitgeverij, 1973] 50–66). Only in the last decade or two have more sophisticated theories of Romantic closet drama emerged, first with Alan Richardson, who, in *A Mental Theater: Poetic Drama and Consciousness in the Romantic Age* (University Park: Pennsylvania State UP, 1988) defines it as drama in which "Dramatic action would not function to portray or set off character; rather, character becomes plot as the dramatic interest centers on the history of a protagonist's consciousness" (1). In her study of Joanna Baillie's drama theory, Catherine M. Burroughs brings together the association of "closet" as a space for women's artistic and intellectual expression and a more modern notion of "closet" emerging from gender and gay studies in order to suggest that closet drama is that which will "problematize the distinctions between the actor's body and the role with which s/he is identified [... in order to] deconstruct the opposition between 'literariness' and 'theatricality'" (*Closet Stages* 15–16).
36. "Remarks" on *De Monfort*.
37. *Closet Stages* 85.
38. "Remarks" on *The Dramatist*; "Remarks" on *John Bull*; "Remarks" on *The Rival Queens*.
39. "Remarks" on *The Mourning Bride*; "Remarks" on *Barbarossa*; "Remarks" on *The West Indian*; "Remarks" on *Othello*; "Remarks on *The Beggar's Opera*.
40. Burroughs, *Closet Stages* 84; Backscheider, *The Plays of Elizabeth Inchbald* xxv.
41. Stillinger, *Multiple Authorship and the Myth of Solitary Genius* 6–7, vi, 183.
42. "Remarks" on *The Careless Husband*; "Remarks" on *The Duenna*.
43. "Remarks" on *Lovers' Vows*.
44. Boaden 2:23–4.

Part II Introduction

1. James Basker, "Criticism and the Rise of Periodical Literature," *Cambridge History of Literary Criticism*, ed. H. B. Nisbet and Claude Rawson, 8 vols, vol. 4, *The Eighteenth Century* (Cambridge: Cambridge UP, 1997) 316. My brief history of literary reviews is summarized from Basker's chapter. On the

growing anxieties around the proliferation of writing during the Romantic years, see Clifford Siskin, *The Work of Writing: Literature and Social Change in Britain, 1700–1830* (Baltimore: Johns Hopkins UP, 1998). Klancher's discussion of the role of periodicals in transforming the Romantic-era public sphere into a fully textual phenomenon, "an image to be consumed by readers who did not frequent it" is relevant here as well (*The Making of English Reading Audiences* 24).
2. Jno. Chas. O'Reid [Josiah Conder], *Reviewers Reviewed; Including an Enquiry into the Moral and Intellectual Effects of Habits of Criticism, and Their Influence on the General Interests of Literature; to Which Is Subjoined a Brief History of the Periodical Reviews Published in England and Scotland* (Oxford: J. Bartlett, 1811).
3. Butler, *Romantics, Rebels and Reactionaries* 70–1.

Chapter 3

1. *Collected Letters of Mary Wollstonecraft*, ed. Ralph M. Wardle (Ithaca: Cornell UP, 1979), 164.
2. Most biographical studies of either writer are interested in the relationship between these two professional women writers primarily because of this influence. Some examples include Gary Kelly, *Revolutionary Feminism: The Mind and Career of Mary Wollstonecraft* (London: Macmillan, 1992) and *Women, Writing, and Revolution, 1790–1827* (Oxford: Clarendon P, 1993); Gina M. Luria, "Mary Hays: A Critical Biography" (Ph.D. Diss., New York U, 1972); Janet Todd, *Mary Wollstonecraft: A Revolutionary Life* (London: Weidenfeld & Nicolson, 2000); Eleanor Ty, *Unsex'd Revolutionaries: Five Women Novelists of the 1790s* (Toronto: U of Toronto P, 1993); and A. F. Wedd, ed., *The Love-Letters of Mary Hays (1779–1780)* (London: Methuen, 1925), 1–14.
3. MacDermott, "Literature and the Grub Street Myth."
4. Siskin's *The Work of Writing* examines the professionalization of literary culture while arguing for the emergence of writing as a new technology. Other recent studies in periodicals and print culture include Kevin Gilmartin, *Print Politics: The Press and Radical Opposition in Early Nineteenth-Century England*, Cambridge Studies in Romanticism 21 (Cambridge: Cambridge UP, 1996); Mark Parker *Literary Magazines and British Romanticism*, Cambridge Studies in Romanticism 45 (Cambridge: Cambridge UP, 2000); Thomas Pfau, *Wordsworth's Profession: Form, Class, and the Logic of Early Romantic Cultural Production* (Stanford: Stanford UP, 1997); and Marcus Wood, *Radical Satire and Print Culture, 1790–1822* (Oxford: Oxford UP, 1994). In her introduction to a special issue of *Victorian Periodicals Review* devoted to women's participation in nineteenth-century periodical publishing, D. J. Trela describes the rapid increase in the numbers of women who were able to earn a living through journalism and editing ("Introduction: Nineteenth Century Women and Periodicals," *Victorian Periodicals Review* 29 [1996]: 89–94).
5. Information about Johnson is summarized from Gerald P. Tyson's *Joseph Johnson: A Liberal Publisher* (Iowa City: University of Iowa P, 1979). A Dissenter himself, Johnson had over the years published an impressive

array of Dissenting authors, many of whose works contained some of the country's most advanced thinking on social, scientific, and theological issues. Johnson also showed astute judgment of art and literature at times, employing William Blake as an illustrator and assisting Henry Fuseli with his "Milton Gallery" plan. Though at this date he rarely published creative works, he nevertheless printed some of William Wordsworth's and Samuel Taylor Coleridge's early work (Leslie F. Chard II, "Joseph Johnson: Father of the Book Trade," *Bulletin of the New York Public Library* 79 [1975]: 51–82). In fact, he might have been the publisher of *Lyrical Ballads* had not contractual complications interfered. Johnson also published Anna Letitia Aikin's (later Barbauld) first volume of poetry. Later, he increased his attention to creative works, and women writers such as Mary Hays, Maria Edgeworth, and Anna Seward joined the ranks of Johnson's authors.
6. Wardle, "Mary Wollstonecraft, *Analytical Reviewer*."
7. *The Making of English Reading Audiences.*
8. On the evolution of literary reviews' purpose, see Basker, "Criticism and the Rise of Periodical Literature;" Marilyn Butler, "Culture's Medium: The Role of the Review," *The Cambridge Companion to British Romanticism*, ed. Stuart Curran (Cambridge: U of Cambridge P, 1993), 120–76; and Roper, *Reviewing before the* Edinburgh.
9. Thomas Christie, "To the Public," *Analytical Review* 1 (May 1788): vi.
10. Butler 126–7.
11. Christie i, iv.
12. In *Mary Wollstonecraft* Wardle, normally dismissive of Wollstonecraft's reviews, concedes that her loose though lively sentences provide a welcome relief from her colleagues' "studied periods" 99.
13. Klancher 23–4.
14. Review of *Observations and Reflections Made in the Course of a Journey through France, Italy, and Germany* by Hester Lynch Piozzi (London: Cadell, 1789), *Analytical Review* 4 (June–July 1789): 301; *The Works of Mary Wollstonecraft*, ed. Janet Todd and Marilyn Butler, 7 vols. (London: William Pickering, 1989) 7:127. The issue of review commentary addressed to benefit the book's author rather than its potential reader is taken up in greater depth in the following chapter.
15. Wardle, *Mary Wollstonecraft* 98. The two reviews that Wardle regards as containing aesthetic criticism are the review of Charlotte Smith's *Ethelinde, or the Recluse of the Lake* (London: Cadell, 1789) in volume 5 (December 1789): 484; Todd and Butler 7:188–90, and Mrs Bennet's *Agnes de Courci; A Domestic Tale* (Bath: Hazard; London: Robinsons, 1789) in volume 6 (January 1790): 96–8; Todd and Butler 7:203–4.
16. Roper, *Reviewing Before the* Edinburgh 124.
17. Review of *Emmeline, the Orphan of the Castle*, by Charlotte Smith (London: Cadell, 1788), *Analytical Review* 1 (July 1788): 333; Todd and Butler 7:26.
18. Samuel Johnson, *Rambler* No. 4 (31 March 1750).
19. *Reviewing before the* Edinburgh 27.
20. Review of the anonymous *Woman. Sketches of the History, Genius, Disposition, Accomplishments, Employments, Customs, and Importance of the Fair Sex, in all Parts of the World* (London: Kearsley, 1790), *Analytical Review* 8 (September 1790): 100–1; Todd and Butler 7:291.

21. (London: Vernor, [n.d]) *Analytical Review* 1 (August 1788): 451–7; Todd and Butler 7:29–32.
22. Review of *The Interesting Narrative of the Life of Olaudah Equiano, or Gustavus Vassa, the African, Written by Himself*, *Analytical Review* 4 (May 1789): 28; Todd and Butler 7:101.
23. Wollstonecraft, review of *A General History of Music, from the Earliest Ages, to the Present Period*, by Charles Burney (London: Robson and Robinsons, 1789), *Analytical Review* 6 (February 1790): 131; Todd and Butler 7:211.
24. "[On Artificial Taste]," was published as a letter with the signature "W. Q." in *The Monthly Magazine* 3 (April 1797): 279–82. It is Wollstonecraft's only known contribution to any periodical other than the *Analytical Review*. The essay appeared again with amendations under the title "On Poetry" in *The Posthumous Works of the Author of a Vindication of the Rights of Woman in four volumes*, ed. William Godwin (London: Johnson, 1798). Most mentions of the essay refer to this second, posthumous version, arguing that this published version is superior and probably represents Wollstonecraft's own final intentions. Examining the manuscripts, however, Eleanor Louise Nicholes dates "On Poetry" as earlier in composition than "On Artificial Taste" (*Shelley and his Circle: 1773–1822*, ed. Kenneth Neill Cameron, 10 vols. [Cambridge, MA: Harvard UP, 1961] 1:177). The latter, then, would be the revised version, and as the version that Wollstonecraft herself published, the most authoritative as well. Comparing the two versions shows most alterations to be minor and nearly as often for the worse as for the better. For example, though Latinate words are sometimes replaced with more pithy Anglo-Saxon equivalents, on other occasions the exact opposite occurs. If any generalization can be made, it would be that the cumulative effect of the revisions is to add to the loose, almost luxuriant flow of Wollstonecraft's sentences – in other words, to make it more characteristic of Wollstonecraft's usual prose. Moreover, the most extensive revision mitigates in "On Artificial Taste" the harsher criticism in "On Poetry" of one of Samuel Johnson's remarks. Considering Wollstonecraft's admiration for Johnson, it seems likely that she would have preferred the second version.
25. *A Vindication of the Rights of Men*, Todd and Butler 5:29.
26. *Analytical Review* 1 (August 1788): 451–7; Todd and Butler 7:29–32.
27. Wollstonecraft, review of *Voyages Made in the Years 1788 and 1789, from China to the North-West Coast of America*, by John Meares, Esq. (London: Walter, 1790), *Analytical Review* 9 (January 1791): 8–16; Todd and Butler 7:332–6.
28. Wollstonecraft, review of *Observation on the River Wye, and Several Parts of South Wales, etc. Relative Chiefly to Picturesque Beauty, Made in the Summer of the Year 1770*, by William Gilpin, 2nd ed. (London: Price, 1789), *Analytical Review* 5 (September 1789): 41–6; Todd and Butler 7:160–4. Wollstonecraft's second review of Gilpin's work, discussing *Observations, Relative Chiefly to Picturesque Beauty, Made in the Year 1776, on Several Parts of Great Britain, Particularly the Highlands of Scotland* (London: Blamire, 1789), appears in the *Analytical Review* 6 (January 1790): 54–9; Todd and Butler 7:196–8. The third reviews *Remarks on Forest Scenery, and Other Woodland Views (Relative Chiefly to Picturesque Beauty.) Illustrated by the Scenes of New Forest in Hampshire* (London: Blamire, 1791) in *Analytical Review* 10 (August 1791): 396–405; Todd and Butler 7:386–8. The fourth review discusses *Three Essays:*

on Picturesque Beauty; on Picturesque Travel; and on Sketching Landscape (London: Blamire, 1792). It appears in the *Analytical Review* 14 (September 1792): 77–9; Todd and Butler 7:455–7.
29. Review of *Tour of the Isle of Wight* by J. Hassell (London: Hookham, 1790), *Analytical Review* 7 (August 1790): 393–5; Todd and Butler 7:279–81.
30. Review of *Letters of the Countess Du Barre* (London: Symonds, 1792), *Analytical Review* 12 (January 1792): 102; Todd and Butler 7:416.
31. Review of *Letters Written in France [...] between the Month of November 1794, and the Month of May 1795* by Major Tench (London: Johnson, 1796), *Analytical Review* 24 (September 1796): 238–43; Todd and Butler 7:467–72.
32. Review of *A View of England towards the Close of the Eighteenth Century*. By Fred. Aug. Wendeborn, LL.D., *Analytical Review* 9 (February 1791): 180–8; Todd and Butler 7:346–51, continued from (January 1791): 45–52; Todd and Butler 7:338–41.
33. Review of *Letters on Education: with Observations on Religious and Metaphysical Subjects* by Catherine Macaulay Graham (London: Dilly, 1790) *Analytical Review* 8 (November 1790) 241–54; Todd and Butler 7:309–22. This review, the issue's lead article, is one of the most important of Wollstonecraft's reviewing career.
34. Review of the anonymous *Female Ruin: A Poem* (London: Forster, 1791) *Analytical Review* 12 (March 1792) 275; Todd and Butler 7:422.
35. Review of *On the Prevention of Crimes, and on the Advantages of Solitary Imprisonment* by John Brewster (London: Clarke, 1792) *Analytical Review* 13 (June 1792): 107; Todd and Butler 7:442.
36. Todd, *Mary Wollstonecraft* 128, 135.
37. Wollstonecraft to Johnson, c. July 1788 *Collected Letters* 178–9.
38. Janet Todd, *Mary Wollstonecraft* 380.
39. See, for example, the discussion of Ralph Griffiths *Monthly Review* in the following chapter.
40. Price quoted in G. J. Barker-Benfield, "Mary Wollstonecraft: Eighteenth-Century Commonwealthwoman," *Journal of the History of Ideas* 50 (1989) 97.
41. Poovey, *The Proper Lady and the Woman Writer: Ideology as Style in the Works of Mary Wollstonecraft, Mary Shelley, and Jane Austen*, Women in Culture and Society, ed. Catherine R. Stimpson (Chicago: U of Chicago P, 1984). Wollstonecraft's letters and early publications demonstrate her absorption in her own sensibility (see, for example, her letter to George Blood, 4 December [1786], *Collected Letters*, 127–9), an issue that is discussed in Wardle's biography, Janet Todd's *Sensibility* and *The Sign of Angellica: Women, Writing, and Fiction, 1660–1800* (New York: Columbia UP, 1989) and Moira Ferguson and Janet Todd's *Mary Wollstonecraft*, Twayne's English Authors Series (Boston: Twayne, 1984), among other places.
42. Wollstonecraft, review of Johnson's *Sermon* 467; Todd and Butler 7:32.
43. Myers, "Sensibility and the 'Walk of Reason': Mary Wollstonecraft's Literary Reviews as Cultural Critique," *Sensibility in Transformation: Creative Resistance to Sentiment from the Augustans to the Romantics*, ed. Syndy McMillen Conger (Rutherford: Fairleigh Dickinson UP, 1990) 129–31.
44. Wollstonecraft's view of sensibility is perhaps one of the most contested issues in Wollstonecraft scholarship. Especially those scholars who concentrate primarily or exclusively on her *Vindication of the Rights of Woman* are

familiar with Wollstonecraft's condemnation of the frivolity, superficiality, and even depravity that can proceed from the cultivation of sensibility. *Rights of Woman* offers an extended critique of the social ills caused by an excessive, artificial sensibility, especially among middle-class women, and advocates as a corrective an educational system that would develop women's reason and prepare them for the active exercise of virtue in both the domestic setting and in at least some appropriate professions. Many scholars have read this work, then, as opposing reason to emotion, and favoring the former to the denigration of the latter. See, for example, Johnson, *Equivocal Beings*; Cora Kaplan, *Sea Changes: Essays on Culture and Feminism* (London: Verso, 1986); Poovey, *The Proper Lady and the Woman Writer*; and Todd, *Mary Wollstonecraft*.

Certainly, *Rights of Women* makes a strong case against excesses of sensibility, especially as they undermined the domestic virtues, but as I argued in my introduction, the domestic virtues were themselves grounded in sensibility, albeit a moderated form – witness, for example, Wollstonecraft's various images of contented domesticity. Thus several scholars point out the various ways Wollstonecraft destabilizes the traditional opposition between the extremes of pure reason and sensibility. Notable contributions to this argument include Barker-Benfield, *The Culture of Sensibility*, especially Chapter 7, "Wollstonecraft and the Crisis of Sensibility in the 1790s"; Guest, *Small Change*; Simpson, *Romanticism, Nationalism, and the Revolt against Theory*, esp. 104–10; and Orrin N. C. Wang, "The Other Reasons: Female Alterity and Enlightenment Discourse in Mary Wollstonecraft's *A Vindication of the Rights of Woman*," *Yale Journal of Criticism* 5 (1991): 129–49.

In addition to sources mentioned above, those interested in the debate over Wollstonecraft's engagement with the discourse of sensibility will wish to consult Syndy McMillen Conger, *Mary Wollstonecraft and the Language of Sensibility* [Rutherford: Fairleigh Dickinson UP, 1994]; Harriet Devine Jump, *Mary Wollstonecraft: Writer* (New York: Harvester Wheatsheaf, 1994); Catherine N. Parke, "What Kind of Heroine is Mary Wollstonecraft?" *Sensibility in Transformation: Creative Resistance to Sentiment from the Augustans to the Romantics* (Rutherford: Fairleigh Dickinson UP, 1990) 103–19; Timothy J. Reiss, "Revolution in Bounds: Wollstonecraft, Women, and Reason," *Gender and Theory*, ed. Linda Kauffman (New York: Basil Blackwell, 1989) 11–50; and Susan Khin Zaw, "The Reasonable Heart: Mary Wollstonecraft's View of the Relation Between Reason and Feeling in Morality, Moral Psychology, and Moral Development," *Hypatia* 13 (1998): 78–117. In discussing Wollstonecraft's views of the relationship between reason and imagination, "the mother of sentiment," Barbara Taylor also contributes to this debate (Taylor, *Mary Wollstonecraft and the Feminist Imagination*, Cambridge Studies in Romanticism 56 [Cambridge: Cambridge UP, 2003] 58 quoting Wollstonecraft to Gilbert Imlay, 22 September 1794, *Collected Letters* 263).

45. Review of *Sermons, on Different Subjects*, published by S. Hayes, A.M. (London: Cadell, [n.d.]) *Analytical Review* 2 (September 1788): 11; Todd and Butler 7:40.
46. Wollstonecraft, review of Burney's *History of Music* 131; Todd and Butler 7:211.
47. Review of *Nature and Art*, by Mrs. Inchbald (London: Robinsons, 1796), *Analytical Review* 23 (May 1796): 511; Todd and Butler 7:463.

48. Myers 138, n. 6. Eleanor Flexner discusses the problems posed by a review of *A Letter on the Practice of Boxing* by Rev. Edward Barry (*Analytical Review* 6 [March 1790]: 351–2; Todd and Butler 7:227) for the issue of review attribution (273–4).
49. "[On Artificial Taste]" 279–82. See Locke's *Essay Concerning Human Understanding* (1690), especially Book II, Chapter 11, where Locke contrasts wit and judgment.
50. Christie i.
51. Review of *Earl Goodwin, an Historical Play*, by Ann Yearsley (London: Robinsons, 1791), *Analytical Review* 11 (December 1791): 427; Todd and Butler 7:398.
52. Review of Wendeborn's *A View of England*, *Analytical Review* 9 (1791): 183; Todd and Butler 347–8.
53. Flexner 110.
54. Tyson 99.
55. Though most of this chapter is argued on the basis of signed reviews only, this claim depends on accepting the view that in addition to signed reviews, Johnson published many Wollstonecraft reviews unsigned. For attribution of unsigned reviews, I have depended on Todd and Butler, eds., *The Works of Mary Wollstonecraft*. Allowing for a margin of error that they acknowledge must accompany the inexact art of hypothetical attribution, I have compared their reprints with the periodicals themselves to determine Wollstonecraft's relative importance as a contributor.
56. Luria, "Mary Hays" 163–7.
57. The letter includes an ambiguous postscript that suggests that although his name does not appear on the title page, Johnson may have had some interest in the publication. Collaborative publishing ventures by congers, loose affiliations between several booksellers, were quite common at the end of the eighteenth century, and Johnson was an active partner in more than one. (See Terry Belanger, "Publishers and Writers in Eighteenth-Century England," *Books and their Readers in Eighteenth-Century England*, ed. Isabel Rivers [n.p., Leicester UP, 1982]: 5–26; Gerring, *Notes on Printers and Booksellers*; Michael Harris, "Periodicals and the Book Trade," *Development of the English Book Trade, 1700–1899*, ed. Robin Myers and Michael Harris [Oxford: Oxford Polytechnic, 1981], 66–94; and Chard, "Bookseller to Publisher.") If Johnson did hold interest in Hays's book, it is clear that Wollstonecraft was handling negotiations between them, and that Hays's connection to Johnson's firm was at that time exclusively through Wollstonecraft.
58. Wollstonecraft to Mary Hays, 12 November [17]92, *Collected Letters* 219–20.
59. *Analytical Review* 27 (April 1798): 418–19. My account here differs from that in Janet Todd's recent biography of Wollstonecraft. More interested in Wollstonecraft's personality, Todd emphasizes the "hauteur" expressed in this letter, downplaying the "genuinely good advice" it contains, and concluding that Wollstonecraft "had little sense that the other woman was a fellow professional" (Todd 193–4). While I could hardly disagree that much of the letter is bluntly phrased, its sheer length when compared with many of Wollstonecraft's other short notes along with the specificity of its criticism seem to belie the notion that the letter was intended as no more than

a dismissal. For the purposes of this study, my interest is in Wollstonecraft's canny understanding of the liabilities inhering in a gendered self-presentation, in Hays's willingness to profit from Wollstonecraft's insight regardless of the unflattering delivery, and in the gradual evolution of a more respectful professional relationship over the course of the same years that witnessed the growth of a warm personal friendship between the two women. As Barbara Taylor has put it, when it comes to women with the intellectual creativity of Wollstonecraft, "paradox and contradiction" can be sources of new meanings rather than "embarrassments to be brushed aside" (21).

60. *Collected Letters* 219.
61. Wollstonecraft to Mary Hays, late 1792, *Collected Letters* 223–4.
62. Derek Roper, "The Politics of the *Critical Review*, 1766–1817," *Durham University Journal* 53 (1961): 117–22.
63. Wollstonecraft to Mary Hays, [15 September 1796], *Collected Letters* 351; Wollstonecraft to Mary Hays, [20 September 1796] *Collected Letters* 353. Both letters show that Hays had begun to bring her sister's work to Wollstonecraft for appraisal as well.
64. Wollstonecraft to Mary Hays, [c. January 1797] *Collected Letters* 375–6. Other evidence for Wollstonecraft acting in an editorial capacity includes her assigning Godwin a review of Isaac D'Israeli's *Vaurien* (Wollstonecraft to William Godwin, Friday morning [17 March 1797], *Collected Letters* 383).
65. Using biographical, stylistic, and documentary evidence, Wardle attributes 412 articles to Wollstonecraft, only about half of them signed ("Mary Wollstonecraft, *Analytical Reviewer*"). Wardle assumes that the *Analytical Review* printed signatures only at the end of any series of articles by the same contributor. Thus, he argues, unsigned articles leading up to a signature can be attributed to the same writer. Most Wollstonecraft scholars find Wardle's arguments for attributing reviews signed "M," "W," and "T" to Wollstonecraft both convincing and supported by subsequently discovered evidence, but his generalization about unsigned reviews has been questioned. Moreover, two of these initials refer to Wollstonecraft's real name, contrary to the usual practice at the *Analytical*. Eleanor Flexner not only questions Wardle's attribution of unsigned reviews, but argues partly on the basis of this departure from usual practice that Wollstonecraft is unlikely to have been the author of some of the signed reviews as well ("Appendix D: Mary Wollstonecraft's *Analytical* Reviews," *Mary Wollstonecraft* 273–4). Nevertheless, her argument has failed to convince. Most scholars have accepted the likelihood that a writer as self-assertive and autobiographical as Wollstonecraft may well have departed from usual practice. Further, Sally N. Stewart has provided convincing evidence to positively identify a few unsigned reviews, for a minimum total of 233 contributions that can be attributed to Wollstonecraft with confidence ("Mary Wollstonecraft's Contributions to the *Analytical Review*," *Essays in Literature* 11 [1984]: 187–99). Other landmarks in the attribution controversy include Derek Roper, "Mary Wollstonecraft's Reviews," *Notes and Queries* 203 (1958): 37–8 and Todd and Butler, where the editors reprint the reviews, attributing over 100 unsigned articles to Wollstonecraft. Todd and Butler's prefatory remarks explain their attribution criteria (7:14–18). Summaries of the arguments on attribution can be found in Stewart's essay and Todd and Butler's

prefatory remarks. While they acknowledge a necessary margin of error in what must at times be speculative identification, Todd and Butler's collection serves as the definitive canon of Wollstonecraft's contributions to the *Analytical Review*.
66. See Luria, *Mary Hays*; Ty, *Unsex'd Revolutionaries*; Todd, *Mary Wollstonecraft*. I thank Gina Luria Walker for alerting me that, at this writing, publication is shortly expected of *The Correspondence (1779–1843) of Mary Hays, British Novelist* ed. Marilyn L. Brooks (Lampeter: Edwin Mellen P, 2004), wherein Brooks identifies several *Analytical Review* articles by Hays.
67. Hays, "On Novel Writing," *Monthly Magazine* 4 (September 1797): 181.
68. Wollstonecraft to Mary Hays, [c. January 1797], *Collected Letters* 375–6.
69. The possibility that, as the editor responsible for a literary department, Wollstonecraft might package single reviews solicited from others along with her own articles could answer a persistent question about Wollstonecraft's *Analytical* contributions. In "Mary Wollstonecraft's Reviews," Roper challenges Wardle's attributions of unsigned articles leading up to a signed article. Roper points out that Wardle thereby attributes to Wollstonecraft an unsigned October 1796 review of Matthew Lewis's *The Monk*, which Roper rightly characterizes as "strongly masculine" in tone (38). He suggests Henry Fuseli, a regular *Analytical* contributor, as a more likely candidate for author. Yet this review falls between two unsigned articles reflecting style and concerns characteristic of Wollstonecraft and which Stewart provides conclusive evidence for attributing to Wollstonecraft. Stewart suggests that this evidence supports the hypothesis that at least occasionally the *Analytical* provided signatures only after the final article in a series by the same contributor. She does not address Roper's objections about the content of the article, nor do Todd and Butler, who reprint the article as a Wollstonecraft contribution in *The Works of Mary Wollstonecraft* (7:473–5). Wollstonecraft's letters indicate that in late September Godwin was reading her copy of *The Monk* (Wollstonecraft to Mary Hays, Tuesday morning [20 September 1796], *Collected Letters*, 353). Since Wollstonecraft asked Godwin to write other reviews, it seems plausible that she asked him to review the novel he had just finished, and she delivered this predictably masculine sounding article to Johnson with her own, so he grouped them together in that month's 'Novels' section.
70. "I send you "P.P. – ," Wollstonecraft writes in early 1797. "[I]f you do not chuse [sic] to review it return it after you have perused it – " (Wollstonecraft to Mary Hays, [c. early 1797] *Collected Letters* 382). Wardle suggests that "P.P. – " might refer to Peter Pindar, the pseudonym of satirical poet John Wolcot (1738–1819). Wardle notes that two reviews of his work appear in the *Analytical Review* around this time, one in February 1797 signed "D.P.," and an unsigned review the following July. In fact, neither review is signed, though the February review, which actually appears in the March number, immediately precedes a review signed "D.M." Neither review shows characteristics that would convincingly attribute it to Hays, and the signature "D.M." is one that belongs to one of the *Analytical*'s most prolific reviewers, probably Dr. John Aikin (Roper 255). Another candidate might be an April review of the more sentimental *Prison Amusements*, by Paul Positive. Again, however, the review is unsigned, the next occurring signature is "D.M," and

the prose seems quite unlike that of Hays. Hays must have declined the assignment, perhaps, if "P.P. – " does indicate Peter Pindar, because Wolcot's satirical and sometimes ribald poetry would have fallen outside the bounds of interest and expertise indicated by Hays's identifiable reviews.
71. Jane Worthington Smyser, "The Trial and Imprisonment of Joseph Johnson, Bookseller," *Bulletin of the New York Public Library* 77 (1974): 418–35. In *The British Periodical Press and the French Revolution, 1789–99* (Houndmills, Hampshire: Palgrave, 2000), Stuart Andrews outlines the *Anti-Jacobin*'s role in the *Analytical Review*'s demise.
72. *The Monthly Magazine* 4 (September 1797): 180–1.
73. Hays, "Improvements Suggested in Female Education," *Monthly Magazine* 3 (March 1797): 193.
74. *Monthly Magazine* 4 (September 1797): 232–3.
75. Luria 422.
76. In addition to the work already mentioned, Hays authored a number of essays for Phillips that were included in his *Public Characters* (1798–1810). Between 1791, when her first book appeared, and 1810, when her last publication with either Johnson or Phillips was issued, Hays was quite active in the literary world, publishing a significant work every two or three years as well as numerous short articles and several reviews. After that time, she published only two minor works in 1815 and 1817, *The Brothers* (W. Button and Sons), and *Family Annals: or, the Sisters* (Simpkin and Marshall), before her last publication, *Memoirs of Queens* (1821). Twenty-two years elapsed between *Memoirs of Queens* and Hays's death. Henry Crabb Robinson notes the modesty of Hays's independent income, a pension of only £70. In addition, by 1805 he comments that Hays was living modestly in retirement. 1813 marks the first of several references to Hays's attempts to find economical lodgings and literary work (*Henry Crabb Robinson on Books and Their Writers*, ed. Edith J. Morley, 3 vols. (London: M. M. Dent, 1938), 1:124–5 and passim). Moreover, along with the evidence offered by Crabb Robinson, Hays's published correspondence with Robert Southey documents her attempts to enlist Southey's advice on potentially profitable literary undertakings, his assistance in marketing literary work that she had already completed, and even his hospitality in providing her with a congenial and, presumably, inexpensive home (Wedd 242–6).

Chapter 4

1. Sources on the *Monthly Review* and its competitors include Wilbur T. Albrecht, "The Monthly Review," *The Augustan Age and the Age of Johnson*, vol. 1 of *British Literary Magazines*, ed. Alvin Sullivan, 4 vols., Historical Guides to the World's Periodicals and Newspapers (Westport, CT: Greenwood P, 1983–86) 231–7; Stuart Andrews, *The British Periodical Press and the French Revolution*; Graham, *English Literary Periodicals*; Benjamin Christie Nangle, *The Monthly Review, First Series, 1749–1789: Indexes of Contributors and Articles* (Oxford: Clarendon P, 1934) and *The Monthly Review, Second Series, 1790–1815: Indexes of Contributors and Articles* (Oxford: Clarendon P, 1955); and Roper, *Reviewing before the* Edinburgh.

2. I am indebted to Basker for this brief summary of the antecedents of literary reviews. For discussions of the "encyclopedic spirit of the culture of knowledge" and its role in shaping Romantic-era periodicals, see also Butler's "Culture's Medium," especially pp. 127–30 and Roper, especially pp. 36–44.
3. During this time, "literature" referred to all branches of letters, and would therefore have included, for example, books and pamphlets on scientific topics. For discussions of shifts in the understanding of the term "literature" from a broad definition that included these types of texts to our modern day usage referring mainly to imaginative writing, see Paul Keen, *The Crisis of Literature in the 1790s: Print Culture and the Public Sphere*, Cambridge Studies in Romanticism 36 (Cambridge UP, 1999) and Jonathan Brody Kramnick, *Making the English Canon: Print-Capitalism and the Cultural Past, 1700–1770* (Cambridge UP, 1998).
4. *The Monthly Review* 1st series 1 (1749): 238.
5. *Critical Review* 1 (January–February 1756): A_2.
6. See Roper, especially pp. 27–32 for a summary of these arguments.
7. Roper 124.
8. At this writing, William McCarthy is researching a much needed new biography of this talented poet who has recently rejoined the Romantic canon after nearly two centuries of relative neglect.
9. John O. Hayden, *The Romantic Reviewers* 53, 58; Derek Roper, *Reviewing Before the* Edinburgh 92 n. 76; Thomas Rees, *Reminiscences of Literary London* 55; Anna Letitia Le Breton, *Memoir of Mrs. Barbauld, Including Letters and Notices of Her Family and Friends* (London, G. Bell, 1874) 144–5 and passim. Roper notes that Barbauld's brother, John Aikin, M. D., was reviewing for the *Analytical* at the time that these initials appear. He conjectures that Aikin had been using the initials D.M., for Doctor of Medicine, and that the D.M.S. signatures that appear in 1798 stand for Doctor of Medicine's Sister, thus indicating Barbauld. Without additional confirmation of some kind, relying on such a speculation is quite risky. The reviews so signed number only four, too few for internal references or stylistic evidence to offer adequate support for Roper's theory. In his defense, however, it must be noted that the reviewer's style does resemble that of Barbauld, and nothing of the contents seems to disallow the possibility that she may be their author. Further, Donald H. Reiman remarks of a "D.M.S." signed review of Coleridge's *Fears in Solitude* (*Analytical Review* 28 [December 1798]: 590–2): "The apologetic tone of this notice and its closing personal wishes suggest that 'D.M.S.' was a friend of Coleridge. Those initials do not, however, belong to any of Coleridge's known correspondents of the period, and they might be a coded signature" (*The Romantics Reviewed: Contemporary Reviews of British Romantic Writers*, 3 vols. [New York: Garland, 1972] 1:10). Barbauld had become acquainted with Coleridge the year before, and though their friendship eventually collapsed, at the time of this review, they enjoyed a mutual regard. William McCarthy and Elizabeth Kraft identify a letter defending Edgeworth's *Tales of Fashionable Life* (1809), signed Y.Z., as authored by Barbauld (*The Gentleman's Magazine* 80 [March 1810]: 210–12, cited in McCarthy and Kraft, eds., *Anna Letitia Barbauld* 456–63).

10. Of Barbauld's over 300 Catalogue reviews for the *Monthly Review*, roughly one third of the articles review novels. Another one fourth each of the total number of reviews are devoted to poetry and educational materials. Foreign language teaching, reading, composition, and conduct and moral works divide between them a two-thirds share of the portion devoted to education, thus making as a group more or less one sixth of the total number of reviews. The remaining third of the educational literature portion is nearly equally divided between various subjects such as geography, arithmetic, educational theory, natural history, and so forth. Around 10 percent of Barbauld's total reviews treat untranslated foreign literature, with French fiction overwhelmingly predominating, and French educational theory holding a distant second place. It is worth noting that although Barbauld was not an expert in German and so did not discuss any untranslated German literature, she did review several German works that had been translated to French, but not English. The remainder of her reviews, some 10 percent of the total, are widely spread over various forms such as travel literature, history, biography, drama, word games and puzzles, children's literature, and others. It is also worth mentioning that only two thirds of the works she reviews have identified authors or permit gender attribution, whether reliably or not, through such signatures as "by a Gentleman" or "by an Englishwoman." Of these, roughly 60 percent are attributed to male authors, 40 percent to female.
11. Nangle, *The Monthly Review Second Series* 67; Hazlitt, *Complete Works*, ed. P.P. Howe, 21 vols. (London: J. M. Dent & Sons, 1930–4) 6:127, cited in Nangle, *Second Series* x.
12. Parker 3, 1.
13. Review of *Ned Bentley* by J. Amphlett, *Monthly Review* 2nd series 60 (September 1809): 94–5.
14. Review of *Sir Owen Glendower*, and other Tales, by Ant. Frederick Holstein, *Monthly Review* 2nd series 60 (September 1809): 95–6.
15. Copeland, *Women Writing About Money*.
16. James Boswell, *Life of Samuel Johnson, LL.D.*, [5 April 1776] (1791, Oxford: Oxford UP, 1966).
17. Letter to Dr. Haygarth dated August 1794, quoted in Lucy Aikin, *Memoir of John Aikin, M. D.* 108.
18. Hayden and Roper comprise two examples. Though Roper notes that such judgments apply today's standards anachronistically, he nevertheless evaluates reviews partly on the basis of the proportion of summary versus criticism, quantified by the number of words devoted to each in any one article. Bad reviews might consist only of extracts with some valueless general remarks. Good reviews, on the other hand, include a substantial proportion of "detailed and thoughtful criticism" (*Reviewing before the* Edinburgh 115).
19. See Roper, *Reviewing before the* Edinburgh 41–5; Butler, "Culture's medium" 126–7. Basker's discussion of the origin of literary reviews is relevant here as well.
20. Review of *The Cottage of Var* [n.a.], *Monthly Review* 2nd series 60 (September 1809): 97.
21. Review of *The Husband and the Lover* [n.a.], *Monthly Review* 2nd series 60 (September 1809): 95.

22. Review of *Poems on Various Subjects* by Henry Richard Wood, *Monthly Review* 2nd series 60 (December 1809): 456; review of *The Towers of Ravenswold* by William Henry Hitchener, *Monthly Review* 2nd series 74 (June 1814): 216.
23. Roper, *Reviewing before the* Edinburgh 26, and passim; Basker 328.
24. Review of *Poems* by Felicia Dorothea Browne [Felicia Hemans], *Monthly Review* 2nd series 60 (1809): 323; review of *Fitz-Gwarine* by John F. M. Dovaston, A. M., *Monthly Review* 2nd series 71 (1813): 99; review of *A History of France, from the Commencement of the Reign of Clovis, in 481, to the Peace of Campo Formio in 1797* [n.a.], *Monthly Review* 2nd series 63 (1810): 423.
25. Review of *Poems* by William Hersee, *Monthly Review* 2nd series 60 (November 1809): 322; review of *Poems, Rural and Domestic* by William Hersee, *Monthly Review* 2nd series 66 (December 1811): 431.
26. Review of *Faulconstein Forest* [n.a.], *Monthly Review* 2nd series 62 (May 1810): 97–8.
27. Review of *An Introduction to the Epistolary Style of the French* by George Saulez, *Monthly Review* 2nd series 76 (January 1815): 103; review of *The Splendour of Adversity* [n.a.], *Monthly Review* 2nd series 73 (March 1814): 310.
28. Basker 328.
29. White 511–33.
30. Davidoff and Hall, *Family Fortunes*.
31. *Memoir of John Aikin, M. D.* 116–17.
32. Moody's reviewing was suspended between August 1791 and January 1800, a gap which, according to Jan Wellington, remains unexplained (*The Poems and Prose of Elizabeth Moody*, diss., U of New Mexico, 1997).
33. In their discussion of the Taylors of Ongar, Davidoff and Hall offer another telling example of a family literary enterprise that, among other efforts, resulted in some of the family's women publishing occasional periodical reviews.
34. Wellington, *The Poems and Prose of Elizabeth Moody* 4, 7. Background information on Elizabeth Moody is here summarized from the introductory chapter of this dissertation, and from "Elizabeth Moody," also authored by Wellington, in *An Encyclopedia of British Women Writers*, ed. Paul Schlueter and June Schlueter (1988; New Brunswick, NJ: Rutgers UP, 1998).
35. Wellington 13.
36. In order, these three reviews discuss *The Denial* by James Thomson ([London: Sewell, 1790], *Monthly Review* 2nd series 3 [December 1790]: 400–2,); *Les Souvenirs de Felicie L**** by Mad. de Genlis ([Paris: 1808] *Monthly Review* 2nd series 56 [Foreign Appendix, May–August 1808]: 542–4); *Lettres de Mademoiselle De Launai, & c* by Mademoiselle De Launai (Madame De Staal) ([Paris 1806; imported by De Conchy] *Monthly Review* 2nd series 49 [Foreign Appendix, January–April 1806]: 541–3); and *Noveaux Contes Moraux* by Marmontel ([Paris: 1801; imported by De Boffe] *Monthly Review* 2nd series 34 [Foreign Appendix, January–April 1801]: 542–4).
37. Review of *Beauties Selected from the Writings of the Late William Paley* by W. Hamilton, *Monthly Review* 2nd series 64 (February 1811): 219. Griffiths also adds to another review beginning on the same page. Barbauld's review of Sarah Trimmer's didactic tales for the lower classes concludes with a paragraph by Griffiths in which, though he acknowledges the inappropriateness of the concern considering the intended audience of

the work, he "animadverts" on numerous class-marking "inelegant phrases" on which Barbauld had remained silent (Review of *Instructive Tales* by Mrs. Trimmer, *Monthly Review* 2nd series 64 [February 1811]: 219–20). His addition here, as in many other instances where he added comments on style, grammar, or usage, supports the view that such exacting commentary was standard practice at this periodical and part of a widely held view that reviews had a role to play in final literary product that reached the reading audience, rather than an indication of one contributor's over-fastidiousness.
38. The article reviewed *Le Paradis Reconquis* by L. R. Lafaye ([London: Bell, 1789] *Monthly Review* 2nd series 81 [December 1789]: 535–7). Other main article contributions by Moody include the reviews of *The Denial* by James Thomson ([London: Sewell, 1790], *Monthly Review* 2nd series 3 [December 1790]: 400–2), *Men and Manners* by Francis Lathom ([London: Wright, 1799] *Monthly Review* 2nd series 31 [February 1800]: 136–41, *The Rival Mothers* by Madame de Genlis ([London: Longman, 1801] *Monthly Review* 2nd series 36 [October 1801]: 186–8) and *The Lamentation* ([London: White, 1801]: *Monthly Review* 2nd series 37 [January 1802]: 9–12).
39. Wellington, *The Poems and Prose of Elizabeth Moody* 21–3. Wellington cites the Moody quotations reproduced here from Moody's reviews of *The Denial* by James Thomson, *Monthly Review* 2nd series 3 (December 1790) 400 and *Rimualdo; or the Castle of Badajos* by W. H. Ireland (London: Longman, 1800), *Monthly Review* 2nd series 34 (February 1801): 203–4.
40. Barbauld, review of *Matilda Montford* by Peter Peregrine, *Monthly Review* 2nd series 60 (September 1809): 97.
41. Moody, review of *The Turtle Dove* from the French of M. de Florian, *Monthly Review* 2nd series 4 (January 1791): 113.
42. *The Poems and Prose of Elizabeth Moody* 20.
43. Review of *Les Voyageurs en Perse* by Mad. Gaçon-Dufour, *Monthly Review* 2nd series 60 (Foreign Appendix): 544; review of *Histoire du Prince de Timor* by M. D. B., *Monthly Review* 2nd series 73 (February 1814); review of *Tableaux de Société* by Pigault Le Brun, *Monthly Review* 2nd series 76 (Foreign Appendix): 544; review of *Poems on Various Subjects* by Henry Richard Wood, *Monthly Review* 2nd series 60 (December 1809): 456; review of *Anatonda* by Anton Wall, *Monthly Review* 2nd series 64 (April 1811): 435.
44. Review of *Raphaël* by Augustus La Fontaine, *Monthly Review* 2nd series 67 (January 1812): 107.
45. Review of *Les Voyageurs en Perse* 544.
46. Review of *Nouvéaux Contes Moraux* by Marmontel, *Monthly Review* 2nd series 34 (Foreign Appendix): 542; review of *Le Malheur et la Pitié* by Abbé de Lille, *Monthly Review* 2nd series 44 (Foreign Appendix): 495; review of *The Rival Mothers* by Madame de Genlis, *Monthly Review* 2nd series 36 (October 1801): 186; review of *Le Divorce* by M. Fie´ve´e, *Monthly Review* 2nd series 46 (April, 1805): 540; review of *Les Amours Èpiques* by Parseval Grandmaison, *Monthly Review* 2nd series 45 (Foreign Appendix): 511.
47. Colley, *Britons*; Newman, *The Rise of English Nationalism*.
48. Andrews, *The British Periodical Press*, Chapter 11, "Reviewers Reviewed: *Monthly* and *Critical*"; Graham, *English Literary Periodicals*; Roper, *Reviewing before the Edinburgh* and "The Politics of the 'Critical Review'" 117–22; *British Literary*

Periodicals, ed. Alvin Sullivan, 4 vols., Historical Guides to the World's Periodicals and Newspapers (Westport, CN: Greenwood P, 1983–86).
49. Chandler, "The Pope Controversy".
50. Roper, *Reviewing before the* Edinburgh 36–7.
51. *Romantics, Rebels and Reactionaries* 9.

Chapter 5

1. Trela 89.
2. Butler 126.
3. Attacks against the writers studied here began in full earnest with the reviews hostile to Wollstonecraft soon after Godwin published his *Memoirs of Author of* A Vindication of the Rights of Woman (1798) and with the appearance of Richard Polwhele's *The Unsex'd Females* (1798) attacking not only Wollstonecraft, but Barbauld and Hays as well. Further examples include Colman's tirade published in Inchbald's *The British Theatre*, and Croker's hostile review of Barbauld's *Eighteen Hundred and Eleven* in the June 1812 *Quarterly Review*.
4. Biographical information on Martineau is summarized from *Harriet Martineau's Autobiography*, ed. Maria Weston Chapman, 4th ed., 2 vols. (Boston: Houghton, Osgood and Company), R. K. Webb, *Harriet Martineau: A Radical Victorian* (New York: Columbia UP, 1960), and Valerie Kossew Pichanick *Harriet Martineau: The Woman and Her Work, 1802–76* (Ann Arbor: U of Michigan P, 1980).
5. *Autobiography* 1:94.
6. The article begins in October 1822 with a second installment in December.
7. *Autobiography* 1:92.
8. Information on Fox was summarized from the *Dictionary of National Biography*, Francis E. Mineka, *The Dissidence of Dissent: The Monthly Repository, 1806–1838, Under the Editorship of Robert Aspland, W. J. Fox, R. H. Horne, & Leigh Hunt, with a Chapter on Religious Periodicals, 1700–1825* (Chapel Hill: U of North Carolina P, 1944), and Richard Garnett and Edward Garnett, *The Life of W. J. Fox: Public Teacher and Social Reformer 1786–1864* (London: John Lane, 1910).
9. Martineau, "To W. J. Fox," November, 1828, *Harriet Martineau: Selected Letters*, ed. Valerie Sanders (Oxford: Clarendon P, 1990) 14.
10. *Autobiography* 1:106–7.
11. *Autobiography* 1:108, 110.
12. Review of *Exposition of the practical Operation of the Judicial and Revenue Systems of India* and *Translations of several [...] Texts of the Veda*, both by Rajah Rammohun Roy, *Monthly Repository* 2nd ser. 6 (September 1832): 609–17.
13. *Autobiography* 1:113.
14. Chapman, "Memorials of Harriet Martineau," *Autobiography* 2:175
15. Letter dated Stamford Hill, 22 January 1830, *Autobiography* 2:176.
16. Mineka 207.
17. *Autobiography* 1:111. Linda Peterson documents that Martineau's account is not strictly true. Early publications such as *Devotional Exercises* (1823), her first book, and the moral tales she sold to Houlston earned her modest but

respectable sums. Peterson argues that the discrepancy supports her position that Martineau saw apprenticeship under an editor and periodical publication as integral to literary professionalism in contrast with these other publishing ventures ("[Re]inventing Authorship: Harriet Martineau in the Literary Marketplace of the 1820s," *Women's Writing* 9 [2002] 337–50). I would agree, adding only that self-publishing, the method by which Martineau brought out *Devotional Exercises*, places a financial risk on the author that Martineau was less in a position to sustain after her family's subsequent financial crises.

18. *Autobiography* 1:135.
19. Review of *Illustrations of Political Economy*, *Quarterly Review* 49 (April 1833): 136–52.
20. In his review of Barbauld's poem, *Eighteen Hundred and Eleven*, John Wilson Croker focuses on the author's gender, castigating her for stepping outside the bounds of feminine discourse. "We had hoped indeed," Croker sneers, "that the empire might have been saved without the intervention of a lady-author" (*Quarterly Review* 7 [June 1812]: 309). After this assault Barbauld continued to write anonymous reviews for several years, and she published several poems and short essays, some signed, others unsigned, in publications such as the *Monthly Repository*. Yet she never again published the sort of signed, freestanding long work that had been so much a part of her social commentary during the 1790s. As the account of Elizabeth Inchbald's response to George Colman's attack (Chapter 2) shows, however, it is risky to assume that such an assault alone can explain a major turn in an author's career.
21. *Autobiography* 1:157, 1:155, 1:158.
22. William Maginn, "Miss Harriet Martineau," *Fraser's Magazine for Town and Country* 8 (November 1833): 576. See Patricia Marks, "Harriet Martineau: Fraser's 'Maid of [Dis]Honour'" [sic], *Victorian Periodicals Review* 19 (1986): 28–33 for a discussion of misogynist imagery in the article's accompanying illustration.
23. "Miss Martineau's Illustrations of Political Economy," *Tait's Edinburgh Magazine* 1 (August 1832): 612–18.
24. Review of *John Hopkins's Notions of Political Economy* by the Author of Conversations on Political Economy [Jane Marcet] and *Illustrations of Political Economy* by Harriet Martineau, *Edinburgh Review* 57 (April 1833): 3–39.
25. William Maginn, "Our Confession of Faith," *Fraser's Magazine for Town and Country* 1 (February 1830): 1–7.
26. Review of *Letters and Journals of Lord Byron* with *Notices of His Life* by Thomas Moore, *Monthly Repository* 2nd ser. 4 (February 1830): 124–8; review of *The Maid of Scio* by Eleanor Snowden, *Monthly Repository* 2nd ser. 4 (May 1830): 332–3.
27. Review of *Library of Ecclesiastical Knowledge*, *Monthly Repository* 2nd ser. 4 (March 1830): 182–4; review of *Lives of Eminent British Lawyers*, by Henry Roscoe, *Monthly Repository*, 2nd ser. 4 (June 1830): 405–6; review of *A Practical Exposition of the Law of Wills* by Richard Dickson, *Monthly Repository*, 2nd ser. 4 (June 1830): 406.
28. The series consists of three articles, two on "Female Writers on Practical Divinity," entitled "Mrs. More" (*Monthly Repository* 17 [October 1822]:

593–6) and "Mrs. More and Mrs. Barbauld" (*Monthly Repository* 17 [December 1822]: 746–50), and a third, "On Female Education," (*Monthly Repository* 18 [February 1823]: 77–81).
29. Martineau, *Monthly Repository* 17:748–9, 593.
30. Mullan 2; Colley, especially her chapter on "Womanpower"; Guest 14, 16, 17.
31. *Monthly Repository* 17:593, 596.
32. *Autobiography* 1:301–3. Discussion of parallels between Martineau's and Wollstonecraft's work can be found in both Webb's and Pichanick's biographies as well as in Shelagh Hunter's *Harriet Martineau: The Poetics of Materialism* (Hants, England: Scolar P, 1995).
33. Kelly, "Bluestocking Feminism," 174.
34. *Monthly Repository* 17:593.
35. *Monthly Repository* 17:594.
36. Simpson 77.
37. "Demonology and Witchcraft," review of *The Family Library* No. XVI, "Letters on Demonology and Witchcraft by Sir Walter Scott," *Monthly Repository* 2nd ser. 4 (November 1830): 744.
38. "On Negro Slavery," review of *The Death Warrant of Negro-Slavery throughout the British Dominions*, *Monthly Repository* 2nd ser. 4 (January 1830): 6.
39. "Godwin's Thoughts on Man," review of *Thoughts on Man, his Nature, Productions, and Discoveries by William Godwin*, *Monthly Repository* 2nd ser. 5 (July 1831): 434.
40. See Webb, *Harriet Martineau*, especially Chapter 4, and Hunter Chapter 3.
41. "On the Duty of Studying Political Economy," review of *Lectures on the Elements of Political Economy* by Thomas Cooper, M. D., *Monthly Repository* 2nd ser. 6 (January 1832): 24–34.
42. "Van Diemen's Land," review of *Sketch of the History of Van Diemen's Land*, by James Bisehoff, *Monthly Repository* 2nd ser. 6 (June 1832): 372.
43. "Van Diemen's Land," 374, 375.
44. "On Prison Discipline," review of *The Eighth Report of the Committee of the Society for the Improvement on Prison Discipline* and *Punishment of Death*, *Monthly Repository* 2nd ser. 6 (September 1832):577–86 and "Secondary Punishments," review of *Thoughts on Secondary Punishments in a Letter to Earl Grey* by Richard Whately, D. D., Archbishop of Dublin, *Monthly Repository* 2nd ser. 6 (October 1832): 667–9.
45. "On Prison Discipline" 578.
46. "Secondary Punishments" 669.
47. *Life of Fox* 95.

Bibliography

Abrams, M. H. *The Mirror and the Lamp: Romantic Theory and the Critical Tradition.* London: Oxford UP, 1953.

Adburgham, Alison. *Women in Print: Writing Women and Women's Magazines From the Restoration to the Accession of Victoria.* London: George Allen and Unwin, 1972.

Addison, Joseph. *Essays in Criticism and Literary Theory.* Ed. John Loftis. Northbrook, IL: AHM Publishing, 1975.

Aikin, Lucy, ed. *The Works of Anna Lætitia Barbauld; with a Memoir by Lucy Aikin.* 2 vols. London: Longman, et al., 1825.

———., ed. *Memoir of John Aikin, M. D. with a Selection of His Miscellaneous Pieces, Biographical, Moral and Critical.* Philadelphia: Small, 1824.

Albrecht, Wilbur T. "The Monthly Review." *The Augustan Age and the Age of Johnson.* Vol. 1 *British Literary Magazines.* Ed. Alvin Sullivan. Historical Guides to the World's Periodicals and Newspapers. Westport, CT: Greenwood P, 1983–86. 231–7.

Analytical Review, The; or, History of Literature, Domestic and Foreign, on an Enlarged Plan. London: J. Johnson, 1788–99.

Andrews, Stuart. *The British Periodical Press and the French Revolution, 1789–99.* Houndmills, Hampshire: Palgrave, 2000.

Anti-Jacobin Review and Magazine, The. London, 1798–1821.

Armstrong, Nancy. *Desire and Domestic Fiction: A Political History of the Novel.* New York: Oxford UP, 1987.

Backscheider, Paula R., ed. *The Plays of Elizabeth Inchbald.* 2 vols. Eighteenth-Century English Drama: A Comprehensive Collection of Over Two Hundred Representative Plays, Reproduced with Critical Introductions by Leading Scholars. New York: Garland, 1980.

Barbauld, Anna Letitia. "On the Origin and Progress of Novel-Writing." *The British Novelists; with an Essay, and Prefaces Biographical and Critical, by Mrs. Barbauld.* Ed. Anna Letitia Barbauld. 50 vols. 1810. London: F. C. and J. Rivington, 1820. 1:1–59.

———. "Life of Samuel Richardson with Remarks on His Writings." *Correspondence of Samuel Richardson, Author of* Pamela, Clarissa, *and* Sir Charles Grandison. *Selected from the Original Manuscripts, Bequeathed by Him to His Family. To Which Are Prefixed, A Biographical Account of That Author, and Observations on His Writings.* Ed. Anna Letitia Barbauld. 6 vols. London: Richard Phillips, 1804. New York: AMS P, 1966. 1:vii–ccxii.

———. "Essay on *The Pleasures of Imagination.*" *The Pleasures of Imagination by Mark Akenside; to Which is Prefixed a Critical Essay on the Poem by Mrs. Barbauld.* London: T. Cadell, and W. Davies, 1794; Philadelphia: B. Johnson, J. Johnson, and R. Johnson, 1804). xiii–xx.

———. "On the Poetical Works of Mr. William Collins." *The Poetical Works of Mr. William Collins; with a Prefatory Essay by Mrs. Barbauld.* 1797. London: T. Cadell, Jun. and W. Davies: 1802. iii–1.

——. "Preliminary Essay." *Selections from the* Spectator, Tatler, Guardian, *and* Freeholder; *with Preliminary Essay by Mrs. Barbauld*. Ed. Anna Letitia Barbauld. 2 vols. 1804. London: Edward Moxon, 1849. 1:v–xxvi.
Barbauld, Anna Letitia [Anna Letitia Aikin] and John Aikin. *Miscellaneous Pieces in Prose*. London: Johnson, 1773.
Barker-Benfield, G. J. *The Culture of Sensibility: Sex and Society in Eighteenth-Century Britain*. Chicago: U of Chicago P, 1992.
——. "Mary Wollstonecraft: Eighteenth-Century Commonwealthwoman." *Journal of the History of Ideas* 50 (1989): 95–115.
Barzun, Jacques. "Cultural Nationalism and the Makings of Fame." *Nationalism and Internationalism: Essays Inscribed to Carlton J. H. Hayes*. Ed. E. M. Earle. New York: Columbia UP, 1950.
Basker, James. "Criticism and the Rise of Periodical Literature." *The Eighteenth Century*. Ed. H. B. Nisbet and Claude Rawson. Cambridge: Cambridge UP, 1997. Vol. 4 of *The Cambridge History of Literary Criticism*. 8 vols.
Bateson, F. W., ed. *The Cambridge Bibliography of English Literature*. 4 vols. Cambridge: Cambridge UP, 1940.
Belanger, Terry. "Publishers and Writers in Eighteenth-Century England." *Books and Their Readers in Eighteenth-Century England*. Ed. Isabel Rivers. N.p.: Leicester UP and St. Martin's P, 1982. 5–26.
Bloom, Harold. *The Anxiety of Influence – A Theory of Poetry*. London: Oxford UP, 1973.
Boaden, James, ed. *Memoirs of Mrs. Inchbald: Including Her Familiar Correspondence with the Most Distinguished Persons of Her Time. To Which Are Added* The Massacre *and* A Case of Conscience; *Now First Published from Her Autograph Copies*. 2 vols. London: Richard Bentley, 1833.
Bonnell, Thomas F. "Bookselling and Canon-Making: The Trade Rivalry over the English Poets, 1776–83". *Studies in Eighteenth-Century Culture* 19 (1989): 53–69.
Boswell, James. *Life of Samuel Johnson, LL.D*. 1791. Oxford: Oxford UP, 1966.
Bradley, James E. *Religion, Revolution, and English Radicalism: Nonconformity in Eighteenth-Century Politics and Society*. Cambridge: Cambridge UP, 1990.
British Theatre Plays. London: John Bell, 1780.
Burney, Fanny. *Camilla; or, A Picture of Youth*. London, T. Payne, T. Cadell and W. Davies, 1796.
——. *Evelina, or, A Young Lady's Entrance into the World*. London, T. Lowndes, 1778.
Burroughs, Catherine B. *Closet Stages: Joanna Baillie and the Theater Theory of British Romantic Women Writers*. Philadelphia: U of Pennsylvania P, 1997.
——. "English Romantic Women Writers and Theatre Theory: Joanna Baillie's Prefaces to the *Plays on the Passions*." *Re-Visioning Romanticism: British Women Writers, 1776–1837*. Ed. Carol Shiner Wilson and Joel Haefner. Philadelphia: U of Pennsylvania P, 1994. 274–96.
——, ed. *Women in British Romantic Theatre: Drama, Performance, and Society, 1790–1840*. Cambridge: Cambridge UP, 2000.
Butler, Marilyn. "Culture's Medium: The Role of the Review." *The Cambridge Companion to British Romanticism*. Ed. Stuart Curran. Cambridge: Cambridge UP, 1993. 120–47.
——. "Revising the Canon." *TLS* 4 (Dec. 1987): 1349, 1359–60.

———. *Romantics, Rebels and Reactionaries: English Literature and Its Background 1760–1830*. Oxford: Oxford UP, 1981.
Calhoun, Craig, ed. *Habermas and the Public Sphere*. Cambridge MA: MIT P, 1992.
Carlson, Marvin. "Elizabeth Inchbald: A Woman Critic in Her Theatrical Culture." *Women in British Romantic Theatre: Drama, Performance, and Society, 1790–1840*. Ed. Catherine Burroughs. Cambridge, Cambridge UP, 2000. 207–22.
Carter, Elizabeth. *All the Works of Epictetus, Which Are Now Extant: Consisting of His Discourses, Preserved by Arrian, in Four Books, Then Enchiridion, and Fragments. Translated from the Original Greek, by Elizabeth Carter. With an Introduction, and Notes, by the Translator*. London: Printed by S. Richardson, 1758.
Castle, Terry. "Women and Literary Criticism." *The Eighteenth Century*. Ed. H. B. Nisbet and Claude Rawson. Cambridge: Cambridge UP, 1997. Vol. 4 of *The Cambridge History of Literary Criticism*. 8 vols. 434–55.
Chandler, James. "The Pope Controversy: Romantic Poetics and the English Canon." *Critical Inquiry* 10 (March 1984): 481–509.
Chard, Leslie F. "Bookseller to Publisher: Joseph Johnson and the English Book trade, 1760–1810." *The Library: Transactions of the Bibliographical Society* 32 (1977): 138–54.
Chard, Leslie F., II. "Joseph Johnson: Father of the Book Trade." *Bulletin of the New York Public Library* 79 (1975): 51–82.
Colley, Linda. *Britons: Forging the Nation 1707–1837*. New Haven: Yale UP, 1992.
Conger, Syndy McMillen. *Mary Wollstonecraft and the Language of Sensibility*. Rutherford: Fairleigh Dickinson UP, 1994.
———., ed. *Sensibility in Transformation: Creative Resistance to Sentiment from the Augustans to the Romantics*. Rutherford: Fairleigh Dickinson UP. 13–19.
Copeland, Edward. *Women Writing about Money: Women's Fiction in England, 1790–1820*. Cambridge Studies in Romanticism 9. Cambridge: Cambridge UP, 1995.
Crane, R. S. "Suggestions Toward a Genealogy of the 'Man of Feeling.'" *ELH: English Literary History* 1 (1934): 205–30.
Crawford, Patricia. "Women's Published Writings 1600–1700." *Women in English Society, 1500–1800*. Ed. Mary Prior. London: Methuen, 1985. 211–74.
Critical Review, The; or Annals of Literature. London, 1756–1817.
Davidoff, Lenore, and Catherine Hall. *Family Fortunes: Men and Women of the English Middle Class, 1780–1850*. London: Hutchinson, 1987.
Donkin, Ellen. *Getting Into the Act: Women Playwrights in London, 1776–1829*. London: Routledge, 1995.
Edinburgh Review, or Critical Journal, The. Edinburgh, 1802–1929.
Eger, Elizabeth. *The Nine Living Muses of Great Britain (1779): Women, Reason, and Literary Community in Eighteenth-Century Britain*. Diss. King's College, Cambridge, 1999.
———. "Representing culture: 'The Nine Living Muses of Great Britain' (1779)." *Women, Writing and the Public Sphere, 1700–1830*. Ed. Elizabeth Eger, Charlotte Grant, Clíona Ó Gallchoir, and Penny Warburton. Cambridge: Cambridge UP, 2001. 104–32.
Eger, Elizabeth, Charlotte Grant, Clíona Ó Gallchoir, and Penny Warburton, eds. *Women, Writing and the Public Sphere, 1700–1830*. Cambridge: Cambridge UP, 2001.

Felski, Rita. *Beyond Feminist Aesthetics: Feminist Literature and Social Change*. Cambridge, MA: Harvard UP, 1989.
Ferguson, Moira, and Janet Todd. *Mary Wollstonecraft*. Twayne's English Authors. Boston: Twayne, 1984.
Fielding, Sarah. *The History of the Countess of Dellwyn*. 2 vols. London: A. Millar, 1759.
——. *The Cry; a New Dramatic Fable*. 3 vols. London: R. and J. Dodsley, 1754.
Flexner, Eleanor. *Mary Wollstonecraft: A Biography*. New York: Coward, McCann and Geoghegan, 1972.
Folger Collective on Early Women Critics, ed. *Women Critics 1600–1820: An Anthology*. Bloomington: U of Indiana P, 1995.
Foxon, David F. *English Verse, 1701–1750: A Catalogue of Separately Printed Poems with Notes on Contemporary Collected Editions*, 2 vols. London: Cambridge UP, 1975.
Fraser's Magazine for Town and Country. London, 1830–82.
Garnett, Richard, and Edward Garnett. *The Life of W. J. Fox: Public Teacher and Social Reformer 1786–1864*. London: John Lane, 1910.
Garside, Peter, James Raven, and Rainer Schöwerling. *The English Novel, 1770–1829: A Bibliographical Survey of Prose Fiction Published in the British Isles*. 2 vols. Oxford: Oxford UP, 2000.
Gentleman's Magazine, or Monthly Intelligencer, The. 1731–1907.
Gerring, Charles. *Notes on Printers and Booksellers with a Chapter on Chap Books*. London: Simpkin, Marshall, Hamilton, Kent, 1900.
Gilmartin, Kevin. *Print Politics: The Press and Radical Opposition in Early Nineteenth-Century England*. Cambridge Studies in Romanticism 21. Cambridge: Cambridge UP, 1996.
Godwin, William. *Memoirs of Mary Wollstonecraft*. [*Memoirs of the Author of* A Vindication of the Rights of Women. London: J. Johnson, 1798]. Ed. W. Clark Durant. London: Constable, 1927.
Goodman, Dena. *The Republic of Letters: A Cultural History of the French Enlightenment*. Ithaca: Cornell UP, 1994.
Graham, Walter James. *English Literary Periodicals*. New York: T. Nelson and Sons, 1930.
Griffith, Elizabeth, ed. *A Collection of Novels, Selected and Revised by Mrs. Griffith*. 3 vol. London: G. Kearsly, 1777.
——. *The Morality of Shakespeare's Drama Illustrated*. London: T. Cadell, 1775.
Guest, Harriet. *Small Change: Women, Learning, Patriotism, 1750–1810*. Chicago: U of Chicago P, 2000.
Haakonssen, Knud, ed. *Enlightenment and Religion: Rational Dissent in Eighteenth-Century Britain*. Ideas in Context. Cambridge: Cambridge UP, 1996.
Habermas, Jürgen. *The Structural Transformation of the Public Sphere: An Inquiry into a Category of Bourgeois Society*. Trans. Thomas Burger with the assistance of Frederick Lawrence. 1989. Cambridge, MA: MIT P, 1991.
"Hack." *The Oxford English Dictionary*. 2nd. ed. CD-ROM. Oxford: Oxford UP, 1992.
Hagstrum, Jean H. *Sex and Sensibility: Ideal and Erotic Love from Milton to Mozart*. Chicago: U of Chicago P, 1980.
Harris, Michael. "Periodicals and the Book Trade." *Development of the English Book Trade, 1700–1899*. Ed. Robin Myers and Michael Harris. Oxford: Oxford Polytechnic, 1981. 66–94.

Hartman, Geoffrey H. *Wordsworth's Poetry, 1787–1814*. New Haven: Yale UP, 1964.
Hayden, John O. *The Romantic Reviewers, 1802–1824*. Chicago: U of Chicago P, 1968.
Hays, Mary. *Cursory Remarks on an Enquiry into the Expediency and Propriety of Public or Social Worship*. London: T. Knott, 1791.
——. *The Love-Letters of Mary Hays (1779–1780)*. Ed. A. F. Wedd. London: Methuen, 1925.
——. *Memoirs of Emma Courtney*. Ed. Marilyn L. Brooks. London: G. G. & J. Robinson, 1796. Ontario: Broadview, 2000.
——. "On Novel Writing." *Monthly Magazine* 4 (Sept. 1797): 180–1.
Hazlitt, William. *Complete Works*. Ed. P. P. Howe. 21 vols. London: J. M. Dent & Sons, 1930–4.
Hogendoorn, Wiebe. "Reading on a Booke: Closet Drama and the Study of Theatre Arts." *Essays on Drama and Theatre: Liber Amicorum Benjamin Hunningher*. Ed. Erica Hunningher. Schilling Amsterdam/Baarn: Moussault's Uitgeverij; Antwerpen: Standaard Uitgeverij, 1973. 50–66.
Holcroft, Thomas. *Life of Thomas Holcroft, Written by Himself*. Ed. Elbridge Colby. 2 vols. London: Constable, 1833.
Hume, David. *Essays Moral, Political and Literary*. London: Oxford UP, 1963.
Hunningher, Erica, ed. *Essays on Drama and Theatre: Liber Amicorum Benjamin Hunningher*. Schilling Amsterdam/Baarn: Moussault's Uitgeverij; Antwerpen: Standaard Uitgeverij, 1973.
Hunter, Shelagh. *Harriet Martineau: The Poetics of Materialism*. Hants, England: Scolar P, 1995.
Inchbald, Elizabeth. *Lover's Vows, a Play, in Five Acts; Performing at the Theatre Royal, Covent-Garden, from the German of Kotzebue*. London: G. G. and J. Robinson, 1798.
——. *Nature and Art*. 2 vols. London: G. G. and J. Robinson, 1796.
——. "On Novel Writing." *The Artist* 1 (June 13, 1807): 9–19.
——. *Remarks for the British Theatre (1806–1809) by Elizabeth Inchbald*. Ed. Cecilia Macheski. Delmar, NY: Scholars' Facsimiles & Reprints, 1990.
——. *A Simple Story*. 4 vols. London: G. G. and J. Robinson, 1791.
——., ed. *The British Theatre; or, A Collection of Plays, Which Are Acted at the Theatres Royal, Drury-Lane, Covent-Garden, and Haymarket, With Biographical and Critical Remarks, by Mrs. Inchbald*. 25 vols. London: Longman, Hurst, Rees, and Orme, 1808.
——, ed. *A Collection of Farces and Other Afterpieces Which Are Acted at the Theatres Royal, Drury-Lane, Covent-Garden, and Hay-Market, Printed under the Authority of the Managers from the Prompt Book, Selected by Mrs Inchbald*. 7 vols. London: Longman, Hurst, Rees, and Orme, 1809.
——., ed. *The Modern Theatre; A Collection of Successful Modern Plays, as Acted at the Theatres Royal, London ..., Selected by Mrs. Inchbald*. 10 vols. London: Longman, Hurst, Rees, Orme, and Brown, 1811.
Ingrassia, Catherine. *Authorship, Commerce, and Gender in Early Eighteenth-Century England: A Culture of Paper Credit*. Cambridge, Cambridge UP, 1998.
Jarvis, Simon. *Scholars and Gentlemen: Shakespeare Textual Criticism and Representations of Scholarly Labour, 1725–1765*. Oxford: Clarendon P, 1995.
Jenkins, Annibel. *I'll Tell You What: The Life of Elizabeth Inchbald*. Lexington, KY: UP of Kentucky, 2003.

Johnson, Claudia L. *Equivocal Beings: Politics, Gender, and Sentimentality in the 1790s: Wollstonecraft, Radcliffe, Burney, Austen*. Women in Culture and Society. Ed. Catharine R. Stimpson. Chicago: U of Chicago P, 1995.

———. "'Let me make the novels of a country': Barbauld's The British Novelists (1810/1820)." *Novel: A Forum on Fiction* 34 (2001): 163–79.

Johnson, Samuel, ed. *The Works of the English Poets*. 68 vols. London: Bathurst, 1779–81.

———. *Rambler* No. 4 (31 Mar. 1750).

Jump, Harriet Devine. *Mary Wollstonecraft: Writer*. New York: Harvester Wheatsheaf, 1994.

Kaplan, Cora. *Sea Changes: Essays on Culture and Feminism*. London: Verso, 1986.

Keen, Paul. *The Crisis of Literature in the 1790s: Print Culture and the Public Sphere*. Cambridge Studies in Romanticism 36. Cambridge: Cambridge UP, 1999.

Keener, Frederick M., and Susan E. Lorsch, eds. *Eighteenth-Century Women and the Arts*. Contributions in Women's Studies 98. New York: Greenwood, 1988.

Kelly, Gary. "Bluestocking Feminism." *Women, Writing and the Public Sphere, 1700–1830*. Ed. Elizabeth Eger, Charlotte Grant, Clíona Ó Gallchoir, and Penny Warburton. Cambridge: Cambridge UP, 2001. 163–80.

———. *Revolutionary Feminism: The Mind and Career of Mary Wollstonecraft*. London: Macmillan, 1992.

———. *Women, Writing, and Revolution, 1790–1827*. Oxford: Clarendon P, 1993.

Klancher, Jon P. *The Making of English Reading Audiences, 1790–1832*. Madison: U of Wisconsin P, 1987.

———., ed. *Romanticism and its Publics: A Forum Organized and Introduced by Jon Klancher*. Spec. issue of *Studies in Romanticism* 33 (1994): 527–88.

Kramnick, Jonathan Brody. *Making the English Canon: Print-Capitalism and the Cultural Past, 1700–1770*. Cambridge: Cambridge UP, 1998.

Landes, Joan, ed. *Feminism, the Public and the Private*. Oxford: Oxford UP, 1998.

———. *Women and the Public Sphere in the Age of the French Revolution*. Ithaca: Cornell UP, 1988.

Lanser, Susan Sniader, and Evelyn Torton Beck. "[Why] Are There No Great Women Critics?: And What Difference Does It Make?" *The Prism of Sex: Essays in the Sociology of Knowledge*. Ed. Julia A. Sherman and Evelyn Torton Beck. Madison: U of Wisconsin P, 1977. 79–91.

Le Breton, Anna Letitia. *Memoir of Mrs. Barbauld, Including Letters and Notices of Her Family and Friends*. London: G. Bell, 1874.

Lennox, Charlotte. *The Female Quixote; Or, The Adventures of Arabella*. 2 vols. London: A. Millar, 1752.

———. *Shakespear Illustrated: or the Novels and Histories, on Which the Plays of Shakespear Are Founded, Collected and Translated from the Original Authors with Critical Remarks in Two Volumes by the Author of* The Female Quixote. 2 vols. London: A. Millar, 1753–4.

Lipking, Lawrence. *The Ordering of the Arts in Eighteenth-Century England*. Princeton: Princeton UP, 1970.

Littlewood, S. R. *Elizabeth Inchbald and Her Circle: The Life Story of a Charming Woman (1753–1821)*. London: Daniel O'Connor, 1921.

Locke, John. *Essay Concerning Human Understanding*. Ed. Peter H. Nidditch. 1690. Oxford: Clarendon P, 1975.

Lott, Anna. "Sexual Politics in Elizabeth Inchbald." *SEL: Studies in English Literature, 1500–1900* 34 (1994): 635–48.
Luria, Gina M. *Mary Hays: A Critical Biography*. Diss. New York U, 1972.
Macheski, Cecilia, ed. *Remarks for the British Theatre (1806–1809) by Elizabeth Inchbald*. Delmar, NY: Scholars' Facsimiles & Reprints, 1990.
MacDermott, Kathy. "Literature and the Grub Street Myth." *Literature and History* 8 (1982): 159–69.
Manvell, Roger. *Elizabeth Inchbald: England's Principal Woman Dramatist and Independent Woman of Letters in 18th Century London, a Biographical Study*. Lanham, NY: UP of America, 1987.
Marks, Patricia. "Harriet Martineau: *Fraser's* 'Maid of [Dis]Honour,'" *Victorian Periodicals Review* 19 (1986): 28–33.
Martineau, Harriet. *Harriet Martineau's Autobiography*. Ed. Maria Weston Chapman. London: Smith, Elder, 1877. 4th ed. 2 vols. Boston: Houghton, Osgood and Company, 1879.
——. *Harriet Martineau: Selected Letters*. Ed. Valerie Sanders. Oxford: Clarendon P, 1990.
Mathur, Om Prakash. *The Closet Drama of the Romantic Revival*. Salzburg Studies in English Literature under the Direction of Professor Erwin A. Stürzl. Poetic Drama and Poetic Theory. Ed. Dr. James Hogg. Salzburg, Austria: Institut für Englische Sprache und Literatur, Universität Salzburg, 1978.
McCarthy, William and Elizabeth Kraft, eds., *Anna Letitia Barbauld: Selected Poetry and Prose* Petersborough, Ont.: Broadview, 2002.
McDowell, Paula. *The Women of Grub Street: Press, Politics, and Gender in the London Literary Marketplace, 1678–1730*. Oxford: Clarendon P, 1998.
McGann, Jerome J. *The Romantic Ideology: A Critical Investigation*. Chicago: U of Chicago P, 1983.
McKee, William. *Elizabeth Inchbald, Novelist*. Washington, DC: Catholic U of America, 1935.
McLachlan, Herbert. *Warrington Academy: Its History and Influence*. Manchester: Chetham Society, 1943.
Mellor, Anne K. "A Criticism of Their Own: Romantic Women Literary Critics." *Questioning Romanticism*. Ed. John Beer. Baltimore: Johns Hopkins UP, 1995. 29–48.
——. *Mothers of the Nation: Women's Political Writing in England, 1780–1830*. Women of Letters. Ed. Sandra M. Gilbert and Susan Gubar. Bloomington: Indiana UP, 2000.
Mineka, Francis E. *The Dissidence of Dissent: The* Monthly Repository, *1806–1838; under the Editorship of Robert Aspland, W. J. Fox, R. H. Horne, & Leigh Hunt; with a Chapter on Religious Periodicals, 1700–1825*. Chapel Hill: U of North Carolina P, 1944.
Montagu, Elizabeth. *An Essay on the Writings and Genius of Shakespeare, Compared with the Greek and French Dramatic Poets. With Some Remarks upon the Misrepresentations of Mons. de Voltaire*. London: J. and H. Hughs, 1769.
Monthly Magazine and British Register, The. London, 1796–1843.
Monthly Repository, The. London, 1806–38.
Monthly Review, The. London, 1749–1844.
Moore, Catherine E. "'Ladies … Taking the Pen in Hand': Mrs. Barbauld's Criticism of Eighteenth-Century Women Novelists." *Fetter'd or Free: British*

Women Novelists 1670–1815. Ed. Mary Anne Schofield and Cecilia Macheski. Athens, OH: U of Ohio P, 1986. 383–97.

Mullan, John. *Sentiment and Sociability: The Language of Feeling in the Eighteenth Century*. Oxford: Clarendon P, 1988.

Myers, Mitzi. "Sensibility and the 'Walk of Reason': Mary Wollstonecraft's Literary Reviews as Cultural Critique." *Sensibility in Transformation: Creative Resistance to Sentiment from the Augustans to the Romantics*. Ed. Syndy McMillen Conger. Rutherford: Fairleigh Dickinson UP; London: Associated UP, 1990. 120–44.

Myers, Sylvia Harcstark. *The Bluestocking Circle: Women, Friendship, and the Life of the Mind in Eighteenth-Century England*. Oxford: Clarendon P, 1990.

Nangle, Benjamin Christie. *The Monthly Review, First Series, 1749–1789: Indexes of Contributors and Articles*. Oxford, Clarendon P, 1934.

———. *The Monthly Review, Second Series, 1790–1815: Indexes of Contributors and Articles*. Oxford, Clarendon P, 1955.

Newman, Gerald. *The Rise of English Nationalism: A Cultural History 1740–1830*. 1987. New York: St. Martin's P, 1997.

Nicholes, Eleanor Louise. *Shelley and his Circle: 1773–1822*. Ed. Kenneth Neill Cameron. Vol. 1. Cambridge, MA: Harvard UP, 1961. 177.

O'Brien, P. *Warrington Academy, 1757–86: Its Predecessors and Successors*. Wigan, UK: Owl Books, 1989.

O'Reid, Jno. Chas. [Josiah Conder]. *Reviewers Reviewed; Including an Enquiry into the Moral and Intellectual Effects of Habits of Criticism, and Their Influence on the General Interests of Literature; to which Is Subjoined a Brief History of the Periodical Reviews Published in England and Scotland*. Oxford: J. Bartlett, 1811.

Parke, Catherine N. "What Kind of Heroine is Mary Wollstonecraft?" *Sensibility in Transformation: Creative Resistance to Sentiment from the Augustans to the Romantics*. Ed. Syndy McMillen Conger. Rutherford: Fairleigh Dickinson UP, 1990. 103–19.

Parker, Mark. *Literary Magazines and British Romanticism*. Cambridge Studies in Romanticism 45. Cambridge: Cambridge UP, 2000.

Patey, Douglas Lane. "The Eighteenth Century Invents the Canon." *Modern Language Studies* 18 (1988): 17–37.

Paul, C. Kegan. *William Godwin: His Friends and Contemporaries*. 2 vols. London: Henry S. King, 1876

Peterson, Linda. "(Re)inventing Authorship: Harriet Martineau in the Literary Marketplace of the 1820s." *Women's Writing* 9 (2002): 337–50.

Pfau, Thomas. *Wordsworth's Profession: Form, Class, and the Logic of Early Romantic Cultural Production*. Stanford: Stanford UP, 1997.

Pichanick, Valerie Kossew. *Harriet Martineau: The Woman and Her Work, 1802–76*. Ann Arbor: U of Michigan P, 1980.

Polwhele, Richard. *The Unsex'd Females: A Poem, Addressed to the Author of The Pursuits of Literature*. London: Cadell and Davies, 1798.

Poovey, Mary. *The Proper Lady and the Woman Writer: Ideology as Style in the Works of Mary Wollstonecraft, Mary Shelley, and Jane Austen*. Women in Culture and Society. Ed. Catherine R. Stimpson. Chicago: U of Chicago P, 1984.

Prior, Mary, ed. *Women in English Society, 1500–1800*. London: Methuen, 1985.

Quarterly Review, The. London, 1809–1962.

Reed, Isaac. *Biographia Dramatica*. 2 vols. London: Rivington, 1782.

Rees, Thomas. *Reminiscences of Literary London from 1779 to 1853. Reminiscence of Literary London from 1779 to 1853* by Thomas Rees and *The Rise and Progress of the Gentleman's Magazine* by John Nichols, The English Book Trade 1660–1853. 1896. New York: Garland, 1974.

Reeve, Clara. *The Old English Baron: A Gothic Story*. 2nd ed. 1778. London: C. Dilly, 1780.

———. *A Progress of Romance*. London: G. G. J. and J. Robinson, 1785.

Reiman, Donald H., ed. *The Romantics Reviewed: Contemporary Reviews of British Romantic Writers*. 3 vols. New York: Garland, 1972.

Reiss, Timothy J. "Revolution in Bounds: Wollstonecraft, Women, and Reason." *Gender and Theory*. Ed. Linda Kauffman. New York: Basil Blackwell, 1989.

Richardson, Alan. *A Mental Theater: Poetic Drama and Consciousness in the Romantic Age*. University Park, PA: Pennsylvania State UP, 1988.

Rizzo, Betty. "Isabella Griffiths." *A Dictionary of British and American Women Writers, 1660–1800*. ed. Janet Todd. Totowa, NJ: Roan and Allanheld, 1985. 143.

Robberds, J. W., ed. *A Memoir of the Life and Writings of the Late William Taylor of Norwich, Containing His Correspondence of Many Years with the Late Robert Southey, Esq., and Original Letters from Sir Walter Scott*. 2 vols. London: Murray, 1843.

Robinson, Henry Crabb. *Henry Crabb Robinson on Books and Their Writers*. Ed. Edith Morley. 3 vols. London: Dent, 1938.

Robinson, Solveig C., ed. *A Serious Occupation: Literary Criticism by Victorian Women Writers*. Peterborough, ON: Broadview, 2003.

Rogers, Katherine M. "Britain's First Woman Drama Critic: Elizabeth Inchbald," *Curtain Calls: British and American Women and the Theater, 1660–1820*. Ed. Mary Anne Schofield and Cecilia Macheski. Athens, OH: U of Ohio P, 1991. 277–90.

Roper, Derek. "Mary Wollstonecraft's Reviews." *Notes and Queries* 203 (1958): 37–8.

———. "The Politics of the *Critical Review*, 1766–1817." *Durham University Journal* 53 (1961): 117–22.

———. *Reviewing before the* Edinburgh: *1788–1802*. Newark: U of Delaware P, 1978.

Ryan, Robert M. *The Romantic Reformation: Religious Politics in English Literature, 1789–1824*. Cambridge Studies in Romanticism 24. Cambridge, Cambridge UP, 1997.

Schofield, Mary Anne, and Cecilia Macheski, eds. *Curtain Calls: British and American Women and the Theater, 1660–1820*. Athens, OH: U of Ohio P, 1991.

———., eds. *Fetter'd or Free: British Women Novelists 1670–1815*. Athens, OH: U of Ohio P, 1986.

Seward, Anna. *The Letters of Anna Seward*. 6 vols. Edinburgh: Constable; London: Longman, 1811.

Sheridan, Frances. *Memoirs of Miss Sidney Biddulph: Extracted from Her Own Journal, and Now First Published*. 3 vols. London: R. and J. Dodsley, 1761.

Sherman, Julia A., and Evelyn Torton Beck, eds. *The Prism of Sex: Essays in the Sociology of Knowledge*. Madison: U of Wisconsin P, 1977.

Sigl, Patricia. "Prince Hoare's *Artist* and Anti-Theatrical Polemics in the Early 1800s: Mrs Inchbald's Contribution." *Theatre Notebook* 44 (1990): 62–73.

Simpson, David. *Romanticism, Nationalism, and the Revolt against Theory.* Chicago: U of Chicago P, 1993.
Smiles, Samuel. *A Publisher and His Friends.* London: John Murray, 1891.
Smyser, Jane Worthington. "The Trial and Imprisonment of Joseph Johnson, Bookseller." *Bulletin of the New York Public Library* 77 (1974): 418–35.
Stanton, Judith Phillips. "Statistical Profile of Women Writing in English from 1660 to 1800." *Eighteenth-Century Women and the Arts.* Ed. Frederick M. Keener and Susan E. Lorsch. Contributions in Women's Studies 98. New York: Greenwood, 1988. 247–254.
Stephen, Leslie and Sir Sidney Lee, eds. *Dictionary of National Biography: From the Earliest Times to 1900.* London: Oxford University Press, 1921–22.
Stewart, Sally N. "Mary Wollstonecraft's Contributions to the *Analytical Review.*" *Essays in Literature* 11 (1984): 187–99.
Stillinger, Jack. *Multiple Authorship and the Myth of Solitary Genius.* New York: Oxford UP, 1991.
Sullivan, Alvin, ed. *British Literary Magazines.* 4 vols. Historical Guides to the World's Periodicals and Newspapers. Westport, CN: Greenwood P, 1983–86.
Tait's Edinburgh Magazine. Edinburgh, 1832–55.
Taylor, Barbara. *Mary Wollstonecraft and the Feminist Imagination.* Cambridge Studies in Romanticism 56. Cambridge: Cambridge UP, 2003.
Taylor, John. *Records of My Life.* New York: J. & J. Harper, 1833.
Thompson, Ann, and Sasha Roberts, ed. *Women Reading Shakespeare, 1660–1900: An Anthology of Criticism.* Manchester: Manchester UP, 1997.
Todd, Janet. *Mary Wollstonecraft: A Revolutionary Life.* London: Weidenfeld & Nicholson, 2000.
——. *Sensibility: An Introduction.* London: Methuen, 1986.
——. *The Sign of Angelica: Women, Writing, and Fiction, 1660–1800.* New York: Columbia UP, 1989.
Trela, D. J. "Introduction: Nineteenth Century Women and Periodicals." *Victorian Periodicals Review* 29 (1996): 89–94.
Turner, Cheryl. *Living by the Pen: Women Writers in the Eighteenth Century.* London: Routledge, 1992.
Ty, Eleanor. *Unsex'd Revolutionaries: Five Women Novelists of the 1790s.* Toronto: U of Toronto P, 1993.
Tyson, Gerald P. *Joseph Johnson: A Liberal Publisher.* Iowa City, U of Iowa P, 1979.
Wang, Orrin N. C. "The Other Reasons: Female Alterity and Enlightenment Discourses in Mary Wollstonecraft's *A Vindication of the Rights of Woman.*" *Yale Journal of Criticism* 5 (1991): 129–49.
Wardle, Ralph M. "Mary Wollstonecraft, *Analytical Reviewer.*" *PMLA* 62 (1947): 1000–9.
——. *Mary Wollstonecraft: A Critical Biography.* Lawrence, Kansas: U of Kansas P, 1951.
Webb, R. K. "The Emergence of Rational Dissent." *Enlightenment and Religion: Rational Dissent in Eighteenth-Century Britain.* Ed. Knud Haakonssen. Ideas in Context. Cambridge: Cambridge UP, 1996. 12–41.
——. *Harriet Martineau: A Radical Victorian.* New York: Columbia UP; London: William Heinemann, 1960.
Wedd, A. F., ed. *The Love-Letters of Mary Hays (1779–1780).* London: Methuen, 1925.

Wellington, Jan. "Elizabeth Moody." *An Encyclopedia of British Women Writers*. Ed. Paul Schlueter and June Schlueter. 1988. New Brunswick, NJ: Rutgers UP, 1998. 461–2.

——. *The Poems and Prose of Elizabeth Moody*. Diss. University of New Mexico, 1997.

Wendorf, Richard. *William Collins and Eighteenth-Century English Poetry*. Minneapolis: U of Minnesota P, 1981.

White, Daniel. "The 'Joineriana': Anna Barbauld, the Aikin Family Circle, and the Dissenting Public Sphere." *Eighteenth-Century Studies* 32 (1999): 511–33.

Wollstonecraft, Mary. *Collected Letters of Mary Wollstonecraft*. Ed. Ralph M. Wardle. Ithaca: Cornell UP, 1979.

——. *Letters Written during a Short Residence in Sweden, Norway and Denmark*. London: J. Johnson, 1796.

——. *Mary: A Fiction*. London: J. Johnson, 1788.

——. [W. Q., pseudo.] "On Artificial Taste." *Monthly Magazine* 3 (Apr. 1797): 279–82.

——. *Original Stories from Real Life, with Conversations, Calculated to Regulate the Affections, and Form the Mind to Truth and Goodness*. London: J. Johnson, 1788.

——. *Thoughts on the Education of Daughters: with Reflections on Female Conduct, in the More Important Duties of Life*. London: J. Johnson, 1787.

——. *A Vindication of the Rights of Men, in a Letter to the Right Honourable Edmund Burke*. London: J. Johnson, 1790.

——. *A Vindication of the Rights of Woman, with Strictures on Political and Moral Subjects*. London: J. Johnson, 1792.

——. *The Works of Mary Wollstonecraft*. Ed. Janet Todd and Marilyn Butler. Vol. 5. London: William Pickering, 1989.

——. *The Wrongs of Woman, or Maria; a Fragment. Posthumous Works of the Author of a Vindication of the Rights of Woman*. Ed. William Godwin. 4 vols. London: J. Johnson, 1798.

——., ed. [Mr. Cresswick, Teacher of Elocution, pseudo.] *The Female Reader; or Miscellaneous Pieces, in Prose and Verse; Selected from the Best Writers, and Disposed under Proper Heads; for the Improvement of Young Women*. London: J. Johnson, 1789.

——., trans. *Elements of Morality for the Use of Children*. By Christian Gotthilf Salzmann. London: J. Johnson, 1790.

——., trans. *Young Grandison*. By Madame de Cambon. London: J. Johnson, 1790.

Wood, Marcus. *Radical Satire and Print Culture, 1790–1822*. Oxford: Oxford UP, 1994.

Woolf, Virginia. *A Room of One's Own*. Norton Anthology of English Literature. Ed. M. H. Abrams, et al. 6th ed. Vol. 2. New York: W. W. Norton and Co., 1993. 1926–86.

Yudin, Mary F. "Joanna Baillie's Introductory Discourse As a Precursor to Wordsworth's Preface to *Lyrical Ballads*." *Compar(a)ison: An International Journal of Comparative Literature* 1 (1994): 101–11.

Zall, Paul M. "The Cool World of Samuel Taylor Coleridge: Elizabeth Inchbald; or, Sex and Sensibility." *The Wordsworth Circle* 12 (1981): 270–3.

Zaw, Susan Khin. "The Reasonable Heart: Mary Wollstonecraft's View of the Relation Between Reason and Feeling in Morality, Moral Psychology, and Moral Development." *Hypatia* 13 (1998): 78–117.

Index

Adburgham, Alice, 4
Addison, Joseph
  Criticism of, 39–47, 48, 126
  The Spectator, 4, 37, 38, 90, 124;
    Sir Andrew Freeport, 41
aesthetics, *see* literary aesthetics
Aikin, Anna Letitia, *see* Barbauld,
    Anna Letitia
Aikin, Arthur, 127
Aikin, John (1713–80), 26, 28,
Aikin, John (1747–1822), 29, 32, 127,
    129, 133–4, 140, 199 n. 9
Aikin, Lucy, 17, 140, 167–8
Akenside, Mark, 20, 31, 37–8, 55–6,
    126
Althusser, Louis, 7
Analytical Review, The, 17, 21, 32, 85,
    87–120, 127, 140, 152, 172
  history and scope, 123–6
  Hays's reviews for, 114–8
  Wollstonecraft's reviews for, 92–104,
Anglicanism, *see* religion: Established
    Church
Annual Review, 127, 140
Anti-Jacobin Review, The, 117
Armstrong, Nancy, 181 n. 48
Artist, The, 186 n. 3
Athenæum, The, 127, 140
Aspland, Robert, 157
Austen, Jane, 36, 52, 58

Backscheider, Paula, 59, 78
Barbauld, Anna Letitia, 5, 17, 19–20,
    21, 22, 25–27, 28–56, 85, 121–41,
    144–50, 153, 155, 166–7, 183
    n. 20
  and audience, 31, 34–8, 149–50
  and class, 34–5, 37–8, 41–2, 44–5,
    47–9, 133–4
  collaborative view of literary
    production, 137–9
  and cultural effects of literature,
    39–43
  dissenting culture and professional
    support of, 28–9, 123, 139–43
  critical values and aesthetic
    concerns, 35–7, 48–9, 122, 132,
    134–7
  and domesticity, 40–2, 47–49, 52–6
  education and expertise, 25–6,
    28–9, 38, 128–131, 149–50
  gender-based attack, 163, 171, 203
    n. 3, 204 n. 20
  intellectual authority, 34–8, 139
  and the literary canon, 31, 42–6,
    48, 50–2
  and *The Monthly Review*, 121–41,
    145–50, 154, 199–200 n. 10,
    201–2 n. 37; review
    identification, 127–8, 199 n. 9;
    titles reviewed in *The Monthly
    Review*: Amphlett, J., *Ned
    Bentley*, 132–3, 137; Browne,
    Felicia Dorothea [later
    Hemans], *Poems*, 137; La
    Fontaine, Augustus, *Raphaël*,
    146–7; Trimmer, Sarah,
    Instructive Tales, 201–2 n. 37;
    topics/types of work reviewed:
    129–131, 135–6
  on nationalism or national
    character, 31, 34–5, 41–56, 73,
    146–50
  and other periodicals: 127, 140, 204
    n. 20
  professionalism, 121–2, 126–9, 136
  and religious dissent, *see* dissenting
    culture
  Works: *An Address to the Opposers of
    the Repeal of the Corporation and
    Test Acts*, 30; *British Novelists,
    The*, 39, 43, 50–6, 58, 126–7,
    128, 185 n. 50; *Correspondence
    of Samuel Richardson*, 43, 47–50,
    126; *Eighteen Hundred and
    Eleven*, 42, 163, 204 n. 20;

Barbauld, Anna Letitia – *continued*
  The Female Speaker, 129; *Hymns in Prose for Children* 30; *Lessons for Children*, 29; "Life of Samuel Richardson with Remarks on His Writings." 43, 47–50, 126; *Miscellaneous Pieces in Prose*, 29, 30, 33, 184 n. 42; "On the Origin and Progress of Novel-Writing," 39, 51–6, 127, 150; "On Romances," 140; *Poems*, 29; *The Poetical Works of Mr. William Collin*, 20, 31, 32–7, 55, 126; *The Pleasures of the Imagination*, 20, 31, 37–38, 55–6, 126; *Selections from the* Spectator, Tatler, Guardian, *and* Freeholder, 39–48, 54, 126; "A Summer Evening's Meditation," 56
Barbauld, Rochemont, 29, 42
Barker-Benfield, G. J., 11, 12, 13, 105
Barzun, Jacques, 16
Basker, James, 84, 138
Beaumont, Sir Francis and John Fletcher, 77
Beck, Evelyn Torton, 1–2
Behn, Aphra, 3, 70
Bell, John, 186 n. 5
Bentham, Jeremy, 164
Blake, William, 25, 190–1 n. 5
  Songs of Innocence, 30
Blood, Fanny, 96, 104
Bluestockings, 5–7
  See also individual names
Boaden, James, 25, 26, 28, 62
Boileau, Nicholas, 45
Bonnell, Thomas F., 16, 43
Bowring, John, 164
British national character, *see* national character
Brooke, Frances, 4
  Old Maid, The, 4
Burgh, James (and wife), 104
Burke, Edmund, 16, 101
  A Philosophical Enquiry into [...] the Sublime and the Beautiful, 100
  Reflections on the Revolution in France, 45, 97

Burney, Fanny (Frances, later d'Arblay), 53, 93, 133, 179 n. 12
Burroughs, Catherine B., 61, 76, 78, 189 n. 35
Butler, Marilyn, 8, 84–5, 91, 150, 153, 170, 182 n. 2 195 n. 55, 196 n. 65, 198 n. 2
Byron, George Gordon, Lord, 52

Cadell, Thomas and William Davies, 31–2, 35, 37, 55
Canon, literary, *see* literary canon
Carlson, Marvin, 59, 66
Carpenter, Lant, 156
Carter, Elizabeth, 5, 169, 179 n. 16
Catholicism, 57, 73–5, 168–9; *see also* religion; *see also* Inchbald, Elizabeth
Cavendish, Margaret; Duchess of Newcastle, 5
Chandler, James, 16, 22, 45–6,
Chapman, Maria Weston, 159, 160
Chapone, Hester, 5, 6
Charles I, 74
Chesterfield, Philip Dormer Stanhope, 4th earl of, 108
Christie, Thomas, 90–2, 99, 102, 103, 110
Cibber, Colley, 59, 80
Class, *see under* individual author names
Colby, Elbridge, 187 n. 16
Coleridge, Samuel Taylor, 17, 93, 190–1 n. 5, 199 n. 9
  Lyrical Ballads, 19, 30–1, 107, 190–1 n. 5
Collaboration, literary, *see* literary collaboration
Colley, Linda, 14, 73–4, 148, 167, 168, 184 n. 26
Collins, William, 20, 31, 32–7, 44, 55, 126
Colman, George (the elder), 77, 187–8 n. 17
Colman, George (the younger), 60–5, 69, 187–8 n. 17, 188 n. 18, 204 n. 20
Conder, Josiah, 84
Conger, Syndy Mcmillen

Copeland, Edward, 3, 133, 185 n. 57
Crane, R. S., 11, 12
Critical Review, The, 84, 114, 118, 123, 124, 125, 130
Croker, John Wilson, 163–4, 171, 204 n. 20

Davidoff, Leonora, 11, 12, 123, 139, 177, 201 n. 33
Davies, William, *see* Cadell, Thomas and William Davies
Defoe, Daniel, 48
Denman, Thomas, 130
Dictionary of National Biography, 163
D'Israeli, Isaac, 64–5
Dissent, religious, *see* religion: religious dissent
Doddridge, Philip, 11
Domesticity, 11–16, 40–2, 47–49, 52–6; *see also* sensibility
Donkin, Ellen, 187–8 n. 17
Drama, criticism of, *see* Inchbald, Elizabeth
Dryden, John, 72
Duchess of Newcastle, *see* Margaret Cavendish
Dyer, George, 111, 114

Edgeworth, Maria, 53, 127, 190–1 n. 5
Edinburgh Review, The, 103, 123–4, 125, 134, 153, 164–5, 170–1
Eger, Elizabeth, 6, 179 n. 21
Eliot, George, 151
Empson, William, 164
Enfield, William, 28, 29, 129
Established Church, 74, 105, 123, 153, 169; *see also* religion
Eyres, William, 29

Fielding, Sarah, 179 n. 12
Finch, Anne, Countess of Winchilsea, 5
Fletcher, John, 77
Flexner, Eleanor, 97, 109–10, 196 n. 65
Flower, Eliza, 160, 162
Flower, Sarah, 160
Fox, Charles, 161–2

Fox, William James, 157–62, 172, 174
Fraser's Magazine, 164–5
French Revolution, 16, 148–9
Fuseli, Henry, 25, 190–1 n. 5, 197 n. 69

Garnett, Richard and Edward Garnett, 177
Garrick, David, 77
Gentleman's Magazine, 127
Gender
and audience, 91, 93–5, 112, 125
-based attacks, 42, 60–5, 162–5, 171, 203 n. 3, 204 n. 20
concerns in women's criticism, 40–2, 51–3, 69, 100
and intellectual or critical authority, 34–7, 68, 87, 92, 104–9, 112–4, 139
literary criticism of women writers, 31, 51–3, 56
performance of, 63, 113, 144–5
and the public sphere, 14–5
see also domesticity, sensibility
Genlis, Stephanie Felicite, Mme. de, 56, 169
George III, 62
Gifford, William, 117
Gilpin, 99–100
Godwin, William, 25, 57, 71, 93, 173–4, 188 n. 28, 197 n. 69, 203 n. 3
Goethe, Johann Wolfgang von, 39
Goldsmith, Oliver, 133, 180 n. 24
Gordon Riots, 73
Graham, Catherine Macaulay, 5
Graham, Walter James, 17
Gramsci, Antonio, 55
Griffith, Elizabeth, 5, 6
A Collection of Novels, 51
Morality of Shakespeare's Drama Illustrated, The, 6
Griffiths, George Edward, 123, 130, 143–4
Griffiths, Isabella, 5, 182 n. 53
Griffiths, Ralph, 5, 123–4, 142, 143, 182 n. 53, 201–2 n. 37
Griffiths, Richard, 57
Guest, Harriet, 14–15, 16, 167–8

Habermas, Jürgen, 13–14
hack writing, *see* literary professionalism
Hagstrum, Jean, 13
Hall, Catherine, 11, 12, 123, 139, 177, 201 n. 33
Hamilton, Elizabeth, 167–8
Hardinge, George, 142
Harris, Benjamin, 4
Harris, Elizabeth, 4
Protestant Post-Boy, 4
Harris, Thomas, 80–1
Hartley, David, 12
Hawsbawm, Eric J., 185 n. 57
Hays, Mary, 19, 21, 22, 85, 87–8, 89, 92, 110–19, 121, 140, 153, 190–1 n. 5, 197 n. 70, 198 n. 76
and *The Analytical Review*, 114–19; works reviewed: West, Jane, *A Gossip's Story*, 114–6
critical values and aesthetic concerns, 117–8
gender-based attack, 203 n. 3
professional expertise and support, 114, 117–9
and sensibility, 115, 117–8
Works: *Cursory Remarks on [...] Public or Social Worship*, 111, 113; *Female Biography*, 118–9; *Fool of Quality, The*, 118; *Harry Clinton, or A Tale of Youth*, 118; *Letters and Essays, Moral and Miscellaneous*, 111; *Memoirs of Emma Courtney*, 118, 119; *Memoirs of Queens*,118; "On Novel Writing," 117–8
Haywood, Eliza, 4
The Female Spectator, 4
The Tea Table, 4
Hazlitt, William, 129
Hemans, Felicia, 137
Hodgson, Francis, 130
Hogendoorn, Wiebe, 189 n. 35
Holcroft, Thomas, 25, 57, 62
Howard, John, 29
Hume, David, 1

Inchbald, Elizabeth, 17, 19–21, 25–27, 57–81, 107, 153, 187 n. 12, 187–8 n.17, 188 n. 18
and audience, 65–7
and closet drama, 75–7
collaborative view of literary production, 77–81
critical values and aesthetic concerns, 67–70
discussions from *The British Theatre*: Baillie, Joanna, *De Montfort*, 76; Brown, John, *Barbarossa*, 77; Colman, George (the elder) and David Garrick, *The Clandestine Marriage*, 75, Colman, George (the younger), *The Heir at Law*, 64, *John Bull*, 76, *The Surrender of Calais* 71; Congreve, William, *The Mourning Bride*, 77; Cumberland, Richard, *The West Indian*, 77; Gay, John, *The Beggar's Opera*, 78; Garrick, David, *The Country Girl*, 78; Lee, Nathaniel, *The Rival Queens*, 76; Macklin, Charles, 78, *Man of the World*, 70; Moore, Edward, *The Foundling*, 77, Morton, Thomas, *The School for Reform*, 72; O'Keefe, John, *Fontainbleau*, 71; Philips, Ambrose, *The Distressed Mother*, 72; Shakespeare, William, *As You Like It*, 75, *Comedy of Errors*, 66–8, *Henry V*, 71, *Julius Caesar*, 70–1, *King Henry VIII*, 74, *King Lear*, 74–5, 186 n. 7, *Othello*, 77, *Twelfth Night*, 74, *The Winter's Tale*, 75; Sheridan, Richard, *The Duenna*, 80, *School for Scandal*, 59; Shirley, James, *The Gamester*, 76; Southern, Thomas, *Oroonoko*; Vanbrugh, John, *The Provoked Husband*, 80
education, 25–6, 188 n. 25
gender-based attack, 60–5, 204 n. 20
intellectual authority, 65–7
and irony, 62–4, 65, 71, 72, 81
and nationalism or national identity, 71–5
politics and social reform, 70–1
and professionalism, 63–5, 81
and religious culture, 57, 73–5

theatrical and playwriting experience, 57–8, 68, 73, 78
works: *British Theatre, The*, 20, 25, 58–81, 186 n. 4; project structure and scope, 58–9; *A Collection of Farces and Other Afterpieces*, 65; *Lover's Vows* 57–8, 80–1; *Massacre, The*, 188 n. 28; *Nature and Art*, 58, 62, 107; "On Novel Writing," 186 n. 3; *Simple Story, A*, 58; *Such Things Are*, 62
Inchbald, Joseph, 57

James II, 74–5
Jenkins, Annibel, 62, 186 n. 5, 188 n. 18, 188 n. 25
Johnson, Claudia L., 185 n. 51
Johnson, E., Mrs., 4
Johnson, Joseph, 22; dissenting publisher, 28–9, 32, 127, 139–40; and Mary Hays, 119; other publishing interests, 183 n. 20, 190–1 n. 5, 195 n. 57; support for women writers, 9, 32; trial for sedition, 117; and Mary Wollstonecraft, 22, 86–90, 96–7, 103–4, 109, 110, 111, 113, 114, 117
Johnson, Samuel, 6, 53, 77, 93, 107, 133
criticism of, 103, 106–7, 192 n. 24
works: *Plays of William Shakespeare*, 66; *Rambler, The*, 94–5, 117; *Works of the English Poets*, 16, 32, 36, 43, 79

Kauffman, Angelica, 5
Kelly, Gary, 6, 169
Kemble, John, 57
Klancher, Jon, 18–19, 67, 90–1, 92, 189–90 n. 1
Kotzebue, August von, 58, 80–1
Das Kind der Liebe, 58
Kraft, Elizabeth, 55, 199 n. 9

La Fayette, Marie, Mme. de, 48, 56
Lanser, Susan Sniader, 1–2
Latitudinarians, 10, 12; *see also* religion: religious dissent

Lee, Vernon, 1
Lennox, Charlotte, 1, 5, 6–7, 179 n. 12
Shakespear Illustrated, 6–7, 51
Linley, Elizabeth (later Sheridan), 5
Lipking, Lawrence, 45, 46
Literary
Aesthetics: Aristotelian, 5; Augustan or neoclassical 16, 17, 20, 22, 33–4, 44–6, 107, 109; concern with moral effect, 18, 51–4, 93–6, 106–7, 136; criticism of publications on, 99–100; realism and probability, 66–8, 117–8, 132, 135; Romantic, 17, 22, 45–6; and sensibility, 12–16; *see also* critical values and aesthetic concerns under individual authors
Canon, 6, 16–7, 20; women writers in, 20, 31, 52; *see also* under individual author names
Collaboration: collaborative view of literary production, 77–81, 137–9; collaboratively composed criticism, 143–4, 159–60; *see also* dissenting culture and professional support under individual author names
Criticism: of drama, 18; 58–81; identification of, 97, 114–5, 127–8, 196 n. 65, 197 n. 69; consumerism and marketability, 30, 32, 41, 55, 59, 64–5, 81, 84, 90–2; and nationalism or national character, *see under* individual author names; of novels, 18, 20, 39, 47–8, 51–6, 93–5; in periodicals, *see* reviews; of periodicals, 18, 20, 39–48, 54, 126; in poetry, 5; as prefatory essays, 4, 25–81, 86; of Shakespeare, *see* Shakespeare, William; by women, 1–7, 17, *see also* individual author names; of women writers, 31, 51–3, 56; *see also* aesthetics

Literary – *continued*
  Professionalism 2–9, 19, 22, 84–5
    see also under individual author names
    Devaluation of, 7–8, 88, 125–6, 131–4
    reviews: catalogues, 124–133, 136–7, 165; format, 91–2, 123–6, 134–7, 152–3, 170–2; history and development, 83–5, 123–6; political slant, 114, 164–5; quality and professionalism, 88, 123, 126–9, 134–7; purpose and significance, 82–5, 91 see also under individual author names, individual review names
  work, see literary professionalism
Locke, John, 12, 108
Lockhart, John Gibson, 163, 171
Longman, Thomas, 31, 58, 60, 67–8, 71, 186 n. 5, 186 n. 7
Lott, Anna, 61–2
Lovibond, Edward, 142
Lowe, Joseph, 130
Lyrical Ballads (Wordsworth and Coleridge), 19, 30–1, 107, 190–1 n. 5

Macaulay, Catherine (later Graham), 5
MacDermott, Kathy, 7, 88
Macheski, Cecilia, 186 n. 4
Manley, Mary de la Rivière, 4
  Female Tatler, The, 4
Manning, James, 130
Marcet, Jane, 161, 164
Martineau, Harriet, 19, 21, 22–3, 85, 151–177
  and audience, 153, 165–6
  and class, 153, 155, 158
  collaboratively composed criticism, 159–60
  critical values and concerns, 165
  dissenting culture and professional support, 152–62
  education, 155–6
  gender-based attack, 162–4
  and *The Monthly Repository*, 152, 156–61, 165–77; Titles of works reviewed in *The Monthly Repository*: Byron, Lord, *Letters and Journals*, 165; Bischoff, James, [...] *Van Diemen's Land*, 174–6; Cooper, Thomas, *Lectures on Political Economy*, 174; *The Death Warrant of Negro Slavery*, 172–3; Godwin, William, *Thoughts on Man*, 173–4; *Report [...] on Prison Discipline*, 174–6; Scott, Sir Walter, *Letters on Demonology and Witchcraft*, 171–172, Snowden, Eleanor, *The Maid of Scio*, 204; Whately, Richard, *Thoughts on Secondary Punishments*, 174–6
  on nationalism and national character, 153, 167–70
  professionalism, 153, 155, 161, 203 n. 17
  and sensibility, 153, 167–70
  social and political reform, 153, 172–6,
  utilitarianism, 174–6
  Works: "Female Writers on Practical Divinity," 156, 166–7; *Illustrations of Political Economy*, 161–5
Martineau, James, 156
Martineau, Thomas, 156–7
Mathur, Om Prakash, 189 n. 35
McCarthy, William, 55, 199 n. 9
McDowell, Paula, 4
McGann, Jerome, 7
Maginn, William, 164
Malthus, Thomas, 28, 165
Marat, Jean Paul, 28
Mellor, Anne, 2, 14, 179 n. 12, 181–2 n. 49
Middle class, *see* class
Mill, John Stuart, 164, 176
Milton, John, 13, 144
  criticism of, 44–8, 108–9, 148
Montagu, Elizabeth, 5–6
Monthly Magazine, The, 118, 127
Monthly Repository, The, 85, 152, 156–61, 164, 204 n. 20
  format, 170–1

perspective, 157, 161, 172, 176
  see also under Martineau, Harriet
Monthly Review, 5, 22, 84, 85, 121–50, 165, 182 n. 53,
  history and scope, 121–6
  see also under Barbauld, Anna Letitia and Moody, Elizabeth
Moody, Christopher Lake, 130, 142–3
Moody, Elizabeth, 21, 22, 85, 123, 141–9, 153, 201 n. 32
  and The Monthly Review, 141–9
  and The St. James Chronicle, 142
Moore, Catherine, 48, 51, 52
moral effect, see literary aesthetics
More, Hannah, 3, 5, 166–8
  Cheap Repository Tracts, 3
Mullan, John, 13, 167
Murray, John, 171, 187 n. 12
Myers, Mitzi, 106
Myers, Sylvia Harcstark, 5

Nangle, Benjamin Christie, 129
nationalism and national character, 14–17, 20, 21; see also under individual author names
national literature, see literary canon
neo-classical aesthetics, see literary aesthetics
Newman, Gerald, 16, 34, 73, 56, 148
Newton, Sir Isaac, 12
Nicholes, Eleanor Louise, 192 n. 24
Nine Living Muses of Great Britain, The (Samuels), 5, 6, 29
Norton Anthology of English Literature, The, 1
novels, criticism of, 18, 20, 47–8, 51–6, 93–5,

Ogle, Thomas, 130
Old Maid, The (Brooke), 4
Opie, Amelia, 25, 57

Paine, Thomas, 188 n. 28
Parker, Mark, 131
Pennant, Thomas, 29
Peterson, Linda, 203 n. 17
Pitt, William, 70
Phillips, Richard, 43, 118–9, 198 n. 76
Plumptre, Anne, 81

Polwhele, Richard, 42, 203 n. 3
Poovey, Mary, 106
Pope, Alexander, 16, 32, 41, 45, 46, 149
  The Dunciad, 4, 7, 59,
Popping, Sarah, 4
Powell, Elizabeth, 4
  Charitable Mercury and Female Intelligence, The, 4
protestantism, 73–4, 168–9; see also religious dissent
Price, Richard, 104, 105
Priestley, Joseph, 25, 28, 29, 104, 105
private sphere, see domesticity
professionalism, literary, see literary professionalism
Protestantism, 73–4, 168–9
Protestant Post Boy, The (Harris), 4
public sphere, 13–15

Quarterly Review, The, 60, 125, 130, 162–5, 171, 187 n. 12

Rambler, The (Johnson), 94–5, 117
rational dissent, see religion: religious dissent
Raven, James, 185 n. 57
Rees, Abraham, 129
Rees, Thomas, 127
Rees, William, 130
Reeve, Clara, 1, 179 n. 12
Reiman, Donald H., 199 n. 9
religion
  Catholicism, 57, 73–5, 168–9; see also Inchbald, Elizabeth
  Established Church (Anglicanism), 10–11, 74, 105, 123, 153, 169
  Latitudinarians, 10, 12
  Protestantism, 73–4, 168–9
  religious dissent, 22, 23, 73, 180 n. 30
    and class, 10, 11–13
    and collaborative culture, 8–9, 12, 15, 22
    and domesticity, 11–12
    history of, 10–11, 105
    Newington Green, 104–5
    Norwich, 154–5, 157

religion – *continued*
    and the publishing industry,
        9–11, 28–9, 85, 104, 122,
        123, 154
    and sensibility, 11–13, 15
    Warrington Academy, 28–9, 129,
        139, 140
    see also under individual author
        names
Richardson, Alan, 189 n. 35
Richardson, Samuel, 43, 47–50, 126
    Clarissa, 48–50
Rizzo, Betty, 182 n. 53
Robinson, George, 114, 118
Robinson, Henry Crabb, 198 n. 76
Robinson, Mary, 25, 57
Rogers, Katharine M., 61
Romantic aesthetics, *see* aesthetics
Romantic ideology, 7, 8
Roper, Derek, 17, 93, 95, 126, 170,
    197 n. 69, 199 n. 9, 200 n. 18
Roscoe, William, 29
Rousseau, Jean Jacques, 34, 39, 53,
    109

St. James's Chronicle, 142
Samuels, Richard, 5
    Nine Living Muses of Great Britain,
        5–6, 29
Schiller, Johann C. F. von, 39
Schwabe, C. E., 130
Scott, Sir Walter, 127, 133, 171–2
Scottish enlightenment, 12
sensibility, 13–16, *see also* under
    names of individual authors
sentimental culture, *see* sensibility
Seward, Anna, 190–1 n. 5
Shaftesbury, Anthony Ashley Cooper,
    3rd earl of, 12, 37, 38, 109
Shakespeare, William, 4–6, 65–75, 77,
    78, 79, 108, 186 n. 7; *see also*
    Inchbald, *The British Theatre*
Shakespear Illustrated (Lennox), 6–7,
    51
Sheridan, Richard Brinsley, 59, 80
Sheridan, Elizabeth Linley, 5
Sheridan, Frances, 179 n. 12
Siddons, Sarah, 57, 77
Sigl, Patricia, 187 n. 12

Simpson, David, 36–7, 169
Siskin, Clifford, 88, 190 n. 4
Smith, Charlotte, 3, 90, 93–4
Smollett, Tobias, 123
    Humphry Clinker, 43
Southey, Robert, 93, 133, 198 n. 76
Sowle, Stacy, 4
    Spectator, The (Addison and Steele),
        4, 37, 38, 39–47, 48, 90, 124,
        126
Staël, Germaine Necker, Mme. de, 31,
    56, 169
    De la littérature, 31, 39
Steele, Richard, 41, 44, 46
    The Spectator, 4, 37, 38, 90, 124
    see also Addison, Joseph
Steevens, George, 66, 79
Sterne, Laurence, 39, 43
Stewart, Sally N., 196 n. 65, 197 n. 69
Stillinger, Jack, 8, 79, 122–3, 137
Sterne, Laurence, 39, 43
Swift, Jonathan, 41, 46
    Tale of a Tub, 7

Tait's Edinburgh Magazine, 164
Talbot, Catherine, 5, 6
Tate, Nahum, 186 n. 7
Taylor, Barbara, 195–6, n. 59
Taylor, John, 188 n. 28
Taylor, William (of Norwich), 129,
    143–4
Tea Table, The (Haywood), 4
Todd, Janet, 102 195 n. 55, 195–6
    n. 59, 196 n. 65
Trela, D. J., 151, 190 n. 4
True Briton, 62
Tyson, Gerald P., 92

Unitarianism, *see* religion: religious
    dissent
Unsex'd Females, The (Polwhele), 42,
    203 n. 3
utilitarianism, 174–6

Voltaire (François-Marie Arouet), 5

Wakefield, Gilbert, 28, 117
Wardle, Ralph M., 17, 93, 191 n. 12,
    191 n. 15, 196 n. 65, 197 n. 70

Webb, R. K., 10, 11
Wellington, Jan, 141, 142, 144–5, 146, 201 n. 32
Wendorf, Richard, 33, 35
Westminster Review, The, 151, 164, 176
White, Daniel E., 139
Wollstonecraft, Mary, 3, 17, 19, 21–22, 36, 42, 53, 85, 86–120, 121, 151, 153, 164, 168, 169, 170, 172, 193–4 n. 44
  And *The Analytical Review*, 86–120, 192 n. 24, 195 n. 55; Titles reviewed in *The Analytical Review*: Burney, Charles, *A General History of Music*, 97, 107; Costigan, William, *Sketches of Society and Manners in Portugal*, 95–6, 98; Equiano, Olaudah, *The Interesting Narrative*, 96, 102; Gilpin, William, *Observaton on the River Wye, Observations, Relative Chiefly to Picturesque Beauty, Remarks on Forest Scenery,* and *Three Essays*, 99–100; Graham, Catherine Macauley, *Letters on Education*, 102, 193 n. 23; Inchbald, Elizabeth, *Nature and Art*, 107; *Letters of the Countess Du Barre*, 100; Meares, John, *Voyages [...] from China to the North-West Coast of America*, 98–9; Smith, Charlotte, *Emmeline*, 93–4; Tench, Major, *Letters Written in France*, 101; *Woman. Sketches of the History, Genius, [...] of the Fair Sex* [anon.], 95; topics/types of work reviewed, 96–7
  and audience, 87, 90–5, 98–9, 100, 102, 111–16, 119–20
  critical values and aesthetic concerns, 93–6, 97–9, 106–7
  editorial responsibilities, 87, 110–11, 113–14, 197 n. 69, 197 n. 70
  education and expertise, 96–100, 103
  gender-based attack, 203 n. 3
  intellectual authority, 92–3 103–9
  on nationalism or national character, 98
  relationship with Mary Hays, 87–8, 89, 92, 110–20; 195–6, n. 59
  politics and social reform in, 100–2
  and professionalism, 86–90, 109–10, 113, 116, 119–20
  religious dissent, 104–5, 140
  review attribution, 97, 196 n. 65
  and sensibility, 97–8, 104, 105–9
  On the French Revolution, 93, 100–1
  Works: *De l'Importance des Opinions Réligeuses* (trans.), 90; *Female Reader, The*, 90; *Mary*, 90; "On Artificial Taste," 97, 107–8; "On Poetry," 192 n. 24; *Original Stories*, 90; *Thoughts on the Education of Daughters*, 89; *Vindication of the Rights of Men*, 87, 100, 102, 119; *Vindication of the Rights of Woman*, 53, 87, 94, 100, 102, 105, 108, 109, 111, 119 193–4 n. 44; *Wrongs of Woman*, 117, 119
Woolf, Virginia, 1
Wordsworth, William, 17, 19, 107, 190–1 n. 5
  Lyrical Ballads, 19, 30–1, 107, 190–1 n. 5
Wycherley, William, 78, 80

Young, Edward, 38

Zall, Paul M., 61, 62, 64, 187 n. 16